The Harper's Quine

THE HARPER'S QUINE

Pat McIntosh

CARROLL & GRAF PUBLISHERS
New York

Carroll & Graf Publishers
An imprint of Avalon Publishing Group, Inc.
245 W. 17th Street
NY 10011
www.carrollandgraf.com

First Carroll & Graf edition 2004

First published in the UK by Constable,
an imprint of Constable & Robinson Ltd 2004

ISBN 0-7867-1349-6

Printed and bound in the EU

Magno amore caris meis,
memoriaeque parentum dilectae.

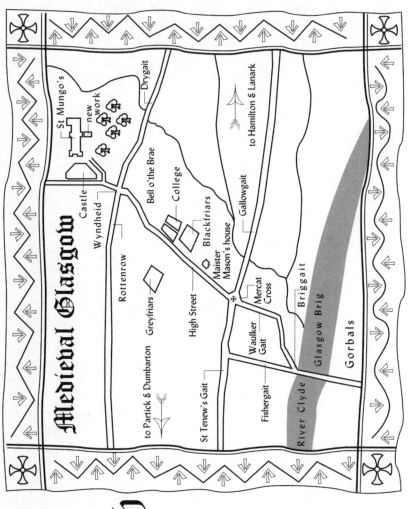

Medieval Glasgow

north

Chapter One

Glasgow, 1492

At the May Day dancing at Glasgow Cross, Gilbert Cunningham saw not only the woman who was going to be murdered, but her murderer as well.

Strictly speaking, he should not have been there. Instead he should have been with his colleagues in the cathedral library, formulating a petition for annulment on grounds which were quite possibly spurious, but shortly after noon he had abandoned that, tidied his books into a neat stack in his carrel, with *Hay on Marriage* on the top, and walked out. A few heads turned as he went, but nobody spoke.

Descending the wheel stair, past the silent chambers of the diocesan court, he stepped out into the warm day enjoying the feeling of playing truant and closed the heavy door without stopping to read the notices nailed to it. The kirkyard was busy with people playing May-games, running, catching, shrieking with laughter. Gil went out, past the wall of the Archbishop's castle, and jumped the Girth Burn ignoring the stepping stones. From here, already, he could hear the *thud*, *thud* of the big drum, like the muffled beat for a hanging.

There was plenty of movement in the steep curving High Street too. Weary couples, some still smelling of smoke from the bonfires, were returning home in the sunshine with their wilting branches. Others, an honest day's work at least attempted, were hurrying from the little thatched cottages to join the fun. Hens and dogs ran among the feet of the revellers, and a tethered pig outside one door had a wide empty space round it.

Further down, where the slope eased and the houses were bigger, a group of students were playing football under the windows of the shabby University building, shouting at each other in mixed Latin and Scots. Gil nodded to the solemn Dominican who was guarding the pile of red and blue gowns, and skirted the game carefully with the other passers-by. Beyond the noise of the players and onlookers he could hear the drum again, together with the patter of the tabor and a confused sound of loud instruments which came to a halt as he drew near to the Tolbooth.

At the Mercat Cross there was clapping and laughter. The dancers were still in the centre of the crossing, surrounded by a great crowd. More people lined the timber galleries of the houses, shouting encouragement, and several ale-wives who had brought barrels of ale down on handcarts were doing a brisk trade.

The burgh minstrels on the Tolbooth steps, resplendent in their blue coats under an arch of hawthorn branches, had added a man with a pipe and tabor and a bagpiper to the usual three shawms and a bombard. As Gil reached the mouth of the High Street they struck up a cheerful noise just recognizable as 'The Battle of Harlaw'.

'A strange choice for the May dancing,' he remarked to the man next to him, a stout burgess in a good cloth gown with his wife on his arm. 'Oh, it's yourself, Serjeant,' he added, recognizing the burgh's chief lawkeeper. 'Good day to you, Mistress Anderson.'

Mistress Anderson, more widely known as Mally Bowen the burgh layer-out, bobbed him a neat curtsy, the long ends of her linen kerchief swinging, and smiled.

'The piper only has the two tunes,' explained Serjeant Anderson, 'that and "The Gowans are Gay", and they've just played the other.'

'I see,' said Gil, looking over the heads at the top dancers advancing to salute their partners, while more couples pushed and dragged one another into position further down the dance. By the time all were in place the top few were already linking arms and whirling round with wild war-cries. A far cry from Aristotle's ideal, he thought.

'It's a cheery sound, yon,' said Gil's neighbour in his stately way. Gil nodded, still watching the dancers. Most were in holiday clothes, some in fantastic costume from the pageant, or with bright bunches of ribbon or scraps of satin attached to their sleeves. Many of the girls, their hair loose down their backs, were garlanded with green leaves and flowers, and their married sisters had added ribbons to their linen headdresses. Students from the College, sons of burgesses in woollen, prentice lads in homespun, swung and stamped to the raucous music.

Watching a pair of students in their narrow belted gowns, crossing hands with two girls who must be sisters, Gil tried to reckon when he had last danced at the Cross himself. It must be eight years, he decided, because when he first returned to Scotland his grief and shock had kept him away, and last year he had been hard at work for his uncle on some case or other. He found his foot tapping.

'See her,' said the serjeant, indicating a bouncing, black-browed girl just arming with a lad in brown doublet and striped hose. 'Back of her gown's all green. Would ye take a wager she's doing penance for last night's work next Candlemas, eh, Maister Cunningham?'

'Oh, John!' said his wife reproachfully.

'She'll not be the only one, if so,' Gil observed, grinning. 'There's a few green gowns here this morning.'

'And I'll wager, this time o' year, Maister Cunningham, you wish you were no a priest,' added the serjeant, winking slyly up at Gil.

'Now, John!'

'I'm not a priest,' said Gil. Not yet, said something at the back of his mind, as he felt the familiar sinking chill in his stomach. When the man looked sceptically at his

9

black jerkin and hose, he added reluctantly, 'I'm a man of law.'

'Oh, so I've heard said. You'll excuse me, maister,' said Serjeant Anderson. 'I'll leave ye, afore ye charge me for the time of day. Come on, hen.'

'I'm at leisure today,' Gil said, but the serjeant had drawn his wife away. Gil shrugged, and turned his attention back to the dancing. The couple he had been watching had completed their turn of the dance and were laughing together, the boy reaching a large rough hand to tug at the girl's garland of flowers. She squealed, and ducked away, and just then the tune reached an identifiable end and the musicians paused for breath. The man banging the big drum kept on going until the tenor shawm kicked him. He stopped, blinking, and the dancers milled to a halt.

Gil took advantage of the general movement to climb a few steps up the nearest fore-stair, where several people were already perched out of reach of the elbows and feet of the mob.

'More!' shouted someone. 'Anither tune!'

The band made its reluctance clear. A short argument developed, until someone else shouted, 'The harper – fetch the harper!'

'Aye, the harper!' agreed several voices at once. The cry was taken up, and the band filed down the steps, carrying its instruments, and headed purposefully for the nearest ale-wife's trestle.

'This will be good,' said someone beside Gil. He looked round, and found the next step occupied by a tall, slender girl with a direct brown gaze above a narrow hatchet of a nose. 'The harper,' she added. 'Have you heard him? He has two women that sing.'

'No, I haven't,' he admitted, gazing appreciatively.

'They sang *Greysteil* at the Provost's house at Yule.'

'What, the whole of it? All four thousand lines?'

She nodded. 'It took all afternoon. It was Candlemas before the tune went out of my head.'

'I have never heard it complete. There can't be many singers could perform it like that.'

'They took turns,' she explained, 'so neither voice got tired, and I suppose neither needed to learn the whole thing. One of them had her baby with her, so she had to stop to nurse it.'

'What about the audience?' said Gil.

The brown eyes danced. 'We could come and go,' she pointed out. 'I noticed the Provost found duties elsewhere in his house.'

'And his lady?' said Gil, half at random, fascinated by her manner. She was dressed like a merchant's daughter, in well-cut brown linen faced with velvet, and she was clearly under twenty, but she spoke to him as directly as she looked, with none of the archness or giggling he had encountered in other girls of her class. Moreover, she was tall enough to look nearly level at him from the next step up. What was that poem some King of Scots wrote in captivity? *The fairest or the freschest yong flower That ever I saw, me thocht, before that hour.* It seemed to fit.

'Lady Stewart had to stay,' she acknowledged. 'I thought she was wearying by the end of the afternoon.'

She spoke good Scots with a slight accent which Gil was still trying to place when there was a disturbance beyond the Tolbooth, and the crowd parted to make way for three extraordinary figures. First to emerge was a sweet-faced woman in a fashionably cut dull red gown and a new-fangled French hood, who carried a harper's chair. After her came another woman, tall and gaunt, her black hair curling over her shoulders, pacing like a queen across the paved market-place in the loose checked dress of a High-lander. In one arm she clasped a harp, and on the other she led a man nearly as tall as Gil. He wore a rich gown of blue cloth, in which he must have been uncomfortably warm, a gold chain, and a black velvet hat with a sapphire in it. Over chest and shoulders flowed long white hair and a magnificent beard. At the sight a child on its father's shoulders wailed, 'Set me down, Da, it's God the Faither! He'll see me!'

The harper was guided up the Tolbooth steps, seated himself with great dignity, accepted harp and tuning-key, and as if there was not a great crowd of people watching, launched into a formal tuning prelude.

'How the sound carries,' Gil said.

'Wire strings,' said the girl. 'I'm surprised you haven't heard him before. Did he not play when the King stayed with the Bishop last winter? Archbishop,' she corrected herself.

'My uncle mentioned a harper,' Gil recalled.

'I thought you would have attended him,' she said. 'The Official of Glasgow is important, no? He is the senior judge of the diocese? His nephew should be present to give him consequence.'

'You know me?' said Gil in French, suddenly placing her accent.

'My nurse – Catherine – knows everyone,' she answered enigmatically. 'Hush and listen.'

The Highland woman on the Tolbooth steps was arguing with some of the crowd, apparently about what they were to sing. The other was watching the harper, who, face turned unseeing towards the Waulkergait, continued to raise ripples of sound from the shining strings. Suddenly he silenced the instrument with the flat of his hand, and with a brief word to the women began to play the introduction to a May ballad. They took up the tune without hesitation, the two voices echoing and answering like birds.

Gil, listening raptly, thought how strong was the rapport between the three musicians, in particular the link between the blind man and the woman in the red dress. When the song ended he turned to his companion.

'My faith, I've heard worse in Paris,' he said over the crowd's applause.

'You know Paris? Were you there at the University?' she

said, turning to look at him with interest. 'What were you studying? When did you leave?'

'I studied in the Faculty of Laws,' he answered precisely, 'but I had to come home a couple of years since – at the end of '89.'

'Of course,' she said with ready understanding, 'the Cunninghams backed the old King in '88. Were all the lands forfeit since the battle? Are you left quite penniless?'

'Not quite,' he said stiffly, rather startled by the breadth of her knowledge. She gave him a quick apologetic smile.

'Catherine gossips. What are they playing now? Aren't they good? It is clear they are accustomed to play together.'

The Highlander woman had coaxed the taborer's drum from him, and was tapping out a rhythm. The other woman had begun to sing, nonsense syllables with a pronounced beat, her eyes sparkling as she clapped in time. Some of the crowd were taking up the clapping, and the space before the Tolbooth was clearing again.

'Will you dance?' Gil offered, to show that he had not taken offence. The apologetic smile flashed again.

'No, I thank you. Catherine will have a fit when she finds me as it is. Oh, there is Davie-boy.' She nodded at the two youngsters Gil had been watching earlier. 'I see he has been at the May-games. He is one of my father's men,' she explained.

The dancers had barely begun, stepping round and back in a ring to the sound of harp, tabor and voice, when there was shouting beyond the Tolbooth, and two men in helmets and quilted jacks rode round the flank of the Laigh Kirk.

'Way there! Gang way there!'

The onlookers gave way reluctantly, with a lot of argument. More horsemen followed, well-dressed men on handsome horses, and several grooms. Satin and jewels gleamed. The cavalcade, unable to proceed, trampled about in the mouth of the Thenawgait, with more confused shouting.

'Who is it?' wondered Gil's companion, standing on tiptoe to see better.

'You mean Catherine did not expect them?' he asked drily. 'That one on the roan horse is some kind of kin of mine by marriage, more's the pity – John Sempill of Muirend. He must have sorted out his little difficulty about Paisley Cross. That must be his cousin Philip behind him. Who the others might be I am uncertain, though they look like Campbells, and so do the gallowglasses. Oh, for shame!'

The men-at-arms had broken through the circle of onlookers into the dancing-space, and were now urging their beasts forward. The dancers scattered, shouting and shaking fists, but the rest of the party surged through the gap and clattered across the paving-stones to turn past the Tolbooth and up the High Street.

Immediately behind the men-at-arms rode Sempill of Muirend on his roan horse, sandy-haired in black velvet and gold satin, a bunch of hawthorn pinned in his hat with an emerald brooch, scowling furiously at the musicians. After him, the pleasant-faced Philip Sempill seemed for a moment as if he would have turned aside to apologize, but the man next him caught his bridle and they rode on, followed by the rest of the party: a little sallow man with a lute-case slung across his back, several grooms, one with a middle-aged woman behind him, and in their midst another groom leading a white pony with a lady perched sideways on its saddle. Small and dainty, she wore green satin trimmed with velvet, and golden hair rippled down her back beneath the fall of her French hood. Jewels glittered on her hands and bosom, and she smiled at the people as she rode past.

'Da!' said the same piercing little voice in the crowd. 'Is that the Queen of Elfland?'

The lady turned to blow a kiss to the child. Her gaze met Gil's, and her expression sharpened; she smiled blindingly

14

and blew him a kiss as well. Puzzled and embarrassed, he glanced away, and found himself looking at the harper, whose expressionless stare was aimed at the head of the procession where it was engaged in another argument about getting into the High Street. Beside him, the tall woman in the checked gown was glaring malevolently in the same direction, but the other one had turned her head and was facing resolutely towards the Tolbooth. What has Sempill done to them? he wondered, and glancing at the cavalcade was in time to see Philip Sempill looking back at the little group on the steps as if he would have liked to stay and listen to the singing.

'Who is she?' asked Gil's companion. 'Do you know her?'

'I never saw her before.'

'She seemed to know you. Whoever she is,' said the girl briskly, 'she's badly overdressed. This is Glasgow, not Edinburgh or Stirling.'

'What difference does that make?' Gil asked, but she gave him a pitying glance and did not reply. The procession clattered and jingled away up the High Street, followed by resentful comments and blessings on a bonny face in roughly equal quantities. The dance re-formed.

'What is a gallowglass?' said the girl suddenly. Gil looked round at her. 'It is a word I have not encountered. Is it Scots?'

'I think it may be Ersche,' Gil explained. 'It means a hired sword.'

'A mercenary?'

'Nearly that. Your Scots is very good.'

'Thank you. And now if you will let me past,' she added with a glance at the sun, 'I will see if I can find Catherine. She was to have come back for me.'

'May I not convoy you?' suggested Gil, aware of a powerful wish to continue the conversation. 'You shouldn't be out unattended, today of all days.'

'I can walk a few steps up the High Street without coming to grief. Thank you,' she said, and the smile flickered again. She slipped past him and down the steps before he could argue further, and disappeared into the crowd.

The harper was playing again, and the tall Highlander woman was beating the tabor. The other woman was singing, but her head was bent and all the sparkle had gone out of her. The fat wife who was now standing next to Gil nudged him painfully in the ribs.

'That's a bonny lass to meet on a May morning,' she said, winking. 'What did you let her go for? She's a good age for you, son, priest or no.'

'Thank you for the advice,' he said politely, at which she laughed riotously, nudged him again, and began to tell him about a May morning in her own youth. Since she had lost most of her teeth and paused to explain every name she mentioned Gil did not attempt to follow her, but nodded at intervals and watched the dance, his pleasant mood fading.

That was twice this morning he had been taken for a priest. It must be the sober clothes, he thought, and glanced down. Worn boots, mended black hose, black jerkin, plain linen shirt, short gown of black wool faced with black linen. Maybe he should wear something brighter – some of the Vicars Choral were gaudy enough. It occurred to him for the first time that the girl had not addressed him as a priest, either by word or manner.

He became aware of a disturbance in the crowd. Leaning out over the handrail he could see one man in a tall felt hat, one in a blue bonnet, both the worse for drink and arguing over a girl. There was a certain amount of pulling and pushing, and the girl exclaimed something in the alarmed tones which had caught his attention. This time he knew the voice.

The stair was crowded. He vaulted over the handrail, startled a young couple by landing in front of them, and pushed through the people, using his height and his elbows ruthlessly. The man in the hat was dressed like a merchant's son, in a red velvet doublet and a short gown with a furred collar caked in something sticky. The other appeared to be a journeyman in a dusty jerkin, out at the elbows. As Gil reached them, both men laid hold of his acquaintance from the stairway, one to each arm, pulling her in opposite directions, the merchant lad reaching suggestively for his short sword with his other hand.

This could be dealt with without violence. Gil slid swiftly round behind the little group, and said clearly, 'Gentlemen, this is common assault. I suggest you desist.'

Both stared at him. The girl twisted to look at him over her shoulder, brown eyes frightened.

'Let go,' he repeated. 'Or the lady will see you in court. She has several witnesses.' He looked round, and although most of the onlookers suddenly found the dance much more interesting, one or two stalwarts nodded.

'Oh, if I'd known she kept a lawyer,' said the man in the hat, and let go. The other man kept his large red hand on the girl's arm, but stopped pulling her.

'It's all right, Thomas,' she said breathlessly. 'This gentleman will see me home.'

'You certain?' said Thomas indistinctly. 'Does he ken where 'tis?' She nodded, and he let go of her wrist and stepped back, looking baffled. 'You take her straight home,' he said waveringly to Gil. 'Straight home, d'you hear me?'

'Straight home,' Gil assured him. 'You go and join the dancing.' If you can stay upright, he thought.

Thomas turned away, frowning, at which the man in the hat also flounced off into the crowd. The girl closed her eyes and drew a rather shaky breath, and Gil caught hold of her elbow.

'This time I will convoy you,' he said firmly.

She took another breath, opened her eyes and turned to him. He met her gaze, and found himself looking into peat-brown depths the colour of the rivers he had swum in as a boy. For an infinite moment they stared at one another; then someone jostled Gil and he blinked. Recovering his manners, he let go of her elbow and offered his arm to lead her.

She nodded, achieved a small curtsy, and set a trembling hand on his wrist. He led her out of the crowd and up the High Street, followed by a flurry of predictable remarks. He was acutely aware of the hand, pale and well-shaped below its brown velvet cuff, and of her profile, dominated by that remarkable nose and turned slightly away from him. The top of her head came just above his shoulder. Suppressing a desire to put his arm round her as further support, or perhaps comfort, he began a light commentary on the music which they had heard, requiring no answer.

'Thomas was trying to help,' she said suddenly. 'He saw Robert Walkinshaw accost me and came to see him off.'

'Is he another of your father's men?' Gil asked. 'He's obviously concerned for you.'

'Yes,' she said after a moment, and came to a halt. Although she still trembled she was not leaning on his wrist at all. He looked down at her. 'And this is my father's house. I thank you, Maister Cunningham.'

She dropped another quick curtsy, and slipped in at the pend below a swinging sign. At the far end of the tunnel-like entry she turned, a dark figure against the sunlit court, raised one hand in salute, then stepped out of sight. Gil, troubled, watched for a moment, but she did not reappear. He stepped backwards, colliding with a pair of beribboned apprentices heading homeward.

'Whose house is that?' he asked them.

'The White Castle?' said one of them, glancing at the sign. 'That's where the French mason lives, is it no, Ecky?'

Ecky, after some thought, agreed with this.

'Aye,' pursued his friend, who seemed to be the more wide awake, 'for I've taken a pie there once it came out the oven. There's an auld French wife there that's the devil to cross,' he confided to Gil. 'Aye, it's the French mason's house.'

They continued on their way. Gil, glancing at the sun, decided that he should do likewise. Maggie Baxter had mentioned something good for dinner.

Canon David Cunningham, Prebendary of Cadzow, Official of Glasgow, senior judge of the Consistory Court of the archdiocese, was in the first-floor hall of his handsome stone house in Rottenrow. He was seated near the window, tall and lean like Gil in his narrow belted gown of black wool, with a sheaf of papers and two protocol books on a stool beside him. In deference to the warmth of the day, he had removed his hat, untied the strings of his black felt coif, and hung his furred brocade over-gown on the high carved back of his chair. Gil, bowing as he entered from the stair, discovered that his head was bare in the same moment as his uncle said,

'Where is your hat, Gilbert? And when did you last comb your hair?'

'I had a hat when I went out,' he said, wondering at the ease with which the old man made him feel six years old. 'It must have fallen off. Perhaps when I louped the handrail.'

'Louped the handrail,' his uncle repeated without expression.

'There was a lass being molested.' Gil decided against asking when dinner was, and instead nodded at his uncle's papers. 'Can I help with this, sir?'

'You are six-and-twenty,' said his uncle. 'You are graduate of two universities. You are soon to be priested, and from Michaelmas next, Christ and His Saints preserve us, you will be entitled to call yourself a notary. I think you should strive for a little dignity, Gilbert. Yes, you can help me. I am to hear a matter tomorrow – Sempill of Muirend is selling land to his cousin, and we need the original disposition from his father. It should be in one of these.' He waved a long thin hand at the two protocol books.

'That would be why I saw him riding into the town just

now. What was the transaction, sir?' Gil asked, lifting one of the volumes on to the bench. His uncle pinched the bridge of his long nose and stared out of the window.

'Andrew Sempill of Cathcart to John Sempill of Muirend and Elizabeth Stewart his wife, land in the burgh of Glasgow, being on the north side of Rottenrow near the Great Cross,' he recited. 'Just across the way yonder,' he added, gesturing. 'I wonder if he's taken his wife back?'

'His wife?' said Gil, turning pages. 'You know my mother's sister Margaret was married on Sempill of Cathcart? Till he beat her and she died of it.'

'Your mother's sister Margaret never stopped talking in my hearing longer than it took to draw breath,' said his uncle. 'Your sister Tibby is her image.'

'So my mother has often said,' agreed Gil.

'There is no proof that Andrew Sempill gave his wife the blow that killed her. She was his second wife, and there were no bairns. John Sempill of Muirend would be his son by the first wife. She was a Walkinshaw, which would be how they came by the land across the way. I think she died of her second bairn.'

'And what about John Sempill's wife?' Gil persisted.

'You must not give yourself to gossip, Gilbert,' reproved his uncle. 'Sempill of Muirend married a Bute girl. While you were in France, that would be. She and her sister were co-heirs to Stewart of Ettrick, if I remember. She left Sempill.'

'There was a lady with him when he rode in just now.' Gil turned another page, and marked a place with his finger. 'Dainty creature with long gold hair. Child in the crowd thought she was the Queen of Elfland.'

'That does not sound like his wife.'

'It's not his wife.' Maggie Baxter, stout and red-faced, appeared in the doorway from the kitchen stair. 'Will ye dine now, maister? Only the May-bannock's like to spoil if it stands.'

'Very well.' The Official gathered up his papers. 'Is it not his wife, Maggie?'

'The whole of Glasgow kens it's not his wife,' said Maggie, dragging one of the trestles into the centre of the hall, 'seeing she's taken up with the harper that stays in the Fishergait.'

'What, the harper that played for the King last winter?' said the Official. 'When was this? Is that who she left Sempill for?'

Maggie counted thoughtfully on her fingers.

'Before Yule a year since? I ken the bairn's more than six month old.'

'There is a bairn, is there? And has she gone back to Sempill? I had not heard this,' said Canon Cunningham in disgruntled tones.

'I don't know about that,' said Maggie with grim significance. Gil rose and went to fetch in the other two trestles. 'But what I saw an hour since was Sempill of Muirend ride in across the way there, and his cousin with him, and Lady Euphemia Campbell tricked out in green satin like the Queen of the May.'

'Ah,' said the Canon. He lifted his over-gown from the back of his chair and began searching among the intricacies of black brocade and worn fox-fur for the armholes.

'Is that something else that happened while I was in France?' Gil asked. 'Maggie, will you take the other end?'

'Aye, it would be,' agreed Maggie as they set the great board up on the trestles. 'Her first man fell at Stirling field – who was he now? I think he was on the old King's side, like the Sempills and the Cunninghams. She never grieved ower lang for him, for she was already getting comfort with John Sempill when you came home, Maister Gil. Or so I hear,' she added piously.

'I think we conclude that Sempill's wife has not returned to him,' David Cunningham said. He and Maggie began an involved discussion of who Euphemia Campbell's first husband might have been, while Gil quietly went on setting up the table for dinner with the long cloth of bleached

21

linen from the smaller carved cupboard, and the wooden trenchers from the open base of the great cupboard. May Day or no, he knew better than to touch the silver dishes gleaming on top of the great cupboard; they were only used when the Archbishop or the other canons dined with them. He added horn spoons and wooden beakers from the small cupboard, lining them up carefully, dragged his uncle's chair to the head of the board, set the two long benches on either side, and said across the genealogy,

'Maggie, will I bring in anything else?'

'Aye, well,' said Maggie, 'I've work to do, maister. Sit you in at the table and I'll call the household.'

She stumped off down the stairs to the kitchen. By the time she returned, Gil had finally assisted his uncle into the long furred gown, and both Cunninghams had washed their hands under the spout of the pottery cistern by the other door and were seated waiting for their food.

'A May blessing on the house,' she said, setting a pot of savoury-smelling stew at the top of the table. Behind her, Matt, the Official's middle-aged, silent manservant, and the two stable-hands echoed her words as they bore in bread and ale, a dish of eggs, a bowl of last year's apples. Last of all came the kitchen-boy, scarlet with concentration, carrying the May-bannock on a great wooden trencher. The custard of eggs and cream with which it was topped quivered as he set it in the centre of the table and stood back.

'May Day luck to us all!' he said breathlessly, and licked custard off his thumb.

Once grace was said and all were served, Maggie and the Official continued their discussion. The men were arguing about whether to graze the horses on the Cowcaddens Muir or to take them further afield, perhaps nearer Partick. Gil ate in silence, thinking about the day, and about the girl he had left at the house of the White Castle. He was surprised to find that he could not remember what she wore, except that it had velvet cuffs, or anything about her other than that direct gaze and the incisive, intelligent voice. What colour was her hair? Was she bareheaded? And yet he could not stop thinking about her.

'Gilbert,' said his uncle sharply. He looked up, and apologized. 'I am to say Compline in the choir tonight. Will you invest me, so that Matt can go to his kin in the Fishergait?'

'I can invest you, sir. I'm promised to Adam Goudie after Vespers. I'll come down to St Mungo's and attend you at Compline, and Matt can go as he pleases.'

Matt grunted a wordless acknowledgement, and David Cunningham said, 'Playing at the cards, I suppose, with half the songmen of St Mungo's.'

'I'm in good company,' Gil pointed out, and seized a wrinkled apple from the bowl as Maggie began to clear the table. 'The Bishop himself plays at cards with the King. Archbishop,' he corrected himself.

'The King and Robert Blacader both can afford to lose money,' said his uncle. 'Neither you nor any of the Vicars Choral has money to lose. Remember the gate to Vicars Alley is locked at nine o'clock.'

'I will, sir.'

'And that reminds me. I have a task for you. You mind the Archbishop's new work? Where he's decided to complete the Fergus Aisle?' Gil nodded, biting into his apple. 'It seems St Mungo's is not big enough now we're an archdiocese. Christ save us, is it only four months since the Nuncio was here? Anyway, the mason wants a word with one of the Chapter, I suppose to talk about some detail or other. You might as well deal with it. Don't promise the Chapter to any expenditure – or the Bishop either.'

'I won't.'

'Before the morn's work starts, he said, after Lauds.' The Official took his hands from the board as the stable-lads lifted it off the trestles. 'Have you found the Sempill disposition yet? I want to see it tonight.'

* * *

Compline, that folding-together of the hands at the day's end, was always a satisfactory service. In the vaulted sacristy, where fingers of late gold sunlight poked through the northward windows, David Cunningham accepted his vestments one by one from Gil, and finally bent his head under the yoke of his own stole from the bundle Gil had carried over before Vespers. He paused for a moment, his lips moving, then said, 'I'll disrobe myself, Gilbert. You may hear the service or go, as you please.'

'I'll hear it, I think, sir,' said Gil politely. He knelt for his uncle's blessing, and slipped out into the nave.

This late in the evening those present were principally servants or dependants of the cathedral community, more familiar to Gil than the habitants of the lower town. Maggie Baxter was there, with her friend Agnes Dow who kept house for the sub-chanter. Adam Goudie's sister Ann, who ran the sub-Thesaurer's household, the Canon himself and some said his share of the Treasury too, had a new gown of tawny wool in honour of the May. Beyond them a flash of black-and-gold caught Gil's eye.

Shifting position he saw John Sempill, with some of the party he had seen ride past the Tolbooth: Sempill's handsome cousin, and also the small dark fellow and one of the men-at-arms, and furthest away, beyond her stout companion, Lady Euphemia Campbell, small and fragile in sapphire-blue with her golden hair rippling from under a velvet hat like a man's. Another quotation popped into his head, from the bawdy tale of the Friars of Berwick: *A fair blyth wyf . . . sumthing dynk and dengerous.* Was such a dainty lady dangerous? he wondered.

At his movement she glanced his way, and smiled at him, then returned to her prayers. Her actions as she stood or knelt, crossed herself, bent her head over her beads, were fluid and graceful, and Gil watched, fascinated, hoping she would look his way again. Beyond the massive stone screen the Vicars Choral launched into the evening psalms. Down here in the nave the other man-at-arms came in with a word for his master, and behind him

24

another expensively dressed man joined the group, hiding Lady Euphemia from his view.

For a while Gil paid attention to the singing; then, as if to a lodestone, he found his glance drawn in that direction again. One of the men was just slipping away to another altar, but it was almost with relief that he found Euphemia Campbell's slight person was still invisible.

When the Office ended and the choir had filed through the narrow door in the screen and back into the vestry, the church slowly emptied. Gil paused by the altar of St Giles to leave money for candles. Earlier the image had glowed in red and gold light from the west windows, and the hind at the saint's side had been resplendent in a coat of many colours, but now the sun had moved round St Giles and his pet stood in their workaday brown and white paint. The holiday was over. Tomorrow, Gil thought, I must go back to the Monteath petition. His heart sank at the notion. Sweet St Giles, he said silently to the remote image, give me strength to face what is set before me.

After a moment he made for the south door. As he reached it Euphemia Campbell rose from her knees before the altar of St Catherine, crossed herself with that distracting grace, and moved towards the door herself. Gil held it open, bowing, and she favoured him with a luminous, speculative smile and went out before him.

Following her, he paused on the door-sill to look around. To the right, the Sempill party was gathering itself together, Sempill himself emerging from a nearby clump of trees scowling and fiddling with his codpiece. Lady Euphemia strolled gracefully towards him and put her hand possessively on his arm. The whole party made for the gate, except for the small sallow man, who stood for a moment longer staring after Euphemia Campbell, one hand on his dagger. Then, as she turned to look over her shoulder, he shied like a startled horse and scurried after her.

Gil stood where he was, admiring the evening. He had no wish to accompany John Sempill and his friends the quarter-mile or so back to the two houses which faced one another across Rottenrow. The kirkyard was in shade, only the high crowns of the trees still catching the light. Before Vespers there had been people about, talking or singing. Someone had been playing a lute, a group of children danced in a ring, their voices sweet on the warm air, and Gil had caught a glimpse of the two youngsters he had seen earlier at the Cross, the boy's striped hose conspicuous under the trees. The children had been called home now, the lutenist had gone to find a more financially rewarding audience, and only a last few parishioners drifted up the path towards the gate.

To the left, against the pale bulk of the cathedral itself, the Archbishop's new work was in shadow. Robert Blacader, Bishop of Glasgow, now since last January Archbishop of Glasgow, wanted to elaborate his cathedral, and his eye had fallen on the Fergus Aisle. If one was precise about it, the little chapel off the south transept was not new work, but something started more than a hundred years ago over the burial-place of that holy man Fergus whose death had brought the young Kentigern to his dear green place. It had been soon abandoned, probably when the Chapter of the day ran out of money, the foundations open to the weather ever since.

Gil considered the building site. The walls had now reached shoulder-height, and stood surrounded by stacks of timber for the scaffolding. A neat row of blocks of stone waited to be cut to shape in the masons' lodge whose thatched roof Gil could see beyond the chapel. Hurdles supported on more scaffolding made a ramp for a wheelbarrow. Tomorrow he must meet the master mason there.

The Sempill party had left the kirkyard. Patting his purse, which was significantly heavier for the evening's card-play, Gil set off for home. Several of the songmen thought they could play Tarocco, but had not learned the game, as he had, from the card-players of Paris.

He wondered later how much difference it would have made if he had gone to look in the building site then, rather than in the morning.

Chapter Two

It was surprising how much of the singing one could hear, sitting shivering outside the cathedral at five o'clock in the morning, trying very hard to remember whether a building site was consecrated ground or not.

Here in the kirkyard the birds were shouting. Inside, the Vicars Choral had dealt with Matins and were cantering through Lauds, with more attention paid to speed than sense. A lot of the sound came through the windows, but a certain amount of it, Gil reasoned, came by the door which used to be the south transept entrance and now stood firmly shut and locked above the muddy grass of the Fergus Aisle, quite near to where someone had recently been sick, and just above where the dead woman was lying.

He sat on the scaffolding, fingering his beads and staring at her. She had given him a most unpleasant turn. Coming out early to meet the mason, since he was awake anyway and there was no chance of breaking his fast until Maggie got the fire going, he had climbed up the wheelbarrow ramp and into the chapel to have the closer look he had passed over last night, and there she was, lying half under the planks by the far wall. He had thought at first she was asleep, or drunk, until he smelled the blood; and then he had touched her shoulder and found it rigid under his hand.

The last paternoster bead reached his fingers. He rattled through the prayer, added a quick word for the repose of the lady's soul, whoever she might be, and rose to have another look, the question of consecrated ground still niggling at his mind.

She was lying on her right side, face hidden in the trampled grass as if she was asleep, one hand tucked under her cheek. The other sleeve of her red cloth gown was hitched nearly to the shoulder, the tapes of the brocade under-sleeve half-torn, and the blood-soaked shift stiffened in sagging folds round her arm. The free hand was strong, white, quite clean, with surprisingly long nails and calloused fingertips. She wore a good linen headdress, with a neat dark French hood over it. Round her waist was a belt of red-dyed leather shod with silver, with no purse attached to it, and she had no jewellery beyond a set of finely carved wooden beads. She looked like a decent woman, not one of the inhabitants of Long Mina's well-known house in the Fishergait. Gil could not rid himself of the feeling that he had seen her before.

The sound of chanting was diminishing towards the vestry on the other side of the nave. He realized Lauds must be over, and there was still no sign of the mason, and nobody to help him move the corpse, which could certainly not stay there.

A door clanked open, east along the buttressed honey-coloured flank of St Mungo's. Children's voices soared, then paused as an angry adult voice entered at full volume.

'Andrew Hamilton! William! Come here this instant!'

That was the chanter himself, sounding surprisingly alert after last night's drinking session. Gil got to his feet, intending to shout to him, and found himself looking out over the roof of the masons' lodge at Patrick Paniter, broad-shouldered and angry in his robes, confronting two blue-gowned trebles.

'What were you about, that you were three beats late in the Gloria? What was so interesting?' The chanter pounced. One boy ducked away, but the other was slower. 'Give me that!'

Strong hands used to forcing music from the cathedral's

two organs had no difficulty with a twelve-year-old's grip.

'Ow! Maister Paniter!'

Maister Paniter's dark tonsured head bent briefly over the confiscated object. 'A harp key? What in Our Lady's name did you want with a harp key? It'll never tune your voice, you timber-eared skellum!'

'It's mine – I found it!' The boy tried to seize it back, but the chanter held it easily beyond his reach.

'Then you've lost it again.' His other hand swung. 'And *that's* for boys who don't watch the beat. What have I told you about that? And you, Will Anderson, hiding behind that tree! What have I told you? It's . . .?'

'It's wickedness, Maister Paniter,' they repeated in reluctant chorus with him.

'Because . . .?'

'Because it interrupts the Office,' they completed.

'Remember that. Now get along to school before you're any later, you little devils, and you may tell Sir Adam why I kept you.'

The fair boy, rubbing a boxed ear, ran off down the path to the mill-burn. His friend emerged from behind the tree and followed him, and they vanished down the slope, presumably making for school by the longest way around.

Gil drew breath to call to the chanter. He was forestalled by a creaking of wood behind him, and a voice which said in accented Scots, 'Well, what a morning of accidents!'

He glanced over his shoulder, then back again, just in time to see Maister Paniter hurl some small object into the trees, and then withdraw, slamming the crypt door behind him.

Gil turned to face the master mason, staring. The man standing on the scaffolding was big, even without the fur-trimmed gown he wore. A neat black beard threatened; under the round hat a sharp gaze scanned the kirkyard and returned to consider the corpse.

'What has come to this poor woman in my *chantier*?' he

demanded, springing down from the planking. 'And who are you? Did you find her, or did you put her there?'

'I am Gil Cunningham, of the Cathedral Consistory,' said Gil, with extreme politeness, 'and I should advise you not to repeat that question before witnesses.' The French mason, he thought. Could this be the father of his acquaintance of yesterday?

'Ah – a man of law!' said the big man, grinning to reveal a row of strong white teeth. 'I ask your pardon. I have other troubles this morning already. I spoke without thinking.' He raised the hat, baring dark red hair cut unfashionably short and thinning at the crown, and sketched a bow. 'I am called Peter Mason, master builder of this burgh. Maistre Pierre – the stone master. Is a joke, no? I regret that I come late to the tryst. I have been searching for the laddie who did not sleep in his bed last night, although his brother was come from Paisley to visit him. Now tell me of this.'

'I found her when I came for the meeting,' said Gil. 'She's stiff – been killed sometime last night, I'd say.'

'Been killed? Here? She has not died of her own accord?'

'There's blood on her gown. Yes, I think here. The grass is too trampled to tell us much, this dry weather, but I would say she is lying where she fell.'

Maistre Pierre bent over the corpse, touching with surprising gentleness the rigid arm, the cold jaw. He felt the back of the laced bodice, sniffed his fingers, and made a face.

'See – I think this is the wound. A knife.' He looked round. 'Perhaps a man she knew, who embraced her, and slipped in the knife, khht! when she did not expect it.'

'How was her sleeve torn, then?' asked Gil, impressed in spite of himself.

'He caught her by it as she fell?' The big hands moved carefully over the brocade of the under-sleeve. 'Indeed, there is blood here. Also it is smeared as if he wiped his hand. There is not a lot of blood, only the shift is stained. I think a fine-bladed dagger.'

'Italian,' offered Gil. The bright eyes considered him.

'You know Italy, sir?'

'There were Italians in Paris.'

'Ah. Firenze I know, also Bologna. I agree. What do we do with the poor soul? Let us look at her face.'

He laid hold of the shoulder and the rigid knee under the full skirt, and pulled. The body came over like a wooden carving, sightless blue eyes staring under half-closed lids. The black velvet fall of the French hood dropped back, shedding tiny flakes of hawthorn blossom and exposing a red scar along the right side of her jaw. Poor woman, thought Gil, she must always have kept her head bent so that the headdress hid that, and with the thought he knew her.

The knowledge made him somehow decisive. He reached out and drew a fold of velvet up across the staring eyes, and the woman's face immediately seemed more peaceful.

'It's one of the two who sings with the harper,' he said.

'But of course! The one with the baby, I should say.'

'A child, is there?' said Gil, and suddenly recalled his uncle using the same words. 'Then I know who must be told, as well as the harper. She is on St Mungo's land, we must at least notify the sub-dean as well, and he is probably the nearest member of Chapter in residence just now. I have no doubt he will want to be rid of her. Do you suppose the Greyfriars would take her until we can confirm her name and where she is and find her kin?'

'But certainly. Go you and tell whom you must, Maister Cunningham. I will bide here, and by the time you return my men will be come back from searching for Davie-boy and we can put her on a hurdle.'

A plump maidservant opened the door to Gil when he reached the stone tower-house by the mill-burn.

'Good day to you, Maister Cunningham,' she said cheerfully. 'Is it the maister you're wanting?'

'It is,' he agreed. 'Can I get a word with him, Kirsty?'

'Oh, aye. He's just breaking his fast. Will you wait, or interrupt him? Mind, he's going out hawking in a wee bit.'

'I'd best see him now. I need a decision.'

Agog, she led him up a wheel stair and into the sub-dean's private closet, where James Henderson, red-faced and richly clad, was consuming cold roast meat with bannocks and new milk in front of a tapestry of hunting scenes.

'Here's Maister Cunningham for you,' she proclaimed, 'and it'll no wait.'

'St Mungo's bones!' exclaimed Canon Henderson. 'What ails ye, Gil? Will ye take bannocks and milk?'

'No, I thank you,' said Gil with regret. 'I've come to report a corpse in the Fergus Aisle. I found her just now.'

'A corp!' said Kirsty. 'Who is it? What's come to her? And at May-tide, too!'

'A corpse,' repeated Canon Henderson. 'In the Archbishop's new work? You mean a fresh corpse?'

'Stabbed, last night, I would say, sir.'

'Save us! I never heard anything last night,' said Kirsty.

'Is she from the Chanonry? A dependant, a servant? Her household must be notified.'

'I think she's one of the harper's singers.'

'Oh, a musician,' said the sub-dean distastefully. 'If she belongs down the town then it's hardly proper for her to stay here. Maybe the Greyfriars –'

'I thought so too.'

'And Gil . . .' The sub-dean hesitated, staring at the woven heron, caught in the moment of its death. He tapped his teeth with a chewed fingernail. 'How did she die? Stabbed, you say? And on St Mungo's land. I suppose we have a duty to look for the man responsible, even if she is a minstrel.'

'We do,' agreed Gil.

'Aye, we do!' said Kirsty. 'Or we'll none of us can sleep easy, thinking we'll get murdered in our beds.'

'Be silent, woman!' ordered Canon Henderson.

'Well enough for you,' retorted Kirsty. 'It's me that's at the side nearest the door!'

'Is there anyone else I should report this to?' Gil asked.

'No,' said the sub-dean hastily. 'Just get her moved. Maybe the mason's men can bear her to the Greyfriars. See to it, Gil, will you? And as for finding the malefactor, you'd be well placed to make a start. After all, you found her. I'll speak to your uncle – perhaps at Chapter.'

Gil, seeing himself out to the sound of a blossoming domestic quarrel, did not take the direct path to the building site, but cut across the slope of the kirkyard to the stand of tall trees opposite the door of the lower church.

He made his way through the trees, scuffing the bluebells aside with his feet, many thoughts jostling in his head. It seemed he would be spending more time away from his books. Surely it should not feel as if he had been let off his leash. And when he finally became a priest, scenes such as this morning's would become part of his existence, both the encounter with a recent corpse and the slice of home life he had just witnessed. The corpse he could cope with, he felt. One would usually have some warning, and there were procedures to be gone through, shriving, conditional absolution, prayers for the dead. One would know what to do. But what could one do about the other matter – the behaviour of what his uncle referred to, with dry legal humour, as *The concordance of debauched canons*. Nothing to do with Gratian's classic text, of course.

He sniffed the green smell of the new leaves he was trampling, and tried to imagine himself, a senior figure in the Church, taking a servant to his bed like Canon Henderson, or setting up a woman of his own class as an acknowledged mistress with her own home, like Canon Dalgliesh. The image would not stay before him. Instead

33

he saw his uncle, whom he knew he would resemble closely in thirty years' time, and the scholar who had taught him logic at the University.

He looked about him, a little blankly. What was it Aristotle said about incongruity? The dead woman was a thing out of place; the harp key the trebles had found was another. There was, of course, a significant and bawdy double meaning attached to the object, but the chanter appeared to have discarded it as an irrelevance, rather than as a source of corruption.

He began to search more carefully under the bluebells, and was rewarded by a lost scrip, empty, a broken wooden beaker and one shoe. He was casting about nearer the church, trying to judge where the implement might have landed after the chanter threw it this way, when a blackbird flew up, scolding, and something snored behind him.

Wild boar! he thought as he whirled, drawing his sword. Then it dawned on him that there could be no wild boar in St Mungo's kirkyard. Feeling slightly foolish, he stared round under the trees, sword in hand, waiting for the sound to be repeated. There it was again – over there among those bushes. He made his way cautiously through the long grass, and carefully parted the leaves with the point of his blade.

The mason's men, three sturdy fellows in aprons, were gathered inside the walls of the chapel, standing on the muddy grass staring down at the corpse. Their master was issuing instructions about a hurdle when Gil climbed the scaffolding.

'Ah – maister lawyer,' he said, breaking off. 'What have you learned? Where does she go home?'

'Greyfriars,' said Gil. 'But we'll need another hurdle.'

The three men turned to stare at him. One was squat and grizzled, one was fair and lanky, and the middle one was the journeyman called Thomas, who had argued with a merchant's son in the High Street. So her father is the master mason? he thought.

'Is your missing laddie about fifteen, wearing striped hose?'

Thomas swallowed.

'Aye,' he said. 'Rare proud of them he is, too. What d'ye mean, a hurdle, maister? Is he – have you –?'

'I've found him,' said Gil.

The boy was not dead. He lay on his face in a little huddle under the bushes, blood caked on a vicious wound on the top of his head, breathing with the stertorous snores that had attracted Gil's attention. There was no other mark on him, but he was very cold.

'It needs that we nurse him,' said Maistre Pierre. 'I have heard men breathe so before.' He looked round, to where two of the men were approaching with a hurdle, and held up one large hand. 'A moment, Wattie. Maister Cunningham, do you see something strange?'

'Very strange,' agreed Gil. 'I wondered if you would see it. There is no sign of the man who struck him that blow. I followed the boy's own tracks into the bushes. Someone else has run by him, a couple of paces that way, but hardly close enough to hit him like that.'

'You must stand still to strike so hard a blow,' said the mason thoughtfully. He scratched the back of his head, pushing the hat forward. 'I have seen a man walk away after he was struck and fall down later. Perhaps he was not struck here.'

'Can we move him, maister?' demanded the grizzled Wattie. 'If he's no deid yet, he soon will be, laid out here in the dew like that.'

'Aye, take him up, Wattie,' said his master, straightening the hat. 'You and Thomas, bear him to our house. Send Luke ahead to warn the household, and bid him fetch a priest,' he added. 'He must be shriven. Ah, poor laddie.'

The limp form was lifted on to the hurdle. Gil, on

sudden impulse of pity, pulled off his short gown and tucked it round the boy.

'His bonnet's here,' said Wattie, lifting it. 'It was under him.'

'Give me,' said the mason. 'Has he been robbed?'

'Two pennies and a black plack in his purse,' reported Wattie, 'and he's still wearing this.' He pulled aside the folds of the gown to display a cheap brooch, the kind exchanged by sweethearts, pinned to the lad's doublet. 'His lass gave him that at St Mungo's Fair.'

The mason turned the bonnet over. It was a working man's headgear, a felted flat cap of woad-dyed wool with a deep striped band.

'There is blood on the inside,' said Gil, pointing. 'He was wearing it when he was struck.'

Maistre Pierre turned the bonnet again. On the outside, corresponding to the patch of blood, was a rubbed place with scraps of bark and green stains. 'With a great piece of wood,' he agreed. He set the bonnet on the boy's chest as the hurdle was borne past him. 'Take him home, Wattie, and come back for the lady. Or if you pass any sensible men send them up to carry her away.'

As the two men plodded up the slope with their burden, Gil said thoughtfully, 'The woman was stabbed, but the boy was struck over the head. Have there been two malefactors at large in the kirkyard last night?'

'And the woman was robbed but the boy was not.' The mason gathered his furred gown round him and strode up the slope in the wake of his men. 'Come, maister lawyer, you and I can at least put her on a hurdle.'

As they rounded the angle of the Fergus Aisle they saw a small crowd hurrying eagerly towards them. Wattie's idea of sensible men turned out to be anyone who had been passing when he reached the Great Cross, and it was with some difficulty that the hurdle with its sad burden was handed up the ramp on the inside of the scaffold-shrouded walls and down the outside, and set on its way. Several prentice-boys who should have been at work tried to climb in to see where the blood was, and a couple of the town's licensed beggars appeared, offering to pray for the lady's soul for ever in return for suitable alms. Once they realized that her kin had not been discovered they lost interest, but a knot of women followed at the rear of the procession, exclaiming and speculating.

Brother Porter at Greyfriars was compassionate.

'Poor lass,' he said, raising the fall of the hood to look at her face. 'Aye, it's the harper's quine right enough. Father Francis is waiting for her in the mortuary chapel. She can lie quiet there till they come for her. They've nowhere they can lay her out, they live in two rooms in a pend off the Fishergait.'

'You know where they live?' said Gil as the small cortège plodded past him, through the gateway and towards the chapel. 'Someone needs to send to let them know.'

'Bless you, son,' said the porter, grinning wryly. 'Half the town's let them know by now. The man's sister'll be here any moment, I've no doubt, if not the harper himself.'

'The other woman's his sister, then?' Gil said. 'True enough, they're alike. I'll wait, if I may, brother. I must speak with her.'

'Then I wait also,' said Maistre Pierre. He drew a well-worn rosary from his sleeve and approached the chapel. Gil turned away to lean against the wall, thinking. The woman had clearly been dead for some hours, perhaps since yesterday evening. If she had reached St Mungo's yard in daylight, she must have been about the place at the same time as he was himself. Alive or dead, he qualified. When he left the cathedral after Compline, was she already lying hidden under the scaffolding?

Over in the church, the rest of the little community of Franciscans were beginning to sing Prime. It felt much later.

As the Office was ending, the harper's sister arrived in a rush, followed by a further straggle of onlookers. It was, as Gil had expected, the other singer, the tall woman in the checked kirtle, now wrapped in a huge black-and-green plaid. He straightened up and followed her to the little chapel, where she halted in the entrance, staring round; when her eye fell on the still figure on the hurdle a howl escaped her and she flung herself forward to kneel by the body, the plaid dropping to the tiled floor.

'*Ohon, ohon!* Ah, Bess!' she wailed, unheeding of Father Francis still reciting prayers before the altar. Gil stepped forward to hush her, but two of the women in the crowd were before him, bending over her with sympathetic murmurs. She would not be stilled, continuing to lament in her own language. The porter hurried in and with some difficulty she was persuaded to leave the body and sit on a stool where she began to rock back and forth, hands over her face, with a high-pitched keening which made the hair on Gil's neck stand up. The two women showed signs of joining in the noise.

The mason said to Gil under his breath, 'Are these all her friends, that they mourn so loudly?'

'I don't know,' Gil returned. 'Er – ladies. Ladies,' he repeated more loudly, without effect. 'Madam!' he shouted. 'Be at peace, will you!'

She drew her hands from her face, still rocking, and showed him dry, angry eyes.

'I am mourning my sister,' she spat at him. 'How can I be at peace?'

'Listen to me,' he said urgently, grasping her wrists. 'Someone killed her, on St Mungo's land.'

'The more ill to St Mungo,' she said, ignoring the shocked response of her companions. 'Oh, Bess, as soon as I saw the gallowglass, *ohon* –'

'Gallowglass?' repeated Gil. 'When was this?'

'Yesterday, after Vespers. Him and his brother, they rode through the dance at noon, and him after Vespers casting up at our door, meek as a seal-pup, with a word for Bess Stewart and no other.'

'You knew him?' said the mason.

'And why would I not know him, Campbell that he is?'
She spat as if the name were poison. 'So what must she do,
just about Compline, once the bairn is asleep, but put her
plaid round her and go out with him, though we would
gainsay her, Aenghus and I.'

'She took her plaid?' said Gil. 'You are sure of it?'

She stared at him.

'But of course. She was a decent woman, and not singing, of course she wore her plaid.'

'It was not with her when we found her,' said Gil.

'He has kept it, the thieving – Oh, and when she never
came home to her bairn, I knew there was trouble, *ohon*,
alas!'

'I want to find out who did it,' said Gil hastily. She
stared at him, and then grinned, showing gapped teeth.

'It will have been the husband,' she said. 'But if it is
proof the gentleman wants, I will help. Then we can
avenge her.' One hand went to the black-hilted gully-knife
at her belt.

'Then tell me what you can about her,' said Gil, sitting
back on his heels. 'Who was she? No, first, who are
you?'

'I?' She drew herself up, and the two weepers beside her
sat back as if to hear a good story at some fireside. 'I am
Ealasaidh nic Iain of Ardnamurchan, daughter of one
harper and sister of another, singer.'

The dead woman was, as Gil had assumed, Bess Stewart
of Ettrick, wife of John Sempill of Muirend. The harper and
his sister had met her in Rothesay in late autumn a year
and a half since.

'She was singing with me first,' said Ealasaidh. 'I was
playing the lute and singing, and she was joining in the
second part. That was in the Provost's house one evening.
Then a day or so later we played at another house, Aenghus and me both, and she was there, and she was singing
with us.'

She paused, remembering.

'French music it was,' she said at length. 'Binchois, and

some other. And it seemed Aenghus must have had a word with her by his lone, for when we came away from Bute before St Martin's tide she came with us. I was not happy about this, the gentleman will be seeing, for it is one thing a willing servant lass and another entirely a baron's wife. So we went to Edinburgh for Yule, and spent a while in Fife, and when we were coming back into the west there was the bother the Sempills had about Paisley Cross, and she was already showing, so we thought the husband would not be pursuing her.'

'Showing?' queried Gil. She gestured expressively.

The child had been born at Michaelmas, and by then Bess had learned to sing a good few of the songs the harper played, and also to play a little on a smaller harp. As soon as she could leave the baby she had begun to help to earn her keep.

'I never had a singing partner I was liking so well,' said Ealasaidh, 'nor never a sister like Bess. Sorrow is on me now and for ever, *ohon, ohon* . . .'

'Tell me something,' said Maistre Pierre suddenly. She had resumed her rocking, but paused to look at him. 'Why did the lady leave her husband so willingly? She had land, I presume there was money, and your brother is – well . . .'

'No doubt,' she said, 'but I would not stay with a man that used his knife on me, neither.'

'His knife?' repeated Gil.

'Why d'you think they called her One-lug Bess?' said one of the other women suddenly.

Ealasaidh turned on her. 'Never in my hearing was anyone calling her that, Margaret Walker,' she hissed, 'and you will not do it again.'

'Who's to stop me?' said the woman. Ealasaidh nic Iain rose to her full height, gathering her checked skirts round her away from the contamination of Mistress Walker's presence.

'It is myself will stop you,' she said wrathfully, 'for you will not be over my doorsill again. And if the gentleman,' she said, rounding on Gil, who had scrambled to his feet, 'wishes to speak with me more, he may find me. We are staying at the sign of the Pelican, in the Fishergait. Anyone will be telling where the harper and his women – his sister are staying.'

She snatched her plaid from the woman beside her, jerked the door open and strode out into the courtyard. The two women got to their feet.

'He cut her ear off,' said one of them. 'That's where she got the scar.'

'That's why she was aye in that French hood,' said the other. 'Take a look under it.'

'She told me once she'd more scars than that.'

'I suppose that would be one advantage of the harper.'

Their eyes slid sideways at one another, and they nodded, and slipped out of the chapel after Ealasaidh. Gil, uncomfortably reminded of Euripides, turned back to the body, which someone had covered with a linen sheet. Father Francis had left, but two of the brothers were pattering prayers at the altar.

'The chorus has gone,' said Maistre Pierre at his side. 'Maister Cunningham, I am wishing to ask at my home how is the boy Davie, and it is a long time since I broke my fast.'

'I'm still fasting,' said Gil frankly.

'Then you will come with me and eat something and we talk. Yes?'

'That would be very welcome,' said Gil. He drew back the sheet and looked at Bess Stewart's still face. She was lying as he had found her, and the scarred jaw was hidden. 'She'll soften by tonight or tomorrow, in this weather, and they can lay her out properly. We should look at her then.'

The mason marched him firmly from the chapel and down the High Street, nodding to acquaintances as he went, and in at the pend below the sign of the White Castle.

They came through the arched entry into a courtyard,

bright with flowers in tubs. The house, like most of this part of the High Street, must be some fifty years old, but it was showing signs of modernization. The range to their right had a row of large new windows set into the roof, and a wooden penthouse ran round two sides of the yard. Gil had no time to look further; Maistre Pierre dragged him across the cobbles and up the fore-stair, in under the carved lintel, shouting loudly in French, 'Catherine! Alys! I am here and I am hungry! Where are you?'

He drew Gil into a large hall, dim after the sunny courtyard, where plate gleamed in the shadows and the furniture smelled of beeswax.

'Welcome to my house,' he said, gesturing expansively, and threw the furred gown on to a windowseat. 'Where are those women?'

'I am here, father,' said a remembered voice behind them. 'No need to make so much noise, we were only in the store-rooms.'

Gil, turning, had just time to recognize the figure outlined in the doorway against the light, before the mason seized the girl, kissing her as soundly as if he had been away for days.

'My daughter, maister! Alys, it is Maister Gilbert Cunningham,' he said, pronouncing the name quite creditably, 'of the Consistory Court. He and I have found a dead lady and a live boy this morning, and we need food.'

'Yes, Luke has told me. I will bring food in a moment, father.' She moved forward, held out both hands to Gil and leaned up to kiss him in greeting. A whisper reached his ear: 'Please don't tell!'

'Enchanted to serve you, demoiselle,' said Gil in ambiguous French, and returned the kiss with careful courtesy. 'How is the boy?'

'We are still washing him. When he is comfortable you may see him.'

'Has he spoken? Where is his brother? Where is that food?'

'The food is in the kitchen, father, and Catherine is

42

supervising the girls who are all helping with Davie. No, he has not roused. His brother is with him. If you take our guest up to your closet I will bring you something to eat.'

Maistre Pierre's closet, on the floor above, was panelled and painted, with a pot of flowers on the windowsill and cushions on the benches. A desk stood in one corner, with a jumble of papers on it; a lute lay on a bench, and there were four books on a shelf near the window.

'Be seated,' said the mason, indicating the big chair. Gil shook his head, and sat politely on a bench. 'Well!' said the mason explosively, dropping into the chair himself. 'What a day, and it not yet past Terce!'

He looked consideringly at Gil, and seemed to come to some conclusion.

'I am concerned in this,' he said. 'That is my boy who is injured, and the lady has come to grief in my *chantier*. Do you know who will pursue the matter?'

'Not the burgh officers,' Gil said. 'I'll speak to the serjeant out of courtesy, but he has no authority on St Mungo's land. It will be someone from the Consistory Court, likely.'

'One of the apparitors? I have the term right? The men who serve notice that one must be present on a certain day or be excommunicated.'

'You have the term right. It might be.' Gil rose as Alys entered with a tray of food. 'I will report to the Official, as soon as I may, and he will make a decision,' he added, setting a stool to act as table, irritated to find himself clumsy.

Unruffled, Alys poured ale for both men and handed a platter of oatmeal bannocks and another of barley bannocks with slices of meat in them. Her father took one of these, jumped to his feet and began to stride this way and that in the small room like a hunting-leopard Gil had once seen in its cage.

Alys sat down, gathering her skirts neatly about her, and watched him with an intent gaze. She was as taking as Gil remembered. She was clad today in a gown of faded blue which set off her young figure to advantage, and her hair was tied back with a ribbon, emphasizing the oval shape of her face with its pointed chin and high-bridged nose. Finer-boned and finer-featured than her father, she still resembled him strongly, although she must have inherited that remarkable nose from someone else.

As if aware of his scrutiny, she glanced up at him and smiled briefly, then turned back to her still-pacing father.

'What do we know?' the mason said. 'This woman who sang with the harper was knifed, there in that confined space, in the Fergus Aisle, Alys, with a narrow blade.'

'Luke told me that too,' said Alys. 'I find it extraordinary. Why was she there? A young man – someone Davie's age – might go in out of curiosity, but a woman in her good clothes would need a sound reason to climb the scaffolding, even by the wheelbarrow ramp.'

'A good point, *ma mie*,' agreed her father. 'It must have been someone she knew, someone she trusted, to enter the *chantier* with him.'

'We know a little more,' Gil said. 'There was not much blood, so he will not necessarily be marked.'

'A negative.'

'But useful. And we know that one of Sempill's men-at-arms fetched her sometime after Vespers. Indeed, I think I saw him come to Compline.' He paused, thinking carefully. 'I saw the whole party at Compline. One of the men-at-arms was late, as I say, and one of Sempill's friends arrived after him, but the rest were under my eye for the most part from the start of the service.'

'Perhaps the man-at-arms – the gallowglass,' said Alys, bringing the word out triumphantly, 'was the one who killed her. Or could the husband have stabbed her after he left the church?' She rose to replenish their beakers.

'I don't think so,' said Gil with regret. 'He left just before me, and when I reached the door he was already returning from the clump of trees opposite.'

44

Alys set the jug down and stood considering him, absently twirling a lock of hair round one finger.

'He came from the trees,' she repeated. 'Not from the Fergus Aisle?'

'No,' agreed Gil. 'Besides, I think even Sempill of Muirend is not so rash as to summon a woman openly in order to kill her. No, and I do not know who had time to get into the Fergus Aisle and out of it again before I saw them all together. It's an easy enough climb over the scaffolding, or up the ramp for the barrow and down again, but it takes a moment, and the scaffolding would creak. On a quiet evening like yesterday you would hear it in Rottenrow.'

'Perhaps the person had not left,' said Alys. 'And what about Davie? Did the same person strike him down?'

'I saw Davie,' Gil said, reaching for another bannock. 'He was in the kirkyard before Vespers, with a lass. I took her to be the same one I saw him with earlier at the dancing.'

'I do not know who she is,' said Alys, 'but the men might. It is urgent that you find her, you realize, whoever is to track down the killer.'

'It is,' agreed Gil.

'I must see the boy,' said the mason impatiently, setting down his beaker. 'Where have you put him?'

Across the courtyard, sacks and barrels had been hastily stacked in the shelter of the new penthouse. In the vaulted store-room thus cleared, worn tapestries hung round the walls for warmth, and a charcoal brazier gave off a choking scent of burning spices. Next to it the boy Davie lay on a cot, curled on his side with bandages across the crown of his head and supporting his slack jaw. A small woman veiled in black knelt at the bed's foot, her rosary slipping through her intent fingers, her lips moving steadily. A stout maidservant sat at the head with her spindle, and a gangling youth with a strong resemblance to the injured boy rose to his feet as Alys put aside the hanging at the door.

'He's no stirred, mem,' he said anxiously. 'But his breathing's maybe a mite easier.'

'I think you are right,' Alys agreed, feeling Davie's rough red hand. 'He seems warmer, too.' She turned to her father. 'We washed the wound, and bandaged it, after we clipped his hair. Brother Andrew came, and said he thought the skull was broken, but to keep him warm and still and nurse him carefully and pray. So Annis is watching and Catherine is praying, and so is Will while he can stay.'

'A broken skull,' the mason said in some dismay. 'It needs a compress of vinegar with lavender and rose petals, hot to his feet, Alys, to restore the spirits and draw excess humours from the brain.'

'So I thought,' she agreed, 'but we are short of rose petals. Jennet is gone out to the apothecary for more.'

'What came to you, boy?' said Maistre Pierre, staring down at the waxy yellow face. 'I wish you could tell me.'

The sandy lashes stirred and flickered. Annis leaned forward with an exclamation, and Catherine paused in her muttering. Alys dropped to her knees, her head near the boy's as the bloodless lips twitched, formed soundless words. Then the eyes flew open and suddenly, clearly, Davie spoke.

'It wisny me. It wisny me, maister.'

His eyes closed again. Alys felt his hand, then his cheek, with gentle fingers, but he did not respond. She rose, and turned to her father and Gil.

'You must find his sweetheart,' she said. 'Before the killer does.'

Chapter Three

Canon Cunningham was in his chamber in the Consistory tower, working at the high desk in an atmosphere of parchment and old paper. When Gil brushed past the indignant clerk in the antechamber and stepped round the door, his uncle was ferreting through more documents in a tray from the tall narrow cabinet behind him. At his elbow were the protocol books and rolled parchments for the Sempill conveyancing, with his legal bonnet, shaped like a battered acorn-cup, perched on top of the stack.

'I'll ring when I am ready,' he said, without looking up.

'May I have a word, sir?' said Gil. At his voice the Official raised his head and favoured him with a cold grey stare. Gil, undaunted, closed the door and leaning on the desk gave a concise account of the morning's discoveries. His uncle heard him in attentive silence, then stared out of the window at the rose-pink stone tower of the Archbishop's castle, tapping his fingers on the desk.

'James Henderson spoke to me at Chapter this morning,' he said at last. 'I think he has the right of it. She died on St Mungo's land, St Mungo's has a duty to find her killer.'

'And to determine whether it was forethought felony or murder *chaud-mellé*,' offered Gil. His uncle glanced at him sharply.

'Aye. Well, you were aye good at hunting, Gilbert, and you have shown some sense making a start on the trail already. You might as well continue. You'll report to me, of course, and I'll take it to Chapter.'

'Of course, sir,' said Gil, blinking slightly at the unaccustomed praise.

His uncle looked again at the parchments at his elbow.

'This must be replait, I suppose,' he said, 'at least until the poor woman is formally identified. Where will you begin? Where is the trail freshest?'

'Two places, I think, sir,' said Gil readily. He and the master mason had already found themselves in agreement on the same question. 'The lass who was with the mason's boy must be found, and I wish to speak to John Sempill of Muirend. And additional to that, St Mungo's yard must be searched carefully, in case we find the great piece of wood with which the boy was struck down. The mason and his men are seeing to that just now. I passed Sempill in the waiting-room here,' he added, 'himself, Philip, two witnesses, and one of the gallowglasses.'

'Well, well,' said Canon Cunningham. He picked up parchments and protocol books, and moved to sit behind the great table, arranging his documents on the worn table-carpet. Clapping the legal bonnet over his black felt coif, he continued, 'Then let us have in Sempill of Muirend and see how he takes the news.'

John Sempill of Muirend, summoned alone, argued briefly with Richard Fleming the clerk in the antechamber, then erupted into the chamber saying impatiently, 'Yon fool of a clerk says you don't want my witnesses. Is there some problem, sir?'

'There may be,' said David Cunningham calmly. 'Be seated, Maister Sempill.'

John Sempill, ignoring the invitation, stared at the Official. He was a solid, sandy man, inappropriately dressed in cherry-coloured velvet faced with squirrel, with a large floppy hat falling over one eye. Scowling from under this he said, 'My damned wife hasn't compeared, no in person nor by a man of law, but she's left me anyway, I suppose you know that, so she isn't concerned in this.'

'When did you last see your wife, John?' asked Gil.

The pale blue eyes turned to him. 'Yesterday, making a May-game of herself at Glasgow Cross. Fine thing for a man to meet, riding into the town – his lawful wife, disporting herself in public for servant-lads and prentices to gape at.'

'And that was the last you saw her?' Gil pressed.

'Yes. What is this?' Sempill pushed the hat back. 'Is something wrong?'

'Did you try to have word with her?'

'Yes, I did, but the bitch never compeared for me either. What is this?' he demanded again. 'What's she done, run off from the harper too?'

'Not quite,' said Gil. 'When were you to have met her?'

'Last night after Compline. Neil Campbell said he fetched her, but when I came out of the church she wasn't to be seen. Turned hen-hearted, I suppose. You saw me,' he added. 'You came out of St Mungo's just behind Euphemia.'

'I did,' Gil agreed.

'Maister Sempill,' said David Cunningham, 'I think you should know that a woman was found in the Fergus Aisle this morning, dead. She has been provisionally identified as Bess Stewart of Ettrick, your wife.'

The blue eyes, fixed on his, grew round with shock. The broad face sagged and stiffened into a mask of astonishment.

'Sit down, man,' said the Official. John Sempill, still staring, felt behind him with one booted foot for the stool and sank on to it.

'Dead,' he repeated. 'When? How? Had she been forced?' he demanded.

'No sign of that,' said Gil. 'She never went back to her lodgings. She must have died sometime last night.'

'Dead,' said Sempill again. 'And in the Fergus Aisle? You mean that bit of building work in St Mungo's yard? Why? What happened to her?'

'That we hope to establish,' said Gil. 'Perhaps you can tell us a few things.'

'So she didn't run out,' said Sempill thoughtfully. 'Poor bitch.' He looked up, from Gil to his uncle. 'That means her interest in the Rottenrow plot is returned to me,' he pointed out firmly. 'We can continue with that transaction at least.'

'That must be for you and your witnesses to decide,' said Gil, rather taken aback. 'My immediate concern is to discover who killed your wife and bring him to justice. Do you tell me that between the time you rode in at Glasgow Cross yesterday and now, you have not seen or spoken with her?'

'That's exactly what I said,' agreed Sempill irritably. 'The woman's dead, what purpose is there in worrying at it?'

'I think the Bishop – Archbishop,' Gil corrected himself, 'could enlighten you on that if your confessor cannot. What was the message that your man took, John?'

Sempill stared angrily at Gil for a moment, then evidently decided to humour him.

'That she should come up and meet me by the south door of St Mungo's after Compline. *And* he delivered it. *And* he came into Compline and told me she was waiting out-by in the trees. The small belt of haw-trees,' he elaborated, 'by the south door. Is that clear enough? You can ask Neil himself if you choose. He's over in Rottenrow.'

'Thank you, I will. Did you offer her a reason for the meeting?'

'Aye, but what's that to do with it?'

'It will tell us why she would come up the High Street at that hour,' said Gil mildly. 'It was late to be out without a reason.'

Sempill stared at him again, chewing his lip. Finally he said, 'I don't know what Neil told her.'

'Understood,' agreed Gil.

'I bid him tell her it was a matter of money. Her money. Knew that would fetch her,' he said, grinning. 'All Stewarts are thrieveless and she's no exception.' The grin

50

faded as the two lawyers looked at him without expression. 'I was going to offer her her share of the purchase if she agreed to this transaction.' He nodded at the desk in front of him.

'You must be desperate for the money,' Gil said.

Sempill scrutinized this, failed to detect sarcasm, and said, 'Aye. Well. The Treasury has a long memory. So we might as well go ahead with it.'

'It seems to me as your conveyancer,' said Canon Cunningham, 'that it is only proper the matter should be replait – that it should be set aside to wait until you have identified the corpse yourself. Perhaps you would discuss this with your witnesses, Maister Sempill. And accept our condolences on your loss.'

'Aye,' said Sempill again. He glared at both Cunninghams, rose and withdrew with dignity, slamming the door behind him so that documents went flying about the room.

'Well!' said Gil, stooping for the nearest. 'Why is he in such a hurry to get the money?'

'Paisley Cross,' said his uncle elliptically.

'What was it at Paisley Cross?' asked Maistre Pierre. He had been waiting near the door at the foot of the stair. Without the fur-lined gown he was less bulky but still big, an inch or two shorter than Gil but far broader. He had unlaced and removed the sleeves of his jerkin and rolled up his shirtsleeves, revealing muscular brown forearms decorated with silver scars. 'This way, maister,' he added.

'It began two years since,' said Gil, following him down the kirkyard. 'The Crown granted Paisley burgh status and a market after Stirling field, you remember, and Renfrew took exception to another market two miles away from theirs.'

'This I knew from Davie. Where does Sempill enter?'

'The burgesses of Paisley bought stones to make a market cross, and some *evil advised persons of the said town of Renfrew,'* Gil quoted with relish, 'came by night and broke up the stones. If Sempill of Eliotstoun –'

'Ah, the Sheriff of Renfrew –'

'Indeed, and head of the Sempills in the west, was not involved, he certainly knew who was. The Earl of Lennox and his son were charged with putting it right, and naturally they pursued the guilty with all rigour, given their –'

'Great love for all Sempills,' Maistre Pierre completed. 'I begin to see. There would be fines to pay, of course. So this particular Sempill is being pursued by the Crown, and having to sell land to raise funds. Is he close kin to the Sheriff of Renfrew?'

'Not close enough for Eliotstoun to pay his fines for him,' Gil said, and realized his companion was not listening. He had come to a halt at the edge of the trees and was casting about.

'Now where – ah, that peeled twig. We search for a weapon, we agreed, or a thing out of place. We have seen no weapon this far, but Luke found this, which is certainly out of place. We left it lying so you also could see where it was.'

He parted the bluebells in front of the marker. Gil leaned down and lifted the harp key which nestled in the long leaves. It was a pretty thing; the metal barrel that gripped the tuning-pins was set into a painted wooden handle. A love-gift, a musician's gift, acutely personal. Surely the dead woman would have kept such a thing safe?

'It has flowers on, it must be hers, not?' the mason continued. 'Has she been here? Was it she who struck the boy down?'

'Her hands were clean,' Gil pointed out. 'She had not handled the kind of stick we are searching for. No, this came here another way.'

He recounted the incident he had seen just before the mason arrived. Maistre Pierre heard him out, and said thoughtfully, 'She must have had a purse, to keep it in. I wonder what has happened to that?'

'My thought,' agreed Gil.

'We must find these laddies and question them. It must be nearly noon – will they sing also at Nones? We can catch them then.'

'More like two of the other boys,' Gil said. 'They take turns. It's cheaper, and doesn't tire their voices. I'll speak to Patrick – no doubt he can help. Where are your men now? Have you asked them about Davie's lass?'

'Alys spoke to them. I am not certain what she learned. They are up-by, searching the top of the kirkyard, since most of Glasgow is now gone home to its noon piece. Maister lawyer, this gallowglass must be questioned, I think. Suppose you leave us here and go see to that?'

The Sempill property was a large sprawling townhouse, an uneasy mix of stone tower and timber additions set round a courtyard. Three hens and a pair of pigeons occupied the courtyard; voices floated from an open window, and someone was practising the lute. Gil paused under the arch of the gateway, then, on the grounds that he represented St Mungo's, moved towards the stairs to the main door.

He had taken barely two steps into the courtyard when sound exploded behind him, an enormous barking and clanking and scrabble of claws. He whirled, drawing his sword, leaping backwards through a flurry of wings, as the mastiff hurtled to the end of its chain bellowing threats. Laughter from the house suggested that he had been seen. He took another prudent step backwards, assessing the huge animal with its rolls of brindled muscle. Ropes of saliva hung from the white fangs in the powerful jaws. He looked carefully at the chain, then sheathed his whinger, turned and strolled to the stairs, controlling his breathing with some difficulty. Behind him the dog continued to bay furiously until Sempill appeared in the doorway.

'Doucette!' he bawled. 'Down! You were safe enough,'

he added, grinning as the noise dropped. He had discarded the cherry velvet, and wore a very old leather
jerkin. 'We only let her loose at night.'

'I hope the chain is secure,' Gil commented. Behind him
metal rattled as the dog lay down with reluctance, still
snarling. 'You could find yourself with a serious action
against you if she got loose and killed something.'

The grin vanished. Sempill grunted in answer, and said,
'I suppose you're here to ask more questions.'

'I wish to speak to the man who took your message last
night,' Gil agreed. 'And perhaps I might ask the rest of
your household if they saw anything unusual in the kirkyard when we left Compline.'

'Why? You were there. You know what there was to
see.'

'Someone else might have noticed something different.'

Sempill stared at him, then said ungraciously, 'Wait in
here, I'll send Neil to you. I'll see if the others will speak
to you as well – but you're not to upset Euphemia,
mind.'

He showed Gil into a small closet off the hall. It
contained a clutter of half-repaired harness, for man
and horse, and some leather-working tools laid on the
windowsill.

'Fool of a groom in charge here,' said Sempill, seeing Gil
looking at these. 'I swear by the Rood, half the leather in
the place is rotted, I'm having to overhaul the lot, but if
I beat him as he deserves, who's to see to Doucette out
there?'

He strolled off, ostentatiously casual, shouting, 'Neil!
Neil, come here, you blichan!' Gil sat down by the window
and studied the array of tools. There were some nasty
triangular needles, a leather palm, a vicious little knife. He
lifted the awl and turned it in his hand, feeling the
point.

'Fery sharp,' said a voice. Gil turned, to see one of the
two men-at-arms occupying most of the doorway. 'The
chentleman wished to see me?'

Gil studied the man briefly. Dark hair cut short to go under a helm, dark eyebrows in a long narrow face, blue eyes which slid sideways from his.

'You are Neil Campbell?'

'It iss myself.' The accent was far stronger than Eala-saidh's. Gil rephrased his next question.

'You were sent with a message for Maister Sempill yesterday evening?'

'I am taking many messages for himself.'

'This one was to his wife.'

'That iss so,' agreed Campbell, the stern face softening momentarily. 'To his wife. In the Fishergait, where she is liffing with the clarsair.'

'What was the message?'

'Oh, I could not be telling that.' The man's eyes slid sideways again.

Gil said patiently, 'Maister Sempill gave me permission to ask you. I know what he bade you say, but I need to know what message reached her.'

'Oh, I would not know about that.'

'You know she is dead?' Gil said.

The blue gaze sharpened. '*Dhia*! You say?' said the man, crossing himself. 'The poor lady!'

'And you may have been the last to see her alive,' Gil pointed out. 'Did she come up the High Street with you, or did she follow you?'

'Oh, I would not know,' said the man again.

Gil drew a breath, and said with some care, 'Tell me this, then. Did the message that John Sempill sent for his wife reach her, or not?'

'Oh, it was reaching her,' said the other man, nodding sadly. 'And then she was coming up the hill, and now she is dead. How did she come to die, maister?'

'Someone knifed her,' said Gil. The narrow face opposite him froze; the blue eyes closed, and opened again.

'What do you know about her death?' Gil asked.

'Nothing. Nothing at all, at all,' said the gallowglass,

55

through stiffened lips. 'The last I saw her she was well and living.'

'Did she come up the hill with you?'

'Not with me, no, she did not.' This seemed to be the truth, Gil thought. The man was too shaken to prevaricate.

'And what was the message?'

'That I cannot be telling you.'

'Why can't you tell me?'

'Chust it is not possible. Is the chentleman finished asking at me?'

Gil gave up.

'Will you tell Maister Sempill I have done with you for the moment,' he said. 'I will need to get another word with you later.'

The man turned and tramped out. Baffled, Gil stared after him, then bent his attention to the tools on the sill again. He was still studying them when John Sempill returned.

'I could have told you you'd not get much out of Neil,' he said. 'Him and his brother, they're both wild Ersche. You need the two tongues to deal with them.'

'How do you manage?' Gil asked, controlling his irritation.

'Oh, they have enough Scots for my purposes. Do you still want to speak to the others?'

'Yes, if it is possible.' Gil rose, and followed Sempill across the hall, picking his way past hunting gear and half a set of plate armour, and up a wheel stair at the other side towards a continuous sound of voices. The room at the top of the stair was hung with much-mended verdure tapestry, and replete with cushions, among which Lady Euphemia Campbell was sewing and chattering away like a goldfinch to her middle-aged waiting-woman.

They made a pleasing sight. Lady Euphemia, wearing a wealth of pleated linen on her head, fathoms more rumpled round her, appeared daintier than ever. Her stout companion, stolidly threading needles, merely served to emphasize this further. Under her coarse black linen veil her face reminded Gil of the dough faces Maggie used to bake for him and his brothers and sisters, with small black currant eyes and a slit of a mouth.

'Here's Euphemia, making sheets to her bed,' said Sempill. 'I can make do with blankets myself, but she's too delicate for that.'

'Venus rising from the foam,' said Gil, and added politely, 'in duplicate.'

This won him a suspicious look from Sempill and two approving smiles. Someone laughed at the other end of the room.

'And there's my cousin Philip and Euphemia's brother,' added Sempill.

'Have some claret, priest,' suggested one of the two men by the blank fireplace, darkly handsome and much Sempill's age. 'Since my good-brother does not see fit to introduce us, let me tell you I am James Campbell of Glenstriven. Are you here to explain why we've to wait to finish this sale?'

'In a way,' agreed Gil, accepting a cup of wine and adding water. 'I am Gilbert Cunningham of the Consistory Court.' He waited until the familiar chill in his stomach dispelled itself, and continued, 'I'll drink to a successful conclusion with you. Perhaps John has already explained that Bess Stewart his wife was killed last night in the kirkyard of St Mungo's. We need to find out who did it and take him up.'

'Why?' said Campbell of Glenstriven. 'She was an adulterous wife, she's dead. Why bother yourself with her?'

'That comes well from you, James Campbell!' said Sempill indignantly.

'I spoke nothing but the truth.'

'She was a Christian soul killed on Church land,' said Gil, 'and she died unshriven of her adultery. St Mungo's owes her justice. Moreover, the manner of her death must be clarified before John's sole right to the land can be certain.'

'Why?' said Sempill blankly. 'What's that to do with it?'

57

Behind him there was a pause in the chatter at the other end of the room.

'You mean in case it was John killed her?' said Campbell of Glenstriven.

Sempill's colour rose. 'I never set eyes on her last night!' he said loudly. 'I wanted her agreement, she'd to turn out today and sign her name – I never killed her!'

'I have not said you did,' said Gil. 'Just the same, that's why the sale must wait.'

Philip Sempill looked up from his wine. Physically he was a paler imitation of his cousin, fair rather than sandy, less stocky, quieter in speech and movement and less forceful in manner. Like him, he was wearing an old leather jerkin, which contrasted oddly with James Campbell's wide-sleeved green velvet gown.

'Och, well,' he said, his voice sounding thickened. 'Ask away, Gil. We'll answer you, at least.'

His cousin stared at him.

'You got the rheum, Philip? You can stay away from Euphemia if you have, I don't want her getting sick just now.'

'It's nothing much,' said the fair man. 'Gil?'

Gil hesitated, considering. The three men watched him; the two women had gone back to their sewing, but he was aware that Lady Euphemia flicked him a glance from time to time. Squaring his shoulders, he began:

'You were all at Compline.' The three men nodded. 'Was the kirkyard busy when you went down to St Mungo's?'

'I wouldn't say so,' said Philip Sempill. 'A few folk coming down from the Stablegreen and Rottenrow, a last few youngsters going home to a beating for staying out. I saw a couple in that stand of haw-bushes.'

'Would you know them again?' Gil asked.

The other man shook his head. 'Likely not. Oh – the boy had striped hose on. The Deil knows where he got such a thing in Glasgow.'

'I saw them,' said Euphemia Campbell, breaking off her chatter. She had a high pretty voice with a laugh in it, and

58

a dimple came and went in her cheek as she spoke. 'But they were further down the hill. I wondered where he got the striped hose too. Surely not in Glasgow, I never saw such a dreary place. I swear you can buy better wares in Rothesay.'

'When did you see them?' Gil asked.

She giggled. 'It must have been later, mustn't it, if they were in the haw-trees when Philip saw them? Maybe after Compline when we all came out?'

'I never saw them,' said Sempill suspiciously.

'Maybe you were looking at me,' she cooed. He stared at her as if he could not help it, and she smiled at him so that the dimple flashed then turned back to her sewing and her chatter, with what appeared to be a highly coloured account of how she had purchased the linen. Her waiting-woman nodded in time to her words.

'Did you see anybody in the kirkyard after the Office?' Gil asked. The men exchanged glances, and all shook their heads.

'Not even Bess, damn her,' said Sempill. 'I told you – Neil came into the kirk, said he'd left her in the haw-bushes, but when I went out she'd gone.' He stared at the empty fireplace, chewing his lip. 'Not a sign of her. I checked through the bushes – you can see right through, but I went to the other side. I looked down the kirkyard, and not a thing was stirring.'

'You are sure of that?' said Gil.

'I keep telling you. Besides,' he added, undermining this statement, 'I assumed she'd run off. If she could do me an ill turn she would.'

'We were close enough behind to see him moving about in the haw-bushes,' said his cousin, and James Campbell nodded and muttered something that might have been agreement.

'And were you all together during Compline?'

Once more they exchanged glances. After a moment Campbell said, fiddling with his embroidered shirt-cuffs, 'There was some coming and going to other altars. You know the style of thing. I was gone long enough myself to say a prayer to St James and come back to the others.'

'I left money for candles to St Thomas,' agreed Philip Sempill. 'It took me the length of a Gloria, I suppose. John was the only one who stood the Office through. Oh, and one of the men. Euan, maybe.'

'I thought you were watching us, Maister Cunningham,' said Lady Euphemia, looking up with her needle poised above her seam. 'Did you not see where we all were?'

'My attention may have wandered,' said Gil drily. Sempill frowned, looking for the insult, but Lady Euphemia cast her eyes down again, and the dimple flashed. 'And the wee dark fellow?' Gil continued. 'What is he, a musician? Where was he?'

'Antonio?' said James Campbell dismissively. 'He'd likely be listening to the music. I'll swear he thinks in tablature.'

'Never in Scots, that's for certain,' said Sempill. Gil, turning to set down his wine-cup, caught sight of Euphemia's expression. She was listening to her companion, but her needle had paused again, and her mouth curved, softly crooked as if she was recalling the taste of stolen fruit.

'And afterwards?' he continued. 'You all came back to the house together?'

'Oh, yes. And sat together afterwards. We were up here for an hour or so listening to lute music.' Philip Sempill looked round, and Campbell of Glenstriven said,

'Aye, that sounds about right. And playing at the cards,' he added.

'Even the two gallowglasses?'

'Neil and Euan?' said John Sempill dismissively. 'They'd be in the kitchen, likely, you could ask Marriott Kennedy.'

'And what about the dead woman?' Gil asked. 'Tell me about her. Why would anybody want to kill her?'

Three pairs of eyes stared, and there was a pause in the chatter behind him.

'I took it to be some beggar or broken man,' said Sempill after a moment. 'Why should it have been deliberate?'

'I hoped you could tell me that.'

'She was a quiet body,' said Philip Sempill thickly, shaking his head.

'Quiet!' exploded his cousin. 'She scarcely had a word, and that not civil.'

'That was after you took your belt to her.'

'And why would I not? I needed an heir – she knew I needed an heir – and then she lost it, the clumsy bitch. So after that she never spoke to me. And if she had I'd have clouted her round the lug for what she cost me.'

Rage boiled up, a physical presence in Gil's chest. He put up a hand to finger his upper lip in concealment, taking a moment to compose himself, astonished at the strength of the response. *Never condemn*, his uncle had said, *you'll get the story clearer*. He had been referring to pleas of divorce, but it applied just as firmly here.

'Cost you?' he asked, when he was sure of his voice.

'Aye. Well. My uncle. He's made it clear I have to settle down, not only wedded but with an heir, if I'm to get his estate. So she lost the brat, and ran off before I could get another, and if the old ruddoch dies at the wrong moment the whole lot goes to Holy Church and I'll not get my hands on it, may they both rot in Hell for it.'

'It might have been a lassie,' Philip Sempill pointed out. His cousin snarled at him.

'Did your wife have friends?' Gil asked.

'Other than the harpers, you mean?' said Euphemia. Sempill swivelled to look at her. 'I'm sorry, John, but it was notorious. Every musician that came to Rothesay was in her chamber.' She giggled, and the dimple flashed at Gil. 'They say she had a key for every harp west of Dumbarton, and her own ideas about speed of performance.'

Sempill glared at her, and her brother said, 'Now, Euphemia,' and raised an admonishing finger in a gesture which Gil found suddenly familiar.

'So it might have been a jealous lover,' she finished

triumphantly. Sempill made a move towards her, but she lifted her chin and smiled at him, showing little white teeth, and he stopped.

'What –' said Campbell of Glenstriven rather loudly. 'What did you mean, Maister Cunningham, about the couple in the bushes? Was it just the state of sin they were in, or had you a purpose asking about them?'

'I did,' said Gil. 'We've found the laddie, but he's no help. We need to find his sweetheart.'

'Can he not tell you who she is?'

'He can tell us nothing. He was struck on the head there in the kirkyard and now lies near to death. There may have been two ill-doers abroad in St Mungo's yard last night.'

Lady Euphemia, suddenly as white as her linen head-dress, stared at Gil for a moment. Then her eyes rolled up in her head and she slipped sideways into the arms of her companion. Sempill, with a muffled curse, sprang forward to land on his knees beside her, patting frantically at her cheek and hands.

'Euphemia! Mally, a cordial! Wine – anything!'

'It's just a wee turn,' said the companion, putting a cushion under the sufferer's head. 'She'll be right in a minute.'

Sempill, still rubbing at the limp little hand in his grasp, turned to glare at Gil over his shoulder.

'I warned you not to upset Euphemia,' he said forcefully. 'James, get him out of here!'

Campbell of Glenstriven got to his feet, and indicated the door with a polite gesture. Gil, aware of unasked questions, considered brazening it out, but something about James Campbell's bearing changed his mind. He rose, said an unheeded goodbye and went down the wheel stair. As Campbell emerged into the hall after him he turned to say, 'You were in Italy after St Andrews?'

'Bologna,' agreed the other. 'I was back there just last autumn, indeed. And you? Glasgow and . . .?'

'Paris,' Gil supplied. 'But of course the subtle doctor is a

Bolognese.' He raised the admonishing finger in imitation, and they both grinned.

'Was it that gave me away, or was it a good guess?' Campbell asked, moving towards the door.

'That and other things. There were Italian students. Dress, deportment, your dagger. Is it Italian? The pommel looks familiar.'

James Campbell drew the blade and laid it across his palm.

'From Ferrara. I brought several home this time. I like the wee fine blade they make. It has a spring to it we can't achieve here. Least of all in Glasgow,' he added.

'Was that all you brought?'

'Five miles or so of lace. Two-three lutes and a lutenist to play on them. Oh, did you mean a sword? No, those were beyond my means. The daggers were dear enough.' Campbell opened the front door, and the mastiff raised her head and growled threateningly. 'Good day to you, brother.'

Maistre Pierre drank some wine and chewed thoughtfully on a lozenge of quince leather. Further down his table two maids were whispering together and the men were eating oatcakes and cheese and arguing about football, ignoring the French talk at the head of the long board.

'Why did she swoon, do you suppose?' he asked.

Gil shrugged. 'Alarm at hearing there were two dangerous persons in the churchyard? Her gown laced too tight? I don't know.'

'These little fragile women are often very strong,' remarked Alys, pouring more wine for Gil. 'Was it a real swoon?'

'Real or pretended, you mean?' Gil considered. 'Real, I should say. Her mouth fell open.'

'Ah.' Alys nodded, as at a bright student, and her elusive smile flickered.

'And what of the boys who found the harp key? Or the

unknown sweetheart?' said her father fretfully. 'She must hold the key to the mystery.'

'Luke tells me,' said Alys, glancing along the table, 'that she is called Bridie Miller and she is kitchenmaid to Agnes Hamilton two doors from here. I thought to go after dinner and ask to speak with her.'

Gil opened his mouth to object, and closed it again, hardly able to work out why he should have anything to say in the matter.

'Very good,' said her father, pushing his chair back. 'That was an excellent meal, *ma mie*. Maister Cunningham, what do you do now?'

'I accompany the demoiselle,' said Gil. Alys, supervising the clearing of an empty kale-pot and the remains of a very handsome pie, turned her head sharply. 'Mistress Hamilton's son Andrew found the harp key,' he elaborated, 'with William Anderson, the saddler's youngest.'

'Better still,' said the mason. 'Take your cloak, Alys, the weather spoils. Wattie, Thomas, Luke! To work! We seek still this weapon.'

'In a moment,' said Alys. 'I must see that Catherine and Annis are fed and set someone to watch Davie. Kittock, do you carry this out, and I will bring the wine.'

The household began to bustle about. Gil, retreating to the windowseat, found not one but two books half hidden under a bag of sewing. When Alys reappeared, in plaid and clogs like any girl of the burgh, he was engrossed.

'Maister Cunningham?' she said. He looked up, tilting the page towards her.

'I like this,' he said. '*Cease from an inordinate desire of knowledge, for therein is much perplexity and delusion.* I've often felt like that when confronted with another pile of papers.'

'*There are many things,*' she agreed, '*which when known profit the soul little or nothing.*'

'You read Latin?' he said, startled.

'It is my copy. I have to confess –' The apologetic smile

flickered. 'I take refuge in Chaucer when it becomes too serious for me.'

'What, this one? The story-tellers on pilgrimage?'

She nodded. 'I am cast out with Patient Grissel at the moment.'

'I never had any patience with Patient Grissel or her marquis.' Gil laid the *Imitation of Christ* on the sill and followed her to the door. 'Any man that treated one of my sisters so would have got his head in his hands to play with as soon as we heard of it.'

'Her lord cannot have loved her, for sure, though he claimed to.' She clopped down the fore-stair into the court-yard. 'And he took all the power and left her none.'

'Power?' said Gil. This girl, he recognized again, was exceptional.

'If the wife has responsibilities,' Alys said seriously, 'duties, about the house, she must have power to order matters as she wishes. Grissel must do all, but has no power of her own. It is as if she is her marquis's hand or foot and must do only as he directs.'

'You think that is wrong? Holy Kirk teaches us –'

'I know the husband is the head of the wife, it's in St Paul's letters somewhere,' Alys said, pausing beside a tub of flowers in the middle of the yard. She had taken the ribbon out of her hair and it hung loose down her back. She pulled at a soft fair lock. 'But what sort of head cuts off its own right hand to test it?'

'I had not thought of it that way, I admit,' Gil said. 'To my mind, she would have had good grounds for a lawful separation *a mensa et thoro*, though I suppose the Clerke of Oxenfoord would not have given us the tale of Patient Grissel Divorced.' Alys giggled. 'We see a lot of marriages,' he said. 'The ones I admire most are those where the wife is allowed to think for herself and decisions are made by both spouses together. Myself, I think . . .' He paused, groping for words to fit his idea. 'Women have immortal souls and were given the ability to seek their own salva-

tion. How can they do that if someone else takes responsibility for their every deed and thought?'

Alys considered this, twirling the lock of hair round one
finger.

'St Paul thought we were capable of more than that. *The
unbelieving husband is sanctified by the wife*,' she quoted, in
the Latin. 'Although,' she added thoughtfully, 'St Paul
contradicts himself more than once. Is that what you think
learning is for? To seek salvation?'

'That was not what I said, but it's surely one of its
purposes. You think so too, do you not? You use yours to
read Thomas à Kempis and the New Testament.'

She nodded, pushing the lock of hair back over her
shoulder, and hitched her plaid up.

'When free of my duties about the house. Shall we go?
Do you know Agnes Hamilton? Or her husband?'

'I was at the College with her brother Hugh,' he said,
accepting the change of subject. 'She was new married,
and generous with the bannocks and cheese when we had
a free hour or two.'

Agnes Hamilton, it was well seen, was still generous
with the bannocks and cheese. She met them in her doorway, vast and flustered, with exclamations of distress.

'And the dinner late, and Andrew in such a mood, and
not a hand's turn done in the kitchen since the news came,
they're all so caught up with Bridie's troubles – my dear,
it's a pleasure to see you any time, you know that, but
maybe not the now. And is that you, Gil Cunningham?'
she said, peering up at him under the folds of her linen
kerchief. 'I'd not have known you, you've changed that
much –'

Distantly behind her there was a great outbreak of wailing. Mistress Hamilton cast a glance over her broad
shoulder.

'Listen to that!' she said unnecessarily. 'The girl will
choke herself weeping! And I can do nothing with the rest
of them. They've let the fire go out.'

'Is it Bridie Miller?' asked Alys briskly. 'May I try? We need a word with her about Davie.'

'He's not – the boy's not . . .?'

'He's not dead,' Gil said, 'but he's still in a great swound. If Bridie knows anything it would be a help.'

'Well . . .' said Mistress Hamilton doubtfully. She led them along the screened passage, past the door to the hall where several men sat about listening glumly to the noise, and out to the yard at the back. The kitchen, built of wattle-and-daub, was set a few feet away from the house, and from its door and windows came the sound of many weeping women. Gil found his feet rooted to the spot.

'Do – do you need me?' he asked, despising himself.

Alys glanced up at him, and said with some sympathy, 'You will be no help. Go and find the boy. Agnes, I will need the key to your spice-chest.'

She took the bunch of keys Mistress Hamilton unhooked from her girdle, hitched up her plaid and plunged forward into the noise. Agnes Hamilton watched her go, hand over her mouth, then turned helplessly to Gil.

'I forget at times she's just sixteen,' she confessed. 'Do you know she reads three languages?'

'Three?' said Gil, and realized this must be so.

'I had a book once, but Andrew sold it. Gil, it's grand to see you, but I can offer you nothing but cowslip wine and suckets –'

'I've had my dinner,' he assured her. 'I need a word with Andrew, and then I'll go, and come back another time.'

Her face changed.

'He's not very pleased at his dinner being late,' she said. 'I don't think he'd talk to you.'

'That's a pity,' said Gil. 'Patrick Paniter bade me tell him –'

'Oh!' said Mistress Hamilton in some relief. 'You mean wee Andrew! Come in here out of all this noise and I'll find him. Drew! Doodie! Oh, that laddie, where has he got to now?'

She disappeared, leaving Gil standing in the hall with

the hungry men eyeing him sideways. After a moment she returned, towing a grubby boy by one ear, exclaiming over the torn hose, of which a good length was visible below his blue scholar's gown.

'And you be civil, mind,' she prompted. 'Maister Cunningham's here from St Mungo's, with a message from Maister Paniter.'

'Not quite that important,' said Gil hastily, seeing all chance of getting an answer from the boy slipping away. 'May I get a word with you, Andrew?'

Andrew stared at him apprehensively. Nudged by his mother he achieved a clumsy bow and muttered something. Gil stepped back out into the yard, where the wailing from the kitchen was not much reduced, and beckoned the boy after him.

'Two boys found something this morning,' he said. 'Maister Paniter was angry, and took it off them, and I found it again.' Well, by proxy, said his conscience. 'I need to ask a couple of questions about it.'

Andrew, fiddling with his belt, said indistinctly that he kenned nuffin.

'Now, that's a pity,' said Gil, 'for the boy who told me what I need to know might get a penny.'

Andrew brightened noticeably. Gil fished the harp key out of the breast of his jerkin and held it up.

'Was that what you found?' he asked. 'I know it was a harp key – is this the right one?'

Andrew nodded eagerly.

'It's got the same flowers on,' he volunteered. 'We saw it shining in the grass when we came to Prime.'

'What, just like this? It wasn't in a purse or anything?'

'No, maister,' said Andrew, a touch regretfully. 'There was never a purse. It was just lying in the grass.'

'Where?' Gil asked. 'Was it among the trees?' I should be dismissed the court, he thought, for prompting the witness, but Andrew shook his head.

'We'd no have seen it among the trees,' he pointed out kindly. 'It was on the grass near the door.'

'Which door?'

'The door we go in by,' said Andrew. 'The south door by St Catherine.'

Gil stood looking down at him, thinking this over. The boy, misreading his silence, said after a moment, 'It's true, maister. You can ask Will. Can I get it back, maister?'

'I've no doubt it's true,' Gil said. 'I need to keep it, but here's your penny, Andrew. Those were good answers.'

Andrew seized the coin, but any thanks he might have returned were drowned in an extraordinary commotion from the kitchen. The multiple sounds of grief suddenly stopped, to be replaced abruptly by a succession of squeals which escalated into a violent outburst of sneezing. The door flew open, and first one, then another girl staggered out, sneezing and sneezing, until the yard was full of spluttering, wheezing, exploding women.

Behind the last one came Alys, her plaid drawn over her face, dusting the other hand off on her blue skirts. Letting the plaid fall, she looked at Agnes Hamilton, who was peering round Gil's shoulder with her mouth open, and said, 'Well, that was a waste of time.'

'What –' said Agnes helplessly. 'What happened? What's wrong?'

'They quarrelled on Good Friday,' Alys elaborated. 'She hasn't seen him for ten days. I can't tell if she was weeping for Davie, or for danger avoided, or lost opportunity, and nor can she, but she can't help us. Agnes, I've a cold pie in the larder. If we send someone up for it, you and the men can eat.'

'And the girls?' said Gil, indicating the suffering household.

'Oh, that.' Alys flapped her skirts again, face turned away. 'I've seen that happen in a nunnery. Everyone weeping and nobody able to stop. It's all right, it isn't the pestilence. Here are your keys, Agnes. I'm afraid I've used up your year's supply of pepper.'

Chapter Four

Out in the street, they stood at the foot of the Hamiltons' fore-stair and looked at one another.

'A false scent,' said Gil.

'Luke was very certain,' said Alys in faint apology.

'Would the other men know any more? Or your maid-servants?' Gil suggested hopefully.

'I asked them first.' Alys looked up and down the quiet street. 'I'll send them out to ask at the market tomorrow. No purpose in searching now, with nobody about. Once they get together with their gossips, the word will pass like heath-fire.' She straightened her shoulders. 'What will you do now?'

'I have to find the other boy,' Gil said, 'the saddler's youngest, and confirm Andrew's story. And since that takes me down the Fishergait I will go by the harper's lodging and ask them about the harp key.'

'May I come with you? I am concerned for them.'

'Do you promise not to throw pepper at them?'

The smile flickered. 'That was a special case. In general I would deplore such a waste.'

'Then it would give me great pleasure,' he said, and offered his arm.

'And after the saddler's house we must stop and buy a jug of spirits to take with us.'

The sign of the Pelican swung crookedly from the front of a tall building, apparently a former merchant's house which had seen better days. Gil, picking a careful path for the two of them through a noisome pend, wondered if he should have brought Alys to the place, and felt his qualms confirmed when they emerged into a muddy yard in which children were squabbling on the midden. Two of them turned to stare at the strangers from under unkempt hair.

'Where does the harper live?' Alys asked.

'Is it the wake ye're after?' asked the taller child. Alys nodded, and the boy gestured with a well-chewed chicken bone at the side of the yard which was probably the original house. 'He stays up yon stair, mistress. Two up and through Jiggin Joan's. Ye can hear them from here,' he waved the chicken bone again. There was indeed a buzz of voices from one of the upper windows.

'Through?' Gil queried, and got a withering look.

'Aye. She's nearest the stair. D'ye ken nothing?'

Gil would have enquired further, but Alys thanked the child and moved towards the stair tower. As Gil turned to follow her, a woman hurried along the creaking wooden gallery opposite.

'Your pardon, maisters!' she exclaimed, with an Ersche-speaker's accent even heavier than the gallowglass's. She leaned over the rail, pulling her plaid up round her head, to ask in a tactful whisper, 'Could you be saying, maybe, when is the poor soul to be buried?'

'I have no idea,' said Gil. 'It's surely a matter for the harper to determine.'

'Oh, 'tis so, 'tis so,' she agreed, 'it iss for mac Iain to decide, but it will be needful to send round to the keening-women, and they will be wishing to know what time to gather.'

'Perhaps Mistress McIan will know,' Gil suggested.

The woman nodded, a dissatisfied look crossing her broad face. 'I will be at the wake as soon as the bannocks is cooked,' she said, drawing back from the railing. 'I cannot be calling empty-handed.'

Alys was waiting at the stair-mouth. Gil followed her up two turns of the spiral, past a doorway where a woman was scrubbing a small boy's face, on up where the protests were drowned by the sound of loud conversation which came from the open door on the next landing. The untidy room seemed deserted, but the noise came from within.

'This should be it,' Alys said doubtfully. 'Dame Joan is not at home, I think.'

'Does the harper stay here?' Gil called loudly. The door to the inner room opened, and Ealasaidh appeared on a redoubled blast of sound and a smell of spirits.

'It is the man of law,' she said, accepting Alys's proffered jug of brandy with grace. 'Come within. Mac Iain is at home.'

The room was crowded, and so noisy that it was a moment before Gil realized there was a baby crying somewhere. Amid the press of people, the harper was seated in a great chair by the fire, dressed in saffron-dyed shirt and velvet jerkin, the formal dress of the Highlander, with deerskin buskins laced up his bare legs. A Flemish harp with a curved soundboard hung behind his head. As Gil entered behind Alys he rose and bowed to them, saying with great dignity, 'I bid you welcome, neighbours.'

He was not as old as Gil had thought at first, possibly not yet fifty. Hair and beard were white, but his eyebrows were dark and shaggy and the high forehead was relatively unlined. He listened courteously to Gil's formal words of sympathy, and bowed again.

'I must thank you for your care of her, sir. Woman, bring refreshment for our guests.'

Ealasaidh was already returning from yet another, further, room, the one where the baby was crying. She handed Gil a tiny wooden beaker brimming with liquid, and offered him a platter of oatcakes. As Gil had feared the liquid proved to be barley eau-de-vie, fierce enough to burnish brass, but he offered a toast to the memory of Bess Stewart and drained his little cup resolutely. Around him, the harper's neighbours and acquaintances were talking, not in the least about the departed. Alys had disappeared.

'You are not yet a man of law,' said the harper suddenly.

'I soon will be,' said Gil, startled.

'But you will not be a priest.'

'I must,' said Gil, utterly taken aback, 'or live on air. Sir, I have a couple questions for you or your sister.'

'In a little space,' said the harper, turning to greet another mourner. Gil stood quietly, wrestling with the surge of conflicting feelings which assailed him. He was used to the sinking in his stomach when he thought of his approaching ordination (Lord, strengthen me, remove my doubts! he thought) but why should he feel panic at the thought of not being a priest?

The baby, he discovered after a moment, had fallen silent.

'Maister,' said the harper. 'We will not talk here. Come ben and ask your question.' He moved confidently towards the other door, and those round him fell back to let him pass.

The inmost room contained three adults and the baby, and a quantity of stained linen drying on outstretched strings. Ealasaidh, by the window, was opening another flagon of eau-de-vie. Before the fire, Alys was dandling the baby while a sturdy young woman looked on. The small head turned when the door opened, but at the sight of Gil the infant's mouth went square and the crying started again.

'What ails the bairn?' Gil asked, dismayed. His sister's children had never reacted like this.

'He is looking for one who will not return to him,' said Ealasaidh remotely.

'Every time the door opens,' said Alys over the baby's head. 'There, now! There, now, poor little man. Nancy, shall we try the spoon again?'

'Ask your question, maister lawyer,' said the harper again. 'Here is mac Iain and his sister both.'

'And I must go out in a little,' said Ealasaidh. 'We will

73

not be having enough usquebae for all the mourners, and
I must borrow more cups.'

Gil drew the harp key from his jerkin again.

'Do you recognize this?' he asked, through the baby's
wailing.

Ealasaidh gave it a glance, then another.

'It is hers,' she agreed heavily. 'The key to her little harp.
Where was it?'

'In the kirkyard,' said Gil. The harper's hand went out,
and he put the key into it. McIan's long fingers turned the
little object, the nails clicking on the metal barrel, caressing
familiar irregularities of the shape, and his mouth twisted
under his white beard .

'It is hers. Where in the kirkyard?'

'By the south door. Could she have dropped it?'

'No,' said Ealasaidh. 'Not Bess – not that.'

'She took care of what I gave her,' said the harper
harshly, 'for that it was given in love. This dwelled in her
purse always.'

'Her purse? There was no purse at her belt. I must talk
to you,' said Gil, 'but this is not the moment.'

'Aye, I must return to my guests. You will come back.' It
was not an order.

Alys handed the baby back to the other girl and rose.

'The bairn will be better with Nancy,' she said, 'and we
should be gone. My father the mason sends his sym-
pathies, maister harper.'

A fine rain was now falling. They walked through it in
silence back to the White Castle, Gil turning over the
harper's words in his mind. As they reached the pend Alys
paused, and he looked down at her.

'I feared you might lead me on up the High Street,' she
said, smiling at him.

'I'm sorry – I was discourteous.'

'You were thinking,' she pointed out. 'And so was I. Will

you come in, Maister Cunningham? My father will be home, it is near Vespers.'

The mason was brooding in his closet with a jug of wine. Alys showed Gil in and slipped away to see how Davie did, and Maistre Pierre said with sour enthusiasm, 'Sit down, lawyer, and have some wine, and we consider where we are at. I think we are no further forward than this morning.'

'I would not agree,' said Gil. 'We have named the lady, and arranged for her burial. Father Francis will accept her – he is willing to believe that since she had gone to meet her husband she may have repented of her adultery. And I told you I have spoken with Serjeant Anderson. He has no wish to meddle in something concerning the Chanonry.'

'Of that I have no doubt. But in everything else we have raised up two problems where one was before,' complained the mason.

'What do we know?' said Gil. 'She went out before Compline, to meet her husband after the Office in St Mungo's yard. She was not waiting for him when Compline ended. I think most likely she was already dead inside the Fergus Aisle by then, for otherwise surely she would have come out to meet him when she heard the Office was ended.'

'I suppose so,' agreed Maistre Pierre, scratching his beard with a loud rasping. 'But how many people could have killed her? We do not look for a beggar or robber, no?'

'I do not think it, although her purse is missing. Why should she follow such into the chapel? There were no signs of violence – fresh violence,' he amended, 'other than the wound that killed her. Her husband is the most obvious, but he was inside St Mungo's at the time I think she died, and I would swear he was shocked to learn of her death today. I saw the gallowglass come in – I suppose he could have directed her there and then killed her. There is also James Campbell, who has an Italian dagger, and I suppose the Italian lutenist must have such a knife, but I do not know why either of them should have killed her.'

'The husband could have killed her quick, there in the trees, before the rest came out of Compline,' Maistre Pierre offered, 'and come back later to move her out of sight.'

'Why would he need to move her?'

'The man-at-arms knew where he was to meet her. He needed to cover his tracks.'

Gil considered this. 'No, I don't think so. Sempill is capable of it, but you saw the body. She lay where she was killed. Who else?'

'This wild woman with the difficult name?'

'Euphemia Campbell, you mean?'

'No, no, the other. The harper's sister. How is it pronounced – Yalissy?'

'Ealasaidh,' Gil corrected. 'I think it is the Ersche for Elizabeth.'

'You amaze me. Could she have killed her? Followed her up the hill and knifed her for jealousy where she could put the blame on the husband? She seems like a woman out of tragedy – Iphigénie, perhaps, or some such. Or could it have been the harper, indeed?'

'The harper is blind.'

'But he was her lover. Who better to get close, his hand round her waist, the knife in his sleeve, a kiss to distract her and the thing is done. If he thought she was returning to her husband?'

'These are wild suggestions,' Gil said slowly, 'and yet we are dealing with secret murder here, the reasons may be as wild as any of these. Euphemia Campbell suggested that Bess had taken other lovers, and that one of those might have killed her, but that seems to me to add unnecessary complication to the matter.'

'It lacks unity of action, for sure,' said the mason, peering into his wine-cup. 'Did she have other lovers?'

'I have no corroboration. I hardly liked to ask the harper today,' admitted Gil. 'And it seems to me that a woman illused by her husband would be slow to trust other men.'

'There is another to consider,' said Alys from the doorway. Her father looked up and smiled at the sight of
her.

'How is the boy?' he asked. She came forward to sit
beside him, straight-backed and elegant in the faded
gown.

'Still in a swound, but I think his breathing is easier.
Kittock reports that an hour or so since he gave a great
sigh, and said something she didn't catch, and from that
time he has ceased that snoring. It is a good sign.'

'God be praised,' said her father.

'Amen. But we must consider, father, whether Davie
might not be the person you and Maister Cunningham are
seeking.'

Both men looked at her, Gil in some surprise.

'The boy would not hurt a fly,' said her father. 'He's a
great soft lump,' he added in Scots.

'But suppose his girl finally said no to him and went off
home,' she offered. 'There is Mistress Stewart standing in
the haw-bushes, he makes a – an improper suggestion, as
I suppose all men do at times, and she is angry with him.
Then the argument grows heated and he kills her and runs
away and is struck down – No,' she finished. 'It doesn't
work.'

'It does not account for her presence in the Fergus Aisle,'
Gil said, 'but you are perfectly right, we must consider
everyone who had the opportunity. Even your father. Even
me.'

'Why would you kill her, father?' she said, turning to
look at him. He looked at her quizzically and shrugged,
declining to join in. 'In fact you were at Compline in the
Greyfriars' church with Catherine and me and half the
household, so we may all stand surety for one another.
And you, Maister Cunningham?'

'Oh, I went out for a breath of air during Compline, and
she took me for a priest and wished to make confession, at
which I grew angry and knifed her,' Gil said, and pulled a
face. 'It isn't funny.'

'Would it anger you, if one took you for a priest?'

'Yes,' he said simply.

'But I thought one must be a priest, to be a lawyer.'

'It isn't essential,' Gil said carefully, 'but I have no money to live on. To get a living, I must have a benefice. To be presented to a benefice, I must be ordained. My uncle has been generosity itself, but he is not a young man, and his own benefices will die with him.'

'So you must be a priest.'

'Yes.'

'When?'

The familiar chill struck him. When it had passed, he said, 'I will be ordained acolyte in July, at the Feast of the Translation of St Mungo. I'll take major orders, either deacon or priest, at Ember-tide in Advent, and my uncle has a benefice in mind for me. Then I can say Masses for my father and my brothers. It will be good,' he said firmly, 'not to have to rely on my uncle. He has fed, clothed and taught me these two years and more, and never complained. At least, not about that,' he added.

'And then you can practise law in the Consistory Court? Is there no other way you may practise law?'

'Alys, you ask too many questions,' said the mason.

'I beg your pardon,' she said immediately. 'I am interested.'

'I am not offended,' said Gil. 'Yes, there are other ways, but I need the benefice. It always comes back to that – I must have something to live on.'

'Let us have some music,' said Maistre Pierre, 'to cleanse the thoughts and revive the spirits.' He turned a bright eye on his daughter. 'Alys, will you play for us, *ma mie*?'

'Perhaps Maister Cunningham would play?' said Alys, turning to a corner of the room. From under a pile of papers, two more books and a table-carpet of worn silk she extracted a long narrow box, which she set on the table.

'Monocords!' said Gil as she opened the lid. 'I haven't seen a set of those since I came home. No, no, I am far too rusty to play, but I will sing later. Play us something first.'

She was tapping the keys, listening to the tone of the small sweet sounds they produced. Her father handed her a little tuning-key from his desk and she made one or two adjustments, then settled herself at the keyboard and began to play the same May ballad that the harper and his two women had performed at the Cross on May Day. Gil, watching the movement of her slender hands on the dark keys, heard the point at which she recollected this; the music checked for a moment, and she bent her head further, her hair curtaining her face and hiding the delicate, prominent nose.

'What about something French?' he suggested as soon as she finished the verse. 'Binchois? Dufay?'

'Machaut,' said Maistre Pierre firmly. Alys nodded, and took up a song Gil remembered well. He joined in with the words, and father and daughter followed, high voice and low voice, carolling unrequited love with abandon.

'That was good,' said Alys as the song ended. 'You were adrift in the second verse, father. The third part makes a difference.'

'Let us sing it again,' said the mason.

They sang it again, and followed it with others: more by Machaut, an Italian song whose words Gil did not know, two Flemish ballads.

'And this one,' said Alys. 'It's very new. Have you heard it, Maister Cunningham? *D'amour je suis désheritée . . .'*

I am dispossessed by love, and do not know who to appeal to. Alas, I have lost my love, I am alone, he has left me . . .

'The setting is beautiful,' said Gil. Alys smiled quickly at him, and went on singing.

. . . to run after an affected woman who slanders me without ceasing. Alas, I am forgotten, wherefore I am delivered to death.

'Always death!' said Maistre Pierre. 'At least let us be cheerful about it.' He raised his wine-cup in one large hand. 'What do they sing in the ale-houses here? *Drink up, drink up, you're deid a long time.*'

'*You're deid a long time, without ale or wine.*' Gil joined in the round. Alys picked up the third entrance effortlessly, and they sang it several times round until the mason brought it to a close and drained his cup.

'I think we finish there. Tomorrow,' he said, 'we must bury Bess Stewart, poor soul, and find out the girl Davie was really with. We must search the kirkyard again, though by now I have little hope of finding the weapon. If it was there, it has been found by some burgess and taken home as a trophy. Half the town came to see what was afoot this afternoon.'

'I will set the maids to ask about the girl,' Alys said, closing up the little keyboard. 'They can enquire at the well, and at the market. Some lass in the town must know.'

'I wish to question that gallowglass further,' said Gil. 'The only Ersche speaker I know of is the harper's sister, and I hesitate to ask her to interpret –'

'I should think she would relish the task,' observed Alys.

He smiled at that. 'You may be right. And I must speak further with Ealasaidh herself and with the harper.'

'Meanwhile,' said Maistre Pierre, 'the day is over. Maister Cunningham, we go to hear Compline at Greyfriars. Will you come with us?'

The Franciscans' church was full of a low muttering, as the people of the High Street said evening prayers before one saint's altar or another. One of the friars was completing a Mass; Alys slipped away to leave money for candles to St Clare, and returned to stand quietly between Gil and her father as the brothers processed in through the nave and into the choir.

Gil, used to St Mungo's, found the small scale of the Office very moving. Kentigern's foundation was a cathedral church, able to furnish a good choir and handsome vestments for the *Opus Dei*, the work of God which was praising Him seven times daily. The Franciscans were a small community, though someone had built them a large church, and the half-dozen voices chanting the psalms in unison beyond the brightly painted screen seemed much closer to his own prayers than the more elaborate settings favoured by Maister Paniter. *I will lay me down in peace and take my rest; for it is thou, Lord, only that makest me dwell in safety.*

Beside him Alys drew a sharp breath. He looked down at her. Light glinted on the delicate high bridge of her nose. Her eyes were shut and her lips moved rapidly as the friars worked their way through the second of the Compline psalms. *For when thou art angry all our days are gone...So teach us to number our days, that we may apply our hearts with wisdom.* Tears leaked from Alys's closed eyelids, catching the candlelight, and Gil thought with a shiver of Bess Stewart lying in the mortuary chapel by the gatehouse, still in the clothes in which she had died, with candles at her head and feet.

For as soon as the wind goeth over it, it is gone, and the place thereof shall know it no more.

The Office ended, the congregation drifted out into the rain. Alys had composed herself, but was still subdued. Gil found it very unsatisfactory to say a formal goodnight at the end of the wynd and watch her go home beside her father, followed down the darkening street by two of the men and several maids. He stood until the household was out of sight and then turned for home.

It had been a most extraordinary day. Almost nothing was as it had been when he got up this morning. He was free of his books, at least for a little while, until he had solved the challenge, the puzzle, with which he was faced. He had a new friend in the mason, whose company would be worth seeking out. His mind swooped away from the suspicion that the mason's company was the more attractive because it promised the company of Alys as well.

Yesterday, the prospect of winning a few groats from the songmen had been something to look forward to.

Past the firmly shut door of the University, beyond the stone houses of the wealthier merchants, at the point called the Bell o' the Brae where the High Street steepened sharply into a slope too great for a horse-drawn vehicle, the Watch was attempting to clear an ale-house. Gil, his thoughts interrupted by the shouting, crossed the muddy street to go by on the other side. Several customers were already sitting in the gutter abusing the officers of the law. As Gil passed, two more hurtled out to sprawl in the mud, and within the lighted doorway women's voices were raised in fierce complaint. One was probably the ale-wife, husky and stentorian, but among the others Gil caught a familiar note.

He paused to listen, then strode on hurriedly. He did not feel equal to dealing with Ealasaidh McIan, fighting drunk and expelled from a tavern.

His uncle was reading by the fire in the hall when he came in, his wire spectacles falling down his nose.

'Ah, Gilbert,' he said, setting down his book. 'What news?'

'We have made some progress,' Gil said cautiously. His uncle indicated the stool opposite. Sitting down, Gil summarized the results of his day. Canon Cunningham listened carefully, tapping on his book with the spectacles, and asking the occasional question.

'That's a by-ordinary lassie of the mason's,' he said when the account was finished.

'I never met a lass like her,' Gil confessed.

The Official was silent for a while, still tapping his book. Finally he said, switching to the Latin he used when considering matters of the law, 'The man-at-arms. The dead woman's plaid and purse. Whatever girl was with the injured boy.'

'I agree, sir.'

'One more thing. Did Maggie not say there was a child?'

'Yes indeed there is, I saw it. Born last Michaelmas, it seems.'

'And when did Mistress Stewart leave her husband's house?'

'Before St Martin's of the previous – Ah!' Gil stared at his uncle. 'Within the twelvemonth, indeed. I think Sempill cannot know of it.'

'Or he does not know it is his legitimate heir.'

'I am reluctant to tell him. What he would do to a child he needs but knows is not his own I dare not think.'

'Keep your own counsel, Gilbert,' said his uncle approvingly. 'Now, what difference will the child make to the disposal of the land? Can you tell me that, hm?'

Trust the old man to turn it into a tutorial, Gil thought. Obediently he marshalled the facts in his head and numbered them off as he spoke.

'*Imprimis*, property the deceased held in her own right, as it might be from her father's will, should go to the child rather than to her kin, unless she has made a will. And even then,' he elaborated in response to his uncle's eyebrow, 'if she has left the property out of her kin, perhaps to the harper, they could challenge it, on their own behalf or the child's.'

'And moveables?'

'*Secundus*, the paraphernal matter, that is her own clothes and jewellery and such items as her spinning-wheel – I hardly think she was carrying a spinning-wheel about Scotland – these are the child's, unless there is a will, but anything Sempill can show he gave her in marriage-gifts returns to him. And, *tertius*, joint property held with her husband also returns to him, to dispose of as he sees fit. Unless,' he added thoughtfully, 'it transpires that he killed her.'

'Unless,' his uncle corrected, 'it can be proven that he killed her. In which case it reverts to the original donor, whether his kin or hers. Very good, Gilbert.'

'I've been well taught,' Gil pointed out.

Canon Cunningham acknowledged the compliment with a quick glance, and pursued thoughtfully, 'And what uncle is it that might leave John Sempill money, I wonder?

Not his father's half-brother Philip, for sure, anything he had would go to his own son, and that's little enough by what I remember. And the Walkinshaws keep their property to themselves.' He paused, lost in speculation, then noticed Gil stifling a yawn, and raised a hand to offer his customary blessing. 'Get you to your bed, Gilbert. It's ower late.'

Gil's narrow panelled room, just under the roof, was stiflingly hot. Whichever prebend of Cadzow had built the house had not lacked either pretension or money, and even here in the attics the upper part of the window was glazed. Gil picked his way across the room in the dim light and flung open the wooden shutters of the lower half, reasoning that the night air was unlikely to do him any more harm now than half an hour since. One would not sleep in it, of course.

Returning to his narrow bed he lit the candle and sat down, hearing the strapping creak, and lifted his commonplace book down from its place on the shelf, between his Chaucer and a battered Aristotle. He turned the leaves slowly. Each poem brought back vividly the circumstances in which he had copied it. Several pieces by William Dunbar, an unpleasant little man but a good makar, copied from his own writing when he had been in Glasgow with the Archbishop. Two songs by Machaut, dictated by Wat Kerr in an inn near St Séverin. Ah, here it was. *The Kingis Quair, made be the King of Scots*, or so Wattie had insisted, when Gil had transcribed it one long afternoon in a thunderstorm from a copy owned by . . . owned by . . . was it Dugald Campbell of Glenorchy? No matter. He skimmed the rime-royal stanzas, his eye falling on remembered phrases. *For which sudden abate, anon astart The blood of all my body to my heart*. Yes, it was like that, the effect of the sight of her against the light in the doorway of her father's house, the blood ebbing and then rushing back so that his heart thumped uncontrollably.

Quite ridiculous. I am to be a priest, he thought.

And here were the descriptions, as if this long-dead king

had seen Alys Mason in his dream. He read on, picking out the cramped lines with satisfaction, until the candle began to flicker.

It was, he realized, very late. He rose, returned the book to its place, and went to the window to close the shutters.

He leaned out first, breathing in the scent of the gardens after the rain. The sky was clearing, and the bulk of the Campsie hills showed against the stars to the north. Late though it was, there were lights in the Sempill house, one where he could see a table with cards and several pairs of hands, and above that and to one side, nearly on a level with him, a room where someone came and went slowly.

It was only when she paused and began to comb her wealth of golden hair that he realized that Euphemia Campbell was undressing before a mirror.

He watched, fascinated, the movement of little white hands and dainty arms, the tilt of the slender neck, the fall of the rippling gold locks as she turned her head before the mirror. How many candles was she burning? he wondered. There was certainly one to one side, and another beyond the mirror, to judge by the way the white shift was outlined, and maybe more. Little surprise that Sempill was short of money.

Euphemia turned her head and moved gracefully out of his sight. The square of light stood empty, while on the floor below the card-game continued, apparently at the stage of declaring points from the new hands dealt. Gil leaned on the sill a moment longer, then drew back into the room and reached for the shutters.

Euphemia came back into view, but not alone. The man with her was still fully clothed, although she was enthusiastically attempting to remedy this, and he had already got her shift down over her shoulders.

Gil stood, hand on the shutter, watching in astonishment. The man's face was buried in her neck and his movements were driven by what could be presumed to be strong passion, but even at a distance and from this angle

85

he felt sure it was not John Sempill. The fellow was not much taller than Euphemia, and his hair was dark in the candlelight and surely longer than Sempill's sandy pelage.

The woman spoke to him, apparently laughing, and he raised his head to answer her. Gil stared, frowning. The urgent manner might be put down to the circumstances but that dark, narrow face, black-browed in the candle-light, was certainly not Sempill's. It was the little dark fellow who had been outside St Mungo's, who had been in the procession which rode through the May Day dancing – dear God, was it only yesterday? – and who had not been present when he questioned the household today. The Italian musician. He suddenly recalled the expression he had seen on Euphemia's face when the man was mentioned.

Euphemia's shift had fallen to her waist. Gil was conscious first of regret that she had her back to him and then of sudden disgust. Such behaviour could be excused in the mastiff down in the courtyard, but not in a human being.

The two entangled figures moved out of sight, presumably in the direction of Euphemia's bed. Thoughtfully, Gil closed the shutters and turned to his own.

He spent longer than usual on his prayers, but nevertheless he found when he finally lay down that sleep was a long time claiming him. Images of women danced behind his eyelids, of Bess Stewart as she lay under the scaffolding in the half-built chapel, of Ealasaidh in her grief, of Euphemia just now in the candlelight wrestling the battle of love, and then of Alys weeping for a woman she had never met while the Franciscans chanted psalms in the shadows. He was disconcerted to find that, though he had spent a large part of the day in her company, and though he could remember the tears glittering under her lashes, his image of Alys was that of the princess in the poem, and he could not remember clearly what she really looked like.

I am to be a priest, he thought again

Exasperated, he turned over, hammered at his pillow, and began firmly to number the taverns on the rue Mouffetarde. In general it never failed him.

He had reached the Bouclier and was aware of sleep stealing over him when he was jolted wide awake by a thunderous banging. As he sat up the shouting started, a piercing voice which he recognized without difficulty, and then a monstrous barking which must be the mastiff Doucette. Cursing, Gil scrambled into hose and shoes, seized his gown and stumbled down the stairs as every dog in the upper town roused to answer its peer. Matt appeared blinking at the Official's chamber door, carrying a candle, as Gil crossed the solar.

'What's to do? The maister's asking.'

'Ealasaidh,' Gil said, hurrying on down.

The moon, not yet at the quarter, gave a little light to the scene in the street. The gate to the courtyard of Sempill's house across the way was shut and barred, but a tall shadowy figure was hammering on it with something hard, shouting in shrill and menacing Gaelic. Shutters were flung open along the street as first one householder, then another leaned out to shout at his dog or to abuse the desecrator of the peaceful night.

Gil picked his way across to the scene of the offensive and caught at Ealasaidh's arm. Above the sound of the dogs and her own screaming, he shouted, 'Ealasaidh! Madam! They will not let you in!'

She turned to stare at him, her eyes glittering in the moonlight, then returned to the attack, switching to Scots.

'Thief! Murderer! What have ye done with her purse? Where is her plaid? Where is her cross? Give me back the plaid I wove!'

'Ealasaidh,' said Gil again, more quietly. 'There is a better way.'

She turned to look at him again.

'What way is that?' she asked, quite rationally, over the mastiff's barking.

'My way,' he said persuasively. 'The law will avenge Bess Stewart, madam, and I hope will find her property on the way. If not, then you may attack whoever you believe stole it.'

'Hmf,' she said. She reeked of eau-de-vie. Gil took her arm.

'Will you come within,' he asked politely, 'and we may discuss this?'

'That is fery civil of you,' she said.

For a moment Gil thought he had won; then, behind the gates, somebody swore at the mastiff, and somebody else demanded loudly, 'Who the devil is that at this hour?'

Ealasaidh whirled to the fray again, staggering slightly, and launched into a tirade in her own language. There was a series of thuds as the gate was unbarred, and it swung open to reveal John Sempill, not entirely sober himself, with his cousin and both of the gallowglasses. Torchlight gleamed on their drawn swords.

'Oh, brave it is!' exclaimed Ealasaidh. 'Steel on an unarmed woman!'

'Get away from my gate, you kitterel besom, you puggie jurrock!' roared Sempill. 'You stole my wife away out of my house! If she had never set eyes on you I would have an heir by now. Away with you!'

'It was not your house,' said Ealasaidh shrilly. Several neighbours shouted abuse, but she raised her voice effortlessly above them. 'It was her house, entirely, and well you know it. Many a time she said to me, how it was hers to dispose of as she pleased, and never a straw of it yours.'

'I will not listen to nonsense at my own gate,' bawled Sempill with stentorian dignity. 'Get away from here and be at peace, partan-faced baird that you are!'

There were shouts of agreement from up and down the street, but Ealasaidh had not finished.

'And you would never have had an heir of her, the

way you treated her! I have seen her back, I have seen what you –'

'Shut her mouth!' said Sempill savagely to the nearest Campbell, snatching the torch from the man's grasp. 'Go on – what are you feart for?'

'In front of a lawyer?' said Gil, without expression, under Ealasaidh's dreadful recital.

Sempill turned on him. 'You call yourself a man of law, Gil Cunningham? You let her stand there and slander me like that in front of the entire upper town –'

'*Rax her a rug of the roast or she'll rime ye*, indeed,' Gil said, in some amusement. Sempill snarled at him, and slammed the gate shut, so fast that if Gil had not dragged her backwards it would have struck Ealasaidh. The bar thudded into place as she reached her peroration.

'And two husbands she may have had, ye countbitten braggart, but it took my brother to get a bairn on her she could carry to term, and him blind and a harper!'

On the other side of the gate there was a momentary silence, then feet tramped away towards the house-door. The mastiff growled experimentally, then, when no rebuke came, began its full-throated barking again. Other dogs joined in, to the accompaniment of further shouting.

Ealasaidh turned triumphantly to Gil.

'That's him tellt,' she said.

Chapter Five

When Gil entered the kitchen, earlier than he would have liked, Ealasaidh was huddled by the kitchen fire with a bowl of porridge under her plaid, the kitchen-boy staring at her across the hearth. Maggie was mixing something in a great bowl at the table and talking at her, getting the occasional monosyllabic answer. Gil cut across this without ceremony.

'Maggie, I have a task for you.'

She eyed him, her big hands never ceasing their kneading.

'Have you, now, Maister Gil?' she said.

'Have you any kin across the way?'

'In Sempill's house, you mean? No what you'd call kin,' she said thoughtfully. 'My sister Bel's good-sister has a laddie in the stable. I say laddie,' she amended, 'but he must be your age, by now. That's as close as it gets.'

'Any friends?'

'Aye, well, Marriott Kennedy in the kitchen's good company from time to time. A rare talker, she is. Sooner gossip than see to the house.'

'Would she need a hand, do you think,' said Gil, 'with the house being so full of people?'

'I've no doubt of it.' Maggie finally paused in her work and straightened up, to look Gil in the eye. 'What are ye at, Maister Gil? Do ye want me in their kitchen?'

'I do, Maggie.' Gil slipped an arm round her broad waist. 'And in as much of the house as you can manage.'

'And for what?' She slapped affectionately at his hand, scattering flour. 'To look for what's lost, is that it? A green and black plaid, a cross, a purse?'

Ealasaidh looked up, but made no comment.

'Maggie,' said Gil, kissing her cheek, 'that's why my uncle brought you to Glasgow, because you're a canny woman, and not because you make the best porridge in Lanarkshire.'

A dimple appeared in the cheek, but she pushed him away firmly, saying, 'If I've to waste my time on your ploys I'll need to set this to rise.'

'Just keep your eyes open,' Gil warned. 'Don't get yourself into any unpleasantness.'

'I'm no dotit yet,' said Maggie. 'Get you away down the town with that poor soul, before the harper calls out the Watch.'

Picking his way along Rottenrow beside a sullen Ealasaidh with her plaid drawn round her head against the early light, Gil said diffidently, 'It seems likely that Bess Stewart was killed by someone she knew.'

'I was telling you already,' said Ealasaidh without looking at him, 'it will have been the husband. Sempill. She went out to meet him.'

'It could have been,' agreed Gil, in an attempt to mollify her, 'but I had him under my eye all through Compline.' She snorted. 'Is it possible Bess could have met someone else in St Mungo's yard, that she would trust at close quarters?'

'Who could she have known that well?' said Ealasaidh, striding past the Girth Cross. 'Here in Glasgow or when she was on the road, she had ourselves and the baby. Before that she was in Rothesay. There is nobody she knew in Rothesay that is in Glasgow just now, except the Campbells and Sempill.'

'She never went out alone, or stayed in the Pelican Court without the rest of the household?'

'No, she –' Ealasaidh stopped in her tracks. A hand shot out of the folds of the plaid and seized Gil's arm in a brutal grip. 'Are you suggesting,' she hissed, 'that Bess had another man?'

'The suggestion was made to me,' said Gil, realizing with dismay that her other hand had gone to the gully-knife at her belt. 'I have to ask.' He kept his voice level with an effort, trying not to envisage a knife-fight here in the street with this formidable woman. She stared at him from the shadows of the checked wool.

'I can guess who suggested it,' she said at length. 'No, she never had the privacy, not while we lived in Glasgow. Besides, you only had to see her with Aenghus.'

'I apologize for asking it,' said Gil. She bowed her head with great stateliness, accepting this, then let go his arm and stalked on down the High Street.

The upper town was still quiet, but below the Bell o' the Brae the street grew busy, with people hurrying to their day's work, schoolboys dragging their feet uphill towards the Grammar School, and the occasional student in his belted gown of blue or red, making his way from lodgings to an early lecture.

At the end of the Franciscans' wynd Ealasaidh halted, and put back her plaid to look at him.

'It is a great courtesy in you to convoy a poor singing-woman,' she said, without apparent irony. 'Do you leave me here, or will you come in? I must wash the dead and shroud her for burial, and there is things I wish to show you. I came by here after Vespers, to say goodnight to her.'

'There are things I wish to see,' said Gil, letting her precede him into the wynd. 'The wound that gave her her death, for one.'

She nodded, and strode in under the stone gateway at the far end of the wynd.

The Franciscans were singing Prime, the chant drifting clearly to meet them on the morning air. Ealasaidh disappeared into the gatehouse, and emerged after a moment bearing a basin of water and a pile of linen. Gil took the basin from her, and followed her as she stalked into the little chapel, where one of the friars still knelt. Ealasaidh nodded briefly to him as he rose and paced quietly out, then she twitched the sheet unceremoniously off the corpse and said,

'As you said, her purse is not here. See, it hung at her belt beside the beads.'

'And that was where she kept the harp key?' Gil prompted. 'How was it taken from the belt?'

'No sign,' said Ealasaidh. 'It was nothing by-ordinary, just a leather purse hung on loops, easy enough to cut them. Little enough in it, too. We never carry much.' She bent her head abruptly.

After a moment Gil said, 'Is there anything else?'

'Yes,' she said. 'I told that good soul in your kitchen about it. Her one jewel. My brother gave her a gold cross on a chain, quite simple. Sweet to hold and comforting, like her, he said. That she always wore under her shift, and that also I miss.'

'So perhaps it was robbery,' said Gil. 'Or made to look like it.' He looked down at the still face. 'After all, why would she go into that place with someone like to rob her?'

The door creaked, and they both looked round. Alys stepped into the chapel, bent the knee in courtesy to the dead, and said simply, 'I was coming in to say my prayers when I saw you. You will need help.'

Ealasaidh's face softened.

'It is not right you should be here now,' she said to Gil. 'She was aye honest and decent, she would not have wished you to see her stripped.'

'I represent justice,' said Gil, and heard the words resonate in the vault. 'I am here on her behalf.'

'There are things we can learn from her,' said Alys. 'Maister Cunningham, have you looked all you wish at the gown? May we remove it?'

'I think so,' said Gil. 'Then I can look at it more closely.'

Ealasaidh nodded and knelt by the corpse. Alys shed her

93

plaid and knelt opposite her, working with gentle fingers at the side-laced bodice. After some unpleasant moments the swathe of red cloth was flung aside, to be followed by the brocade kirtle and its sleeves. Gil lifted these and retreated across the chapel, to Ealasaidh's obvious relief.

The clothing told him nothing new. There was blood dried in the back of both garments, some soaked in the brocade under-sleeve, but not as much as might be expected from a death-wound. The left side of the red gown, which had been uppermost, was slightly stiffened from the dew, and there was a small patch of mud on the elbow of the other sleeve. There were two careful mends in the kirtle, and fresh tapes had been stitched into the under-sleeves. Gil thought of the sweet-faced woman he had seen at the Cross, and imagined her sitting, head bent, stitching by the window of their inmost room in the Pelican Court. It was suddenly unbearably poignant.

Taking up the shift he inspected it gingerly. It was soft and white with much laundering, trimmed with a little needlework at neck and cuffs. There was a large bloodstain on the back and sleeve, matching those on gown and kirtle, and sour-milk stains across the breast; apart from that it told him nothing. Wondering if he was simply looking for the wrong answers, he folded all three garments and set them in a neat pile.

At the other side of the chapel, Alys had removed the French hood and was unpinning the cap which was under it so that Bess's hair fell loose in two long braids. Gil lifted the headgear. The cap was of well-washed linen like the shift, threads pulled here and there by the pins which had secured it to the dark braids. The hood was a structure of wire, velvet and buckram, which he studied with interest, having wondered more than once how such things were constructed. Two small starry shapes floated down from the black velvet as he turned it; lifting one on a fingertip he held it to the light and recognized a five-petalled flower of hawthorn, turning brown now.

Ealasaidh was speaking.

94

'Here is the wound that killed her, maister, and here is what I wanted to show you.'

They had her half-shrouded, turned on to her face so that the final offence showed, a narrow blue-lipped gash between the ribs on the left side.

'Such a little wound, to end a life,' said Ealasaidh.

But it was not the only offence committed against this woman. Red marks, some raised, some turning silver, patterned her back. Neat parallel lines decorated one buttock. And fat and red on her right shoulder-blade, carved with some care, were the letters I S.

'John Sempill's initials,' said Gil, as the bile rose in his throat. 'And she could still sing. Lord send me courage like hers.'

'Amen,' said Alys.

Ealasaidh was silent, but the tears were dripping from her chin on to the linen shroud.

'Forgive me,' said Gil. 'Are there other scars? The jaw I have seen, but –'

'That and her ear,' said Alys. 'And these. No more.'

Ealasaidh muttered something in her own language. Alys touched her hand in sympathy, and without further comment they completed the task of arraying Bess Stewart for burial, turning her head to show Gil the sliced ear-lobe and scarred jaw before they combed out her hair to hide it.

'Will your brother wish to say farewell?' Alys asked at length.

Ealasaidh shook her head. 'I do not know. He was strange, last night. He is saying he may never play again.'

'Could he give it up like that?'

'If he says he will, then he will. Thus far he has only said he may. Cover her face, but do not tie the cloth, I think.' She helped Alys fold the linen over the still face, and got to her feet, lifting the basin and cloths. 'These belong to Brother Porter. Lassie, I still do not know your name, but I thank you, as Bess would, for your charity to her.'

Alys, rising, embraced her, and turned to lift her plaid. Gil said suddenly, 'Ealasaidh, what like was her plaid? Bess's plaid that is lost? You said she was wearing it when she went out.'

'Her plaid?' Ealasaidh stared at him. 'Aye, indeed, her plaid. It is like mine, only that I had more of the green thread when I wove it, so the sett is four threads green and eight of black, not two and ten. She said she never had a plaid like it. I wove it when I was a girl in my mother's house.'

'So where is it, then?' Gil wondered.

'The same place as her cross, likely,' Ealasaidh said fiercely. 'And both in John Sempill's hands, I have no doubt. Go you and ask him, since he would not answer me.'

She lifted the basin and the clothes and stalked out of the chapel, passing one of the brothers without apparently noticing him. He came forward, offered a blessing to Alys and to Gil when they bent the knee to him, and settled himself at the head of the shrouded corpse with his beads over his hands. Gil, after one glance at Alys's face, put a hand under her elbow and steered her out into the courtyard.

'I would give a great deal that you had not seen that,' he said.

She shook her head, biting her lip, and gestured helplessly with her free hand. Gil clasped it too, and in a moment she said, 'She had survived so much, and now she is taken from those who love her and the child who needs her.' She looked up at him in distress. 'What did she think of, when the knife went in?'

'She may not have known it,' Gil said. 'It was a narrow blade, one could see that, and she may not have felt it.' He fell silent. Then he added, 'She had mended the kirtle.'

Her hand tightened in his, and suddenly they were embracing, a warm exchange of comfort from the closeness of another. After a moment she drew back gently, and Gil let her go, aware of the scent of rosemary from her hair.

'Will you come back to the lodgings with me,' said Ealasaidh beside them. 'There were things you wished to ask himself.'

'May I come too, to see the baby?' Alys asked. 'The maids will be a while at the market, I have time.'

They went back out on to the High Street and down the hill, past Alys's house, to where the market was setting up in the open space around the Cross. Those traders lucky enough, or prosperous enough, to have shops which faced on to the market were laying out their wares on the front counter. The centre space was already in good order, with traders from other streets setting out bales of dyed cloth, hanks of tow for spinning, cheeses, leather goods. On the margins, others were arranging trestles or barrows, with much argument about position and encroachment. The serjeant, waiting with the drummer on the Tolbooth steps to declare the market open, favoured Gil with a stately bow as they passed.

They turned into the Thenawgait, encountering a pair of baker's men hurrying to their master's stall with a board of warm loaves, and followed the new-bread smell back down the Fishergait. Past the bakehouse, the painted pelican still hung crooked, and the children were playing on the midden as if they were never called in.

This time, as they stepped out of the stair-tower, a drowsy greeting came from the shut-bed in the outer room. Ealasaidh strode on, ignoring it, and into the room beyond.

For a moment, following her, Gil thought the place empty. A great clarsach was now visible at the far wall, two smaller ones in the corner beyond. The Flemish harp still hung by the cold chimney, and below it the harper sat erect and motionless in his great chair, the determined mouth slack, hands knotted together so that the knuckles showed white in the dim light.

'Aenghus,' said his sister. He did not answer. She closed the door, crossed the room to fling open the shutters, and turned to stare intently at him. Alys slipped to the further door.

'You see,' said Ealasaidh to Gil. 'He has never moved since the mourners left last night.'

'Nancy is not here,' said Alys in the other doorway. 'Nor the baby.'

Ealasaidh, with a sharp exclamation, strode past her. The room was clearly empty but for Alys, but Ealasaidh peered into the shut-bed and felt the blankets in the wicker cradle next to it. Then she turned on her heel, meeting Alys's eye briefly, and came back into the outer room.

'Aenghus!' she said loudly. 'Where is the bairn? Where are Nancy and the bairn?'

She began to repeat the question in her own language, but the harper turned his head to face her voice.

'Gone,' he said. She stiffened, but he went on harshly, 'They are all gone. Bess, and Ealasaidh, and my son. The bairn wept sore for his mammy. The lassie took him to her own mother.'

'When? When was this?'

'All gone,' he said again.

'Aenghus.' She spoke intensely in her own language. After a moment, one hand came up and grasped her wrist.

Gil, still watching, said, 'When did he eat last?'

'The dear knows. He would not eat yesterday, only the usquebae. Aenghus –'

'I will get the fire going,' said Alys in practical tones. 'Maister Cunningham, can you fetch in some food? The market should be open by now.'

He did not need to go as far as the market. By the time he returned, with two fresh loaves from the baker across the Fishergait, a quarter of a cheese from the man's back shop, and a jug of ale, the harper was combed and tidied and wearing a leather jerkin over his saffron shirt. Ealasaidh was clattering pots in the inner room, and as Gil set down his purchases she bore in a steaming dish of sowans.

'Eat that, mac Iain,' she said, putting dish and spoon in her brother's hands. He began obediently to sup the porridge-like mess, and she carried off the loaves and cheese. 'Here is the lawyer to learn about Bess.'

'Where is the demoiselle Alys?' Gil asked.

The white eyes turned to him. 'She has gone too. They are all gone.'

'Ealasaidh is come back,' said Ealasaidh firmly. 'Stop your wandering and speak sense to the man of law.' She gestured helplessly with her gully-knife at Gil, and went on cutting wedges off a loaf. 'The lassie went home, I think. She slipped away once the fire was hot.'

'Tell me about Bess,' said Gil gently. 'How old was she? Who was her first husband? What happened to him?'

'She was the bonniest thing that ever stepped through my life,' said the harper, setting down his spoon in the half-eaten sowans. His fingers clenched and unclenched on the rim of the dish.

'She was quiet,' said Ealasaidh, 'and kind, and sensible. A woman to take her turn at the cooking and do it well, for all she owned a house in Rothesay.'

'She was a good woman,' said the harper. 'It was always a great wonder to me,' he said distantly, suddenly becoming rational, 'that she came away with me, for she was devout, and honest, and lawful. And as my sister says, she owned a house and land, and yet she crossed Scotland with us, laughing when she fell in the mud, and said she was happy with us, for that we loved her.'

'And in especial after the bairn came,' said Ealasaidh. 'It was a great joy to her that she had given himself a son.'

She was, it seemed, five- or six-and-twenty. Her first husband had been a Bute man, and had died of plague leaving her a very young widow with a respectable tierce and a couple of properties outright. Neither the harper nor his sister knew his name.

'He was kind to her,' said the harper. 'She told me that once. Not like the second one.'

'She lost the tierce, of course, when she took Sempill,'

Ealasaidh observed, 'but there was jewels and such, and two plots in Rothesay, and a bit of land at Ettrick that was her dower.'

'What happened to them?' Gil asked, more at home with this kind of enquiry.

'She still had the land,' Ealasaidh said. 'She said time and again, if she could get to Rothesay to sign a paper, we would have money.'

'I wonder where the deeds are,' said Gil.

'Maybe in her box,' said Ealasaidh. 'But we will not have the key. I have never seen it opened.'

The box itself, when dragged from under the shut-bed, was sturdy enough, but the lock was no challenge to Gil's dagger. He said so.

'Then if it will help you, open it,' said the harper.

'You are certain that you wish me to open it?' said Gil formally. The harper, recognizing his intention, bowed his head regally.

'I am certain,' he agreed. Gil brought out his dagger, and was turning the box so that light fell on the lock when the harper put out a hand.

'Wait,' he said, head tilted, listening. Ealasaidh looked from him to the window, then rose to go and look down into the yard.

'Campbell,' she said. Her brother asked a question. 'Eoghan Campbell, the same as brought the word to Bess the other night. There is Morag nic Lachlann getting a crack with him across the way, he will be here in a moment.'

Gil sheathed his dagger.

'Let us put this out the way, then,' he said. 'Euan Campbell? You are certain it is Euan and not Neil? And that Euan brought the word to Bess?'

'How would I not know him?' said Ealasaidh, as she had before, stooping to help Gil drag the box into a corner. 'My mother was wisewoman at their birth, for all they were Campbells.' She stacked a folded plaid, two German flutes and a bundle of music rapidly on top of the box. 'Not that

100

she would have withheld aid if their father had been the devil himself,' she added thoughtfully.

'Wisdom and a gift is both to be shared,' said the harper. He rose as feet crossed the outer room. 'Ah, *Mhic Chaileann* . . .'

The man in the doorway was, to Gil's eye, the same man he had questioned yesterday. He watched the formal exchange of Gaelic, trying to gauge the mind of each contestant. The gallowglass was pleased with himself about something, and also dismayed by Gil's presence, though he hid it well. The harper, his great grief overlaid by his greater dignity, was harder to read; beside him Ealasaidh had a tight rein on her anger. She said suddenly,

'We will be speaking Scots, in courtesy to Maister Cunningham. What brings Eoghan Campbell to this door?'

Gil, startled to find she remembered his name, almost missed the man's slight recoil.

'It iss a word from Maister Sempill,' he said cautiously. 'It iss to say that he is in grief at the death of his wife, and iss wishing her things back for a remembrance. That is the word from Maister Sempill.'

Ealasaidh appeared to be silenced by rage. McIan inclined his head.

'I hear Maister Sempill's word,' he said formally. 'I will consider of my answer.'

'Euan Campbell,' said Gil. The dark-browed face turned to him. 'Did you bring a message to Bess Stewart from Maister Sempill on May Day evening?'

'Of course he did!' hissed Ealasaidh.

'Let him answer for himself,' said Gil. 'There is not only a man of law here, there is a harper. He will speak the truth, will you not, Euan?'

'Yes,' said the gallowglass, in some discomfort.

'Then answer me,' said Gil.

The man took a deep breath. 'I did so,' he admitted.

'What was the message?'

'That she should be meeting him outside the south door of St Mungo's after Compline, in a matter of money. Her money.'

Gil considered the man for a moment. Out in the yard a child wailed and was hushed, and the harper turned his head to listen.

'Did you speak the message in Scots?' Gil asked. 'Or in Ersche?'

Something unreadable crossed the narrow face.

'Of course he was speaking Gaelic at her!' said Ealasaidh impatiently. 'She had the two tongues as well as any in the land, what else would he be speaking?'

'Is that right?' Gil said. The man nodded. 'Tell us what you said to her. Say it again in Ersche – in Gaelic.'

Euan's eyes shifted, from Gil, to the harper standing isolated in darkness, to Ealasaidh's vengeful countenance. After a pause, he spoke. Ealasaidh listened, snapped a question, listened to the answer. There was a short, acrimonious discussion, which ended when Ealasaidh turned to Gil.

'The word he is bringing from Sempill is just as he is saying,' she reported. 'But she asked him how she could trust John Sempill, and he, fool and Campbell that he is, promised to protect her while she spoke with Sempill and see her back here.'

Gil, unable to assess this, said to give himself time, 'Why did Maister Sempill think it was your brother who took the message?'

'He is never telling us apart,' said the gallowglass.

'They were forever playing at being the one or the other,' said Ealasaidh in disgust. 'There is only me and Mairead their sister can tell them apart now, and she is married to a decent man and living in Inveraray.'

'And I,' said the harper. 'It was this one came with the message on Monday. I know the voice.'

'Sorrow is on me,' said the gallowglass, 'that ever I crossed your door on such an errand.'

They went off into Ersche again, a rapid exchange

between Ealasaidh and Campbell. Gil, watching, felt the man was still hiding something. The harper suddenly spoke, a few quick words which silenced the other two, and turning to Gil he said, 'Maister Cunningham, have you more to ask?'

'I have,' said Gil.

'Then ask it, so Eoghan Campbell can go about his lord's business.'

Gil, thanking him as one would a colleague, found himself exchanging bows with a blind man.

'Euan,' he said, 'tell me how Mistress Stewart went up the High Street on May Day evening.'

'Chust like any other,' said the man blankly.

'Did she follow you, or walk beside you? Did you talk? Was she apprehensive? Was she worried about meeting her husband,' he amended. 'You may answer me in Gaelic.'

Ealasaidh said something sharp, and Euan spoke briefly, shrugging.

'He says,' she translated, 'that Bess walked up the street beside him, talking in the Gaelic about the weather, and about where he was coming from, and she did not seem low in her courage at all in any way.'

The harper made a small sound in his throat. Ealasaidh flicked a glance at him, and added, 'What else do you wish to ask, Maister Cunningham?'

'When you got to St Mungo's,' said Gil, 'what then?'

The gallowglass had left Bess Stewart in the clump of hawthorns and gone into the kirk to report to his lord. She had been standing, quite composed, with her plaid over her head. He had never seen her again.

'Was there anyone else in the kirkyard?' Gil asked. The sly grin predicted the answer he got.

'There wass two youngsters, away to the burn from where she was, sitting in the grass, though I am thinking they would shortly be lying in it.'

'What were they wearing?' asked Gil hopefully.

'Oh, I would not be knowing that. The light was going. Chust clothes like any others. The boy's hose was stript.'

'Just now,' said Gil, 'before you came up this stair, what did the neighbour across the way tell you?'

'Oh, nothing at all,' said the gallowglass airily, but Gil had not missed the flicker of self-satisfaction.

'It took a long while to say nothing,' he observed. Ealasaidh said something sharp. She got a sulky answer, then a defiant one; she glanced threateningly at the small harp, and there was an immediate reaction.

'Mistress nic Lachlann and I were chust passing the time of day, and I was asking her would himself be at home chust now, and she was telling me who would be in the house.'

'And who did she tell you would be in the house?' Gil prompted.

'Himself, and herself,' said the man, nodding, 'and a visitor, which I am thinking would be Maister Cunningham.'

'And what more did she tell you?'

'Oh, nothing of any importance. Nothing at all, at all.'

Gil moved over to look out of the window.

'So you promised to protect Mistress Stewart,' he said, his back to the man, 'and to see her safe home. Why, then, did you not search for her after the service?'

'I thought she was gone home without speaking to the maister.' There was what seemed like genuine feeling in the voice. 'He was in the kirk, under my eye, from when I left her in the trees till he went out again and found she wass not there. I thought that was protection enough!' he burst out. 'I did not know –' He broke off. Gil turned, to look into patches of green dazzle.

'What did you not know?' he asked. Ealasaidh had to repeat the question; she got a reluctant, muttered answer, which she translated baldly:

'That he would use witchcraft.'

'Do you think it witchcraft, Maister Cunningham?' asked the harper.

'I don't believe in witchcraft,' said Gil apologetically. 'Do you?'

'What do you call the power of a harper?'

'Ah, that is different. Anyway, he had no evidence,' Gil said, watching the gallowglass cross the yard. 'Supposition is not sufficient. I do not think that John Sempill killed her, though I do not yet know who did. What worries me is how much he learned from your neighbour. Where is the bairn?'

'If Nancy took him to her mother's,' said Ealasaidh, 'he is up the next stair.'

'I thought as much.' Gil turned away from the window. 'Euan has just gone up that stair. Ealasaidh –'

The door was swinging behind her. When Gil caught up, she was just wading into a very promising argument three turns up the next stair, where Euan was holding his ground with difficulty against two kerchiefed women.

'No, I will not tell you where she's gone. I don't know who you are, but my Nancy's none of your business, and less of your master's. Be off with you before I call the serjeant on you, pestering decent women –'

'The bairn's –'

'The bairn's none of hers, and everyone in this pend knows that.'

'I never said –'

'Bel!' said Ealasaidh. 'This one iss from Bess's man!'

'Oh, it's like that, is it?' said Bel. 'See me the besom, sister. I'll *Where's Nancy* you, you great –'

Gil flattened himself against the wall as the gallowglass broke and ran, followed by shrieks of laughter, and loud and personal comments. As the sound of his feet diminished down the stairs the three women nodded in satisfaction.

'So where is Nancy?' he asked. The satisfaction vanished, and two hostile stares were turned on him. He was aware of sudden sympathy with Euan.

'It iss the man of law from St Mungo's,' Ealasaidh explained. 'Looking for proof it was Sempill killed her.'

105

'Looking for proof of who killed her,' Gil amended. She shrugged, and turned to the two women.

'So where is Nancy? And the bairn?'

'She went off this morning. Less than an hour since, it would be, wouldn't it, sister?'

'Who with?' Gil said patiently. 'Did she go alone?'

'Oh, I never saw. We were no here, were we, Kate?'

'We were out at the market,' amplified Kate. 'After Prime.'

'We came back, and she was gone, and the bairn's gear with her. Tail-clouts, horn spoon, coral –'

'And her plaid.'

'Has she left no word?' asked Gil. The two women turned kerchiefed heads to one another, then to him, wearing identical expressions of surprise.

'Why would she do that?'

'She's likely at her married sister's. Isa has a bairn ages with your wee one.'

'And where does her sister live?' Gil persisted.

'On the High Street. Isn't it no, sister?'

'In Watson's Pend,' agreed the other one. 'Second stair. You'll not miss it.'

Ealasaidh turned on her heel and hurried down the stairs, her deerskin shoes making little sound on the stone. Gil, with a hasty word of thanks, followed her. In the yard she hesitated, glancing up at her own windows.

'I must go,' she said. 'I must know the bairn is safe. But to leave him yet again –'

'I will go,' Gil offered, 'and send you word when I have found the bairn.'

She looked from his face to the windows and back. 'What word? I cannot read Scots.'

'I will send that I have found the harpstring,' he said quietly.

Her face lit up in that savage smile. 'Mac Iain and I will wait your messenger,' she said, and strode into the mouth of her own stair.

The market was past its climax when Gil reached the

corner of the Fishergait. Many stallholders were beginning to pack up by now, and the wives and maidservants of the burgh were beginning to turn for home with their purchases, but the bustle, the hopeful whine of the beggars, the cries of fishwives and pedlars, still spread out from the Mercat Cross.

Gil made his way through the noisy scene with difficulty. Here and there a little group of giggling girls whispered and huddled. Beyond the Tolbooth he saw, quite clearly, both the gallowglass brothers, in deep and separate conversation with more young women. A little further on, James Campbell of Glenstriven, in a green velvet hat of identical cut to John Sempill's cherry one, was laughing with another girl. Gil hurried on, avoiding all these as well as raucous attempts to sell him eggs, cheeses, ham, a clutch of goose eggs warranted to hatch, and a toebone of the infant St Catherine.

'The infant St Catherine?' he repeated, pausing despite himself. 'What did she walk on when she was grown?'

'Ah, your worship,' said the pedlar, leering at him. 'Who am I to say what the holy woman walked on? Sure, and if her feet touched the earth at all it was only to bless it.'

'I should report you,' said Gil. 'Put that one away and find something more probable to cry, before the Consistory finds you.'

'Yes, your honour,' said the pedlar hastily. 'Forgive me, father, I didn't see you was a priest, father . . .'

Gil moved on, his jaw tightening. Not yet, he thought, not yet.

'Why, Maister Cunningham!' said a voice at his elbow. He turned in sudden hope, and found himself looking into the sparkling, elfin countenance of Euphemia Campbell. 'Good day to you, sir.'

'Good day, madam,' he returned, bowing. She curtsied in reply, her cramoisie velvet pooling on the damp flagstones. It was already marked at the hem. Her neck bent elegantly under the mass of folded linen, and a heavy waft of perfume reached him. 'Exploring the market?'

This close, he could see that she was older than one thought at first. The fine skin round her eyes was beginning to sag, and there were lines coming between the insignificant nose and the mouth which was now pouting prettily.

'There's not much to explore, is there? The apothecary can't supply enough ambergris for my perfume – I have my own receipt, you know – so I came to look at the rest of the town. Where do Glasgow wives go for linen and velvets?'

'I have no idea,' he admitted.

'Perhaps Antonio knows. Tonino?' She smiled along her shoulder at the small dark man who stood watchfully at her side, his hand on the hilt of his sword, and spoke briefly in Italian. He shook his head, and she laughed. 'No? Men never know. Mally can find out for me. Are you for the Upper Town, Maister Cunningham? Can you convoy me?'

'As far as Greyfriars, gladly,' he said perforce, offering his arm. Lady Euphemia laid her hand on it, the elegantly embroidered glove in contrast with the dusty black of his sleeve, and turned with him, the small man always at her other elbow.

'You aren't much like your brother, are you?' What does she mean by that? Gil wondered, but she chattered on. 'Greyfriars? Oh, of course, that poor woman's to be buried this afternoon, isn't she? John will be there. It's only proper.'

'I'm sure Sempill of Muirend will do what is right,' said Gil, and was aware of sounding fatuous.

'And have you come any nearer finding who killed her? Or who struck down the mason's boy? What about his lass? It must be very difficult for you, with so little evidence.'

'We are searching for evidence,' he assured her.

'I suppose if you find all her missing possessions it will help,' she chattered. 'The plaid, the purse, the harp key and – what was it? A cross? That the poor mad woman was screaming at the gates about last night. I thought at first it was the devil himself come to get us all!'

As well you might, thought Gil, trying to suppress the image of her bare back by candlelight.

'And John was furious.' She giggled throatily. 'Such a rage he was in. It took me the rest of the night to soothe him.'

Gil, grasping her meaning, wondered if his ears were going red. He risked a glance at her and found her suddenly very like her brother, smirking at him sideways like a well-fed cat, the dimple very much in evidence. Beyond the piled-up linen of her headdress he met a burning stare from the small man.

'How is the mad woman?' she went on. 'I heard you took her away – is she locked up? She certainly ought to be out of harm's way. She needs to be tied to St Mungo's Cross for the night, like one of Colqhoun's servants at Luss. They brought him all the way in and tied him to the Cross. It cured him, too, at least he died, but he was sane when he died.'

'She is safe enough,' Gil began.

'And the dogs barking like that. I thought I would die laughing when all the neighbours woke and started shouting too. I'm surprised the Watch didn't come to see what the trouble was. I'm sure they could hear the noise in Inveraray.'

'Nobody shouted for the Watch.'

'I saw a lovely piece of black velvet when I was last in Rothesay. It was very dear, so I just left it, but I wish now I'd bought it, for there's not a scrap fit to wear in Glasgow and I've nothing suitable to go to a burying in. If I can borrow a black mantle I'll be there, but I don't know. Antonio can bring me, or Euan. He ought to be there, dear knows – after all,' Euphemia said, giggling again, 'he promised to see her home.'

'Maister Cunningham! Maister Cunningham!'

Feet hurried in the muddy street. Gil halted, and looked back over his shoulder, to see Alys pattering towards them past a group of maidservants, her brown skirts hitched up out of the mud, neat ankles flashing.

'Oh, Maister Cunningham, well met!' she exclaimed as she reached his side, taking his outstretched hand, answering his smile. She looked beyond him and curtsied to Euphemia. 'Forgive me, madame. I hope I don't intrude. I am sent with a word from my father to Maister Cunningham.'

'Not at all, my dear,' said Euphemia in execrable French. 'We were merely discussing the markets of the burgh.' Her eyes flicked over Alys's linen gown. 'I don't imagine you can tell me where to buy cloth in Glasgow.'

'Then you haven't seen Maister Walkinshaw's warehouse, madame?' responded Alys politely. Two apprentices passed them, leather aprons covered in mud, rolling a barrel up the street.

'Oh, that,' said Euphemia. 'But we are forgetting your errand. What did your father send you to say? Tell Maister Cunningham, and then you may go home safely.'

'Yes, indeed,' said Alys, 'for my father sends to bid you to the house, sir.'

'Is that right?' said Lady Euphemia, raising her finely plucked brows. 'I am sure Maister Cunningham will have time for your father when he has convoyed me home.'

'No, madam,' said Gil in Scots, aware of a level of this conversation which he did not fully understand. 'I undertook to see you as far as Greyfriars, and here we are.' He nodded at the end of the wynd beside them.

'What, are we here already?' She looked round, startled. 'And I was wanting to ask you –' She glanced sideways at the group of maidservants, who were just passing them, and lowered her voice. Gil bent his head to hear her, uneasily conscious of how intimate it must look to the passers-by. 'Have you found that girl? The one that was with the boy?'

'We have,' Gil said, 'but –'

'And did she tell you anything?' Glittering green eyes

stared up at him, holding his gaze. 'Surely she was able to help?'

'We haven't questioned her,' said Gil, 'because –'

'Oh, but you should have! You must see that! Didn't you want to find out what she knew?'

'We do,' said Alys at Gil's other side, 'but she is the wrong lass. Forgive us, Lady Euphemia. I am sure Signor Antonio can see you safe home.'

Euphemia stared from Gil's face to Alys's, apparently startled into silence. Gil seized the opportunity to disengage his wrist from her grasp. Stepping away, he bowed and strode off down the High Street with Alys hurrying at his side.

'All is well,' she said quietly. 'You may come to the White Castle and eat with us.'

'Shortly,' he said. 'I have an errand up the town once they are out of sight.'

'They are still watching us,' she said, with a covert glance over her shoulder, 'but you have no errand. All is well. I have found the harpstring.'

He checked, staring down at her, and she tugged him on by the hand which still clasped hers.

'How? How did you know?'

She let go of him and gathered up her skirts again.

'Come and eat, and I will explain.'

'There are others must be told.'

'No, I have seen to all of it. Come and eat – there is just time before the burial. I asked the harper and his sister too, when I went back there, but they wished to be early at the kirk. He has his farewells to make.'

'I am right glad you found me,' he said, following her. 'I can still smell that woman's scent. It must have been on her glove.' He sniffed at the wrist of his doublet. 'Ugh – yes.'

Alys turned in at the pend.

'Where?' she asked, pausing in the shadows. 'Let me . . .?' She bent her head to his offered wrist. 'No, your nose must be keener than mine. I will give you some powdered herbs to rub on the cloth, if you like, to take the scent away. Mint and feverfew should mask it for you.'

'That sounds like what Maggie uses against fleas,' he observed, following her into the yard.

'It is,' she agreed, her smile flickering, 'but it has other uses. Maister Cunningham, the child is here. He and his nurse both. The harper knows.'

'So you didn't come straight home.'

'I went to speak to Nancy,' she agreed, 'and persuade her to bring the child here. She knew me by repute, at least – her sister is Wattie's wife, and Luke is winching their cousin – so she was willing enough to accompany me.' Her eyes danced. 'It was exciting,' she admitted. 'We spied out of the window till the gallowglass was gone up the harper's stair, and hurried across the yard with the bairn hidden in Nancy's plaid. Then we cut round by the back lands, and across Greyfriars yard, and so down the High Street.'

'And the harper?'

'I went back after they were settled. You were not long left, it seems.'

'This is a great relief,' he said. 'How did you – what made you –'

'I thought about it last night,' she said, moving towards the house stair, 'and it seemed to me a baby with two fathers and a murdered mother should be in a safe place until the thing is untangled.'

'Alys, you have *the wisdom of an heap of learned men*,' he said.

She laughed. 'Come and eat, Maister Cunningham.'

On the long board set up in the mason's well-polished hall, there was cold cooked salmon, for which Alys apologized, and a sharp sauce, and an arranged sallet with marigold petals scattered over it. Further down the table the men had bannocks and cheese as well, but the maids had eaten earlier and were hard at work in the kitchen again. The mason, greeting Gil with enthusiasm, drew him to the seat at his right. He was in funeral black, a great black gown flung over the back of his chair, and wearing a self-satisfied expression which he accounted for, as soon as he had said grace and seen everyone served, by saying,

'Maister lawyer, I have something to show you in St Mungo's yard. We go up there after the Mass.'

Gil raised his eyebrows.

'Not the weapon, no,' Maistre Pierre continued with some regret. 'I think we search no longer. It cannot be there. But something strange, which I think you must look at.' He pushed salmon into his bannock with the point of his knife. 'Alys, how does Davie?'

'Still sleeping, father. Brother Andrew says the longer he sleeps the better. We cannot know until he wakes what sort of recovery he will make, but the good brother is optimistic.'

'Hm,' said the mason, chewing.

'Nancy will help to watch him.'

'Ah, yes. This baby. Why are we harbouring a baby?'

'Because,' said Alys patiently, 'although the harper is its father, it was born less than a year after its mother left John Sempill. He could claim it as his own in law, and he says he needs an heir, you heard Maister Cunningham tell us last night.'

'Can the law not count?' asked Maistre Pierre curiously.

'Stranger things have happened,' said Gil.

'And are we any closer to finding what girl it was with Davie, since it was not Bridie Miller?'

'No word yet,' said Alys, 'but I sent the maids into the market this morning to learn what they could. It is too soon, I think, for word to have got back to us.' She poured ale for Gil and for her father. 'They tell me Bridie herself was there, making great play of how she has had a narrow escape. She should be here soon – Agnes promised to send two girls round to help. And they saw you, Maister Cunningham, and Lady Euphemia and her man. Who

113

I think would do anything at all for his lady,' she added thoughtfully.

'The musician?' said Gil, startled.

'Oh, yes. That was how I managed to find you. Kittock said when she came in that Lady Euphemia had gone up the street with that wee Italian lutenist on one arm and you on the other, and looked like two weans being led to the school,' she quoted, in excellent mimicry of Kittock's broader Scots.

'Alys,' said her father reprovingly. She blushed, and apologized. Gil, contemplating the remark, found it more comforting than offensive. He said so, earning a grateful smile from Alys.

'And what did the Campbell woman say?' asked the mason. 'Anything to the purpose?'

'God, what was she not saying? Her tongue's hung in the middle, I swear it,' said Gil intemperately. 'Questions, questions, about how far we have got. John Sempill will be at the burial, and she may come if she can find anything to wear.' Father and daughter made identical long faces, and he nodded. 'Asking about Bridie Miller – you heard her, Alys – had we questioned her.'

He frowned, trying to recall the flood of words.

'I'm sure she said something I should note, but I can't pick it out among all the nonsense.'

'If you leave it, it will come to mind,' said Alys sagely.

'Speaking of the burial . . .' said Maistre Pierre, and pushed his chair back.

Chapter Six

It was cool and dim in the Greyfriars' church.

In the side-chapel, candles flickered on the altar, their light leaping on the painted patterns on the walls, outlining cowl and rough woollen habit where the half-dozen friars stood waiting, catching the knots in Father Francis Govan's girdle as the Superior stood bowing gravely to the mourners as they entered from the transept. It gleamed on the harper's white hair combed down over his shoulders, on Ealasaidh beside him at the head of the bier, sword-straight, mouth clamped shut, and on the white tapes which bound the shroud about Bess Stewart's knees and shoulders, so that she was reduced within her wrappings to the essence, neither male nor female, neither young nor old, but simply human.

Gil, pacing solemnly in behind Maistre Pierre in an atmosphere of mint and feverfew, was taken aback by the number of people already present. Still more were making their way through the church.

'Are all present?' asked Father Francis at length. 'May we begin?'

'Yes,' said Ealasaidh.

'No,' said Gil in the same moment. 'John Sempill –'

Ealasaidh drew a sharp breath, and was checked by a small movement of her brother's hand. Feet sounded in the transept, and Sempill of Muirend entered the chapel swathed in black velvet, a felt hat with a jet-encrusted brim perched on his head. He dragged this off, glared round, then tramped forward to genuflect, glanced once at the bier, and stood aside. As he stared grimly at the harper from under his dishevelled thatch of sandy hair, his cousin and James Campbell of Glenstriven, also draped in black, followed him in and took up position beside him. The two gallowglasses tramped in, crossed themselves, and took up position either side of the entry like a guard of honour. Sempill nodded and gestured to the Superior, who, waiting a few heartbeats longer, opened his book and began.

'*De profundis clamavi ad te* . . . Out of the deep have I called unto thee, O Lord . . .'

Gil looked round, counting heads. Aside from the mason and his men and the Sempill party, there was another man who looked like a harper, led by a shabby boy; a flamboyant fellow with a lute across his back; and more than a dozen townsfolk, among whom he recognized Nancy's mother and aunt, and a man from the Provost's household, presumably sent as a nicely judged courtesy. The Provost, as a Stewart, was related to the Earl of Lennox, and therefore at odds with the Sempills, and although Sempill of Muirend was a fellow landowner he had lost only an adulterous wife and was in no favour with anyone who mattered in the burgh, such as the Archbishop. Sending one's steward in a black mantle was quite enough.

The brothers were chanting the Miserere. Beside him the mason hitched at his velvet gown, crushing the great bow of the black silk funeral favour tied on his arm. Gil glanced down at his own. Alys had tied it for him after she had seen to her father's, standing in the paved yard with the sunshine bright on her bent head. Her hair, it occurred to him now, was the warm tawny colour of honey just run from the comb.

Movement by the entrance to the chapel made him look round, in time to see David Cunningham enter quietly, followed by his taciturn servant, genuflect, and move into a corner. Catching Gil's eye he nodded briefly, and turned his attention to the service.

'*Requiem aeternam* . . . Grant them rest eternal, O Lord . . .'

The words unfolded, with their promises of eternal life, their reminders of judgement and the end times. Father Francis delivered a brief address in which he managed to suggest rather than state his hope that the deceased, having agreed to meet her husband, had repented of her adultery. Ealasaidh stirred restively, and was checked again.

The Mass drew to its end, and Father Francis stepped down from the altar to stand by the bier. Bowing to the shrouded corpse, he drew breath to address it, but Ealasaidh spoke first, her accent very strong.

'Chust one thing, father. There iss people here who have not seen her. We should make it clear who it is we are burying.'

The Franciscan looked steadily at her for a moment, then bowed. She reached forward and tugged at the ribbons which tied the shroud at the crown of the unseen head, then folded back the linen to reveal the still face, softened now into the calm acceptance of the dead. Tenderly she smoothed at a lock of the dark hair with its dusting of silver threads.

'There,' she said, looking defiantly at John Sempill. 'Now who else will say farewell to Bess Stewart?'

'I will,' he said, accepting the challenge. He stepped forward, and first made the Cross with his forefinger and then bent to leave a rather perfunctory kiss on the white brow. Ealasaidh, watching, smiled grimly as he turned back to his place.

'Now you,' she said to his cousin.

'I can name her from here,' said Philip Sempill, dismay in his tone.

'Come and say farewell,' she commanded. He would have objected, but John Sempill nudged him, and he came reluctantly to touch the corpse's cheek with the back of his hand, then suddenly bent and kissed the cold lips. He turned away, his eyes glittering in the candlelight, and James Campbell stepped after him with a short and sonorous prayer, the palm of his hand on the shrouded breastbone.

'And you,' said Ealasaidh to the two gallowglasses. They strode forward as one, to touch fearlessly, murmuring something in Ersche which sounded like a blessing, and turned away to move back down the chapel to their place.

Gil, from where he stood, had an excellent view of the way their faces changed. Astonishment was succeeded by staring fear, which gave way to horror. Turning his head to look where they did, Gil felt the hair stand up on his neck.

Out in the dim church, a white figure approached, gliding slowly between the pillars of the crossing, hazy and silent, its scale impossible to determine in the shadows. It came nearer, and paused. Others had seen it. Gil noticed the mason's man Luke crossing his fingers against ill luck, and there were muttered exclamations of prayer or blessing. Then the figure moved, and spoke, and became human-sized.

'Am I late? I'm so sorry.'

'Euphemia!' said John Sempill. 'Come and say farewell to Bess, since we're all laying hands on her.'

'I hardly think that necessary,' said Father Francis, regaining control of the situation. '*Oremus . . .*'

As the Latin words rolled over the corpse Euphemia moved gracefully through the screen gate into the chapel, her watchful Italian at her back. She had clearly failed to borrow a black mantle, for she was in full white mourning: a satin gown, without ornament, and a cloak fit for a Carmelite were garnished with an extensive veil of very fine gauze with spangles. Gil heard several people draw in their breath at the sight.

Under the strident keening of the women, as they followed the bier out into the kirkyard, the mason said quietly, 'What do you make of that, maister lawyer?'

'Interesting,' said Gil. 'That is five people who are either innocent or not affected by superstition.'

118

'Would you have touched her, there before all the congregation? And run the risk of being accused of her death, if fresh blood appeared?'

'I already have – and I know myself to be innocent.' Gil eyed the back of John Sempill's sandy head, visible beyond the shrouded form on the bier. 'I am convinced that one is innocent too, at least in himself, though the Fury is equally convinced of his guilt.'

'And she – the Fury – what is she screaming about now?'

'It is an Ersche custom,' Gil explained. 'She and the others are addressing the dead, reproaching her for leaving us, probably listing all the people who will miss her. So I am told.'

'It is a horrible noise. Has she mentioned the child?'

'I would not know.'

'No, but anyone who understands Ersche will,' said the mason significantly. 'Who are all these? I expected an empty church.'

Gil looked round again.

'Two musicians at least. Neighbours. Serjeant Anderson – he's worn that favour to a few funerals. A few others out of compliment to the harper, or to Sempill.'

The pallbearers, selected evenhandedly by Father Francis, halted before the open grave and lowered the bier. Sempill and his cousin stepped back immediately, glaring at the other two, and Euphemia Campbell moved forward to stand between them, leaning on John Sempill's arm with a pretty solicitude as he glowered at the lutenist opposite him. The women fell silent, and four of the Franciscans took up the cords to lower Bess Stewart into her grave. Gil edged back from the sight.

'I cannot bear the way they bend in the middle,' he confessed in Maistre Pierre's ear.

The mason turned a bright eye on him, but moved companionably to the edge of the group, saying, 'There is a bite to eat after this at my house. You will come back, no? There may be something to be learned.'

'I should be grateful.' Gil looked over the heads. 'But I think you have competition. Look yonder.'

James Campbell, in a pose comically mirroring the mason's, was speaking low and sideways to the Official. Since Canon Cunningham's attention was on Father Francis he received only a stiff nod in reply, but this seemed to satisfy him, for he moved casually off to speak to the Provost's steward. Maistre Pierre said something inappropriate to the occasion, and set off in opposition as the singing ended and Father Francis pushed back his hood and turned to John Sempill with calm sympathy. At the grave's foot, Philip Sempill stood, bare head bent, the light breeze ruffling his fair hair.

Gil remained where he was while the mason secured a word with both musicians and several neighbours. James Campbell seemed unaware of the situation until he sidled up to someone with whom the mason had already spoken. Gil was watching the resulting exchange with some amusement when his uncle spoke in his ear.

'We may learn more in different courts.'

'Yes, sir,' he said gratefully, thinking, God, the old man's quick on the uptake.

The Official sniffed. 'Mint and feverfew. Flea repellent?'

'It has other uses, I'm told,' Gil said, annoyed to hear himself defensive.

'Aye, well. Is there anything I should raise in particular?'

'Money. Who is the better for her death.'

'*Cui bono*. Aye. I cannot think it Sempill.'

'Not directly,' Gil agreed, watching Father Francis decline politely. 'I cast Maggie in there this morning to see what she could put up. Best not to see her if you see her, sir.'

'I take your point.' The Official, with another hard look at the borrowed gown and favour, moved away to condole with John Sempill. Gil found Serjeant Anderson approaching in his blue gown of office.

'A sad business, Maister Cunningham,' he said conventionally.

'Aye, indeed,' agreed Gil.

'And I hear you've no put her killer to the horn yet.'

'We only found her yesterday morning,' said Gil. 'I am working on it.'

'Aye,' said the serjeant. 'No doubt. And is that right, that there's a bairn?'

'What makes you ask?' countered Gil.

'Girzie Murray yonder's first man spoke the Ersche. She was telling me what the women were saying, when they were caterwauling there.'

'And what were they saying?'

'Oh, the likes of, Who will stroke the small harp, who will tune the big harp, who will comfort the man-child. All very poetic, though you'd not think it to hear it sung,' said Serjeant Anderson trenchantly. 'So it seems there's a bairn.'

'So what have we learned today?' asked the mason, strolling up the High Street in the late afternoon sun.

'Little enough,' admitted Gil. 'I have another sighting of Davie and his girl, but no description. I have learned that Bess Stewart had property on Bute, and spoke Ersche, and that the gallowglass promised to see her home.' He ticked the points off as he spoke. 'We know that Sempill is after the baby. And I had a long word with that musician.'

'Who was he?'

'He calls himself Balthasar of Liège, but I suspect Leith is nearer it.'

The flamboyant man with the lute had approached Gil in the courtyard of the mason's house. The long trestle table was laden with food, and maids hurried about with wicker dishes containing more food; avoiding a girl with a handful of empty beakers, the man had said, 'Poor Bess. And poor Angus. She's a great loss. Didn't I see you at their lodgings last night? Had you known her long?'

'I never met her,' Gil said. 'I found her dead.'

'Stabbed, so Ealasaidh tells me. By the husband.'

'There is no proof of that,' Gil said firmly. 'Tell me about Bess – how did you know her?'

'I've known Angus for years – you meet folk, on the circuit. Then he turned up with this new singer. More than one of us envied him – I'd have been happy to lift her away from him,' he admitted frankly, 'but she'd none of any of us. Angus it was for her.'

'I heard her sing, on May Day. She'd a bonnie voice.'

'And a rare hand with the wee harp.' The lutenist's own hand shot out and seized a pasty from a passing tray. 'And always a greeting and a friendly word for Angus's friends, for all she was stolen away from her own castle. A good woman and a good musician, and few enough of either come from baronial stock. I saw her on the High Street on May Day evening,' he said abruptly.

'You don't say?' said Gil. 'On May Day evening?'

'I do. I'm in Glasgow for the dancing, see,' he said, indicating the lute, 'and I picked up enough to go drinking. So I was sizing up the howffs on the Bell o' the Brae when she came up the hill with a good-looking young fellow. I'm about to say something tactless when I catch what they're saying, and he's addressing her as *Mistress Bess*, and it's clear they know one another.'

'They knew one another?' Gil repeated.

'By what I heard, aye. In Bute it was, from the sound of it.'

'What language were they speaking?' Gil asked.

'Oh, Ersche, of course.' The lutenist eyed Gil. He had one blue eye and one brown, a most distracting attribute. 'Are you thinking I don't speak Ersche? You're right, of course, but I can sing in it, and I understand it when I hear it. She knew his name, and she sounded like a woman speaking to a trusted servant.'

'I see,' said Gil, digesting this. 'And then what? Did you speak to her?'

'Aye, briefly, and she bade me goodnight, and told me where they were living, and went on up the brae, rattling away in Ersche with the young fellow. And when I went round there yesterday, looking for a crack with the three of them, this was the word that met me.' He gestured largely round the yard and bit into the pasty. 'What a waste.'

'What a waste, indeed,' said Maistre Pierre, pushing open the gate into St Mungo's yard. 'So the gallowglass knew her already. Should we speak to him again, think you?'

'We must,' said Gil. 'And I wonder about going down to Bute.'

'Is it far?'

'You take a ship from Dumbarton, or maybe Irvine.'

'I have contacts in Irvine,' said the mason thoughtfully. 'Alys can manage for a day or two without me.'

'Alys can manage anything, I think,' said Gil. 'Did she organize that by herself this afternoon? As well as fetching the child and its nurse home.'

'She did,' agreed Maistre Pierre, completely failing to conceal his pride. 'When I suggested it to her it was already in hand. And all without a cross word in the kitchen, so Catherine tells me, although Bridie Miller never came to help.'

'Her mother is dead? Who was she?'

'Yes, in '88, just before we came to Scotland, poor Marie. Who was she? She was the niece – well, he said she was his niece – of a parish priest, poor as a grasshopper in all but his learning, in a God-forsaken place inland from Nantes. Claimed to be of the same family as Peter Abelard, if you'll believe it. He dropped dead an hour after he handed me the patron's money for the new east window, so I married the girl and took her back to Nantes with me, and never regretted it in fifteen years.'

'And just the one child?'

'Just the one. She has run my household for four years now. I suppose I should find her a husband, if only to be rid of Robert Walkinshaw, whom she does not affect, but what would I do without her, Maister Cunningham?'

'I find it extraordinary,' said Gil, 'that you and the

123

demoiselle should have been in Glasgow since before I came home, and our paths never crossed. I've been mewed up in the Chanonry, I suppose, learning to be a notary, and seen little enough of the town.'

'And before that you were in Paris, as we were. You were recalled after Stirling field?'

'There was no more money,' said Gil frankly. 'I had studied long enough to determine – to graduate Bachelor of Laws – in '89, but there was no chance of a doctorate. And my father and both my brothers died on Sauchie moor, most of the land was forfeit, my mother needed things sorted out. I had to come home as soon as I was granted my degree.'

He was silent, recalling the scene in the Scots College when the news of the battle arrived, the strong young men weeping in the courtyard, and the unlikely sympathy of the English students who had experienced the same shock three years earlier when Welsh Henry took Bosworth field.

The Cunninghams were not the only family to have been affected, when the young Prince of Scotland and his advisers took up arms against his father, the third King James, and met on a moor near Stirling in a tiresome affray which ended in the mysterious death of the elder James. There had been some strange alliances and enmities forged in that battle and in the troubled weeks which followed it.

'Well,' said Maistre Pierre, 'we grow melancholy again. Come and look at this.'

He led Gil down the slope, past the thatch of the lodge, across the path that led to the crypt door, into the clump of trees where they had found Davie.

'The boy was here, no?' he said, gesturing. 'The mark is still to be seen where he lay. Now look at this.'

He indicated the branch of a sturdy beech which leaned above the recovering grasses and green plants where the boy had huddled. The branch was perhaps chest-high to either of them, and on its western side, about three feet from the trunk, was a scraping bruise in the bark.

'Interesting.' Gil bent closer. The bark was damaged and split, and the powdery green stuff which coated trunk and branches had been rubbed away. 'What has happened here?'

'Has whoever struck the boy hit the branch as well?'

'Why should one do that?'

'By accident, naturally. On the way down, or on the back-swing. Or – what do golfers call it? – when the swing continues after you have hit the ball?'

'We never thought of a golf-club as a weapon.'

'Whatever he used, it is not here,' said Maistre Pierre firmly, wiping his hands on his jerkin. 'I will swear to that. We have searched every ell of this kirkyard, from the gates up yonder down to the Molendinar, and Luke spent this morning guddling in the burn itself.'

'Very strange,' said Gil. 'I wish the boy would waken. Has Alys learned anything about the girl? If we could find her –'

'Ah!' The mason dug in his pouch. 'Alys was much concerned with our guests, she had not time to speak, with having less help than she had depended on, but she gave me this.' He unfolded a slip of paper. 'Annie Thomson, in Maggie Bell's ale-house at the Brigend,' he read carefully, and showed it to Gil.

The writing was neat and accomplished, the spelling no wilder than Gil's own. Admiring the economy of 'elhus', Gil commented, 'That's in the Gorbals – the Brigend. By the leper-house. I've heard of it.'

'Well, even on the other side of the river they must drink,' said the mason, putting the paper back in his pouch. 'Come, let us leave this place, I have seen enough of it for now.'

'I want to look at something else.' Gil set off up the slope. 'You know, if you found yourself a son-in-law who could move in with you, Alys would not have to go away.'

'I thought of that. The trouble is, I would have to live with him too, and she and I would look for different qualities. It isn't easy. You'll find that yourself when you –'

'If I am to be a priest,' said Gil, the familiar chill knotting in his stomach, 'I will never have to seek a son-in-law.'

'The two are not necessarily separate. Many of those in the Church have children and acknowledge them. Look at Bishop Elphinstone in Aberdeen. His father did well by him, from all one hears.'

'A vow is a vow,' said Gil, 'and a promise is a promise. Robert Elphinstone's father was not yet priested when he was born – and by what my uncle says he would never have been allowed to marry the lady anyway. No, some are able to break their vows daily and still sleep at night, but I am not among them.'

'Where are we going?'

'I want to look in the haw-bushes opposite the south door where the gallowglass left Bess Stewart waiting for her husband. These bushes.'

'What do you hope to find?'

'After two days, not a lot.' Gil stepped into the ring of trees, looking round in the dappled, scented light. 'Now if I was a woman waiting for someone I barely trusted . . .'

'The weapon is not here,' said Maistre Pierre doggedly, and sneezed.

'No, I agree. Whoever struck the boy, wherever he has gone, he kept hold of the weapon. How tall was she?'

'About so? A little more than Alys?'

Gil measured off the level which Alys's head had reached as she tied the fringed black silk on his arm before the funeral. Holding out his hand at that height, he turned from tree to tree, parting the young leaves and peering under them. Maistre Pierre did likewise at the other side of the circle, sneezing from time to time. Birds chirruped above their heads.

'What are we looking for?' the mason asked.

'Any sign that she was here. There were hawthorn flowers in her headdress, but there are other haw-bushes. If we find nothing, it does not disprove Euan's story, but . . .' Gil paused, looking closer at the spray of may-blossom he was holding back. 'Ah. Come and look at this.'

Maistre Pierre obeyed, with another explosive sneeze.

'The smell of these flowers!' he complained. 'What have you here?'

'There.' Gil pointed. 'A scrap of thread, look, on that thorn.' Carefully he dislodged it. 'The shade of green is certainly very like Ealasaidh's plaid.'

The mason, covering his nose with one big hand, peered at the little twist of colour.

'And this atomy,' he said, wondering, 'tells us she was here.'

Gil looked round.

'She stood under this tree,' he agreed, 'waiting while Euan went into the kirk and her killer came out to meet her. May I have that paper? It would do to keep it safe.' He folded the wisp of yarn close in Alys's writing and stowed both carefully in his purse.

'You know, it's a strange thing,' he added, looking round at the encircling trees. 'We had evidence, and now we have more, that Bess was here. We have repeated sightings of Davie and whatever girl it was – they were here, they were there, they were yonder down the slope. But after all the people went in to Compline we have no sign of anyone else in the kirkyard. It's as if whoever struck Davie was as invisible as his weapon.'

'Perhaps it was the same person that stabbed Bess.'

'No,' said Gil regretfully. 'We abandoned that hypothesis early, remember. The knife is not here – if it was the same person, then he still had the knife, so why use an invisible stick? We are missing something, Maistre Pierre.'

The mason, turning away, sneezed explosively,

'Let us go away,' he said plaintively. 'I will not miss these confounded flowers. What do we do now? Go down to cross the river and question Annie Thomson?'

'That, or go to my uncle's house,' said Gil, following him out of the kirkyard. 'I set Maggie that keeps house for us to find out what she could, and my uncle accepted Sempill's invitation this afternoon. There may be information. Or – wait. Do you speak Italian? I've only a little.'

'Italian? I do. Oh, you think of the musician? Why not, indeed? We question him, and then we are next to your uncle's house.'

'My thought also. The lassie Thomson will keep, I hope.'

The mastiff had clearly been shut up for the afternoon, and was still raging fruitlessly in the darkness of her kennel as Gil and the mason crossed the courtyard of the Sempill house. When she stopped baying to draw breath they heard her claws scraping on the stout planks which contained her.

'I hope that creature is securely chained,' observed Maistre Pierre.

'Sempill claims she is,' Gil answered.

The house door was open, and within was a noisy disorganized bustle of servants shouting and hurrying about with plate and crocks from the hall. Euphemia's stout companion backed out of a door with an armful of ill-folded linen, shouting, 'And the same for your mother's brat, Agnes Yuill!'

'My mother!' Another woman erupted after her into the screens passage, brandishing a bundle of wooden serving-spoons. 'I'll tell ye, Mally Murray, what my mother says of yon yellow-headed strumpet! It's no my place to clean blood off her fancy satin –'

Catching sight of their audience, she turned to bob a curtsy. 'Your pardon, maisters,' she said in more civil tones, tucking the spoons out of sight behind her skirts. 'What's your pleasure? Are you here for the burial, for if so I'm feared you're too late.'

'It's that lawyer,' said Mistress Murray, her plump face suspicious. 'If ye're wanting a word with Euphemia, maister, it's no possible, for she's away to lie down. She's had a busy day of it, what with one thing and another.'

'No, I thank you,' said Gil. 'No need to disturb her if she's in her bed. Would you ask Maister Sempill if we might get a word with the Italian musician?'

'What, Anthony?' said Mistress Murray. 'You'll no get much out of him. If he's got ten words of Scots he's no more.'

'Nevertheless,' said Gil politely, 'we would like a word with him.'

She stared at them, then sniffed and said, 'Aye, Agnes. Away and tell the maister what they're asking.'

'Where is he?'

'How should I know? I wish that friend of Marriott Kennedy's had stayed longer. We could ha done with her.' Mistress Murray hitched her armful of linen higher and set off purposefully for the door at the far end of the passage. Agnes shrugged, and ducked back into the hall, past two men carrying a bench.

After some time, during which the visitors had ample opportunity to study the temperament of the household, she returned, dragging the alarmed lutenist.

'The maister says, what's your will wi him, maisters?' she reported. 'You can talk in the yaird, he says, and no to be long, for he's wanted to play for them up the stair.'

'Agnes!' said the Italian, twisting in her grasp. *'Cosa succede?'*

'May we speak to you?' said Gil. 'I wish to ask you some questions.'

The mason translated, and the musician stopped squirming and gaped at him.

'Che hai detto? Questione? Perché, messeri?' He broke into a torrent of speech and gesture which appeared to deny all knowledge of anything.

Gil gestured at the fore-stair, and Agnes said robustly, 'Away out and talk to them, man, and get out from underfoot.' She pushed him forward and slammed the door behind him.

Antonio was coaxed down into the yard with some difficulty, and stood, apparently on the point of flight, looking from Gil to the mason and back. Feeling like a man baiting a suckling calf, Gil looked down at him and said, 'You know that a woman was killed in the churchyard on May Day?'

The mason translated this, and the musician looked even more alarmed.

'*Non so niente! Niente, niente.*'

'He says he knows nothing,' the mason translated.

Gil nodded. 'I surmised that. Ask if he saw anything unusual when he came out of St Mungo's.'

The dark gaze flicked from his face to the mason's, a hint of – surprise? relief? – in the man's expression.

'San Mungo?' It sounded like relief. '*La cattedrale? No – vedevo niente insolito.*' He shook his head emphatically. Gil studied him, considering his next question.

'You didn't see the woman standing in the trees?'

Maistre Pierre translated this, and got a blank look and a surprised answer.

'He says the lady was by the church, not in the trees,' he reported.

'By the church?' repeated Gil. 'What lady does he mean? Lady Euphemia was by the church, but –'

'*Si, si, Donna Eufemia, accanto a la cattedrale,*' agreed Antonio enthusiastically.

'Did he see another lady in the trees?'

The answer was emphatic, and scarcely needed to be translated. There was no lady in the trees.

'And he saw nothing suspicious? I thought he had his hand on his dagger.' Gil demonstrated, and the small man tensed warily. Maistre Pierre translated, and there was a longer exchange.

'This is not satisfactory,' the mason complained at length. 'I cannot make sense of what he says. I ask about his knife. He says he drew because he thought he saw something – an *uomo cattivo*, a *ladro* – in the kirkyard. I say you have not mentioned such to me.' He raised his eyebrows, and Gil nodded in confirmation. They turned to study the lutenist, who was now holding the knife across his palm, looking at them with an ingratiating expression. The knife was a little one, with a narrow springy blade, much like the one James Campbell carried.

'I don't think he can tell us anything,' said Gil. 'It seems clear he saw nothing, like everyone else in the household.'

'He seems afraid of something,' the mason said.

'He does, doesn't he? Ask him what it is he's afraid of.'

The small man ruffled like a fighting-cock, in the same way as the Italians Gil had known in Paris. Slamming the dagger back in its sheath he conveyed in indignant tones that Antonio Bragato feared nothing and no one. The mastiff, roused, barked again, and he flinched and glanced over his shoulder, then squared up to Gil again.

The door above them opened, and James Campbell said, 'Antonio, *vieni suonare. Dai!* Oh, your pardon, maisters. Are you still questioning him?'

'No, we've done,' said Gil, and nodded to the lutenist, who hurried up the steps and past James Campbell without a backward glance. 'Good of John to spare him for a quarter-hour.'

'I think you were wasting your time. If a broken man knifed Bess under his nose,' said James, 'Antonio would see nothing. He's a rare good lutenist, but that's all I can say for him.'

He withdrew, slamming the door with finality. Gil and the mason looked at one another.

'Let us go and enquire of your uncle,' said Maistre Pierre. 'I feel sure he will provide us something to drink.'

'The man is certainly afraid,' said Gil thoughtfully, moving towards the gate.

'Did we ask the right questions?' wondered the mason.

'I keep asking myself that,' Gil admitted, 'but I think in

this case we would have got no different answers. *Niente, niente,*' he quoted, crossing Rottenrow.

'But is he afraid,' said Maistre Pierre, avoiding a pig which was chasing two hens, 'because he is guilty, or because he knows who else is guilty?'

'Or is he afraid of being suspected, or of casting suspicion?' Gil countered, and opened his uncle's front door.

Canon Cunningham was seated by the fire in the hall, reading as usual, but set his book aside and rose when he saw the guest. Gil, bowing, began to introduce the mason, but his uncle cut across that.

'We have met more than once. Good evening, Maistre Mason. I hope I see you well?'

'Except for these confounded flowers,' said the mason, sneezing again. 'Good evening, sir.'

'Gilbert, Maggie's in the kitchen. Bid her fetch ale for our guest.'

'No need, maister.' Maggie appeared in the doorway to the kitchen stairs, a tray in her hands. 'I brought mine as well, seeing it was poured.' She set the tray on a stool and began to draw others forward to the fire. 'Maister Gil will be wanting to hear about Sempill's idea of a funeral feast, I've no doubt.'

'You listen too much, Maggie,' said the Official.

'That was a remarkable funeral,' said Maistre Pierre, accepting a beaker of ale. 'I had not witnessed that wailing over the dead before. A local custom, I hear.'

'Aye,' said David Cunningham grimly. 'And they'd have been better to keep quiet. Someone in Sempill's household understood fine what was said, and I was questioned about the bairn. Fortunately I could say I knew nothing.'

'The gallowglass brothers are Erschemen,' Gil pointed out.

'And that Euphemia Campbell speaks their tongue,' Maggie said. 'I heard her, rattling away with one of them. Seems she speaks Italian and all, for I heard her with the wee dark lutenist. And Campbell of Glenstriven too.' She nudged the mason with a plate of girdle-cakes. 'Take a pancake, maister. My granny's receipt.'

'But did you learn anything, sir?' Gil asked hopefully.

'Not to say learn,' the Canon said, pushing his spectacles back up his nose. 'Elizabeth Stewart or Sempill's tocher I think was in coin or kind, which simplifies that.'

'Tocher?' queried the mason. 'I would say her *dot*, her dowry. Is it equivalent in law?'

'Her bride-portion, aye.' Canon Cunningham nodded approvingly, as at a bright student, and continued, 'It is clear that there is also property in Bute. Some of it was Mistress Stewart's own outright, some of it was left her by her first husband –'

'I never knew she was married before,' said Maggie.

The Official glared at her and continued, 'And some of it was the conjunct fee from her kin.'

'Land given them jointly in respect of their marriage,' Gil translated for Maistre Pierre, who nodded, absently taking another girdle-cake.

'However,' continued the Official, 'it is not clear who now has control over these properties. Even if Mistress Stewart made a will, and disposed of nothing which it was not her right to dispose of, we have still to consider the questions of the bairn's inheritance, the conjunct fee property, and the precise terms of her first man's will.'

Gil, recognizing the tone of voice, settled back. Not for nothing did his uncle lecture at the College from time to time. Maggie was less patient.

'So will that be written down somewhere?' she demanded. 'And will it tell us who put a knife into the poor woman?'

'Not immediately,' said Canon Cunningham, put off his stride. 'But it may tell us who benefits from her death.'

'The information may be in her box,' said Gil. 'I was on the point of opening it this morning when something else happened. It is at the harper's lodging.'

'At my lodging,' corrected Maistre Pierre. 'Alys sent Wattie for it.'

133

'It must certainly be opened,' agreed the Official. 'There is of course the further point that, whoever finally benefits, and this is not immediately clear, the person who knifed Mistress Sempill may have been under the erroneous impression that he would be a beneficiary.'

There was a pause.

'You mean he might not have been aware of the bairn's existence,' Gil said. 'I agree, sir.'

'It's all mixter-maxter,' complained Maggie. 'You've made things worse, maister.'

'And we still have no proof it was someone of that household,' said Maistre Pierre, 'although I do not know who else it could be.'

'Nor do I,' said Maggie, 'seeing I found this.'

She dug in the placket of her capacious skirt and produced, from whatever pocket lurked there, a bundle of grimy cloth. This she unfolded to reveal a limp object which she planted triumphantly on the stool in front of her in a waft of rotting cabbage smells. Maistre Pierre snatched the plate of girdle-cakes away and peered past it.

'Bones of St Peter, what is it?' he demanded.

'The purse?' said Gil.

Maggie nodded. 'The purse.'

'A purse,' the Official corrected. 'Where, Maggie?'

'On the midden. That's why it stinks a bit,' she admitted, 'it was on a heap of kale. Why throw away a perfectly good purse, maister, only because the strings is cut? Someone with a bad conscience pitched it there.'

'Particularly since John Sempill can work leather,' Gil observed. 'He could mend it readily enough if it was his own.'

'It's empty,' Maggie said regretfully.

'Well,' said the mason. 'At last, something concrete.'

'Anything else, Maggie?' Gil asked.

'A lot of gossip,' she said. 'Marriott Kennedy's a terrible gossip, which is no more than you'd expect from a woman who keeps a kitchen like yon. A lot of gossip, and most of it not to the point.' She cast her mind back. 'She was telling me how long Mistress Campbell's been visiting the house. Since the year of the siege at Dumbarton, she said, only it was the autumn. And she'd known Sempill well for a year or more before that.'

'The siege was in '89,' Maistre Pierre supplied.

'Near three years, then,' said Gil.

'As Sempill's mistress?' asked Canon Cunningham.

'So she had me understand. Her brother's as bad, Marriott says. Aye out in the town after the servant lassies, for all he's a married man. And it seems now Mistress Campbell's no content with Sempill, for Marriott keeps finding the tags off someone else's points in her chamber.'

'Oh, aye?' said the Official hopefully. 'And whose might they be?'

'That wee lutenist. The Italian.'

'Well!' said David Cunningham, in some pleasure. 'Do you say so?'

'Did you learn anything else?' said Gil, before his uncle could begin to explore this topic. 'Or find the plaid? The cross?'

'I never got into her chamber,' said Maggie apologetically, 'though I tried, for that Mally Murray that calls herself her waiting-woman was fussing about seeing to her clothes. I never saw a sign of the plaid elsewhere in the house. There were other plaids in plenty, in any colour you can name, but not a blink of that green.'

She turned her head, listening.

'Is that someone in my kitchen? Your pardon, maisters.'

She rose, setting down her ale, and made for the kitchen stairs. Gil prodded the purse, and teased out the strings which had hung it to its owner's belt.

'Cut,' he said. 'I wonder.'

'It shows a connection with that household,' Maistre Pierre observed.

'If it is the dead woman's purse,' reminded the Official.

Maggie's voice on the stair preceded her entry into the hall.

'Come away up, ye daft laddie, and tell Maister Gil your message to his face.'

'A message for me?' Gil turned as she dragged the mason's man Luke in by his wrist.

'Here's this laddie sent with a word for Maister Gil,' she reported, 'and trying to teach it to wee William, that can hardly remember his own name, rather than come up and disturb us.'

'Bring him in then,' said the Official.

'And it's for the maister too,' mumbled Luke, trying to cling to the doorpost.

'Then come in, Luke, since Maister Cunningham gives you leave,' said his master, 'and tell us what your word is.'

'It's from the mistress,' said Luke, bobbing. 'I was to find Maister Cunningham and yourself, and tell you, Bridie Miller's no been seen since she went to the market this morning, and now they've picked her up dead in Blackfriars yard. Mistress Hamilton's in a rare taking, and I've to come home after I've tellt you.'

Chapter Seven

'She was certainly in the market this morning,' said Alys, patting Mistress Hamilton's hand.

'She never came back,' sobbed Mistress Hamilton, 'and I had to make Andrew's dinner without the beets she was to bring.'

'Did any of the other girls go with her?' Gil asked uncomfortably. Alys threw him an approving smile, and Mistress Hamilton wiped her eyes on one long end of her linen headdress, hiccuping.

'They all went,' she said, 'but they came back by their lones. They do that, they tarry, if they've met a friend, or a sweetheart. She was a good girl, she knew the beets were for the dinner, she'd have brought them straight back.' She dissolved into tears again. 'Alys, what can have happened?'

'Where is she?' asked the mason. 'Did they bring her back here?'

'Come ben and see her.' Mistress Hamilton rose, still dabbing at her eyes, and led them out across the yard, past the silent kitchen and into a store-room in one of the other outhouses. One of the dead girl's colleagues rose from her knees and stepped back as they entered. 'It's not right, laying her here, but it's quiet, and fine and cold. Oh, the poor lass!'

'Where was she found?' Gil asked, drawing back the linen. 'What happened?'

'A corner of Blackfriars yard. Dear knows what she was doing there, she'd gone down to the market, she'd pass the house on the way back up before she got to Blackfriars. Mally Bowen that washed her says she was stabbed. She thought maybe sometime between Sext and Nones, by the way she was stiffening.'

'She looks as if it was quick,' said Maistre Pierre. 'She had not been forced, then?'

'Mally says not. But she'd been robbed. The money I gave her to go to the market – a couple of groats, no more – that wasny on her.'

Gil looked down at Bridie Miller. Young, moderately pretty, quite ordinary, she lay as if asleep on the board set up to receive her, and kept her secret.

'May I see the wound?' he asked. Alys glanced quickly at him, and stepped forward past Mistress Hamilton's flustered exclamations.

'It's very like the one that killed Mistress Stewart,' she said, 'save that it is at the front.' She drew the shroud further back, exposing the rigid hands with their bitten nails, crossed and bound neatly over the girl's belly. Under one muscular upper arm, just below the girl's small breast, a narrow blue-lipped wound showed between two ribs. Gil bent close to study it, smelling the harsh soap Mally Bowen had used to wash the body. He sniffed, and sniffed again.

'There is, isn't there,' said Alys. 'Just a trace of a scent.'

'Like a privy,' said Gil. 'And something else as well.'

'She'd void herself,' Mistress Hamilton pointed out practically, and wiped her eyes again.

'Mally must have washed that off,' Alys said. Gil leaned over the corpse, sniffing.

'It's on her hair,' he said finally. 'Mally wouldn't wash that. It smells of . . .' He tested the air again. 'Aye, like a privy. Stale. Not from when she voided herself but older, like the spillage outside a dyer's shop. But there's something else.' He frowned. 'It's familiar, but I can't place it.'

Maistre Pierre came forward curiously, peered at the

wound, and sniffed cautiously at the lank brown locks coiled by the dead girl's shoulders.

'How did she wear her hair?' he asked, and sneezed.

'Like any other lass,' said Mistress Hamilton. 'Loose down her back, with a little kerchief tied over it for going outside.'

'Is her kerchief here?'

'It's yonder,' said the maidservant still standing by the wall, pointing at the side of the room. Gil looked around, and found a pile of garments on a barrel.

'Is this it?'

'Aye, likely. Yes, take it, if you need it.' There were voices out in the yard, and Agnes Hamilton turned her head. 'That's likely the serjeant. He sent word he'd come by before he had his supper.'

Gil hastily folded the kerchief and stowed it in his pouch as Serjeant Anderson proceeded into the store-room.

'Good evening, maisters,' he said, nodding. 'What's all this then? One dead lass, as notified.' He touched Bridie's cold cheek with a massive hand, twitched back the linen shroud to look at the wound, and nodded again. 'Aye, aye. She's dead, for certain. Between Sext and Nones, eh? A wee foreign kind of knife, would it be, maybe?'

'Maybe,' said Gil despite himself.

'Found in Blackfriars yard, you tell me,' said the serjeant, covering the corpse's face again. 'Simple enough. Knifed in Blackfriars yard this forenoon by some foreigner, no doubt when she wouldny do his will. Murder *chaud-mellé*. A lesson to all Glasgow lassies no to take up with foreigners. No offence, maister,' he said belatedly to the mason, who eyed him quizzically, and sneezed.

'But is that –' Gil began.

The serjeant smiled indulgently. 'See, Maister Cunningham, I've a burgh to watch and ward. I've no time to run about the streets asking questions. Now, once I've called to mind what foreigners are in Glasgow the now, I can lift someone for it, and get a confession, and that's the end of it.'

'But suppose he was somewhere else at the time?' said Gil helplessly.

'Who?'

'This man you're going to seize for the killing.'

'How could he have been elsewhere,' said Serjeant Anderson, 'when he was in Blackfriars yard knifing Bridie Miller? Now, I've more to do than stand around all evening. God save ye, maisters.'

He raised his bonnet to them, and left. Gil stared after him, and Agnes Hamilton drew a gusty breath.

'I must set someone to watch,' she said. 'The lassies are barely fit for it, what with the last two-three days. Alys, Maister Mason, Gil, I must not keep you. You've been good neighbours. Candles,' she muttered, leading the way from the store-room. 'Flowers. Would St Thenew's send someone to watch?'

She ushered them out with incoherent thanks and shut the door with great firmness behind them. Out on the step, at the head of the Hamiltons' handsome fore-stair, they all paused, Gil watching the serjeant's back retreating towards the Tolbooth as he headed majestically for home and supper. Alys said, 'I think she was no more than eighteen.'

'Hush a moment,' said her father softly. 'Maister Cunningham, look here.'

Gil turned to look up the High Street. There were not many people abroad, although it was still full daylight, but a few stalwarts drifted from door to door in search of variety in their evening's drinking. Among them, conspicuously sober and wearing a short gown of blue velvet which must have cost a quarter's rents, was James Campbell of Glenstriven.

'He has seen us,' said Maistre Pierre. The comment was unnecessary. Gil had also recognized the tiny pause in the sauntering gait. He moved forward, to descend the fore-stair, and Campbell altered direction to meet him, waving his blue velvet hat in a bow. The dark hair was receding unkindly up his high forehead.

'What, are you still at your questions? Don't say you

suspect Andrew Hamilton?' he asked, with slightly artificial lightness.

'No,' said Gil, as Alys and her father came down the stair behind him. 'But someone suspected Bridie Miller of knowing too much.'

The handsome, narrow face froze.

'Bridie Miller?' Campbell repeated. 'Is Bridie dead? But she – are you saying that's the girl that was in St Mungo's yard?'

'The point is that she wasn't in St Mungo's,' Gil reiterated. 'She had quarrelled with Maister Mason's laddie before Easter. Someone else was in St Mungo's yard with the boy, and not Bridie. Nevertheless, she is dead.'

'Poor lassie,' said Campbell, with a hollow note to his voice. 'What happened? When was this?'

'She was found stabbed in Blackfriars yard,' said Maistre Pierre behind Gil.

'Stabbed,' repeated James Campbell. 'Like Bess, you mean? Then surely the same broken man or – When did this happen?'

'She never came back from the market this morning,' said Gil.

'Oh,' said Campbell, his face changing.

'Do you know something to the purpose?' asked the mason. James Campbell glanced at him and shook his head.

'She was found this evening.' Gil gestured down the hill. 'Are you for the lower town? Maister Mason goes home, I believe.'

'Poor wee trollop,' said Campbell. 'Had she been forced?'

'It seems not.'

Campbell looked about him, and frowned.

'Forgive me,' he said, 'I must away back up the hill. I am forgetting. I – I'm to meet Sempill before Compline. Good e'en to ye, maisters. Good e'en, demoiselle.'

He raised the hat again, bent the knee briefly and strode

off rapidly up the High Street, the breadths of velvet in the back of his gown swinging.

'That is a very unpleasant man,' said Alys, 'and his eyes are too close together, but I think he was upset to hear about Bridie.'

'I thought so too,' said Gil.

Maistre Pierre tucked his daughter's hand under his arm, and drew her down the street, saying with rough sympathy, 'You go home now and help Catherine. She is still praying for Davie, no?'

'She is.' Alys looked up at him. 'What did you think of that man, father?'

'He was hiding something,' said the mason firmly.

Gil, with a covert look over his shoulder, said, 'He has just stepped into Greyfriars' Wynd. I wonder where he is meeting Sempill?'

'We have already questioned him,' said Maistre Pierre, 'and I can think of a better errand.'

'Where are you going, father?'

'There is yet an hour to Compline,' said the mason, glancing at the sky. 'Maister lawyer, are you of a mind with me?'

'We must find Annie Thomson,' Gil agreed. 'Thirsty, are you?'

'I knew I could depend on you.' Maistre Pierre stopped outside his own house, and patted his daughter's hand. 'Go in, *ma mie*, and we will go drinking. You will not be shocked, I hope.'

'Catherine says one should never be shocked by the things men do,' she reported primly. 'I wish I could come to the ale-house too.'

'Now Maister Cunningham will be shocked,' reproved her father. She smiled wryly, tilting her face to share the joke with Gil.

'Women are always restricted in what they can do,' she complained. 'Like priests. You must make the most of this visit, Maister Cunningham, for you won't be able to make many more. You should join the Franciscans or the

Blackfriars instead of being a priest – they like the inside of an ale-house, by what I hear.'

'If we are not back, you do not go to Compline. Understood?'

'Luke and Thomas –'

'Understood?'

'Very well, father.' She kissed him. 'Will you both come in later?'

'There is Mistress Stewart's box to inspect,' said Gil, speaking quietly, although they were using French. 'I would like to do that before the day's end.'

'Then I shall see you later.' She smiled at him, and slipped into the shadowy tunnel of the pend. The mason watched her fondly out of sight, and turned to go on down the hill.

'Is the demoiselle truly only sixteen?' Gil asked, falling into step beside him. 'She seems much older.'

'She will be seventeen on St John's Eve,' said Maistre Pierre. 'Her mother was prettier, but I think Alys is a little the wiser.' He sighed. 'Who would be a father?'

They passed the Tolbooth and Gil said, 'What do you think about this second killing?'

'I think it is either connected or coincidence,' said the mason, 'and I do not believe in coincidence. Well, maybe I do,' he conceded, 'but not here. And you?'

'I agree.' Gil tucked his hands behind his back under his gown. 'The means of killing looked very similar. To get close enough to kill in that way one must be trusted, or much stronger than one's victim, I suppose, and there were no bruises on her wrists. I would have liked to look further. I wish we had seen her before she was washed.'

'Before she was lifted from Blackfriars yard would have been better,' said Maistre Pierre. 'And why was she killed? She knew nothing.'

'Either she knew more than she realized –'

'Or we, indeed.'

'Or we. Or as I said to James Campbell, her killer did not know it was the wrong lass. In which case we are responsible for her death.' They paused, looking at one another in dismay.

'Who knew we were searching for her?' asked the mason.

'Your man Luke told Alys who she was,' said Gil, pacing onward. 'All her household knew it when Alys learned that she had quarrelled with the boy, although they may not have been paying attention,' he added, recalling the scene in the Hamiltons' yard. 'But she went on talking about it. Alys said she was at the market today, very full of her narrow escape.'

'Poor lass,' said the mason after a moment. 'And little older than Alys, by what Agnes says. So who could have killed her? Do we look for the same person?'

'Serjeant Hamilton is looking for a foreigner,' Gil reminded him. 'We are hunting off our own land down here.'

'Aye, true. So would we be looking for the same person? In hypothesis?'

'In hypothesis, yes. The existence in the one small burgh of two killers, with two causes for killing, using the same means and method, is not a reasonable postulate.'

'I saw John Sempill coming down the hill as I went up this morning.'

'When was that?'

'After Prime? Maybe later. He and his – cousin, is it? – the fair-haired man who came to the burial – they passed the cross at the Wyndhead to go down as I went up, talking loud about black velvet and leather for a girth. Did you say Sempill works leather? Does he use a knife?'

'Aye. I saw the tools, and some harness he was working on. I would say the knife was the right shape, but too short in the blade.'

'I suppose so, but we should bear it in mind.' Maistre Pierre paused on the crown of the bridge to look down at the water forty feet below. 'We have not simplified matters, have we? The more we look, the more complicated it gets.'

'My mother embroiders bed curtains,' said Gil, and got a startled look. He drew his companion into one of the boat-shaped niches in the parapet as a late cart ground its way up the long slope from the Gorbals side. 'When the cat gets at her thread, it falls into knots and tangles, and I have to untangle it. The best method is to loosen this, and tease at that, and the tangle gets bigger and takes in more thread, and then suddenly you find the end and you can unravel the whole.'

'I see,' said Maistre Pierre. 'So we are not hunting, we are untangling things. Your mother is yet living, then?'

'She and my two youngest sisters live on her dower lands by Lanark.' Gil leaned on the parapet, looking at the green banks of the river in the evening light. 'Let us consider this morning. The girl who has died was at the market,' he said carefully, conscious of ready ears passing as people crossed the bridge to go home or to go out drinking. 'We know that from several sources. Who else was there?'

'Most of the women of the burgh,' Maistre Pierre pointed out. Gil ignored him.

'You saw two of – of the quarry at the Wyndhead. I saw two more in the market.' He gestured quickly, sketching a man's jack and helm, and Maistre Pierre nodded. 'That was just before I met the lady and her escort. Oh, and her brother whom we saw just now. Assuming that her waiting-woman was not –'

'Can we assume anything?'

'True. Well, the waiting-woman was probably not in the town this morning, since they had a funeral feast to arrange, but seven others of the household were. The men I saw were likely gathering information.'

'Are they capable of doing so?'

'I think we should not underestimate the wild Ersche only because they do not speak Scots,' Gil said. 'They think differently because their language is different, but Ealasaidh for one is no fool.'

'Because the language is different,' Maistre Pierre

repeated thoughtfully. 'And any of these,' he added, 'could have stepped aside into Blackfriars yard with that poor girl and knifed her.'

'Once again, we are faced with the same questions. Why knife her? And why would she go aside to a secluded spot like that with someone like to kill her?'

'There is no telling what some girls will do,' offered Maistre Pierre. 'My friend, if we do not proceed across this bridge and find the ale-house, my tongue will cleave to the roof of my mouth, and it will be too dark to find the door of the place. Let us move on.'

'Very true.' Gil straightened up.

Maistre Pierre remained a moment longer looking down at the swirling water of the river. 'You know, God is endlessly good. Look how he has arranged that the tide reaches to the bridge and no further.'

The Brigend was a sizeable community of mingled wattle-and-daub cottages and tall imposing houses, inhabited by those for whom it was not necessary to be indwellers in the burgh, whether because they were too poor to become burgesses or because they were wealthy enough to ignore the by-laws. Maggie Bell's ale-house was perhaps a hundred yards beyond the ancient stone-built leper hospital, and was easy enough to find, with its ale-stake thrust into the thatch over the door. Someone had gone to the trouble of painting the likeness of St Mungo's bell on a piece of wood to hang from the stake. Gil paused below the image and looked along the empty street to where a dog was attempting to round up a handful of hens.

'It is said to be healthier living here,' he remarked to the mason, 'out of the smells of the burgh.'

'I do not see how that can be true,' objected Maistre Pierre. 'There is St Ninian's, after all.'

He ducked to go into the house, and Gil followed him.

A tavern was a tavern, whether on the banks of the Seine or the Clyde. Inside this one there was firelight, and the smell of many people, fried food and spilled ale. Several girls were hurrying about with armfuls of wooden beakers, jugs, plates of food. The long tables were crowded, people stood in groups near the door and the tiny windows, and from the great barrel of ale in the corner Maggie Bell herself kept an eye on the proceedings and removed the money from her girls as they collected it. She was nearly as tall as Gil, broad-shouldered and grey-haired, and put him strongly in mind of Ealasaidh.

'We can learn nothing here, surely!' the mason bawled, his mouth inches from Gil's ear.

'It will clear in a while,' Gil answered. 'Many of these have yet to go home for supper.'

A girl appeared in front of them smiling hopefully. She wore a greasy canvas apron, but she herself seemed fairly clean.

'What's your will, maisters?'

'Two mugs of ale,' said Gil, trying not to look down her bodice. She held out her hand for the money, contriving to brush his hip with hers, and slipped away through the crowd. When she returned, Gil said to her, 'Does Annie Thomson work here, lass?'

'Why? Will I no do?'

'I am suited, thanks. I want a word with Annie.' Gil produced another coin. 'Can you point her out to me?'

'She's out the back the now. Here she comes.' She jerked her head at a girl just pushing in from the kitchen. Gil, peering in the dim light, thought he recognized the build and movements.

'Thank you,' he said, and dropped the coin into the cavity being thrust at him. He got a gap-toothed grin, and the girl slipped away again.

'Is that the girl you saw with Davie?' asked the mason.

'I think it is.' Gil was watching, trying not to stare. The big-framed girl with the black brows distributed the food she had brought in, a plate of fried meat here, bannocks and cheese there. The bell of St Ninian's began to ring, and several groups of customers downed their drinks and left.

'Are these all going to hear Compline?' said Maistre Pierre incredulously.

'Probably not,' said Gil, claiming two stools at the corner of a table. 'But master or dame will bar the door when the Office is done, and there you are in the street shouting to be let in.' He frowned, as the girl who had served them paused by Annie Thomson and spoke in her ear, jerking her head towards their side of the room. Annie answered, without looking round, and went out to the kitchen again. Something about the set of her back made Gil uneasy.

Under the other window, a large group began singing. Gil could make out neither words nor tune above the hubbub, but Mistress Bell straightened up, glared at the singers, and rapped on the ale barrel with an old shoe which lay conveniently to her hand. This had no effect, so she tried again, shouting, 'No singing!'

The noise receded, leaving the singing isolated like rubbish cast up by the tide. One or two of the singers, realizing what was happening, fell silent, but the rest roared on, oblivious to tugged sleeves and nudged ribs. Mistress Bell, leaving her post at the barrel, stalked across the room in a widening hush, and bellowed, 'No singing in my house!'

The singing broke off in a ragged diminuendo.

'Och, Maggie, it's just –' began one of the minstrels. Mistress Bell tucked the shoe behind her busk, removed his beaker and gave it to his neighbour, then lifted him by one arm and the seat of his hose, and carried him without another word to the door. Someone standing by it hastily opened it for her and she stepped out, dropped her burden in the gutter, dusted her hands together and marched back into the house.

'And the rest of ye,' she said, withdrawing the shoe in a threatening manner.

Under her eye the rest of the group finished their drinks and left quietly, while the other customers pretended not to watch. Finally, satisfied, Mistress Bell went back to the tap of the great barrel, making shooing motions at the huddle of grinning serving-lasses in the kitchen doorway.

'Monday!' she shouted after the last miscreant. He nodded, and slunk out. She nodded at another table. 'And you, Billy Spreull. Ye've had enough the night. Finish that and get away to your bed.'

'Ah, Maggie,' said the man next to the red-faced customer she had addressed.

'Will I cross this floor?' she offered, elbows akimbo.

'No, no,' said Billy Spreull hastily. 'We're jush – just going, Maggie.'

'*Mon Dieu!*' said the mason devoutly, as the noise returned and Billy and his friend left.

'The singers are barred until Monday,' Gil interpreted. 'Habbie Sims told me about this place. It's the only alehouse the Watch never has to clear.'

'Surely the Watch has no jurisdiction outside the burgh?'

'They come over occasionally. Probably to drink at Maggie's.' Gil peered into his beaker. 'Maistre Pierre, look into that corner, and tell me what you see.'

The mason turned to cast a casual glance beyond where the singers had been.

'Interesting,' he said. 'Two of those we discussed earlier. So Maister Campbell was not meeting them. I wonder what he was doing?'

'Further,' said Gil, his back to the Sempills, 'I no longer see Annie Thomson. She has not returned to watch the house being cleared, like the other girls. Do you need another drink?'

'My turn.' The mason crooked a finger at the girl who had brought their ale. 'Two more mugs of that very good ale, hen, and where is Annie? Has she left? We wanted to ask her a question.'

'She's likely out the back again, her belly's bothering her,' said the girl, lifting their empty beakers. 'It's funny –

149

there's another two fellows asking for Annie over there, and I never noticed her spitting pearls.'

Another group of customers left. By the time the girl returned with their drinks, the room was half empty.

'Could you find Annie?' Gil said. 'It's important.'

'That's what the other body said,' she retorted, tossing her head at him. 'What's Annie been up to?'

'Nothing you wouldn't do, I'm certain,' said Gil. He produced another coin, and made it slide in and out between his fingers. The girl watched it, fascinated. 'Find Annie for us?' he coaxed.

'Joan!' shouted her employer across the room.

'I'll try,' she said grudgingly, and hurried off.

'Where did you learn that trick with the coin?' the mason asked.

'Paris.'

'I must remember not to play cards with you.'

Gil grinned. 'I don't cheat at Tarocco. No need.'

Joan came back into the room, a loaded tray of food in her hands. She distributed this to a group at the long table beyond where the Sempills were sitting, to the accompaniment of complaints that it was cold, and began collecting empty beakers. Pausing by Gil's elbow she announced, 'Annie's no there. She was to bring that tray in, and she's just no there.'

'Not in the privy?' Gil prompted, dismayed.

'Can ye no understand? I'm saying she's no there.'

Gil dropped the coin after its fellow.

'Thank you for looking,' he said. 'Where might she have gone?'

'Joan!' shouted Mistress Bell again.

'The deil knows,' said Joan, and whisked off. Gil turned to look at Maistre Pierre.

'Another broken scent,' he said, and felt something nudge at his memory.

'Perhaps that formidable woman at the tap could tell us more,' suggested the mason. His eyes flicked beyond Gil, and he sat back a little, so that Gil had a moment's warning before John Sempill of Muirend said at his shoulder,

'And what brings you out this side of the Clyde, Gil Cunningham?'

'I was born this side,' Gil pointed out unwisely.

'Aye, but ye don't hold the Plotcock and Thinacre now. How's your mother?'

'She's well, John. Regrets her sister Margaret yet,' said Gil, giving as good as he got. 'Do you know Maister Peter Mason?'

Sempill nodded at the mason, hooked a stool out with his foot and hunkered down, hitching up the hem of his short black gown to avoid sitting on it. Firelight glinted on the jet beads on his doublet.

'You were at Bess's funeral. Sit down, Philip, in God's name, don't stand over me like that.' His cousin sat obediently beside him, staring heavy-eyed at the wall behind Gil's head. Sempill looked at him and shrugged. 'Gil, I want a word with you.'

'You're getting one.'

'It's about . . .' Sempill hesitated, turning his beaker round, apparently counting the staves of which it was constructed. 'It's about Bess,' he said at length.

'I'm listening.'

Sempill turned the beaker round again.

'I know fine,' he said, picking at the withy hoop that held the staves together, 'that Bess had a bairn and that it was none of mine.' Philip turned and looked at him, then faced the wall again. Ignoring him, Sempill continued, 'I can count as well as the next man, and I'd been at the Rothesay house once in the three months before she left it. At the quarter-day,' he added. 'There was rents to collect. But is that right, that in law I could claim the bairn as mine, because it was born within twelve months of her leaving my house?'

'You were not separated?' Gil asked. 'She had not applied for a divorce?'

'She wouldn't have dared,' said Sempill rather grimly.

151

His cousin turned to look at him again. Recollecting himself, he said more circumspectly, 'Not that I know of.'

'Then I think that is probably the case,' Gil said.

'I need an heir,' Sempill said, 'and I need it now. My uncle is making a will.'

'What uncle would that be?' Gil asked curiously.

'Old John Murray, canon at Dunblane. He's done well for himself, and I'm his nearest male kin, since his sister was my grandam but no Philip's. If it's any business of yours. His mind's going as well this time,' he said viciously, 'and if I can show him an heir he'll leave me the lot. Failing that it goes to Holy Kirk.'

'You are asking Maister Cunningham to bilk Holy Kirk of your uncle's estate?' said the mason. Sempill snarled at him.

'He's asking for advice,' Philip Sempill said, and leaned forward, putting his leather-clad elbows on the table. 'It could benefit Bess Stewart's bairn.'

'I'm asking for more than that. Will you take a proposition to the harper for me? If he will let me recognize the brat as my heir, I'll see him right after I get the money.'

'By *him*, do you mean the harper?' said Gil. 'Or the baby?'

'So it is a boy!' said Sempill triumphantly, and Gil suppressed a wave of annoyance. 'I mean the harper, gomerel.'

'There's Euphemia,' said his cousin.

Sempill glared at him. 'I need a bairn now. This one's here, it's a boy, it's legally mine. Even if I was to marry Euphemia –'

'If Euphemia Campbell were to give you a legitimate heir,' said Gil carefully, 'it would have to be born at least nine months from now. Furthermore, because she has been your mistress in open notoriety, I am not certain you are able to marry Lady Euphemia in any case, though you would be best to take advice on that.'

The two men stared at him, open-mouthed, for a moment.

152

'So I need to recognize the harper's brat,' said Sempill, recovering quickly. 'Will you put it to him? I suppose there'll be a fee to yourself and all.'

'For a fee,' said Gil, 'I will.'

'Thank you.' Sempill slammed his beaker down on the table and rose. 'Come on, Philip. That lass is not here, and it's a long way up the brae.'

'Tom-catting in the Gorbals now?' said Gil innocently.

'Just as much as yourself, Gil,' said Sempill.

Gil caught at his arm, and felt the man tense angrily. 'Now I want a word with you, John.'

'What, then?' Sempill stared down at him.

'What did you come down the market for this morning?'

'If it's any of your business, to get another couple of hides off Sandy the tanner in the Waulkergait, who's sitting over yonder just now with two of his cronies, and to get a word with them at Greyfriars about the burial. Why?'

'And to run up a bill for black velvet with Clem Walkinshaw,' said Philip.

'Aye. You'd think when we're cousins he could let me have it at cost, but not him.'

'And when did you go back up the brae?'

'Oh, well before Sext. Right, Philip?'

Philip Sempill nodded. 'They were just beginning Sext at St Nicholas, at the Wyndhead, when we passed.'

'Who else of the household was down at the market?'

'How the devil would I know? Neil and Euan both, likely, but who knows what Marriott Kennedy chose to send down the brae?'

'What about Lady Euphemia? Her brother? What was her brother doing? And Mistress Murray?'

'I don't lead Euphemia out on a chain,' said Sempill forcefully, 'and I'm not my good-brother's keeper. It's very possible. Ask them. What is this about?'

'Another lass died today,' Gil said, 'and there may be a connection.'

'Well, it was nothing to do with me,' said Sempill. 'And

you'd best find who it was, Gil Cunningham, or there'll be no lasses left in Glasgow. Come on, Philip.'

He tugged his arm free of Gil's grasp and marched out. They heard him in the street cracking his plaid like a whip.

His cousin hesitated.

'Who killed Bess?' he asked quietly. 'Do you know yet? John'll not be fit to live with till it's discovered.'

'Does it worry him?' Gil asked, surprised by this image of the man. 'I never thought he cared a spent docken for her, except as his property.'

'Exactly.' Philip Sempill finished his ale and rose, shaking out his grey plaid. 'And his property's getting scarce enough, without folk putting knives through it.'

'Philip!' shouted Sempill from the street.

'So you'll let us know the answer,' said Philip Sempill ambiguously, and followed his cousin.

Gil turned his head to watch the door swing shut behind him, and Maistre Pierre said, 'Interesting.'

'More than that.' Gil watched the latch click and said thoughtfully, 'He must be desperate for money. He knows it is a boy – that is my fault,' he said ruefully, counting off the points, 'he either cannot find it or knows he cannot reach it, he seems willing to acknowledge it although he knows it is not his.'

'Why can he not marry his leman? He seems to consider her his wife already.'

'Simply because she is his leman. His adultery has been publicly recognized while his wife was alive. Canon law is quite specific on that point.'

'So he must acknowledge this baby which is not his. For how long?' asked Maistre Pierre.

Gil shrugged. 'He was a year or two above me at the Grammar School. I would trust him about as far as I could throw him. Until he gets his uncle's money, I imagine the bairn would be safe.'

'Will you put his proposition to the harper?'

'I will – and whistle for my fee, most likely.' Gil pushed

back his stool. 'We have a long walk over the bridge too, but first I think there is something we must do here.'

Maggie Bell eyed him with disfavour as he approached her. Ignoring this, he took up a position where he did not impede her view of the room, and said quietly, 'Mistress Bell, I owe you an apology.'

'How so?' she said, startled.

'It seems I may have driven one of your lasses away.'

'Annie Thomson.'

'The same. I came looking for a word with her, and so did the two that have just left, and the girl Joan says she has vanished.'

'I'm no surprised. My girls are good girls, maister. What they do in their own time's their own concern, but there's no assignations made in my house. Four of ye in one evening, michty me!'

'I wanted a word,' Gil said, 'because it was Annie who spent May Day with the mason's boy. The one that was taken up for dead in St Mungo's yard. Maybe you've heard about that. And now Annie has disappeared, and the other men who wanted to speak to her have left.'

'I've heard about it,' said Mistress Bell with a sniff, measuring a huge jug of ale for another girl, 'but I don't pay much mind to what happens up-by.'

'I hoped,' Gil pursued, 'that she might be able to tell me who struck him down. Since the boy is still in a great swound, he can tell us nothing. But now I am concerned for Annie, since there's another girl dead.'

'I remember now,' she said unexpectedly. 'Annie came back late on May Day. About this time, it was, or later, after Compline anyway. I would have fetched her a welt for it, for we'd been busy, but she seemed owercouped by something.'

'She said nothing?'

'No to me.' She poured two beakers of ale for one of the girls. 'Mysie, when you've served these, get out the back and search for Annie. All of ye. Take torches to look in the

155

buildings, work in pairs, look in all the corners. All of them, mind, and the yard as well.'

'Why? What's come to her?' asked the girl pertly. Mistress Bell raised her arm to her and she ducked, grinning, and spilled some of the ale. 'I hear ye, mistress.'

'Maybe we should lend a hand,' offered Gil as the girl hurried off. Mistress Bell eyed him carefully.

'Maybe ye should no,' she corrected. Gil, understanding her, felt his face burning, but nodded in acknowledgement.

'You keep your girls well, mistress. Supposing she is not to be found out the back, can you tell me where she might have gone?'

'I can not. Do ye think I've the sight like an Ersche henwife? Her mother's at Dumbarton, she might run home if she's feart for something.' She grinned at him. 'Get you out my way and wait, maister. Unless you like to lend a hand here fetching jugs of ale, since I've sent all the lassies out hunting for Annie.'

But Joan, reporting back after a quarter-hour or so, had no information.

'Not a sign of her, mistress,' she said. 'No in the outhouses, no in the brew-house, no in the yard. Mysie and Peg looked behind the kindling, Eppie and me checked the sacks of malt, but there'd been nobody there, you could see that.'

'Could you?' asked the mason. She threw him a challenging look.

'Aye, you could. Because Rob Morrison tore a sack when he unloaded this afternoon, and there was no fresh footprints in the spilt grain. But we did find the side gate unbarred,' she added to her mistress.

'Ye did, did ye? Was it closed over?'

'Oh, aye. Ye'd never have seen from outside that it was unfastened. I think she's away, maisters, and I think she went that way.'

'May we see it?' Gil asked.

Mistress Bell scowled, looked round the room and

156

finally said, 'Joan, mind the tap a wee while. This way, maisters.'

The light was at that difficult stage where it was too dark to see clearly, but torches helped very little. The yard where Mistress Bell brewed her ale was surrounded by a stout fence of cut planks, as high as Gil's shoulder. Near the house there was a narrow gate for foot traffic, closed by a latch and a bar the thickness of the mason's forearm. It conveyed no information whatever. Gil, holding his torch high, peered round at the dancing shadows of barn and brew-house.

'This is the only gate?' asked the mason.

'No, there's the gate for the carts, yonder by the barn. This is the gate the lassies use in the morn, it's the one she'd think of first. The cart-gate's barred, maisters, I can see it from here.' She strode down the yard and brandished her own torch at the big double leaves.

'May I open this?' Gil asked.

'If it makes ye happy.'

Beyond the gate was the muddy track which led between the ale-house and the next cottage. On one side it went out on to the street, on the other it disappeared into the shadows between the two tofts. Mysterious vegetable shapes jumped in the dimness.

'Out there's only Neighbour Walker's grosset bushes,' Mistress Bell informed him. 'If ye're ettling to search those in this light ye're a better man than I am. Walker could sell the thorns for whingers.'

Gil shut the gate from the outside. It dragged over the ground, but with one hand in the latch-hole he contrived to close it completely. As Joan had said, from the outside all looked secure, and he judged that the hefty girl they were looking for would have had no difficulty in doing the same. He opened the gate and stepped back in.

'Thank you, mistress,' he said, settling the bar in place.

'Seen enough?'

'I have, for one,' said the mason. 'May we now leave the neighbour's gooseberry bushes and speak to the girls?'

Joan, handing responsibility for the tap back to her mistress, admitted that she had no idea what was troubling Annie.

'She's no been right,' she admitted, 'she's been as if the Bawcan's after her, peering in corners and ducking at shadows. She's been taking more than her turn at the dishes, which is no like her.'

'But kept her out of the way of customers,' Gil interpreted.

'Aye,' agreed Joan. 'But as for telling anyone, no. Mysie says she tried, and Peg tried, but she'd tell nobody. She said she'd the toothache, but we thought maybe someone forced her,' she admitted.

'And why did none of you tell me?' demanded her mistress. 'What a flock of haiverel lassies!' She cast a glance round the emptying room, and raised her voice. 'Last orders, neighbours! It's near curfew.'

'Do you know where Annie's mother lives in Dumbarton?' Gil asked.

'No,' said Maggie Bell bluntly. 'And if you've to get home to the Wyndheid before they bar the door, you'd best get away over the river.'

'You know me?' asked Gil.

'I know you're from St Mungo's.'

'Then if you hear any word of Annie – good or bad,' he said earnestly, 'will you send to me? I stay in the Official's house – the Cadzow manse.'

She nodded impatiently.

'I'll do that. Goodnight, maister. I'll put Sandy the tanner out in a wee bit and he'll shut the Brig Port on his way home.'

Out in the darkening street Maistre Pierre said thoughtfully, 'She left well before the Sempills.'

'Aye. She may simply have run, as the other girl says.' Gil looked up and down the street and turned towards the bridge. 'Providing she has not met James Campbell in a kirkyard, she is probably safe enough.'

'You think he knifed the other girl?'

'What do you think?'

The mason remained silent until they had crossed the bridge with a few last revellers, who vanished in ones and twos into the closes of the Waulkergait. Finally he said, 'I do not know. Nevertheless I think we have learned something useful tonight, even if the scent is broken.'

'We have.' Gil hitched his gown round his shoulders. 'Now – shall we try opening Bess Stewart's box?'

Chapter Eight

'But can you believe anything he says?' Alys asked, jiggling the baby on her hip. 'Dance a baby, diddy!'

'It is obvious he needs the child,' said Gil, looking at it with more interest. 'And if he's wise, he'll try to convince his uncle without showing it to him. Even by candlelight, it's clearly the harper's get.'

The baby grizzled at this, but Alys said indignantly, 'It's a boy. Aren't you, my little man?' she crooned to the baby.

'Why is he crying?' asked her father resignedly. 'Is he hungry?'

'No, because we fed him just now. And he's all clean . . .' She sniffed at the child's nether regions. 'Yes. I think he wants his mammy, poor little boy.'

'May I take him?' Gil put his hands out. She hesitated. 'I am an uncle,' he assured her, and after a moment she handed him the bundled baby.

He had forgotten what it felt like to hold a child this age, small and solid and totally dependent on the adult arms. By the time he remembered, his left elbow was crooked to support back and swaddled legs, and his right thumb was offering itself as a grasp for the small hands. The baby, perhaps hoping this new person might be the one he was looking for, stopped wailing long enough to inspect him.

'There's a bonnie fellow,' said Gil, and was suddenly assailed by longing. He bounced the baby gently, and turned the little face to the light. Dark wispy eyebrows and deep-set blue eyes scowled at him; the lip quivered above a jaw alarmingly like Ealasaidh's. 'What a bonnie boy,' he said hastily, and tried one of the tossing-up tricks other babies had enjoyed. Although this baby did not laugh as his nephews did, he showed no immediate signs of disapproval, but waved his arms as he was caught. Gil tried it again, and the bells on the coral pinned to the infant's chest rang merrily.

'He's not long been fed,' Alys pointed out. 'Shall I take him?'

'That's what my sister always said.' Gil handed the baby over reluctantly. As Alys left, the small face peered round her shoulder, looking for Gil. He waved, feeling rather foolish, and sat back as the door closed behind them both, wondering why there seemed to be less light in the room.

'It is late,' said the mason. 'We only got over the bridge because Sandy the tanner had not yet returned to shut the Brig Port. If you are to go back up the brae before the moon sets –'

'True.' Gil turned his attention to the box in front of him. 'Have we something on which to make an inventory?'

'I have,' said Alys, returning. 'And pen and ink.' She stood at her father's tall desk, clearly well accustomed to the position, and lit another candle, which gleamed on the honey-coloured fall of her hair.

'Then let us commence,' said Gil, drawing his gaze with reluctance from the sight.

The box was not a large one, but sturdy, the kind of thing a country joiner might make for a woman to keep jewellery in. The lock gave way after a little persuasion, and they raised the lid.

'Documents!' said Maistre Pierre eagerly.

'A bundle of five documents,' Gil agreed, dictating slowly to Alys. 'Tied with a piece of red ribbon. We'll look at them in a moment.'

'They were at the top,' Alys said. 'Had she looked at them recently, do you suppose?'

'Before she went out to meet Sempill,' speculated Gil, 'to

161

refresh her memory or to be sure of the wording.' He had a sudden vision of Bess Stewart, the fall of her French hood swinging forward past her scarred jaw, fingering through the handful of parchments, and then going up the hill to her death, trusting that Euan her familiar servant would see her home.

'What else is there?'

'Not a great deal. She did not bring much away from Bute with her.' Gil peered into the box. 'A gold chain for a jewel, in a little bag. A remarkably good Book of Hours.' He turned the pages respectfully. 'This is old. See the strange clothes the saints are wearing. Two more letters. A round stone. And a roll of cloth containing . . .' He untied the tapes. 'Ah, here is her jewellery. I wonder which of her husbands gave her these?'

'Now you have unwrapped it, it must be inventoried,' said Alys practically. 'Item, one pin, set with a sapphire.' She wrote carefully. 'Item, one pair of beads with enamelled gauds. Item, a necklace of pearls. *Mon Dieu*, father, look at those pearls! I think they are better than mine.'

'And she was carrying these about Scotland in a wooden box,' said Gil, letting the string glimmer over his fingers in the candlelight. 'Ealasaidh described the cross that is missing as her one jewel. She cannot have worn these since she left Bute. If Sempill ever got his hands on them he could settle his debt to the Crown at a single stroke.'

They completed the list of Bess Stewart's jewellery, and turned to the packet of documents. Gil untied the red ribbon and spread the five slips of parchment out on his knee.

'In fact,' he said after a moment, 'these are not all full documents. This and this,' he lifted the two longer missives, 'are attested copies of the title deeds to land on the Island of Bute. It seems as if she held that in her own right.' He set those aside. 'This is a memorandum of an item in the will of one, Edward Stewart of Kilchattan, whom I take to be her first husband, leaving her a property in the burgh of Rothesay outright, and the interest in two more until her remarriage. And these two are memoranda of grants of land in respect of her marriage to John Sempill.' He tilted them to the light. 'The wording is not at all clear. They might be her tocher, though my uncle thought that was in coin, or they might be conjunct fee –'

'Land given jointly in respect of their marriage,' Maistre Pierre translated for his daughter.

'I know that,' she said absently, her pen scraping on the paper.

'What these do,' said Gil, 'is confirm what we already knew by hearsay in respect of her own property, and if you like confirm how little we know in respect of the conjunct property. Even the names of the grantors are omitted.'

'I do not like,' said the mason gloomily, 'but I take your meaning.'

Alys bit the end of her pen, frowning.

'What difference does it make whether it was her tocher or a conjunct fee?' she asked.

'Quite a lot, now,' said Gil. 'Sempill keeps the conjunct property, the tocher may well go back to her family.'

'So if we are still pursuing *cui bono* we need to know,' said Maistre Pierre. He scratched at his beard, the sound loud in the quiet room. 'Do you suppose Sempill will tell us?'

'I had rather speak to the man who drew these up,' said Gil. 'We need to go to Rothesay.'

'Ah. When do we go?'

'And we need to find Annie Thomson, if she really has gone to Dumbarton.'

'If we go by Dumbarton and not by Irvine, we may look for her on the road. That is if the boy can still tell us nothing.'

'Davie is still asleep,' said Alys. 'He is no worse, but he is no better either. Brother Andrew says we must continue to pray and keep him warm and still.'

'So we must rely on finding Annie. We also need to think about Bridie Miller. I would like to look at Blackfriars yard

163

where she was found. There may be some sign for us there.'

'The beets,' said Maistre Pierre.

'I take it they had not come home with her?'

'Agnes did not mention them,' said Alys, 'and I had a rather detailed account of the event from her.' She smiled quickly. 'Poor soul, she has had a trying two days.'

'So have I,' said her father. 'So we go to Rothesay after we look at Blackfriars yard, yes?'

'I must speak to my uncle,' said Gil. 'But, yes.'

The great door of the house in Rottenrow was barred. Gil, untroubled, went along the house wall and in at the little gate to the kitchen yard. To his surprise, there was a light showing in the window there.

Within, the kitchen smelled of tomorrow's bread, which was rising in the trough near the fire. Beyond the hearth, William the kitchen-boy was already asleep, curled up on his straw mattress in a bundle of blanketing. Beside it, Maggie was on the settle, spinning wool by firelight. She looked up when he came in.

'My, you're early home, Maister Gil.'

'It's all this loose living,' he said, sitting down beside her. 'Did you wait up for me, Maggie?'

'Someone had to. The maister wanted the door barred. Do you want a bite?'

'I'm well fed, thank you.'

'So what's come to Bridie Miller?'

He told her what they had learned. She listened carefully, watching her spindle twirling at the end of the yarn.

'She'll have stepped aside from the market,' she said when he had finished.

'What do you mean?'

'To ease herself. Men can make use of a dyer's tub, or a tanner's, but a modest lass canny hoist her skirts in the

164

street.' She picked up the spindle and began to wind on the new thread.

'In Blackfriars yard?'

'It's where we mostly go. It's a long way back up the brae to your own privy, Maister Gil, and there's a wee clump of bushes where prying laddies'll not get a sight of your shift.'

'That would account for the smell on her hair,' said Gil, startled by this glimpse into another world.

'Aye, it would. It gets a bit rich by the end of a morning.'

'Why was she not found, I wonder? How many women step aside like this in a day?'

She shrugged, and set the spindle twirling.

'I've never stood around counting. You don't often meet anyone else.'

'And somebody followed her, or lay in wait – no, that would mean he was expecting her. Someone saw her step out of the market and followed her, took her unawares – I must speak to Mally Bowen.'

'I could do that for you,' said Maggie. 'What do you want – just the state she was in when she was washed?'

'Yes,' he said gratefully. 'How much blood was there, and where was it, and had she been forced? Were her hands clean? That kind of thing. Oh, and Maggie. I never said. Thank you for today's work in the Sempill house.'

'Oh, that,' she said, and lifted the spindle again. 'Aye. There's more.'

'More?'

'See, I was sweirt to tell you this in front of the maister.' She hesitated. 'I don't know. It's no very nice, and it might just be Marriott Kennedy spreading gossip, but . . .'

'Go on,' Gil encouraged.

'Aye. Well. Marriott says. She took her time to it, and went all round about, but in the end she came out with it that Euphemia Campbell's one of those with a taste for wee games.'

'Wee games?'

165

'And I don't mean merry-ma-tansy,' she said grimly. 'Marriott says – this is just what she says, mind – she's forever washing blood off shifts, and no just where you'd expect blood on a decent woman's shift. And off his shirts as well.'

'Agnes Yuill was complaining about having to get blood off her satin clothes today,' Gil recalled.

'No doubt. And there's aye pieces of rope hidden in her chamber. Quite well hidden, it seems, but you'd need to be right fly to hide something from Marriott.'

'Well,' said Gil. 'That is interesting, Maggie.'

'You mean it's likely true?'

'It fits with another piece of information.'

'Oh, aye?' she said hopefully.

'Sempill used his knife on Bess Stewart.' He could not bear to detail the scars on that slender white back, but suddenly remembered the visible mark. 'He had scarred her jaw, remember? And cut off the lobe of her ear.'

'So maybe she'd not play his wee games, so he found one that would,' she speculated.

'I think you may be right,' he agreed. 'Thank you, Maggie. That's very useful.' He got abruptly to his feet. 'I'm for my bed. And so should you, if you're to make the old man's porridge before Sext. Can I have a candle?'

'In the box yonder. You see why I didn't like to say in front of the maister?'

'What's different about me?' he asked, in some amusement. She eyed him in the firelight.

'You've been longer in the world,' she said. 'He's been a priest, and one that won't take his promises lightly, for near forty year. He can still be shocked, though you'd not think it.'

'I will be a priest,' said Gil, experiencing the familiar knotting in his stomach. Maggie nodded, still eyeing him.

'And what sort of a priest you'll make there's no knowing. You'll find it hard going, Maister Gil. You were aye one that was hungry as soon as the larder door was barred.'

She watched as he bent to light his candle from the fire's glow, and then said, 'Euphemia Campbell killed your good-sister.'

'She *what*?' Gil straightened up, staring at her in the dim light. William's slow breathing checked, and resumed.

'Oh, not herself, not herself, but it was her doing.'

'This is my brother Hughie's wife we're talking about?' Gil searched his memory. 'Sybilla, wasn't it? Sybilla . . .'

'Napier,' Maggie supplied. 'Aye.'

'I thought she died in childbed, poor soul. My mother wrote me at Paris.'

'Aye, she died of their first bairn.' Maggie crossed herself. 'But that woman had been sniffing round your brother more than six months – and you know what Hughie was like.'

'I know what Hughie was like,' Gil agreed ruefully. 'Euphemia would be just to his liking. And Sybilla took it ill out, did she?'

'She moped and dwined, poor wee mommet,' said Maggie, staring into the fire. 'Your mother tried, and I tried, but nothing we said could bring him to his senses. And when it came her crying-time, he was from home.' She paused, seeing something Gil could not.

'Go on,' he prompted.

'Och, it's five year since. The woman Campbell was married on a Murray at the time, though that never stopped her. When your father sent after Hughie, the man had to go to Stirling for him, and he wasn't to be found at his own lodgings. They'd to get him out of Euphemia Campbell's bed to tell him his wife and son were dead, and her barely sixteen.'

'Oh, Hughie!' said Gil in exasperation. 'He never could get it right, could he?'

'Likely he's paying for it in Purgatory now,' said Maggie, crossing herself again with the bundle of wool. 'The maister's never heard this either, Maister Gil.'

'No,' he said, staring at the dark window. He thought of Euphemia wrestling with Hugh by candlelight, and was aware of several conflicting emotions, including distaste and what he recognized with shame as a prurient curiosity. 'No, I can see that.'

The hall was dark and silent. Gil crossed it slowly, and on a sudden impulse turned aside and ducked behind the curtain into the window-space which his uncle used as a tiny oratory. He set his own candle beside the two silver candlesticks on the shelf which served as an altar, and knelt, fixing his gaze on the small Annunciation scene propped behind them. Gabriel, wings and draperies blowing in a great wind, held out a stem of lilies to Mary, who turned, startled, from her reading desk. Through the painted window between them could be seen the towers of St Mungo's.

Out in the house he could hear the quiet sounds of Maggie shutting up the kitchen and shaking out her bed before the fire. Boards creaked. A distant dog barked and was answered.

Trust Hughie, he thought. The oldest, the handsome one, the admired big brother with Edward in his shadow. Gil had spent his childhood trying to catch up, but by the time he could shoot with the little bow both Hugh and Edward had been given crossbows, by the time he could ride his pony they were on horseback.

Everything came easily to Hughie, and he took it for granted, even the admiration of his siblings. Likely he thought he could make it up with his wife when he got the chance. But the chance was taken from him, and he had lost something else taken for granted, something other people – something Gil would give his right hand for.

There, it was out in the open.

Please, God, give me strength, he prayed. Blessed Mother of God, give me strength. Sweet St Giles, pray for me, that I may be free of my doubts.

The decision had been taken imperceptibly, over the slow months. At the beginning, shocked by grief, without

168

land or future, he had been willing enough to do from day to day what David Cunningham directed. He had never got up one morning and said, Yes, I will be a priest. It had simply, gradually, become obvious as the sensible thing to do, and at length he and his uncle had both come to take it for granted. But now – now that it was so close – with the vows and injunctions which he took so seriously . . .

Never to hold a bairn like that and know it was one's own.

Does any man know that? asked a cynical portion of his mind.

A man married to a good woman can be reasonably sure, he answered himself. Unbidden, the image of Alys with the child on her hip rose before him.

And what about her? The mason must find her a husband. He would look for a good match for her, but Sybilla Napier's family had accepted his brother Hugh, and presumably Bess Stewart's kin had thought John Sempill a good match. Would Alys go to a man who would abuse her like that? Or one who would sell her books?

Coherent prayer on his own behalf was beyond him, but he bowed his head and petitioned every saint he thought appropriate for Alys. When he ran out of requests he simply knelt, emptying his mind, concentrating on the wind which blew Gabriel's painted garments.

After a while he became aware that, although nothing had changed, he felt lighter, as if a burden had been lifted. Unlocking his stiffened limbs, he rose and took up the remnant of his candle, and made his way to the attic and sleep.

'Do you think the harper will accept Sempill's offer?' enquired David Cunningham, stirring almond butter into his porridge.

'Who knows?' said Gil. 'I think it is more a matter of whether Ealasaidh will accept.'

'It seems as if the bairn may well be a person of substance in his own right, even without being declared John Sempill's heir.'

'Aye, and sorting that out might prove illuminating. Have you ever been to Rothesay, sir?'

'I have not. You take a boat from Dumbarton, likely, you could ask the harper's sister. Eat your porridge, Gilbert. You think you need to go to Rothesay?'

'We are not doing well on the direct trail. Davie's elusive lass is the only witness, and the tracks are confused.' Gil stared out of the window at the house over the way, where nobody appeared to be stirring. 'But before I can answer the question of *cui bono* with certainty I need to talk to the man who drew up the dispositions.'

'That would be Alexander Stewart. He was in Inveraray but I heard recently he has now settled in Rothesay, which is certainly easier to get to. I can give you a letter for him. I will give you a docket for the Treasurer here as well. St Mungo's should pay for the journey.'

'And I am curious about Bess's first husband,' Gil said. 'He was a Bute man, so I suppose their marriage would have taken place in Rothesay.'

'Likely so. I would have heard, otherwise. When will you go? Not today, surely. It is Friday.'

'So it is!' said Gil, dismayed. 'With the holiday on Tuesday, my reckoning's out. How long does the journey take?'

'Four or five hours to Dumbarton by horse, I should think. Another five with a good wind after that, or several days' waiting if the wind is wrong.'

'Better if we leave in the morning, then, rather than this afternoon. Maister Mason goes too, I will need to speak to him.'

'And what's for today?' said the Official, scraping his bowl. 'This other lass that's dead?'

'I must be careful,' said Gil, 'not to offend the serjeant. But, yes, if he won't ask questions, I must.'

*　　*　　*

As Gil reached the Wyndhead, Maistre Pierre in his working clothes emerged from the High Street, followed by his men.

'Good morning, maister lawyer! I have thought, no one will put to sea on a Friday, so we will get a day's work done and travel tomorrow. I cannot pay these sloungers to play at football any longer.'

'Then I will go and get a word with the harper,' said Gil, nodding to the grinning men. 'Will you stay at St Mungo's all morning?'

'Indeed not. Once Wattie knows what is doing he will work better without the maister breathing down his neck. I meet you at Blackfriars? After Terce?'

Gil agreed to this, and the mason marched purposefully off along the flank of the Bishop's castle, heading for the gate into St Mungo's yard. Gil turned and made his way down the hill, past the houses of the Chanonry, past thatched cottages and the ale-house from which Ealasaidh had been thrown out. The street became busier as he descended, with people going out for work, taking down the shutters on the burgh's scattered shops, beginning the day's round of housework.

At the mouth of the wynd that gave on to Blackfriars kirkyard he paused. He ought, he felt, to go and inspect the scene of Bridie's death as soon as he might. Then again, it had probably been well trampled when she was found. He stood for a moment, considering, then shrugged and turned to walk on, and a voice called across the street, 'Maister Cunningham! A word with you, maister!'

The odd-eyed lutenist, Balthasar of Liège, crossed to him, avoiding a gathering of kerchiefed women who to judge by their gestures were discussing the death of Bridie Miller.

'Good day to you, sir,' he said as he reached Gil, and made a flourishing bow in the French manner. Gil, amused, responded in the same style, and the huddled women stared at them both.

'Shall we walk on?' suggested the lutenist.

'I am bound for the Fishergait,' Gil said, falling into step beside him.

'To call on Angus and his sister?' Gil nodded. 'You'll be a bit early. I went round there after things broke up yesterday, and we made rather a night of it. Harry was there – you saw him at the funeral maybe – and a couple more singers that knew Bess. The neighbours were not very pleased with us.' Quick gestures suggested a displeased neighbour at a window. 'We sank a lot of eau-de-vie between us, and the McIans had the lion's share. They'll neither of them be fit to talk before Nones, I would estimate.'

'Thank you for the advice.'

'That wasn't why I stopped you.' Balthasar halted, to look Gil earnestly in the face. 'Something came back to me I thought you might find important.'

'Oh?' said Gil encouragingly.

'And when I heard of this new killing down in the town it seemed even more important.'

'Go on,' said Gil, well used to the kind of detail which witnesses thought important.

'You mind I said I'd met Bess on the way up the High Street on May Day evening? Well, when I saw her, I'd just come out of an ale-house, and across the street there's a vennel, and in the vennel there's a couple playing May-games, if you follow me. His hand down her neck, and so on, and a lot of giggling. I was just thinking the fellow was well dressed to be tousling a servant-lass in an alley when I heard Bess coming up the hill, talking away in Ersche.'

'Yes?' said Gil.

'Well, the fine fellow opposite heard her too, and he reacted. Grabs his lass by the hand, looking alarmed, and tiptoes away along the alley with his back to the street. He didn't want Bess Stewart to see him.'

'Perhaps he didn't want anyone to see him,' Gil suggested.

'There were others abroad who didn't worry him. He'd

thrown me a wink already. The point is, I saw him at the burial.'

'Ah. Who?'

'One of the two who came in with the husband. Not the cousin, the other one. The very decorative one.' He struck a brief pose, quite unmistakable.

'James Campbell of Glenstriven,' said Gil, grinning.

'Aye, that would be the name. I knew him when I saw him, but it took till this morning to fit it together and think, That's odd.'

'Was he avoiding Bess, or the gallowglass with her, do you think?'

'Ah . . .' The musician paused, casting his mind back. 'No way to be sure, of course, but I think it was Bess's voice he heard first, that caused him to hide. I take your point, maister. But now here's another girl dead, and the word is that she knew too much about Bess's death. I just wondered if this fellow with the bad conscience was connected in some way.'

'It is certainly possible,' Gil said cautiously. 'Thank you. This may prove to be valuable.'

'Glad to be of use to somebody,' said Balthasar off-handedly. 'If you'll forgive me, I have to go and see about some lute-strings. I'm due in Kilmarnock tomorrow.' He performed another grand flourish, to which Gil replied, and strode jauntily off in the direction of the Tolbooth.

Well! thought Gil, staring after him. That rearranges matters slightly. He turned and walked slowly up the hill, deep in thought. James Campbell had come into St Mungo's late, just ahead of the gallowglass who reported Bess's arrival. He had certainly been in the market yesterday morning, talking to a girl with a basket. (A basket of what?) He carried a narrow Italian dagger.

'But what reason?' he said aloud. 'Why should he –?'

His own voice startled him. Looking about him, he was astonished to find himself in the courtyard of the mason's house. As he took this in, the house door opened, and Alys appeared, smiling broadly.

173

'Maister Cunningham! My father is gone out, but there is good news. Come in, come in and hear it.'

'What news is that?'

She stood aside for him to enter.

'Davie has wakened. Just a short while ago. He is weak, and he can remember nothing – but he is awake and in his right mind.'

'Christ and his saints be thanked!'

'But yes, I was just going to do that when I saw you in the yard. Kittock is feeding him. I am sorry – I know it can't help you, since he doesn't remember – but I can't stop smiling.'

'You are so fond of the boy?'

'He is a good laddie,' she agreed, 'and we are all fond of him. Come and sit down, and Catherine shall bring you bread and ale while I see if he is still awake and able to speak to you.'

'I have only just broken my fast,' Gil pointed out.

The smile became apologetic. 'Catherine will insist. Sit here, Maister Cunningham. I won't be long.'

He went over to the window, rather than sit in her father's great chair, wondering at himself. If she had not opened the door, what would he have done? It could have been very embarrassing. Bad enough hanging about on street corners like any servant laddie, hoping for a glimpse of . . . Even if it paid off and you got a word with the lass, it was certainly something Uncle David would call undignified.

'*Eh, bonjour, maistre le notaire,*' said a gruff voice at his elbow. He turned to find the small woman in black studying him. Seen close up, her liver-spotted hands and wrinkled nutcracker face reminded him of nothing so much as a mummified saint he had seen once in a small church north of Paris. Behind her a servant-girl carried a tray with a jug and two little glasses. 'You are admiring our garden, no?'

'I am indeed,' he said, seizing gratefully on this topic. 'Who works it? Is it the demoiselle?'

'She orders it. It is not so good as the one we had in Paris, but it is pleasant to look at.' She sat down, straight-backed, and waved him to another stool. 'You will take our elderflower wine, *maistre*? This is also Alys's work. She can bake and brew with the best.'

The wine was light and delicate in flavour. Gil drank her health, and took a marchpane sucket from the tray when it was offered, saying, 'Had you a large garden in Paris?'

'Sufficiently large.' She sipped elderflower wine. 'And you, *maistre*? Does your family own land for a garden?'

'My uncle has a very agreeable garden in Rottenrow,' he answered.

'And your parents? But perhaps they are no longer alive.'

'My mother lives. She has a charming garden to stroll in, and a good kail-yard.'

She lifted her little glass of wine again, turning it grace-fully by the foot in her twisted fingers.

'You visit her, one hopes? She is not far from Glasgow?'

'Of course. Her home is near Lanark, not thirty miles away,' he supplied, recognizing the style and purpose of the questions. She must be more governess than nurse, if she took it upon herself to inspect her charge's acquaint-ance like this. Her hair, which appeared to be still black, was dragged back into a cap like a flowerpot and covered by a fine black linen veil through which the embroidery showed; her neck and bosom were concealed by a snowy linen chin-cloth. The style was old-fashioned; he remem-bered his grandmother in something similar. It was cer-tainly not that of a peasant or even, he reflected, a woman of the tradespeople. Her French, despite her want of teeth, was clear, elegant, but not that of Paris.

'One hopes she does not lack,' she was saying now. 'The lot of a widow is not easy.'

'Bishop Muirhead was her cousin, and her remaining kin will not see her reduced to begging.' It felt like the bidding round in a game of Tarocco.

'Ah, she is a Muirhead?'

'Of Lauchope. And the present Dean of St Mungo's is also a kinsman.' Gil smiled at the black eyes glittering at him, and drained his glass. She replenished it without consulting him.

'And your father, *maistre*? What land did he hold? I believe he fell at the late battle, just before we came into Scotland.'

These cards were not so good.

'He did,' agreed Gil. 'With my two older brothers. We held lands here in Lanarkshire, near to my mother's dower lands, but I am heir to nothing, because all was forfeit after the battle, and there were no funds to recover it with.' And was that Hughie's doing too? he wondered, for the first time.

'And so you must be a priest,' said the gruff voice. 'One must condole with you and your mother. And our master thinks you do not wish to be a priest.'

'I have no choice. I must live on something.'

'Is this a right way to approach Holy Church?'

'I have prayed over it,' he admitted, 'but St Giles has not yet shown me another path.'

'Perhaps you have not prayed enough, or asked in the right way.' She set her little glass on the tray and rose. 'Alys has not returned, which makes me think the boy is still awake. Come and see him, but do not start asking him questions.'

In the tapestry-hung store-room, Alys and one of the maidservants were watching while Brother Andrew, the nearest thing the burgh possessed to a doctor, examined his patient by the light of a branch of candles. The boy was a curious yellowish white, and had lost substance so that all the angles of his bones showed through the skin, but he was answering the little Franciscan's questions about his physical state coherently enough.

'And what is the last thing you remember?'

Alarm crossed the thin face.

'I was playing at football. Did I take a tumble? I'll need to get up! The maister'll need me to mix the mortar.'

176

'Do not worry about that, Davie,' said Alys. 'You can mix mortar again when you are well.'

Brother Andrew nodded approvingly at her, and drew the cover over the boy's chest.

'Your dame is quite right,' he said comfortably. 'You are proof of the good effects of strong prayer and careful nursing. You have been ill, laddie, but you will recover if you lie quiet and get your strength back. I will come and see you again tomorrow.'

He turned away from the bed, lifting his uroscope and scrip of medicines, and paused in the doorway to bestow a blessing on all present. Alys, with a quick smile at Gil, followed to see him out.

Davie lay back against his pillow as if he would dissolve into it, and said weakly to the maidservant, 'What was it? What's come to me, Kittock?'

'You hit your head,' said Gil, moving forward. Davie's eyes flicked to him and back to Kittock. 'I found you.'

'I dinna mind that.'

'Don't fret about it,' said Gil. 'It often happens after a bang on the head. It addles one's wits. You will find it comes back bit by bit.'

The boy stared blankly at him.

'Don't fret,' he said again. 'And, no, you do not know me. I found you.'

The yellowish face relaxed, and the eyes closed.

'I think he's sleeping, maister,' said Kittock. Alys slipped back into the room and lifted the bowl and spoon from the floor by the bed.

'We are to tell him as little as possible,' she said. 'Answer his questions, but don't add anything. He will be quite childish for a while, Brother Andrew says.'

'He's away now,' said Kittock, sitting down with her spindle. 'Is he still to be watched, mem?'

'Until he is stronger, yes,' said Alys. She went out, and Gil followed her.

'He remembers nothing,' he said, drawing the door to behind him.

'And may never remember,' she answered. 'Brother Andrew says we still cannot tell how well he will mend. It is clear he will be able to walk and talk, but his thinking is still to recover.'

'So we must continue to pursue the other girl.'

'And quickly, before she too is knifed. I hope she has really gone to Dumbarton.'

Gil glanced at the sky.

'I must be gone. I am to meet your father in Blackfriars yard after Terce, to look at where Bridie Miller was lifted up.'

Alys paused on the fore-stair and turned to him with that direct brown gaze. She was wearing the faded blue gown again, and Gil found himself admiring the way her hair fell across the tight wool sleeve.

'May I come too?' she said. 'Not to stare at where she died, never that – but you and my father learned such a lot just by looking in St Mungo's, and I would like to see how it is done.'

'About time, too,' said the wiry Dominican in the porter's lodge. 'I've turned away a many gapers this morning already. It's down yonder corner, my son, not the College corner but the other one, and watch where you put your feet.'

He gestured back towards the wall which divided the small public graveyard from the back of the High Street tofts. In the south-western corner, further from the friars' obstreperous neighbour, was the clump of bushes Maggie had described.

'I suppose you saw nothing?' Gil asked. Brother Porter shook his head regretfully.

'Nothing I can recall. A good few lassies wandered in, with it being market, casual the way they do, trying to pretend they're not here, but no fellow with a foreign knife came in when I was looking. I'd have chased him out of that corner,' the brother declared. 'It's hardly proper, what

178

they're doing in a kirkyard, but spying on decent lassies is even less right.'

Thanking him, Gil made his way towards the place, Alys behind him with her skirts held fastidiously up off the grass.

'This does not make sense,' she said as they reached the bushes. 'The market is all down by the Tolbooth. Bridie would have passed her own house to get here.'

Gil turned to stare at her.

'Agnes Hamilton said the same thing. I never paid any attention,' he admitted. 'So she must have accompanied her killer here for some other reason, rather than have been followed.'

'And why come here to talk or – or anything else, when there are prettier and more comfortable corners to be private with another person?'

'We asked ourselves the same question in St Mungo's,' Gil said, gazing round him. 'Ah – that trampled space.'

He picked a careful path between the bushes, inspecting each one and the grass beneath it as he went. His movements stirred up wafts of a scent which made his nostrils flare. It reminded him of a dyer's tub, which he felt was not surprising, but there were overtones which puzzled him. He found himself thinking, with great clarity, of Euphemia Campbell as he had seen her two nights since, half naked by candlelight, wrestling passionately with her lover.

'What are you looking for?' asked Alys from where she stood. He dragged his mind back to the task at hand.

'Anything. Sign. Broken branches, trampled grass. There will be very little of use, I suspect, the searchers have been everywhere.'

'Footprints? That kind of thing?'

'Yes. In fact I can see prints of many feet, going in different directions.'

'That's just like hunting, isn't it?'

'It is very like hunting,' said Gil. 'I find myself trying to judge the mind of the quarry in the same way, as well as identifying sign.'

'There are fewmets here, too.'

'I had noticed that.' Gil was at the centre of the trampled patch. 'Now, I think this is blood. She must have fallen here.' He looked round, to see her buckle at the knees. 'Ah, Alys, I am sorry!'

Three quick steps took him to her side, but she was already straightening up.

'No, I am sorry. I was interested, watching you, and forgot that that poor girl died here. It took me by surprise.'

'Do you want to go into the church? Perhaps sit down, pray for her?'

'I can pray for her here.' She pressed his hand gratefully, and moved towards the wall, skirts held up again. 'Ugh, more fewmets. And someone has been sick.'

'That's odd.' Gil followed her, to look down at the unpleasant splatter. 'Someone had been sick in St Mungo's, near where Bess lay.'

'Do you think it is important?'

'It might be, or it might be nothing.' He turned his head. 'Maister Mason. Come look at this. And I have found where she fell.'

The mason, after a cursory glance, offered the opinion that some girl was regretting St Mungo's Fair.

'What, last January?' said Alys. 'She would have stopped throwing up by now, father. It's too soon for it to be the effects of May Day, I suppose it could be from Fastern's E'en.' She smiled a little tremulously at Gil, who was gaping at her. 'One has to know these things when one runs a house, Maister Cunningham.'

'And where did Bridie Miller lie?' asked her father.

'Here. You may step as you please, the searchers have trampled everything. See, there is blood, though there was none in St Mungo's, but that may have been due to the way she fell. I wish we had seen her before they took her up.'

'I think we should have come here sooner,' admitted the mason. 'And have we found the beets yet?'

'I can see them,' said Alys, from where she stood by the wall. 'Under that bush to your left.'

Gil and her father both looked round without success.

'No, that one there. The elder-bush with the low branches.'

Gil pulled back the branches, to find a basket lying on its side, a bunch of beets beside it.

'Curious,' he said. 'It was never dropped here, under the branch like that.'

'It is more as if it was set down and then overturned,' the mason agreed. He bent to lift basket and greenstuff.

'Those little new ones are dear on the market just now,' observed Alys. 'Agnes will be glad to get them.'

'I hope she washes them well,' said Gil. 'Do you suppose Brother Porter has water at the lodge? I must get the smell of this place off my hands.'

They turned, after a final look round, and began to walk towards the buildings.

'Now what must we do?' said Maistre Pierre.

'I need to get a word with the harper, and I must speak to the other girls at the Hamiltons',' said Gil. 'To ask if Bridie had a new sweetheart.'

'I could help you do that,' said Alys hopefully.

'If you can spare the time from your duties,' said Gil, 'I would be grateful.'

'Talking of St Mungo's,' said the mason, 'we found a plaid.'

'A plaid? Where?'

'Is it hers?' demanded Alys.

'I do not know. It is black and green, quite vivid, and it was folded up neatly in the lodge, up out of the way under the roof.'

'In the lodge?' repeated Gil incredulously.

'In the lodge. It seems Luke found it spread out on the ground the morning all this began, Tuesday or whenever it was, and folded it up and put it away all tidy.' He looked

181

from one to the other, well pleased with his effect. 'He never thought it might be important.'

'In the lodge,' said Gil again, thoughtfully. 'On the other side of the wall from where Bess died.' He followed the mason towards the gatehouse, abstracted. 'Bess was in the trees. Suppose she left her plaid there when she went into the building site –'

'Why?' asked Alys.

'So John Sempill would know she was not far away? But Davie and his new girl found it, and took it into the lodge to make the ground more comfortable, and overheard – part of the conversation? Bess's death?'

'And ran away in fear and were pursued? But I thought we agreed it was someone else who struck the boy down.'

'Oh, it was,' said Gil. 'We have been very slow. It was someone else, and he is still there, with his weapon.'

'Still there?' Maistre Pierre turned to stare at him.

'I know,' said Alys, pulling her plaid tight round her. 'The tree.'

'The tree?' repeated her father, but Gil nodded.

'The boy was running bent over, with his head down.' He demonstrated. 'That's why the mark on the branch is so low.'

'He ran into the tree,' said Alys. 'And the girl ran on and never looked back, thinking they were still pursued. Maister Gil, you must find her. It becomes more urgent every hour.'

Chapter Nine

'Oh, aye, she had a new sweetheart,' said Kat Paton. She looked speculatively from Alys to Gil, and giggled.

Agnes Hamilton, when asked for the name of the girl closest to the dead Bridie, had become flustered, counted off her entire household one by one, and finally selected this one. She was a small, lively, chattering creature, who had eyed Alys warily at first but seeing no signs of pepper had accompanied her willingly. She was not at all overwhelmed by sitting with her in the best bedchamber talking to a man of law, and Gil was having difficulty getting a word in.

'She told us all about it when she quarrelled with the mason's laddie,' she assured them, 'and she wept for him a day or two, so she did, and then she cheered up. So I asked her, and of course she said not, but I kept at her about it, and finally she said she'd a new leman, and not to tell anyone. So I didn't. Well, not hardly, only Sibby and Jess next door.'

Alys, with fewer qualms than Gil, cut briskly across this.

'Did she tell you anything about him, Kat?'

'Oh, no. Well, she wouldn't, would she? But I think maybe he had money. He gave her a great bunch of ribbons for May Day. Only he wasn't in Glasgow on May Eve for the dancing, so she said she'd mind the kitchen if she could get away on May Day after dinner, and we all went off and left her happy enough.'

'Did she go out on May Day?' Alys broke in ruthlessly.

'Indeed she did, with her new ribbons in her hair, and came back late. She wouldn't tell me where she'd been, but it had been good, you could tell.' Kat giggled merrily, then suddenly sobered and crossed herself. 'She's dead, poor soul, and no in her grave yet, I shouldn't be talking about her this way.'

'When did she first meet him, do you think?' Gil asked, seizing his chance.

Kat looked up and made a face, shrugging her shoulders.

'Last week sometime,' she said vaguely.

'Can you be more certain than that? Had she met him on Easter Monday?'

'No,' she said, and then more confidently, 'no, for her brother that's a ploughman out at Partick came to see her. And it wasn't the next day, for that was the day we burned the dinner. Nor the next, because . . .' Kat giggled again, but would explain no further. 'I know!' she said suddenly. 'It was at the market last week. She came back looking happier than she had since Good Friday, and she slipped out again after her dinner and when she came back she had the ribbons. And she saw him again on the Friday,' she went on fluently, 'but after that he wasn't in Glasgow. Not till May Day.'

'What about yesterday morning?' Gil asked. 'Did you all go out to the market together?'

'Oh, yes. Well, not together, exactly, the mistress called Bridie back to tell her where to ask for the beets she wanted, so she was behind me a bit.'

'And did you see her in the market?'

'No,' she said regretfully. 'I was looking, for I wanted a sight of her new man. I thought I saw her a couple of times, but I was wrong.'

'So you haven't seen the new sweetheart?' said Alys.

'No. Well, just the once.'

'And can you tell us what he looks like?' asked Gil.

184

'Just ordinary, really,' she said dismissively. 'Not as good-looking as my Geordie,' she added, and giggled again.

'How tall is he? What colour is his hair?' Gil persisted.

'I never got a right look at him,' said Kat evasively. 'Just a quick glance. I never saw his hair, for he'd a hat on.'

'A hat? Not a blue bonnet?'

'A big sort of green velvet hat with a feather in it,' she said, 'all falling over his eyes. Daft-looking, I thought it was.'

'What else did he have on?' Alys asked.

Kat looked shifty. 'I never saw him very well,' she admitted.

Alys studied her for a moment, and then said shrewdly, 'Were you somewhere you shouldn't have been?'

The bright eyes rolled sideways at her.

'I won't tell, and nor will Maister Cunningham.'

'Unless it becomes necessary in the course of justice,' said Gil scrupulously.

Kat rubbed the toe of her shoe along the line of the floorboards.

'Well,' she said. 'I just happened to be looking out of the window of the maister's closet, see, when she came back on May Day. There was no harm, really, seeing that the maister was out at supper at the Walkinshaws and no in his closet. And if the marchpane suckets got dislodged when I was there, that the mistress put to dry and never told us, well, it wasn't –'

'I'm sure it was completely accidental,' said Alys. 'And certainly nothing to do with Maister Cunningham.'

'Oh, quite!' Gil agreed hastily.

'And the closet overlooks the street?' said Alys. 'So you got a sight of them from above.'

'Yes.' The cracked leather of the shoe went back and forth. 'So I didn't really see him very well. But I did see one thing,' said Kat, sitting up straighter. 'It wasn't any of the laddies in the town. And he was gey fine dressed, to go with the hat. I thought he was a gentleman.'

*　　*　　*

185

Gil, leaving Alys at the White Castle to oversee the dinner, went on down the High Street, taking more care over where he was going this time. Round the Tolbooth, into the Thenawgait, he passed a baker's shop where hot loaves steamed on the boards, the apothecary's where the scent of spices tickled his nose, the burgh's one armourer with two sullen apprentices rottenstoning a breastplate at the door. He reached the Fishergait without straying from the route, and there encountered Ealasaidh buying bread.

'Good day to you,' she said, unsurprised. 'Himself is waiting on you.'

'You were expecting me?'

'Himself is, certain. He woke me to say you would be here, he had seen it. It is a thing he does now and then.'

'He did not see what came to Bess, I suppose?'

'If he did he has not told me.' She took the change the baker's man offered her and turned towards her lodging. 'I am troubled about him, maister. His women come and go, though never none like Bess, and I have never seen him shaken like this, not even when the servant lassie at Banff drowned herself. He is still saying he may never play again.'

She strode through the pend, nodding to neighbours as she emerged into the yard.

'And Eoghan Campbell was here again yesterday before Vespers,' she said, 'getting another crack with her in there, and then round our door asking where was Bess's things. I sent him away,' she said with some satisfaction.

The harper was seated in the great chair where Gil had seen him before. He was in formal dress again, as if for a great occasion, finished off with the gold chain and velvet cap which he had worn at the Cross on May Day. Gil, distracted, counted hastily and discovered this was still only the fourth of May. The harper had risen and was bowing to him.

'A blessing on the house,' he said.

'And on the guest in the house,' said the harper. 'Good

186

morning to you, maister. Woman, bring refreshment for our guest.'

To Gil's relief, Ealasaidh brought him not usquebae but ale in a wooden beaker and a platter of fresh bannocks. He drank the health of his hosts, and hesitated, wondering where to broach the subject of Sempill's offer.

The harper, after a moment, gave him help.

'It is as a man of law you are here, not my son's tutor,' he stated. 'Put your case, maister.'

'It is hardly a case,' said Gil. My son's tutor? What does the old boy mean? he wondered.

'It is a heavy thing,' said the harper. 'The burden of it woke me. Speak, and make the matter clear to us.'

'It is a word from John Sempill of Muirend,' said Gil.

Putting matters as fairly as he could, he explained Sempill's offer. Ealasaidh listened with growing fury, and as soon as Gil stopped speaking she exploded with, 'The ill-given kithan! The hempie! Does he think we would let a gallows-breid like him raise Bess's bairn?'

'Woman,' said her brother, 'be silent. He has not offered to raise the bairn.'

'He has not,' agreed Gil. 'The offer is only to recognize the child as his heir. I think he is aware that that would give him some control over it, and hence the promise to see you right.'

'Does he mean money?' said Ealasaidh suspiciously.

'Those were his words,' said Gil. 'I offer no interpretation.'

The harper sat silent for a little, his blank stare directed at the empty hearth.

'What would your advice be?' he asked at length.

'Aenghus!'

'Let Maister Cunningham answer, woman. We must do something for the bairn, for we can hardly be trailing him about Scotland with Nancy, and it is best to consider everything. Maister?'

'I am acting for Sempill of Muirend in this,' Gil pointed out, rather uncomfortable. The harper bowed his head with great stateliness. 'However, if I was advising a friend in such a case, I would suggest at least talking to Sempill, to find out what more he intends. There might be some benefit in it –'

'But at what cost!' exclaimed Ealasaidh.

'Further, if you were to pursue the matter, I would recommend that a written contract be entered into, and that it be made out with great care, to protect the bairn in the first instance. He is Bess Stewart's heir, you realize that, with land in his own right so soon as the matter is settled –'

'Is that what Sempill is after?' asked the harper. 'The boy's land?'

'I do not know that,' said Gil.

'Aenghus, we cannot trust him! Bess did not trust him! He will smother the bairn as soon as he gets his hands on him, he only wants the property –'

'Bess's family could contest that if the bairn were to die in infancy,' Gil observed.

'And he will not love him!'

'That I think may be true,' said Gil.

The harper suddenly rose to his feet. 'Woman, give me the small harp,' he said. She stared at him, and slowly reached out and lifted the smallest clarsach. Clasping it, he paused for a moment, then pronounced, 'This is my word to John Sempill of Muirend. I will meet him, upon conditions, to talk more of this, though I promise nothing.'

'And the conditions?' prompted Gil.

'That yourself be present to see fairness, and that another man of law be present on the bairn's account. Myself can speak for myself.'

'Those are reasonable conditions,' said Gil formally. 'I will bear your word to John Sempill.'

'And then he began tuning the harp.'

'It would need it, by now,' agreed Maistre Pierre. 'Have another bannock.'

Gil, turning in at the pend of the White Castle, had met Alys hurrying out to help at the Hamiltons' house. Greeting him with pleasure, she had sent him in to share her father's noon bite of bannocks and potted herring, and hastened on her way.

'Oh, it did. The point was that Ealasaidh was fearing that he might not play again. So whatever else Sempill has done, he has got the harper's hands on the harp again. I won't tell him that.'

'What will you tell him?'

'Exactly what McIan told me. It was a formal statement of intent, given with the harp in his hands – it is binding.'

'I had not known that.' The mason chewed thoughtfully. 'Who will act for the bairn?'

'My uncle may. Failing him, there are other men of law in the Chanonry. I would be more comfortable acting for John Sempill if I knew his intention regarding the bairn, and particularly if I were not investigating the murder of his wife.'

'And of that poor girl.'

'Indeed. Did Alys tell you what we learned from her friend? A very poor witness, but it is reasonably clear what she saw.'

'It is clear that Bridie had a rich lover, but how much can we rely on the other girl's description? I thought all servant lassies sighed for a rich lover.'

'Some are more practical than that. Kat herself is winching with one of Andrew Hamilton's journeymen. Her description is not very detailed, but listen – there is more. Balthasar of Liège stopped me this morning.'

He summarized the musician's observation.

'Aha,' said Maistre Pierre. 'And you saw James Campbell in the market yesterday. What time would that be, think you?'

Gil cast his mind back.

'It feels like last week,' he complained. 'It was before I met Euphemia Campbell and her Italian, and when Alys

189

caught up with us at Greyfriars it was just Nones. Say about half-way between Sext and Nones, at the foot of the High Street near the Tolbooth. He was talking to a lassie with a basket.'

'He was, was he?'

'We don't know which lassie it was,' Gil pointed out. 'As you said, every woman in the burgh was out at the market. No, I must go back to the Sempill house and speak to James Campbell, to Euan, and to Sempill himself.'

'Shall you ask your uncle to act for the harper's bairn?'

'Not to say ask. I will tell him the story, and he will likely offer.'

The mason drained his beaker and set it down.

'I will come up the hill with you,' he said. 'To cut short the noontime football and see what Wattie has done. Will you ask your uncle if I may call on him after Vespers?'

The mastiff Doucette was barking. Gil heard her as he parted from the mason at the Wyndhead, baying angrily like a dog confronting a larger enemy. Several other dogs added their comments occasionally, but the deep regular note continued while he walked up Rottenrow past a group of children playing a singing-game. Entering the gateway of the Sempill house, he was surprised to see Euphemia, seated on the mounting-block and teasing the dog by throwing it a crust from time to time, watched by her silent Italian. He paused, studying her. She was pretty enough to attract any man, and that trick she had of clinging to Sempill's arm and smiling up at him was certainly one which would have appealed to Hughie.

Euphemia tore off another crust and threw it to the dog with a graceful movement, the wide green velvet sleeves of her gown falling back from her hands.

The musician's dark gaze fell on Gil, and he said something to his mistress. She looked round, slid off the mounting-block and came towards the gate, sidestepping quickly as the mastiff rushed at her snarling, and smiled brilliantly at him, pushing back the fall of her French hood with a graceful movement.

'Maister Cunningham, how nice to see you. Have you found who killed Bridie Miller yet? Will the serjeant take someone up for it?'

'Not yet,' said Gil, crossing the yard to meet her, staying carefully outside the mastiff's range. 'Good day to you, madam. I have a –'

'Oh, but he must! Have you never a word of advice for him? Was it the same ill-doer who killed Bess? Is Glasgow full of people killing young women?' She shuddered, biting a knuckle. 'None of us is safe. What if something came to that little poppet who summoned you yesterday? Such a well-mannered child, a pity she's so plain.' Gil recognized Alys with difficulty. 'Or to Mally here, or those bairns out at the Cross?'

'*Calma, calma, donna mia,*' said the Italian beside her. She threw him a glance, and smiled again at Gil, a little tremulously.

'Forgive me,' she said. 'What brings you here, Maister Cunningham?'

'I have a word for Maister Sempill,' said Gil, 'and I wanted to speak to your brother. Are they at home?'

'I think John's in the stables.' She lifted the bread from the mounting-block, looked down at it, and threw another lump, rewarded by further round of barking. 'Ask them at the house.'

Gil left her breaking a new loaf, and climbed the fore-stair to the house door, aware of the lutenist's dark gaze on his back. Hughie, he reflected, if confronted by that lovely smile, those taking ways, would not have troubled to resist Euphemia. And how did he feel, he wondered, when he realized what she had cost him? Not guilty, most like. Few things were ever Hughie's fault.

The door stood open, but the hall within was deserted. After some calling, he raised Euphemia's companion, who emerged from a door at the far end of the hall exclaiming,

'Your pardon, maister! I never heard you, the dog's that loud. Oh, it's Maister Cunningham, is it, the man of law? And what are you after today?'

Gil explained his errand, and she sniffed.

'Maister James is in the tower room with his books, I think Sempill's out the back docking pups' tails. Here, you go down this stair.'

She turned towards another doorway, picking up her dark wool skirts.

'No need to trouble you,' Gil said. 'I can find my own way.'

'Oh, it's no trouble,' she said a trifle grimly, as if she was protecting the house from unauthorized invasion. She stumped down the stair, the rosary and hussif at her belt clacking together at each step, and said over her shoulder, in unconscious echo of her mistress, 'And have you found who's running about knifing women? We'll none of us be able to sleep till someone's taken up for it. Euphemia's quite ill with the worry, the wee sowl, and it's not good for her.'

'I'm still searching,' said Gil, emerging after her into the reeking stable yard. John Sempill was just going into the cart-shed opposite, but seeing Gil he turned and waited for him to cross the yard.

'Well, Gil?'

'Well, John. Finished with the pups?'

'Oh, that was an hour since. I'd ha been quicker with it, but Euphemia helped me.'

'Oh, she never!' exclaimed Mistress Murray. 'In her green velvet, too! It'll be all over blood.' She turned and hastened back across the yard.

Gil, suppressing an image of Euphemia Campbell being stripped of the green velvet gown, said, 'I've had a word with the harper, John.'

'Aye?'

He recited the statement the harper had delivered. Sempill glared at him.

'Better than nothing,' he said grudgingly. 'Aye, I'll meet

192

him, and his conditions. Do you want to name someone yourself to stand for the brat, or will I find a man?'

'I thought to ask my uncle.'

Sempill shot him another look, scowling.

'Aye,' he said at length. 'That makes it clear I'm dealing straight with him.'

'It does that, John,' agreed Gil.

Sempill opened his mouth to speak, closed it, and finally said in exasperation, 'So when can we meet? I need to get this over with.'

'I have still to speak to my uncle, but if he was free this evening –'

'Not this evening. I'm promised to Clem Walkinshaw.'

'Then it needs be a few days hence. I've an errand that takes me out of town.'

'What errand? I thought you were hunting down Bess's killer?'

'I am. This is to that end. What can you tell me about Bess's property in Bute?'

'In Bute? There's the two farms from her father, and the burgage plot from Edward Stewart, with the house on it. Then there's the two joint feus, which will be mine now, I suppose, little use though they are. One's a stretch of Kingarth covered in stones, and the other's between the castle and the sea. Gets burned every time the burgh's raided, it seems. God, I'll get back at him for that. Little benefit she'll have got from the rents, mind you,' he added thoughtfully.

'And the other property? Whose is that now?'

'What the devil's it to do with you?'

'It may have some bearing on her death.'

Sempill stared at Gil. 'Are you still harping on that one? It was some broken man, skulking in the kirkyard, that's obvious.'

'Not to me. Do you know whose the other property is now?'

'I suppose,' said Sempill, chewing his lip, 'it depends on how it was left. Alexander Stewart would know, he likely drew up both wills. Is that where you're going? To poke about Rothesay asking questions that don't concern you?'

'They concern your wife's death, which I am investigating,' Gil said. 'Another thing, John. Did you know that that pair of gallowglasses knew your wife before?'

Sempill stared at him.

'Of course I did, gomerel. Where do you think I got them from? She hired them, after Stirling field when the country was unsettled and I was away. John of the Isles was raging up and down the west coast, and who knew what he'd do next. So of course I sent Neil down with the message for her on May Day. I knew he'd deliver it to the right woman.'

'Can I speak to them?'

'You can not. They're away an errand. Both of them.'

'When will they return?'

'When they've completed it, I hope. I'll send them over to you when they get back, but it'll likely be Sunday or Monday.'

'Thank you. Then can I speak to Maister Campbell of Glenstriven?'

James Campbell was in the chamber at the top of the wheel stair, where Gil had first spoken to the household. He was seated by the window, one expensively booted leg crossed over the other, with a book of Latin poetry in his hands, but he closed this politely enough, keeping a finger in his place, and allowed Gil to take him back over the events of May Day without revealing anything new.

'Where is this leading?' he asked at length. 'I have answered these questions before.'

'Some new detail might emerge,' said Gil inventively. 'Now – do you have a green velvet hat? What shape is it?'

'This one, you mean?' Campbell nodded at the gown on the floor beside him, and lifted it to untangle a hat from the folds of material. 'See for yourself.'

Gil turned the hat in his hand. It was a floppy bag-like

object, with a couple of seagull feathers secured to one side by a brooch with a green stone. It smelled of musk and unwashed hair.

'And were you wearing this,' he said carefully, 'when you were in Glasgow last market day? Not yesterday, but a week ago?'

'I likely was,' said Campbell easily. 'I stayed here, and left that here with my other gear.'

'How long were you in Glasgow?'

'A few days – from the Wednesday to the Saturday. Then I went out to Muirend where Sempill was, to persuade my sister home. I'm still trying, without much success.'

'And that was when you met Bridie Miller?'

There was a silence.

'It was,' said Campbell finally.

'When did you last see her?'

The green eyes flickered. Gil could almost hear the other man recognizing that it was useless to deny it. With a barely perceptible hesitation, Campbell admitted, 'On May Day. Before Compline.'

'That was why you were late to the service?'

'It was. But Neil came in just ahead of me, and Bess was live when he left her. That's certain enough. And before you ask, yes, I did see the two of them in the kirkyard. They were just going into the trees as I came through the gate, and Neil crossed to the south door and went into the church before me.'

'I am looking at what happened to Bridie,' Gil said. 'It is likely but not necessary that the two deaths are connected.'

'Is that what it seems to you?' said Campbell, his tone challenging. 'An exercise in logic?'

'No,' said Gil a little defensively, 'but it helps. Now, I saw you in the market yesterday,' he continued, going on the attack, 'talking to another servant lass. What was in her basket?'

'Her basket?' repeated Campbell. Gil waited. 'Green stuff. Let me think. A pair of smoked fish, a package of laces and a great bundle of something green. Long narrow leaves.' His fingers described them. 'I know – leeks.'

'You seem very sure of that,' Gil commented. Campbell grinned without humour, showing his teeth in the same way his sister did.

'I offer you the advice for nothing, brother: there's always a good line to be spun from a lassie's marketing. Believe me, they love it if you take an interest in what they have bought.'

'Thank you,' said Gil politely. Try spinning that line with a girl who reads Chaucer and Thomas à Kempis, he thought. 'What were you talking about this time, apart from leeks and smoked fish?'

'Where was Bridie.' The handsome face with its lopsided mouth twisted. 'And she, poor lass, was probably getting stabbed about then, by what you said. I had trysted to meet her after Sext by St Mary's down the Thenawgait and she never showed. It was another lassie from the same household I was speaking to, Maister Cunningham. She said they had all left the house before Bridie, but she'd seen her at first up and down the market. I looked further, but I never saw her, and then you told me last evening she was dead, poor wee limmer.'

'So you never saw her yesterday?'

'That's what I have just said.'

'Do you know the name of the girl you were speaking to?'

'No, but she was certainly one of Agnes Hamilton's household, for I asked that.'

Gil set the hat aside and said, getting to his feet, 'Thank you, Maister Campbell. That is all I wish to ask you just now.'

Something like surprise crossed James Campbell's face, but he rose likewise and bowed. When Gil left he was still standing, holding his closed Horace, looking thoughtful.

Gil made his way down the stairs and out to the yard, which he crossed in a wide curve to avoid the furious mastiff, with a nagging feeling of questions unasked. There was something he had missed, or not uncovered, or not noticed, about the whole business. Perhaps in Rothesay, he thought, crossing Rottenrow to his uncle's house. All may be clearer from a distance.

Maggie Baxter was disinclined to talk.

'Aye, I did speak to Mally Bowen,' she said, 'but she had little enough to tell me. Dead between Sext and Nones, she estimated, no struggle, not forced. There was blood on the front of her kirtle, quite a lot, and a kind of odd smell on her hair. That's all, Maister Gil, and I'll thank you to get out of my way till I get the dinner ready. Go on!' She made shooing motions with her floury hands.

'Thank you, Maggie,' said Gil, making for the door. 'I noticed the smell on her hair too.' He remembered the kerchief in his purse, and pulled it out. 'It's on this. I don't know what it is, but it's familiar. You try.'

'I haven't the time to be bothered,' said Maggie, sniffing at the kerchief. 'Aye, I know it, but I can't name it the now. It'll come to me. Now get out my way, you bad laddie, or the dinner will be late!'

Gil left obediently, and went to look for his uncle. Finding him at prayer in his little oratory, he crossed the hall quietly and went up to his garret to find what he needed for the journey.

Over dinner, the Official gave out a stream of instructions and advice about travel. Gil nodded politely from time to time, and forbore to point out that he had gone to France at eighteen and returned alone five years later.

'I promised you a docket for the Treasurer,' his uncle recalled, 'for funds for the journey, and I'll give you a letter for William Dalrymple in Rothesay. We were at the College together, and I believe he is still chaplain of St Michael's. In the castle,' he added helpfully. 'And James Henderson has given me a letter for you to take to the steward at the Bishop's palace. One of them should be able to offer you a bed.'

'And a bed for Maister Mason,' Gil pointed out.

'Indeed.'

'He bade me ask if he might call on you after Vespers.'

'Did he so? Well, I'll be here. And what have you learned today, Gilbert?'

'Little enough.'

Canon Cunningham listened to Gil's account of his day while Maggie cleared the table round him, and at length said thoughtfully, 'James Campbell knew Mistress Sempill was out in the trees. Could he have gone out of the kirk during the service?'

'He could,' Gil agreed. 'He uses a wee thin knife, and he admitted to having slipped away, he said to say a prayer to St James.'

'Reasonably enough.'

'But though he might have stabbed the servant lassie, I do not know why he should have killed Bess Stewart. What could he gain from her death?'

'Some benefit to his sister, perhaps? Many are unaware,' said the Canon, settling into his lecturer's manner, 'of the restrictions which canon law places on the remarriage of adulterers. He may have thought –'

'He has studied at St Andrews and Bologna,' Gil interrupted.

'Ah. Well, Gilbert, you must follow the scent where it leads you, and hope you have not gone astray. Meanwhile there is this matter of the harper's bairn. Do you know, I might act for the laddie. He needs someone to see him right, poor bairn.'

'That would be a great relief to me,' Gil said.

His uncle shot him a look, and a crease appeared at the side of his mouth. All he said, however, was, 'You are enjoying this hunt, aren't you, Gilbert?'

'I am,' he admitted. 'It seems wrong, when two women have died, but I feel as if I have woken up after months asleep, like the lassie in the old tale.'

'I hope not,' said his uncle drily, 'considering what came to the lassie. Well, well, you must make the most of what God sends you. I will write you out that docket for the

Treasury, and then I am for the Consistory, to look over the papers for a matter tomorrow morning. I will be back after Vespers.'

Gil, having exchanged the docket for a satisfactory sum of money, returned to the house and finding his uncle still out retreated to his garret again, to go over the evidence he had collected and to consider what he hoped to find out in Rothesay. Seated cross-legged on his bed, he worked through what he knew, dogged by that same feeling of something missed, or not noticed, or not asked. The man with the best reason for killing Bess Stewart had witnesses to show he had not, including Gil himself. The men with the best opportunities had no reason that he had yet uncovered for doing so. The death of Bridie Miller must be connected, since as he had said to the mason it was not logical to assume two killers with the same method of working, loose at the same time in a town of five thousand souls, but John Sempill had a witness to show he was on his way up the High Street when she died, and if James Campbell was telling the truth he had been down the Thenawgait at Sext waiting for a girl who never showed. Gil himself had seen him only a little later, just beyond the Tolbooth.

'If he killed Bess,' he said aloud, 'then he might have a reason for killing Bridie. But if not the one, then not the other.'

Glancing at the window, he was surprised to realize that it must be well after Vespers. He unlocked his legs, and rubbed the circulation back into them, reflecting that Aristotle had less application to real life than he had hoped.

By one of the hall windows, David Cunningham and the mason were discussing a fine point of contract law over a plate of Maggie's girdle-cakes. They greeted him with pleasure, but returned immediately to the question of what constituted attendance on site, dark red head and black coif nodding in time to one another's words. Gil looked in the small cupboard for a wine-cup, and failing to find one made for the kitchen. The mason's voice floated after him as he went down the stairs.

'And at Cologne, a friend of mine . . .'

Maggie and the men were round the kitchen fire, gossiping. Gil found a cup and was returning to the stair when one of the stable-hands said, 'Maister Gil, did ye know the serjeant's planning to make an arrest?'

'I did not,' said Gil. 'Who is it?'

'He never said,' admitted the man regretfully. 'But it's someone for the lassie Miller, that had her throat cut in Blackfriars yard.'

'It was not her throat,' said Maggie quickly, with a glance at William the kitchen-boy. 'I spoke to Mally Bowen that washed her.'

'And I saw the body,' said Gil. 'She was knifed in the ribs, poor lass. When is the serjeant planning this, Tam?'

'He never said that neither,' said Tam. 'Just that he knew who it was. I got this off his man Jaikie when we went to fetch the horses in.'

'Ah, hearsay,' said Gil.

'It's just as good,' said Tam. 'Jaikie knows all the serjeant's business, he tells me all kind of things.'

'I hope not,' said Gil.

'Never worry, Maister Gil,' said Maggie cheerfully. 'The half of it's likely made up.'

Up in the hall, the Official and Maistre Pierre had moved on to the question of whether the stoneyard at the quarry qualified as the site. Gil sat down and poured himself wine, quite content to listen to the argument, but they left it unresolved and turned to him.

'Well, Gilbert,' said his uncle. 'I have had a profitable discussion with your friend here. He has a very generous suggestion to make concerning the harper's bairn which we can put to John Sempill when we can meet him.'

'John's out this evening. What would that be?' Gil asked.

'Provided the harper agrees,' stipulated the mason.

'Oh, understood. But I would be greatly in favour of it,

as the boy's legal adviser. Maister Mason is offering to foster the child into his own household and raise him.'

'Alys would like that,' Gil said.

Alys's father nodded, smiling fondly at the sound of her name. 'So long as she stays under my roof,' he added.

'And we must hope that will continue to be possible.' The Official glanced at the mason, and a portentous look passed between them. 'A very profitable evening, Maister Mason.'

'More than I have had,' began Gil, and was interrupted by a furious barking.

'What is going on across the way?' His uncle craned to look out of the window. 'Why, there is the serjeant at Sempill's door.'

The gate to the Sempill yard was open, and through the gateway they could see Serjeant Anderson making his stately way to the house door, taking the long way round past Doucette, who was out at the end of her chain hurling abuse. The burgh's two constables trailed cautiously after him.

'Has he decided to arrest John Sempill?' Gil speculated. Maggie arrived, with another hastily poured jug of wine, and stood staring across the street.

'I tried to get a word with Tammas Sproull,' she said with regret, 'but he was past the kitchen gate before I could speak to him.'

The serjeant vanished into the house, his men after him. Someone emerged briefly to shout at the dog, who went sullenly back to her kennel. Maggie inspected the plate of girdle-cakes and lifted it to be replenished.

'They're taking a while,' she said hopefully. 'He's maybe putting up a fight.'

'He's not there, whoever it is,' said Gil, looking along the street. 'Here they all come back from Compline.'

Philip Sempill, James Campbell, resplendent in their expensive clothes, picked their way along the muddy street. Euphemia Campbell and her stout companion followed, the Italian just behind them, and to Gil's great annoyance one of the two gallowglasses came into sight bringing up the rear.

'Sempill said those two had gone on an errand. I want to talk to them.'

'Could that be why he denied them?' said his uncle, still watching the Sempill house. The returning party crossed the yard, the dog emerged to bark and was cursed back to her kennel, and all six vanished into the house as the serjeant had done. 'You might as well fetch more girdle-cakes, Maggie. They'll be a while longer.'

On the cue, the door of the Sempill house opened. The mastiff rushed across the yard bellowing threats, and the constables and the gallowglass emerged dragging a strug-gling figure. The swaying group got itself down the stairs with difficulty, followed by the serjeant. Behind him came a gesticulating James Campbell, seriously impeded by his sister, who was clinging to him and screaming. They could hear her quite clearly above the dog's clamour.

'My!' said Maggie with delight.

'Who is it?' said David Cunningham. 'Who have they arrested?'

'The Italian,' said Gil. 'He's found his foreigner.'

The serjeant, ignoring the Campbells, sailed across the street to hammer on the Cunningham house door. Maggie, muttering, was already on her way to answer it. They heard her questioning the caller through the spy-hole, then the rattle of the latch, and her feet on the stairs again.

'It's Serjeant Anderson,' she announced unnecessarily, stumping into the hall. 'Wanting a word with the maister.'

'And with Maister Gilbert Cunningham and all,' said the serjeant, proceeding into the room in her wake. 'Good evening, maisters.'

'Well, well, Serjeant,' said the Official, pushing his spec-tacles up and down his nose. 'What is this about, then?'

'Just to inform you, sir,' said the serjeant, with some relish, 'that we've just lifted the man that knifed Bridie Miller. Seeing Maister Gilbert Cunningham was seeking her the length and breadth of the town these two days,

202

I thought you'd want to know we've got the man, since he's likely the man you want as well.'

'But what proof have you –?' Gil began.

'Well, I looked at the body,' said Serjeant Anderson, 'and I saw she'd been stabbed with a wee little knife with a long blade. And I thought, Who carries a knife like that? An Italian, that's who. And where is there an Italian in Glasgow? In Maister Sempill's house. So we're just lifting the Italian and his wee knife now, and if you'll come down to the Tolbooth in the morning, when I've got him to confess to my killing, we'll see if we can get him to confess to your killing.'

'But that's not proof!'

'Proof? We'll get a confession in no time, and who needs proof then? I've a burgh to watch, Maister Cunningham. I've more to do than go about asking questions,' said the serjeant kindly. 'It's far quicker my way.'

'Serjeant, I thank you for your offer, but I saw the Italian inside St Mungo's at the time Bess Stewart was killed. He's not my man, and I'm not certain he's the man you're after either. Why should he kill Bridie Miller?'

'Why should anyone kill a bonnie lass?' said the serjeant. 'One reason or another, no doubt. Now I'd best get back to my men, so if you'll excuse me, sirs –'

'I'll come out with you,' said Gil, as shouting floated up the stairs from the front door.

He and the mason followed Serjeant Anderson down and across the street, where a small crowd had gathered and was watching through the gates with interest as the Italian was dragged across the yard of the Sempill house. The mastiff was adding her contribution, but over the thunderous barking Gil heard a number of comments.

'What's he done?'

'If he's no guilty now, he will be by the morning.'

'How will they get a confession? He doesny speak Scots.'

'That's no bother. Write something down and make him put his mark to it.'

The lutenist saw Gil and attempted to fling out a beseeching hand.

'*Signore avvocato! Aiutarmi, aiutarmi!*'

The man holding his left arm buffeted him casually round the head, and he went limp.

'What did you do that for?' said the other man in disgust. 'Now we'll have to carry him.'

'What did he say?' Gil asked Maistre Pierre.

'"Maister lawyer, help me."'

'What the devil is going on here?' demanded John Sempill in his own gateway, his voice carrying without effort over the dog's noise.

Euphemia Campbell uttered a shriek which hurt the ears, let go of her brother and sped across the yard to her protector, pursued vengefully by the dog until it was brought up short and choking at the end of its chain. A great waft of her perfume reached them on the evening air, making the mason sneeze, as she exclaimed shrilly, 'Oh, John! John! He says Antonio killed Bridie Miller and maybe Bess as well!'

The Italian, hearing her voice, roused himself with an effort and broke free of the loosened grasp of his captors to fling himself at her feet, clinging to the hem of her dress.

'Donna Eufemia! *Donna mia, cara mia bella! Aiutarmi! Non so niente!*'

'Oh, God, the poor devil,' said Gil, and moved forward.

Euphemia Campbell, staring down at her servant, said, 'John, do something! He says he killed them!'

'Oh, he did, did he,' said John Sempill, and swung an arm. Everyone else stood frozen for a moment. There was a choking gurgle which was not the dog, and one of the constables stepped forward and tipped the lutenist over with his foot. The small man turned a dulling, incredulous gaze on his mistress. Then blood burst from his mouth and he was still.

'Oh, God,' said Gil again. The mason, beside him, was muttering what sounded like prayers. Euphemia Campbell stared open-mouthed at the dead man, and down at the blood on her gown. A groan escaped her, and she shivered.

'Euphemia!' said John Sempill. She turned to him, still shuddering, and he held her with one arm, staring hungrily down at her as the final drops of the lutenist's blood dripped off his whinger into the dust of the courtyard.

'Take me in, John. I must lie down!'

'Now, I wish you'd not done that, maister,' said Serjeant Anderson majestically, 'but there's no denying it's saved me a bit of bother. Come on, lads,' he said, beckoning his constables away. 'We'll away down the town. Don't fret, you'll get your groat, you'd made the arrest.'

Chapter Ten

'It was murder,' said Gil. 'And the devil of it is, he'll get away with it.'

'You think the Italian was innocent?' said Maistre Pierre.

They were riding along the north bank of the Clyde, and Dumbarton's rock and castle were just coming into view ahead of them down the river. Maistre Pierre, on a sturdy roan horse, his stout felt hat hanging down his back on its strings, was the image of a prosperous burgess on a journey. Behind them, Matt had not uttered a word since they left Glasgow. Gil himself, in well-worn riding-boots and a mended plaid, felt that he did not live up to the quality of his own mount or Matt's. David Cunningham had always had a good eye for a horse.

'Innocent of the two women's deaths, certainly,' he said. 'I saw him in St Mungo's all through Compline, at the time when Bess was killed, which in turn makes it less likely that he killed Bridie Miller.'

'I think so also,' said the mason, 'because how could he persuade a girl like Bridie to go apart with him when he had no Scots?'

'Some men have no trouble,' said Gil fairly, 'but this one seemed to have eyes for nobody but Euphemia Campbell. And what she thought would happen if she screamed at John Sempill like that, is more than I can guess. She has known him several years, she must know how he acts first and violently and thinks after if at all.'

'He certainly acted this time.'

'And it was murder,' said Gil again.

'And he had been her lover also – the Italian.'

'Yes.'

'She seemed greatly moved by his death. I thought of Salome.'

Gil rode on in silence for a time, digesting this remark. On the other bank, the tower of Erskine dropped behind them.

'And where had the gallowglass been?' he said at length. 'Sempill said they were on an errand and would be back on Sunday or Monday. Yet there was one of them last night. Matt,' he said over his shoulder, 'do you know where the Campbell brothers had been sent? Does Tam?'

'No,' said Matt.

'And do you know where the horses may lie while we are on Bute?'

'Aye.'

'Perhaps Matt should stay with them,' suggested the mason. 'We should be back by Monday, God willing, and can shift without him for two days.'

'Aye,' said Matt. Gil twisted in the saddle to look at him, a small fair man perched expertly on one of David Cunningham's tall horses.

'You could ask about for Annie Thomson,' he suggested, and was rewarded by a lowering glance. 'If I leave you ale-money, you could keep your ears open.'

'Hmf,' said Matt.

They rode on, in the growing warmth of a May morning. Birds sang, the distinctive smell of hawthorn blossom drifted on the air, making Maistre Pierre sneeze. Lambs bleated on the heights above them, and the cattle of Kilpatrick lowed on the grazing-lands, where the herd laddie popped up from under a gorse-bush to watch them pass.

'It is beautiful countryside,' said Maistre Pierre. 'So much cultivated, so pastoral.'

'It's nothing compared to Lanarkshire,' said Gil, and Matt grunted agreement.

'And this is an excellent road.'

'It's well used. Argyll took half the guns down here to the siege at Dumbarton in '89. They'd need to level the way for those.'

'I had forgotten. Alys told me of seeing them go through Glasgow, and the teams of oxen hauling the big carts. I missed the sight. I was out looking for building-stone in Lanarkshire.'

'You haven't travelled this way, then?'

'I have not. Parts of Ayrshire and Renfrewshire I know also, and the quarries about Glasgow, but not this ground. What is the stone hereabouts, do you know?'

'Just stone, I suppose,' said Gil blankly. 'Isn't it all?'

'Assuredly not.' The mason leaned over the saddle-bow again, peering at the road-metal under his horse's hooves. 'No, it is still too dusty to distinguish. However these hills have the appearance of trap, which is not good to build with, but makes excellent cobbles. Perhaps on the way back I explore a little. A piece of land to quarry out here, with a good road to Glasgow, would be a valuable investment.'

'Be sure to contract for the mineral rights, then,' Gil said, and got a quizzical look in reply.

Dumbarton town, tucked in the crook of the Leven behind its rock, was not impressive, a huddle of wattle-and-daub roofed with furze or turf. Here and there a stone-built structure had an air of greater permanence, but most of the houses looked as if they had sprouted, possibly by night, since the end of the siege of three years since. There did not appear to be a cobble-stone in the burgh.

'It has a market on Tuesdays, and a wealthy church,' said Gil, guiding his reluctant horse along the muddy curve of the High Street. 'You wouldn't think it paid customs about fifth in the kingdom, would you?'

'Clearly, you have not seen Irvine,' said the mason. 'Where shall we go first? I am both hungry and thirsty.'

Finding an inn, arranging for Matt to stay with the horses, consuming bannocks and cheese and a jug of thin ale, took a little time, and it was past Sext when Gil and the mason walked down to the strand.

There were several boats of varying size drawn up on the shore, loading and unloading. At the far end of a narrow stone wharf, several men were shouting round a crane which they were using to hoist barrels out of a sturdy cog. Larger ships lay in the river, and out in the Clyde, beyond the confluence, two carvels swung at anchor.

'Where do we begin?' said Gil in bewilderment.

'You have been to sea, have you not?'

'Aye, from Leith. From there everything's bound for the Netherlands. Some of these could be headed for Ireland, or for France or even Spain. Or for the North Sea, indeed. How do we tell which will be willing to leave us at Rothesay?'

'You are looking too high. I consulted a map,' said the mason grandly, 'and I find that Bute is the island most near to here. We want a fishing-boat.'

'Does one go through this every time one travels to the place?' Gil wondered, following his companion along the strand. 'It would certainly put me off living on an island.'

'Oh, indeed. Why anyone would go there is beyond me, if he did not have business there. Though at least,' added the mason thoughtfully, 'the sea air is good. There is no smell of hawthorn to make one sneeze. Ah – good day, gentlemen.'

The last three vessels drawn up on the shore were smaller than the others. Above them, on the grassy bank, a group of men sat mending nets. They looked up briefly, and one or two nodded in answer to the mason's greeting, then returned to their task.

Undaunted, Maistre Pierre began talking. Gil, watching in some amusement, appreciated the way the fishermen, tolerant at first, were gradually played in by questions about the weather, the tide, the best course for Rothesay, the best man to sail it. At this point, recognizing that success was in sight and money would shortly be discussed, he turned away to study the fishing-boats.

He was watching the gulls swooping across the sandy causeway to the Castle rock when Maistre Pierre said beside him, 'Done. We sail in an hour. I have said we return to the inn, tell Matt who we sail with, fetch our scrips. There will be time also to look in at that handsome church and say our prayers.'

'Good work,' said Gil. 'You do realize, don't you, that you have just contracted to cross the sea in a basket?'

The mason's jaw dropped, and he whirled to look at the boats. The fishermen looked up at the sharp movement, and Gil saw them grinning.

'They are quite safe,' he said. 'Corachs. I have never set foot in one, but I've heard of them. All the old saints used to tramp up and down the sea-roads in these.'

'Yes, but I am not a saint,' said Maistre Pierre, staring at the leather side of the nearest boat. It was tilted so that they could see clearly how the hides were stretched outside the interlaced laths and finally stitched to the wooden keel, or perhaps the other way about. *'Ah, mon Dieu!'*

From the stern of the *Flower of Dumbarton* as she slipped creaking down the Leven on the current, out past Dumbarton Rock and into the main channel of the Clyde, there was an excellent view of the scars of the bombardment which had eventually ended the siege of '89. Gil commented on this.

'And that was a waste of time,' said Andy the helmsman.

'How so?' said Maistre Pierre beyond him.

'They'd ha given up soon in any case. I heard they were about out of meal. But Jamie Stewart,' said Andy, by whom Gil understood him to mean the young King, fourth of that name, 'wanted back to Edinburgh for Yule, and he had this

210

fancy great gun, so they had to bring it down the water and flatten poor folks' houses with it.'

'It meant money for some, surely,' said Gil.

'Aye,' said Andy, and spat over the side. 'And a lot of inconvenience for the rest of us.'

'And what speed will this excellent vessel make?' asked the mason, settling himself gingerly on the stern thwart. The woven structure gave noisily under his feet.

'Three knots,' said Andy. 'Maybe four.'

'A fast walk,' the mason translated for Gil.

'If you can walk on the water,' said Andy, and laughed. 'That's a good one, eh, maisters? If you can walk on the water!'

'Andy, shut your mouth,' said the master from the bows. He and the ship's boy were doing something complicated to a mound of ginger-coloured canvas.

'She may not be so large or so fast as Andrew Wood's *Flower*,' said the mason, 'but I dare say she knows these waters.'

'Better than Andrew Wood,' said the master, and grinned. 'This *Flower*'ll no go aground on the Gantocks.'

Gil sat silent in the stern of the boat, letting the talk flow past him like the grey water, barely aware of the mason's gradually improving confidence. He was feeling very unsettled. He had been more than five years in France, but since his return he had scarcely left Glasgow, except to spend Yule or his birthday in familiar territory in Carluke. Now here he was travelling again, exploring new places, crossing the water –

'It is extraordinary,' said the mason. 'This river runs not into the open sea, but deeper into the hills, which grow higher everywhere one looks. Tell me, maister, how do you know which of these roadways to follow?'

He gestured at three identical arms of the river.

'Lord love you,' said the master, 'what's your trade? Mason, aren't you,' he added before Maistre Pierre could speak. 'I can tell by your hands. How d'you know which

211

stone will stay on another and which will fall down? Tell me that?'

'I see,' said Maistre Pierre. 'It is a thing learned at one's father's knee.'

'And that's a true word,' said the master. 'Int it no, Billy?'

'Aye,' said Billy.

'And there's the tide,' said Andy.

'True enough,' agreed the master. 'When the tide's on the ebb, she'll take you down the water and out to sea easy enough. But when the tide's on the make, what then? You've got to know where you're steering for, all right. Billy, have you done with that sheet? We've a sail to hoist here.'

And where am I steering? wondered Gil. Which of the arms of the river am I headed for, and will it bring me safe to port, or does it only strike deeper into the hills?

His uncle, bidding him farewell in the dawn, had taken his elbow and said with unaccustomed strength of feeling, 'You're a good lad, Gilbert, and I want to see you right.'

'I know that, sir,' he had answered, startled.

'Aye.' There was a pause, then the Official said abruptly, 'There's more roads than one leads to Edinburgh, or Rome for that matter. Are you content with the road we've planned for you? The law and Holy Kirk?'

'How should I not be, sir? It's a secure future.'

His uncle studied him carefully.

'You've not answered my question,' he said, then raised a hand as Gil opened his mouth to speak. 'No. Dinna forswear, Gilbert. I want you to think about it while you're away. When you come back, you can give me the answer, and I want the truth.' He fixed his nephew with an eye as grey as St Columba's. 'You were aye a poor liar. Like your father.'

'Yes, sir,' said Gil helplessly, and knelt for the blessing.

So now, attempting to put in order the things he needed to ask about in Rothesay, he kept finding his thoughts sliding back to his uncle's words. Was he happy with the road before him, whether it led to Edinburgh or Rome? If he turned back from that road, what other way through life was there? Bess Stewart had turned aside from the road before her, to snatch at happiness with the harper, and look where it got her. And why did the old man pick just now, of all times, to ask a question like that?

A wave slopped over the strake beside his elbow. Gil hitched his plaid up, and the master, having set the sail to his liking, made his way aft and took the helm from the mate. The *Flower* creaked happily in the wind.

'Now you'll see,' said the master instructively, adjusting the rope at his other hand, 'that when we get out yonder, off Kilcreggan, we'll take a point or two to larboard, because that's what the channel does. And I'll tell you, maisters, that if the weather doesny shift southward from here, you'll be kept in Rothesay a day or two.'

'She'll shift,' said Andy, looking at the sky.

'And where is this Kilcreggan?' asked Maistre Pierre.

'Yonder,' said Andy, gesturing to starboard. Gil, peering, made out a scattering of thatched roofs under a haze of peat smoke. How strange, he thought. It is a village, where people live their lives, as important to them as the Chanonry and the High Street are to me, and yet I would not have known it was there. What other havens are out here, invisible until pointed out by someone who knows the coast?

Rothesay Bay was full of shipping. There seemed to be more ships here than at Dumbarton. Several large vessels were anchored in the bay with ferries plying to and fro, a number of ships lay alongside a wooden jetty, and two galleys were beached west of the castle. There were carts and wheelbarrows on the foreshore, and a bustle of people beyond. Over all the gulls swooped, screaming.

'That is a strong fortress,' Maistre Pierre observed. 'Also very old, I should say.'

It stood on a mound, less than a hundred paces from the

213

water, its red stone drum towers dwarfing the houses round it. The light caught the helmet of a man on the walkway, and Gil, looking closer, realized there was a competent guard of five or six on the battlements.

'And what is that yonder?' asked the mason, nodding at a tall building some way to the left of the jetty.

'Bishop's house,' said the master, easing the rope in his hand. 'Let go, Andy.'

The sail clattered and flapped into a heap in the bows again, and the mate and the boy shipped the oars and hauled for the shore.

Gil studied the town. It lay snugly between two small hills, facing the bay. As well as the castle and the Bishop's house, there were a number of stone buildings, certainly more and better than at Dumbarton. A handsome plastered barn stood between the castle and the shore, and there were some timber-framed houses further inland, but most of the dwellings were low structures covered in thatch or turf, each at the head of its toft. Pigs, children and small black cows roamed freely between them, and hens pecked about everywhere. The smell of the middens reached them on the breeze.

'Where are ye for, maisters?' asked the master. 'The Bishop or the castle? Just I need to know which side of the burn to set ye down.'

'The castle,' said Gil. 'I've a letter for the chaplain.'

Sir William Dalrymple, stout and red-faced, his jerkin caked with food under a hastily assumed moth-eaten gown, peered anxiously at the letter Gil presented to him under the interested gaze of the two guards on the gate.

'Lachie Beag stepped on my spectacles,' he said apologetically, handing it back. 'I can make out the salutation, but David's wee writing's beyond me. Mind, I'd know his signature anywhere.' He added something in Gaelic to the guards, and one of them nodded and opened the barrier to let them pass. 'Come into the yard and tell me what it's about. Are ye hungry, maisters?'

'We have not eaten since Sext,' said Maistre Pierre, following the portly outline of the priest along the passageway into the bustling courtyard.

'Come to the buttery, then, and see what we can find.' Sir William led the way round the end of the chapel, past the smithy where several men were discussing crossbow bolts, and up a narrow stair. 'And is your uncle well, Gilbert?'

Dinner was long past but the buttery men, obviously used to their priest, found half a raised pie and some roasted onions which nobody was using. Seated at the end of one of the long tables with these and a plate of bannocks and a jug of claret, Sir William rattled through a short grace and said as the mason grimaced over the wine, 'Now. This letter. Why is David sending to me after all these years?'

'It explains why we're here,' Gil said, and read the letter aloud. Sir William listened attentively, with muffled exclamations, and nodded emphatically at the end.

'Very proper, very proper,' he said. 'It's high time that was cleared up. And so Bess Stewart is dead, then? I'm sorry to hear it, indeed, for she was a bonny girl and a good Christian soul, until she did what she did. That would explain the word from Ettrick, certainly.'

'From Ettrick?' Gil prompted, when the stout priest did not continue.

Sir William nodded deprecatingly. 'News came in this week that the *beann nighe* had been heard at Ettrick, washing linen at the ford, on May Day at twilight.'

'Washing? What is this?' asked the mason, perplexed.

Sir William sighed. 'It is a pagan thing, an evil spirit I suppose, and I should stamp out the belief, but to be honest, maisters, I've heard it myself once or twice. If you are near a ford by night and you hear a sound like someone washing linen, slapping the wet cloth on the stones, go away quickly and do not disturb the washer-woman, or

215

she will have the shirt off your back. And then who knows what will happen? But if she is heard, a death in the parish follows.'

'But what does she wash?' asked the mason. 'How can you tell it is a spirit?'

'Who washes clothes by twilight?' said Gil. 'I have heard of such a thing, in my nurse's tales. Did one of the old heroes not meet her? Finn, or one of those?'

'Aye, very possibly,' said Sir William. 'Anyway she was heard at Ettrick, so they were all waiting for a death in the parish, and when nobody seemed like to die and there were no accidents, of course the entire parish began to reckon up who was off the island that she might wash for. They will certainly believe it was for Bess, if she is dead.'

'She is dead,' Gil agreed, 'under sad circumstances. There is no doubt it was secret murder, forethought murder, and I am charged with finding the killer.'

'Well,' said Sir William. 'And how can I help you? What do you need to know?'

'Tell me about Bess Stewart,' Gil said. 'Did you know her, sir?'

'I baptized them both. Bonny bairns they were, too, her and her sister. Well-schooled, obedient lassies, able to read and write their names, modest and well-behaved for all their mother died when they were young.' He sighed. 'I wedded her to Edward Stewart, and I witnessed his will. He was a good man, and a loving husband to her. Then her good-brother handfasted her to the man Sempill, after Edward died, and I think she was never happy again.'

'You witnessed her first husband's will,' Gil repeated. 'Do you remember the terms? How was the outright bequest worded?'

'Oh, I canny mind that. It was near ten years ago,' Dalrymple pointed out. 'She'd lose the tierce when she remarried, of course, but there was the house, and I suppose the use of the furnishings.'

'That would be the house she left when she ran off with

the harper,' said the mason, cutting another slice off the pie.

'Aye, it was. That was a mystery.'

'Tell us about it,' Gil prompted. 'It was November, wasn't it? Before Martinmas?'

'It was,' said Dalrymple, giving him a startled glance. 'Janet McKirdy the Provost's wife was full of guilt after it happened, for they'd met in her house at Allhallows E'en when she had the guizers' play acted in the yard. Then not ten days later the harper left in a night, and Bess Stewart with him.'

'And what was the mystery?' asked the mason, chewing. 'What was it that must be cleared up?'

'Why, the money,' said Sir William. 'She took every penny there was in the house away with her, and the plate, and her jewels, but the next we heard she was in Edinburgh, and living on the harper's earnings. Whether she'd lost it, or spent it, or given it away, nobody knows.'

'There was no money in her box,' said Gil. 'How much plate would this be?'

'Edward Stewart was cousin to Ninian Stewart the Provost,' said Sir William. 'He was a bien man, very comfortable. I remember a considerable amount of plate when I was in the house. All silver, of course, gold's not to be found in Rothesay, except when the King's in residence, but nevertheless . . .' He took the last roasted onion and bit into it reflectively. 'Twenty-five or thirty pounds weight, maybe.'

The mason whistled.

'Did his kin not reclaim it when she remarried?' Gil asked.

'They tried to, but the man Sempill resisted. It was to come to the head court in the February. They made an inventory, and lodged it with Alexander Stewart, and got Sempill to sign it as well. We're honest folk on Bute, maisters. Well, mostly.'

'How would she carry that much?' the mason wondered. 'It is a great burden, even as far as the shore.'

217

'Oh, she'd not go by the shore,' said Sir William. 'You can wait days for the right wind, in November. They would go round by Rhubodach, to the ferry.'

'When was all this discovered?' Gil asked.

'Not till the morning. Her good-brother came calling, and found the servants in disarray, and her chamber door shut. It seems she'd barred it with a kist and climbed out of the window. He raised a band to follow, but they'd made good time and she was off the island, so he turned back. Once they got in among the hills, there'd be little hope of finding them.'

'Burdened by a chest containing twenty-five or thirty pounds of silver,' said Gil, 'as well as money and jewels, they had made such good time that a mounted band could not catch them?'

There was a short silence.

'It is strange, when you look at it,' admitted Sir William.

'Who else lived in the house with her?'

'She'd a waiting-woman, a kinswoman of some sort, and two-three kitchen girls, of course, and two outside men and a pair of swordsmen.'

'So her kinswoman did not share her chamber? Quite a household.' Gil pushed the crumbs of his bannock into a heap. 'That is strange, for the harper's sister never mentioned that Bess had money. Indeed, she told me that as soon as the bairn could be left, Bess was helping to earn her keep.'

'There was a bairn, was there? Poor Bess.' Sir William looked blankly at the empty dishes. 'Is that all the food there was? Come and leave your scrips in my chamber, and I will lead you to Alexander Stewart.'

The lawyer, it seemed, lived away up the Kirkgait. Having left their baggage in the priest's stuffy chamber in the loft above the chapel, they went out at the postern, into the busy little town.

There were still a lot of people about, even this late in the afternoon, men from the foreshore in tarry jerkin and hose, shipmasters and merchants in furred woollen gowns and felt hats, Highlanders in shirt and belted plaid. The women gossiping at one street corner wore checked gowns like Ealasaidh's, those at the next were in good wool. Many of the passers-by greeted Sir William, who had a name and a blessing for everyone.

They turned inland and walked round the castle walls, passing the mercat cross where a man with a tabor and pipe had an audience of children and time-wasters. Sir William, ignoring this, pointed out one of the stone houses as the Provost's.

'Same stone as the castle,' said the mason. 'I know that soft stuff. You can shape it with axes.' He stopped. 'Maister Cunningham, do you need me to help you talk to a lawyer?'

'I could likely manage without you.'

'Then I will go and walk about this burgh a little way. I can get back into the castle, no?'

Armed with the password for the day, he set off briskly for the shore, and Gil and the stout priest went on inland, Sir William still nodding to passers-by.

'I wonder is the Provost here any kin of Stewart of Minto who is Provost of Glasgow,' Gil speculated. 'I know they say *All Stewarts areny sib to the King*, but are they all sib to one another?'

'Oh, I don't think so,' said Sir William seriously. 'Although I believe a cousin of Janet McKirdy's wedded one of the Stewarts of Minto a few years back. And that is Bess Stewart's own house,' he continued, pausing casually a few tofts along before a substantial timber-framed building, set back from the roadway. Before it, at some time, someone had made a small pleasure-garden, which was now struggling against the depredations of the roving hens. 'It seems she got out of that window there.'

Gil eyed the window. It was just under the thatch, twenty feet above the ground, and the shuttered lower portion was no more than eighteen inches deep.

219

'Was there a rope?' he asked. 'Or marks of a ladder? What time would this have been?'

'You think she might not have climbed down? I thought the same,' confessed Sir William. 'And another thing I thought was, a woman's kirtle is a lot of cloth. Would it all fit through there?'

'Did you mention this at the time?'

'What would be the point? She'd run off, poor lass, and her kin were pinning their mouths up about it. Who was I to argue with her good-brother's version?'

Gil nodded absently, studying the house. It was not being well maintained. He could see several places where the clay and plaster infill between the sturdy timbers of the frame was crumbling under its limewash, exposing the wattle.

'That rose will be through the wall shortly,' he commented. 'What is it, a white one? We have one in Rottenrow which spreads like that. Who was covering up for whom, I wonder?'

'I wondered if her sister might have helped her,' said Dalrymple. 'It would be a sin, of course, to help a woman to leave her lawful husband, but they were very close. If Bess asked for help Mariota would give it. I thought likely Mariota's man suspected that had happened, for he closed up his own house in Rothesay, just down yonder, and moved all out to the farm at Ettrick. He would beat her for it himself rather than have it known publicly that he couldn't control her.'

'The waiting-woman knew nothing?' Gil swung his foot at a hen which was inspecting his boots. It flapped away, squawking, and two more hurried over to see what it had found.

'She slept at the back of the house. The first she heard was when the servants woke her.' The priest's breathing had settled down. He moved on, walking slowly among the homeward-bound workers. 'It's let now, of course. Probably for a good rent, it's a good family in it. Another

220

cousin of Ninian Stewart's. No, I have it wrong, a cousin of his wife's.'

There were a few more timber-framed houses, none quite as grand as Bess Stewart's house, interspersed with long low cottages of field stones. Beyond these were even lower structures which, to Gil's astonishment, proved to be composed of alternating layers of turf and stone, their roofs turfed over and sprouting happily. Women in loose chequered gowns called in Gaelic from house to house as they passed, until they came to one with two goats tethered above the door, and four or five half-naked children in successive sizes tumbling in the street next to its rounded end.

'This is Alexander's house,' said Sir William, turning off the main track towards the door. The children halted their playing to stare as he shouted something in Gaelic.

There was a reply from within, and the leather curtain across the doorway swung back. A woman in a plaid and a checked gown stared at them, then made a gesture of invitation with a dignity quite unimpaired by the fact that she was barefoot and had a sucking child in the crook of her other arm.

Inside the house the smell was almost solid. To the right, clearly, the goats, the hens and at least one cow spent their nights.To the left a peat fire glowed on a square hearth, and by its light a man rose from a stool and bowed to them. He was clad, like the harper, in a saffron shirt and buskins. Several of the children squeezed in past Gil to crowd into a corner, watching the guests with big dark eyes. The priest offered a blessing, to which they all said fervently 'Amen!' with a strange turn to the vowels. Then he made a speech, apparently introducing Gil and explaining his errand.

'I can speak Latin,' said the man of the house at length. 'It is a sight of the title deeds to Bess Stewart's property you are after, yes?'

'I need to know who benefits,' Gil said. At the sound of his voice the children giggled, and their father turned and spoke sharply in Gaelic. They sobered immediately. 'The title deeds, the terms of Edward Stewart's will, Bess's father's will, the conjunct fee or whatever it was, Bess's own will if she made one. I need to know what happens to all that property now, because I suspect that is how I will learn who killed Bess Stewart.'

'You don't ask much,' said the other man drily. 'I have the title deeds and the two wills here in one of the protocol books, I can be finding them for you in a little while, but the other, the conjunct fee, I never drew up. I can tell you it was conjunct fee, it will certainly be going to the husband now, but I have not the details. And if she was making a will, it was not when she was in Rothesay. I have no knowledge of such a thing.' He looked about him, and spoke to the children. Two of them dragged a long bench near the fire. 'Be seated, guests in my house, and the woman of the house will bring you something. I will be looking for the papers.'

He threw a brief word to the woman, who was settling the baby in a strong-smelling nest of sheepskins at the foot of what must be their bed. She straightened up, fastening her gown, and moved to a carved court-cupboard opposite the door. Her man made for the shadows in the corner, and began to search in a kist full of books and papers.

The refreshment proved to be oatcakes with green cheese, and usquebae in a pewter cup. Gil drank his share of the spirit off quickly, to get it over with, and to his dismay was handed another cupful. The oatcakes were light and crisp, and the cheese was excellent. He said as much to the woman, and got a blank smile, until Sir William translated. The smile broadened, and she offered him more, but he refused in dumbshow, fearing he might be eating the children's supper.

'There is plenty,' Sir William assured him. 'Mairead makes excellent oatcakes.'

Gil was about to answer when two more of the children tumbled in from the street shouting in Gaelic. A man's voice spoke indistinctly outside and Gil turned to listen, sure he knew the accents. The woman, pulling her plaid over her head, slipped out past the tall desk which stood at the light, and Gil heard her speaking softly beyond the leather curtain.

'Here it is, maister,' said Alexander Stewart. He brought an armful of books forward into the firelight. 'If we take it to the door there will be light for reading.'

He moved to the door, and pulled back the curtain. Gil, following him, was aware of swift movement and the certainty that someone had ducked round the end of the house. The woman went past them into the shadows, to offer Sir William another oatcake, and the lawyer opened one of the books on the desk to show Gil his own copy of the first of the documents.

'Torquil Stewart of Ettrick,' he said. 'His will. You see, he left his property divided between the two daughters, held in their own right, to leave as they see fit.'

'This is very clear,' said Gil. 'A nice piece of work.'

'He was very clear about his wishes himself,' said Maister Stewart modestly. Seen by daylight, he was dark of hair and eye like his children, the neatly combed elf-locks hanging round a pale, intent face. He seemed, Gil thought, to be not much past thirty. 'He had raised his daughters to know how to run a property, he trusted them to go on as he had taught them. And this is Edward Stewart's will,' he continued, setting open another book. 'More complicated, because more clauses, but in essence the same in respect of the property itself. The house outright to his wife Elizabeth, in her own right, to dispose of as she sees fit. The use of the contents of the house entire, with provision for it to be inventoried at his death, for the rest of her life. Requirement that she does not sell any item, and replaces items worn out or broken. All the liferent goods to revert to his kin after her death. In fact when the house was let the remainder of the contents went to Ninian Stewart like the residue of the estate.'

'This matter of the plate and money is very strange,' Gil said. He skimmed down the careful Latin sentences of

Edward Stewart's will, aware out of the tail of his eye of a steady sauntering of passers-by out in the street, as Maister Stewart's neighbours came to admire his Latin conversation with the colleague from Glasgow. 'There is no sign that she came to the harper with a fortune in her kist. If it were to surface, whose would it be?'

'Interesting,' said Alexander Stewart thoughtfully. 'The plate would certainly be the Provost's, like the furniture. The money I suspect was hers, or perhaps her husband's. It would have been rent for the land at Kingarth and the two farms at Ettrick, all good land. Some of the rent would be in kind, you understand, and some in coin. As to jewellery, some of that would be paraphernal, and should return to her kin, or I suppose it now belongs to the bairn, but any the husband gave her would revert to him. All subject to discussion, I suspect. An interesting question, Maister Cunningham.'

'Had she made a will herself?' Gil asked.

'Not one that I knew of, since her second marriage.'

'I wish we had a copy of the conjunct settlement. What was the value of the two properties? You say the land at Kingarth is good? I had heard otherwise.'

'I do not know who could have told you that,' said Maister Stewart disapprovingly. 'It is very good land. Further, it is beside the St Blane's Fair gathering-place, so it is used for grazing and pound-land at the Fair, and the rents for that every year would ransom a galley. As for the other, it lies between the castle and the harbour, and is rented to two merchants for a good figure. One of them has built a barn on his portion.'

'I saw it as we came into the bay. Trade through the burgh is rewarding, then?'

'Rothesay is the only burgh in the Western Isles licensed to trade overseas,' said Maister Stewart with some pride. 'This is why I moved here last year, to be closer to the centre of trade. There was no man of law here anyway, I came here often or folk came to me in Inveraray to draw up documents, and after I lost two or three clients in bad weather I thought, well, well, better to move the inkstand than the mounting-block.'

'Very wise. I hope it has been good for business.' Gil, only half attending, looked from one will to the other. 'These properties,' he said slowly, 'I think are now the bairn's. There is no indication that either husband had a claim on them. Do you have paper to spare? Would you object to my having a true copy? I need to show them to John Sempill, and to my uncle, who acts for the bairn. And can you tell me who was the grantor of the conjunct fee? Who gave them these two valuable properties? And who is collecting the rents while Bess has been away from Bute?'

'The same man in both cases. Even if I did not draw up the deeds, I know that. It will be the good-brother. Her sister's man, out at Ettrick.'

'And who is he?'

'Alexander makes a good living,' said Sir William as they made their way back down towards the castle. The street was much quieter now, with only a last few townspeople making their way home before curfew. 'He is the only man of law in Rothesay at present, and for some distance round about, and he is a good lawyer.'

'Where did he study, do you know?' Gil asked. 'I meant to ask him, but we were so busy writing these copies that it slipped my mind.'

'St Andrews, I think. Yes, surely. If it had been Glasgow I would have remembered, because he would have met David – your uncle. Yes, indeed, I am sure it was St Andrews. He is Master of Arts as well as Bachelor of Laws. He told me so.'

'He is certainly a good lawyer, and his Latin is excellent. Why does he stay here? Could he not do better in Stirling or Edinburgh?'

'I believe he is happy here. There is plenty of business.

Besides, he is one of the wealthiest men in the burgh,' said Sir William with vicarious pride.

'Wealthy?' said Gil despite himself.

'Oh, yes. Did you not see the court-cupboard at the door, and that desk? Those cost him a penny or two. He gives very generously to the poor, and they always have food on the table. I have eaten there myself when the Provost has been invited, and I am sure you could not have dined better in Glasgow. And he goes daily in that saffron shirt.'

But his children played half-naked in the street, and they all slept under one roof with the cattle, like any poor peasant and his family. Could I live like that, Gil thought, if I remained a layman?

Entering by the postern gate as the curfew bell began to ring across the burgh, Gil and the stout priest found Maistre Pierre seated in the castle courtyard enjoying the evening light and watching the guard detail gathering by the main gateway.

'And was that helpful?' he asked as they reached him.

'Oh, very useful,' said Dalrymple immediately. 'Maister Stewart was very helpful, very helpful. Maister Cunningham has seen and copied all the documents he needs, I think. Forgive me, maisters, I must say Compline. I believe it is late.'

'How was your walk?'

'Interesting.' The mason rose to follow Sir William into the chapel. 'That cog at the wharf had lately been to Nantes. I had a word with her skipper.'

Gil looked at him consideringly.

'You have more news than that,' he observed. 'I can tell.'

'I have indeed.'

'And so have I. What is yours?'

'Guess who I saw in the town?'

Gil paused in the chapel doorway. A seagull screamed from the wall-walk, and then broke into a long derisive cackling. As well it might, he thought. I have been slow.

226

'Was it by any chance,' he said, suddenly sure of the half-heard voice at the door of the lawyer's cottage, 'was it one of the gallowglasses? Neil or Euan?'

'It was,' said the mason, slightly disappointed, 'though I do not know which. Did you see him too?'

'No, but I heard him. Now it is your turn. Can you guess who is Bess Stewart's good-brother, the man who is collecting her rents and who granted the two properties in conjunct fee?'

'Now that,' said the mason triumphantly, 'is easy. It must be James Campbell.'

Chapter Eleven

'But should one of us not stay in Rothesay,' said the mason, 'in the hope of laying hands on that gallowglass?'

They were riding out of the burgh in the wake of one of the castle scullions, who had reluctantly volunteered, when cornered by Sir William after Sunday morning Mass, to guide them to Ettrick and the farm where Bess Stewart's sister lived. Their mounts were the best the stout priest had been able to coax out of the stables, stocky, shaggy creatures with large unshod feet and no manners, and none was willing to go faster than a trot.

Grinning shiftily, their guide had led them over the headland and round a broad sandy bay where the gorse bushes grew down close to the shore, and then turned inland. He appeared to know where he was going. They were now bumping along a track which appeared to lead westward through a broad shallow valley. The occasional spire of sweet blue peat-smoke suggested that the place was inhabited, but they had encountered nobody.

'Whichever brother it was you saw yesterday, if we do not find him in Rothesay we can surely find him in Glasgow,' said Gil. 'I feel happier meeting Mistress Mariota Stewart with some company at my elbow. She may not yet know her sister is dead, poor lady.'

'Ah,' said the mason. 'And apart from that, what do you wish to say to her?'

'I wish to ask her where the money is.' Gil looked about him. 'This is good land. These cattle are sturdy and the crops look healthy, and that was a handsome tower-house we passed a while back.'

'It is when you make remarks like that,' said Maistre Pierre in resentful tones, 'that I recall that you are of baronial stock. Do not change the subject. Are we riding into the wilds, on these appalling beasts, with a guide who does not speak Scots, merely to ask the lady where the money is? And which money, anyway?'

'Well,' said Gil. 'Yes. And no. The money and plate which vanished when Bess did, and the rent for her land and the joint land. John Sempill doesn't appear to be receiving much for it, from what he said, and it must be going somewhere.'

'If it is going into James Campbell's coffers, why should she tell us?'

'A good point.'

'How much further are we going? Do we enter those mountains?' Maistre Pierre nodded towards the blue saw-toothed mass in the distance to their left.

'Sir William said it was two-three miles. I think those mountains must be the next island, for there is the sea.'

Their guide, whom Sir William had identified as Lachie Mor, turned and gave them a snaggle-toothed, shifty grin.

'Arran,' he said, pointing at the mountains. Then, pointing to the other side of their path, 'Ettrick. Mistress Stewart. *Agus* Seumas Campbell,' he added, with great feeling, and spat.

'What is wrong with being a Campbell?' asked Maistre Pierre curiously. 'The Fury – the harper's sister – felt the same way.'

'If you're a Campbell, nothing,' said Gil. 'But my understanding is that they all reserve their first allegiance for the Earl of Argyll, the head of the surname, and next to another Campbell. Local ties and feus, obligations to the lord they hold their land from, come a long way after. And since any Campbell worth the name can manipulate that position to his own benefit, many people distrust them.

229

These two, of course – James and Euphemia – are the grandchildren of the present earl by one of his younger daughters, and so even closer.'

'I suppose that accounts for the air one detects in both of them, of being accountable to no one else for their actions.'

'You could be right,' said Gil, much struck by this. Their guide, listening intently, nodded, spat again, and turned his pony off the track on to a narrower path, down towards a stony ford.

'Ettrick,' he said again, pointing to a thin column of blue smoke visible over the near skyline.

The house, though not a tower-house, was at least stone-built, with shuttered windows tucked under its thatch, and contained a long hall and a small chamber at its far end, well away from the byre. Two little boys practising their letters were dismissed to see Seonaidh in a separate kitchen out the back, quite as if they were in Rothesay. Gil, seated on a morocco-leather backstool in front of Flemish verdure tapestry, sipped the inevitable usquebae out of a tiny footed Italian glass, eyed the woman opposite him and said carefully,

'Mistress Stewart, what is the latest word that has reached you about your sister Bess?'

Mariota Stewart, in her woollen gown and white kerchief, gazed back at him. She was unnervingly like her sister, with the same oval face, the same build and well-bred carriage, but Bess's sweet expression was lacking. This woman looked out at a world which held no illusions for her.

'Word of her death reached me yesterday, maister.' Her voice was quite steady. 'It was no surprise to me. Half the parish heard the washing at the ford yonder, on Tuesday night, so we were waiting for something of the sort.' She sipped at her own glass. 'I understand she was murdered.'

'Yes. I found her. She had been stabbed, without struggling. She probably felt nothing.'

The white kerchief bowed. After a moment, still quite steady, she said, 'Thank you. Do you know who . . .?'

'I am acting on behalf of St Mungo's, to find out who. Maister Mason, here, is also concerned, in that it was on his building site that she was found.'

Maistre Pierre offered some conventional words of sympathy, at which Mistress Stewart bowed her head again and said levelly, 'If I can tell you anything that will help, ask it.'

'Thank you.' Gil paused, and took a bite of yesterday's oatcake to blot up the spirits. 'Mistress, you and your sister both inherited land. The rents are clearly valuable, but your sister had not received hers since she left Bute. Can you tell me where the money might have gone?'

She stared at him.

'My husband collected them,' she said, 'coin and kind both. The grain and kye he would store, or maybe buy in, and the coin went to John Sempill, as was his legal right.' Only the absence of expression conveyed what she thought about Sempill's legal right.

'And yet,' said Gil, equally expressionless, 'John Sempill is convinced that Bess was receiving the rents of her own property, and also that the two conjunct properties, the land by the shore and the plot in Kingarth, are worthless. This suggests to me that very little rent is reaching him.'

'I do not know how that can be,' she said, and took refuge in the married woman's defence. 'My husband deals with all the money.'

'How does the coin go to John Sempill?' asked the mason. She flicked a glance at him, and considered.

'If my husband is to go to Renfrewshire, it goes with him. Otherwise we send a couple of men. We have trustworthy servants.'

'That would be the Campbell brothers,' Gil prompted, and she nodded, taking his knowledge for granted. 'So they take the money to John Sempill?'

'Wherever he chances to be.'

'Which of them brought you word yesterday?'

231

'Neil,' she said indifferently.

'And which of them helped your sister to get out of her house, the night she left with the harper?'

'What does that have to do with –' She stopped, looking out of the window. 'I suppose you need to know,' she said reluctantly. 'It might all have a bearing on the matter.'

'Exactly,' said Gil in some relief. She sighed.

'Her husband – John – was in Renfrewshire, and Bess was here in Rothesay. Last time John was on Bute he had been – displeased, because the rents were less than he wanted. The factor had given the coin to James, and James counted it and gave it straight into his hand,' she added, without seeming to hear what she was saying. 'So John took it out on Bess. And the harper and her – it was like in the ballads, the old romances. One word together and it was as if they were the two halves of an apple. I tried to speak to her,' she said, biting her lips, 'but she would not listen. I knew no good would come of it.'

'If it's of any comfort,' Gil said gently, 'she seems to have been happy while she was with the harper and his sister.'

She smiled bitterly. 'For a year and a half. Aye, well, it's longer than some folk get. So anyway he was leaving and she would go with him. I made sure both the Campbell brothers were in Rothesay for her, and lent her a horse, one that would come back to me on its own from the ferry, and I hugged her and wished her Godspeed, for all she was going into sin, and went back to my own house that night, and I never saw her again.' She stopped speaking and put the back of her hand across her mouth, apparently unaware that tears were pouring down her face. Gil reached out and touched her other hand.

'Drink some usquebae, mistress,' he suggested.

'Perhaps we should be going,' said Maistre Pierre uncomfortably.

'There is still something I need to ask.'

Mistress Stewart poured herself another glass of spirits and took a gulp.

'Ask it,' she said.

'The plate and money –'

'No,' she said firmly. 'I know nothing. I do not believe my sister took them with her, for the plate was not hers, and she was angry at John Sempill for not returning it to the Stewarts when she wedded him. She kept it, you understand, to make a good showing at the wedding, and then he insisted it was part of her tocher, though it was all clear in her first man's will. She would not have taken it away. Nor any money that was not hers,' she added. 'Jewels, now, that was different, and our grandmother's prayer-book that we learned our letters out of, but never a thing that was not hers.'

'What do you suppose might have happened to it?' Gil asked.

She shook her head.

'Ask Neil Campbell. It was him was there when James went in the morning to call on her. I think James suspected what we had done,' she said, taking another mouthful of usquebae.

'When did the horse come home?' asked the mason.

'That was what sent James round to her house. It came in as soon as the Gallowgait Port was opened in the morning, and one of the stablemen must have told him I'd lent it to Bess.'

'What was the name of your sister's waiting-woman?' Gil asked.

'Oh, it wasn't likely her. She was another of the Provost's cousins, an auntie of Edward Stewart's. She'd an interest in making sure it went back to her kin.'

'I had wondered if she might have been your good-sister Euphemia.'

'Her?' Mariota Stewart looked genuinely startled by the idea. 'Euphemia go for a waiting-woman? Not till the sky falls in! She's got ideas beyond her means, that one. It was a great pity her man fell at Stirling, particularly with him being on the wrong side.'

233

'I thought Chancellor Argyll was for the present King,' said Maistre Pierre, 'with all his kin.'

'Someone married Euphemia to the wrong man. He was a Murray, and hot-headed like all of them, so Euphemia trying to argue with him only brought him out the more strongly for the late King. So her ladyship had to see all the property she'd married him for handed over to the Crown in fines. What she lives on now I don't know. To be honest,' she confided, taking another sip of usquebae, 'I don't care either. She's not a nice woman, with her airs and her graces, and her fancy clothes, and her scent to her own receipt, that smells of something else when it gets stale. She's not a nice woman at all, and I don't like her round my bairns.'

She sighed, and hiccuped.

'Where is my sister laid?'

'In Greyfriars kirkyard,' said Gil gently. 'Maister Mason and I were at the burial. It was well attended, by Sempill's kin and the harper's friends, and she was properly keened. There are a number of Ersche speakers in Glasgow.'

She nodded, and went on nodding for some time before she collected herself and said formally, 'Will you eat, maisters?'

'No, no, I thank you,' said Gil, getting to his feet. The mason did likewise, and she sat looking from one to the other. 'We must get back to Rothesay and find Neil Campbell. Mistress . . .' He hesitated, looking down at her. 'Did Neil tell you that there was a bairn?'

'Why are we being sidetracked by this money and plate?' asked Maistre Pierre. 'Is it relevant? Will it tell us who stabbed Bess Stewart in my building site?'

'I feel it is involved,' said Gil, hitching his plaid up against the fine smirr of rain. 'I don't know about you, but I am beginning to see a pattern. One name keeps coming to our attention.'

'How does he benefit?'

234

'If Campbell of Glenstriven has been diverting the rents to his own use rather than give them to Sempill, it was in his interest to prevent Sempill speaking to Bess.'

'Killing her is rather final.'

'Nevertheless, it is effective. Since he did not know about the bairn, he could assume the Ettrick lands would go back to his wife as Bess's surviving kin. The house in Rothesay might go to Sempill of Muirend, which could not be helped, and so would the conjunct fee lands, but since in law Sempill could not dispose of those without first offering them to Bess's kin, Campbell's next step, I should think, would be to buy them in at a bargain price, so his lies might not be detected.'

'And the plate?'

'It is at least curious that he was the first on the scene after Bess left her house to run off with the harper.'

'But what of the other girl? Surely if he was with Bridie on the High Street before Compline, he must know she was not in the kirkyard during the Office. He had no need to kill her. And I thought he was distressed to learn of her death.'

'I thought about that.' Gil counted off the points. '*Imprimis*, he might not be certain of where she went after he left her. She could have been in the kirkyard, half the town heard us say she was there, he might have killed her to be certain.'

'A poor reason.'

'Someone killed her. *Secundus*, perhaps she did know something. What if she followed him and saw what happened –'

'Whatever that was.'

'Whatever that was, and when they met, yesterday at the market – no, the day before, now – she tried to threaten him, or get money from him.'

'Give me some ribbons or I'll tell what I saw, you mean?'

'Precisely. *Let's step aside here and discuss this, my doo.* And in goes the knife.'

'Are there more possibilities?'

'Perhaps he was simply tired of her, and thought her death could be blamed on the same broken man as killed Bess.'

'Not so probable, surely. Do we know him to have behaved like this in the past?'

'No, but we don't know him to have knifed his sister-in-law before this either. He was concealing some strong emotion when he heard of Bridie's death,' Gil pointed out. 'It is hard to be sure whether it was grief, or alarm that we knew of it already, or something else. Even if he killed her, he might have felt grief for her death.'

'Hmm.' The mason rode in silence for a few minutes, considering this. Then, looking about him at the woodland through which they rode, he said in some alarm, 'This is not the path we took! Where are we?'

'The track's about a half-mile that way.' Gil nodded to their left. 'I don't think this fellow means us any harm. I've been keeping an eye on him, and Sir William knows where we are.'

Lachie Mor, obviously understanding this, grinned his unreliable grin and pointed ahead.

'Eagleis,' he enunciated. 'Eagleis Chattan.'

'A church?' said the mason.

Gil nodded. 'The church of the cat?' he hazarded.

Their guide shook his head emphatically. 'Chattan,' he repeated, and gestured: a halo, a benediction.

'St Chattan?' Gil offered, and got another grin and a nod. 'How far?'

'Not far,' said the mason. 'We are here.'

They emerged into the open, and the ponies stopped and all three raised their heads, ears pricked, as if they had seen someone they knew approaching. Gil stared round him in the sunshine. They were in a circular clearing in the trees, perhaps fifty paces across. A small burn trickled at their feet, and a grassy bank beyond it sloped gently up to the remains of a small stone building. It was now roofless, but the walls and the two gables with their slit windows still stood, silent witness to the craft of the old builders who had fitted silver-grey slabs and red field-stones together, course after ragged course, apparently without benefit of chisel.

'Eagleis Chattan,' said their guide again. He dismounted, and from his scrip produced a cloth bundle. He mimed eating this, with an inclusive gesture, then led his pony across the burn and tethered it within reach of the water.

'A good idea,' said the mason, dismounting likewise, 'and a pleasant spot for a meal.'

It was indeed pleasant enough to make stale oatmeal bannocks and hard cheese palatable. They shared out the food and ate, seated on the grass bank while the burn chattered at their feet and birds darted among the branches. The ponies drowsed in the shade. Then Lachie Mor lay back on the grass and drew his plaid over his face in a way that brooked no argument.

'A valuable example,' said the mason, brushing crumbs from his hose. 'I think I also rest a little. I have not slept well.' He lay back and tipped his round hat forward, hiding all but the neat black beard.

Gil, though he forbore from contradicting this statement, did not feel like joining the soporific scene. Instead he rose, checked the ponies' tethers, and strolled up to investigate St Chattan's Kirk.

A grassy path led round the little building to a narrow doorway in one side. Gil stepped in, and found that the place was in use.

It had the same impact on him as stepping into one of Glasgow's little chapels. The walls blazed with colour, and a dark figure bent over the lit and furnished altar. He could hear the rhythmic mutter of the Office.

Astonished, he dropped to his knees on the packed bare earth, groping for words of prayer as his beads almost fell into his hands. Gradually, as the familiar phrases slipped past, he realized that he had seen something other than what was there. The red-and-silver walls were not painted, but dappled with the sunlight which came through the overhanging trees; the crucifix on the clean-swept altar was not of silver, but worked from a gleaming slab of rock, and the bright-coloured candle flame beside it was in fact a bunch of wildflowers in a horn cup. And the sound of the Office was the burn, bubbling away somewhere.

He completed the last paternoster, and turned to his own prayers. But in this extraordinary place his habitual request for freedom from doubt seemed inappropriate. He emptied his mind, and after a while words floated up. *Thank you for showing me this. Please show me the next step.*

He had no idea how long he knelt. After a while the light changed, and he saw without surprise that what bent over the altar was not a priest but a briar-bush, the only thing growing inside the walls. There were no other furnishings. Crossing himself, he rose, bent the knee to the silver stone image, and went out of the narrow door.

Lachie Mor and the mason still lay on the grass. One of them was snoring. Gil grinned to himself and turned to pick his way round the church right-handed.

Clearly, others did the same. The grassy path which led to the door continued round the west gable and into the trees. The sound of water grew louder as he rounded the corner, and he found himself looking at the spring from which the burn rose. The well had been built up with red and silver stones, now mossy, and the water spilled out and chattered away round the other gable of the little building. A thorn tree bent over the pool, shedding may-blossom into the water, its branches decked with rags and ribbons. Clumps of primroses studded the grass.

'A clootie well,' he said aloud, and bent to drink. As he raised a dripping palm to his mouth a twig cracked sharply in the trees. He froze, staring, and the shadows congealed into the form of a red deer hind, her head up, staring back at him unafraid. She stood for five or six heartbeats, then wheeled and trotted off between two beech-trees, her little feet brushing among the pale prim-roses. Gil stared after her, open-mouthed. Almost he could

believe he had seen St Giles's own pet. And something else
– a message . . .

More twigs crackled behind him.

'What do you call it?' said the mason. 'A clootie well?
Clootie pudding I know. How can you boil a well in a
cloth?'

'The ribbons – cloths – are offerings,' Gil explained.
'I believe such wells are very old. St Tennoch's well, out
the Thenawgait, is a clootie well.'

'I have seen it.' The mason gave the well a cursory
glance and turned to study the wall of the church. 'This is
rough work, but they had talent, the old builders. If my
new work is still standing in five hundred years, I shall be
pleased.' He prodded the mortar between two slabs of
ribbed grey rock. 'Our guide is awake and wishes to
leave.'

Lachie Mor slipped out of the little chapel as they passed
the door. For a moment he wore a distant, bemused look
which chimed well with the way Gil felt; then his customary unreliable expression took over, and he leered at them,
gap-toothed.

'Tobar Chattan,' he said, jerking a thumb at the burn.
Then, pointing to their mounts, 'Rothesay.'

'We might be in time for dinner in the castle,' said
Maistre Pierre hopefully, as they rode south around the
bay towards Rothesay. 'You think Sir William will feed
us?'

Gil, still grappling with a strong sense of unreality, made
no answer, but found himself dragged back to the problems confronting them when the mason continued, as if
they had never halted, 'But had Campbell the time? He
said himself he saw Bess Stewart with the gallowglass,
going into the trees, when he came to the kirkyard. She
was still alive then.'

'He was not with the rest of the group throughout the
whole length of Compline,' Gil pointed out. 'He was one of
those that came and went, he said to say a word before St
James's altar, which is nearer to the south door from where

they were standing. He could have slipped out and spoken to her, taken her into the building site for a word in private – perhaps he claimed to have a message from her sister. He carries a fine-bladed knife like the one we think was used. It fits together.'

'You think the money is the only motive?'

'If I had cheated John Sempill out of the best part of a hundred merks' rent,' said Gil frankly, 'I'd go to considerable lengths to conceal it. I have known of men killed for a couple of placks, maister.'

'So have I. I think perhaps you are right. So what do we do next?'

Gil hitched up his plaid against the rain. If it had rained all afternoon, why had there been sunshine at St Chattan's Kirk?

'I wish to talk to Neil Campbell, and then I think we try for a passage back to Dumbarton tomorrow. The wind has changed, with this rain, so we may be lucky.'

'Gil,' said the mason. Gil turned his head to look at him. 'You will stop calling me maister, no? We use names between us?'

'I should count it a privilege, Pierre.'

They grinned at one another.

'*Ah, mon Dieu,*' said the mason. 'Does that mean another night in that little chamber? On the straw mattress with fleas in, and Sir William snoring?'

They went in by the Gallowgait Port, and clattered up to the castle where they dismounted with some relief in the courtyard. Gil thanked their guide in Scots, now quite certain of his understanding; he certainly understood the coin which made its way into his grubby fist. Whistling cheerfully, he led the horses off towards the stables.

'Now we find Sir William,' said Maistre Pierre, turning towards the chapel. 'You think he is in his chamber?'

'He will be in the buttery,' said Neil Campbell, straightening up from the chapel doorway. 'He is sending me here

240

to wait for the gentlemen. There is things I should be telling them.'

'Can you tell us them over some food?' asked the mason.

Sir William was seated in a corner of the buttery, beyond a noisy game of Tarocco. The gallowglass looked longingly at the cards as he passed with his bowl of pease broth. Gil, with a cursory glance at the play, recognized it as the kind of game in which someone who won twice would be accused of cheating. He abandoned interest, slid along the bench beside Sir William, and said, 'Now what is it you should be telling us?'

The long dark face, intent on the bowl of broth, gave nothing away.

'Go on, Neil,' prompted the priest. 'Tell them what you told me.'

'Is it about Edward Stewart's silver plate,' asked Gil, 'or about how Bess Stewart left Bute, or is it about how Maister Sempill sent you down here to ask about Bess's money again?'

'Or is it about how you and your brother killed Mistress Stewart and then the girl Miller?' said the mason. Neil exclaimed something in Gaelic and leapt up and away from the table, knocking over the bench as he went. The players at the next table paused, watching with interest.

'I never –! She was our lady, she was good to us! We never did nothing to harm her!'

'Sit down,' said Gil. 'Sit down and tell us the truth, man.'

After a moment the gallowglass bent, set the bench up, and sat down slowly. The Tarocco game resumed, with an air of disappointment hanging over the table.

'It is about all those other things. I do not know where to be starting.'

'At the beginning,' said Gil, taking a spoonful of his own broth. 'When Bess Stewart ran off with the harper. What was your part in it? When did she go?'

'She left the house before the curfew.'

241

'So early?' said Maistre Pierre. 'I am sorry – go on.'

'She went out to the place the mac Iains were staying, near the Bishop's house with kin of theirs from Ardnamurchan. A while later my brother went after her with her box and a bundle with all the clothes she was bringing with her. I stayed back, and the old dame sent the maids to bed and went herself, for I said I'd wait up for Mistress Stewart.'

'Why this secrecy?' Gil asked. 'Why could she not just walk out of her own house?'

'She knew fine her good-brother would be after her as soon as he knew. Nor she did not want the old dame to be blamed, for she was fond of her.'

'And then what? Did you bar her chamber door with the kist and climb out by the window?'

'No.' The gallowglass crumbled pieces of his bannock into the broth. 'No, I – my brother went with them as far as the ferry at Ardbeg.'

'Not Rhubodach?' said Sir William.

'Why would they be going so far? It was not a bad evening, it was raining hard but not windy, they went by Ardbeg to Ardyne. They left the burgh quietly after the gates was shut. One man can open the Gallowgait Port, and that was my brother's task, and then to close it again when he came back, after he had seen them on the boat. Then he came back to the house.'

'To Bess Stewart's house?' Gil asked, wishing to be certain. The man nodded. 'It was dark by this time, of course, in November. What about the curfew? The Watch?'

'The curfew was a good thing,' said Neil earnestly. 'It meant there was nobody out and nobody looking out. Not when someone goes quiet past the house in the dark, nobody is looking out, not in Rothesay. As for the Watch, well, there is ways to avoid being seen. Particularly in the rain, when the man on the walkway has his plaid well up and his chin down.'

'I wonder if John of the Isles knows he could take Rothesay in the rain,' said Gil speculatively. 'Well, go on.

What happened in the morning? Which of you let the horse loose?'

'I do not know how Maister Cunningham would be knowing about that,' said the gallowglass, 'but that was an accident, indeed. I was grooming it, and it got free, and took itself home. It was only five doors away, after all. I did not want to run after it in the street, for fear of attracting attention, but Maister James Campbell was in his stable-yard, and when the beast came in he had to know where it had been, and then he came round to Mistress Bess's house demanding to know where she was.'

'Who did he speak to?' asked the mason.

'Me,' said the man reluctantly, 'and my brother. We was in the hall, and he came in furious, and demanded to know where was Mistress Bess. So we said, In her chamber. Then he said, No she is not, and shouted, and called us liars, and said he would see her chamber.'

'Where were the maids?' Gil asked, fascinated.

'In the kitchen screaming, for he frightened them. They were just lassies. So we took him up to her chamber, and he looked in, and dragged a kist to look as if it had been behind the door, and opened the window, and then he took the plate-chest and put some more money in it out of the kist and bade us hide it in the hayloft. Then he called the old dame and shouted at her too. Mind, she shouted back,' he said thoughtfully.

'Ah,' said Gil. 'And what happened to the plate-chest?'

'I have never again set eyes on it,' said Neil with finality.

'Never?'

'He sent the old dame to her kin, and turned the maids away, and got all Mistress Bess's own possessions packed up and out of the house by Terce, before he took the armed band looking for her. I doubt the plate-chest must have gone with them. Me and my brother looked for it, but we never found it.'

'Well!' said Maistre Pierre. 'What a history!'

243

'It's the truth,' said the gallowglass desperately. 'Maisters, it's the truth, and now I am not knowing what to do, for Maister Sempill has sent me down here to hunt for Mistress Bess's money and everything. If I am not finding it Lady Euphemia will not be pleased, and if I am telling him where I saw it last Maister James will not be pleased, and either way Maister Sempill will be very angry.'

'Why not go and take service somewhere else?' the mason suggested. 'Somewhere safer, like England, or Germany.'

'They would be finding me when I came back to Ardnamurchan.'

'You see why I said he must tell you,' said Sir William.

'Indeed,' said Gil. The Tarocco game, which had been getting steadily noisier, suddenly erupted in loud disagreement. Whingers were drawn. Sir William got hastily to his feet and moved in on the altercation with a courage Gil would not have expected.

'Peace, peace, my sons!' he exclaimed, and switched to Gaelic.

'He'll be lucky,' said the mason.

'No, I think he will succeed.' Gil was watching the bearing of the two principal antagonists, who were now shouting at their priest as much as each other. 'Meanwhile, what can we do with Neil here?'

'What should we do?'

'I think he deserves some return for telling us all this. Will you come back with us to Glasgow?' he asked the gallowglass, who looked alarmed.

'I have no word yet to tell Maister Sempill. He will be angry when I am coming back without the money.'

'No, but I must go home, for I have learned a lot. Not from you alone,' he said reassuringly. 'We are going down to the shore now to bargain for a boat to Dumbarton in the morning. Once we get back to Glasgow we will see about taking the person who stabbed Mistress Stewart –'

'And Bridie Miller,' said Maistre Pierre.

'And Bridie Miller.' Gil paused to think about that. Deciding that it could be made to fit, he went on, 'If you come with us, we can shield you from Maister Sempill until all is made clear.'

'But can you tell who has the plate-chest?' persisted Neil, staring in awe.

'It may tell us who had it last,' said Gil.

Outside, the rain had ended, though a brisk southwester was herding white clouds across the sky. Down on the strand, they arranged a passage for three without difficulty, and agreed a time for departure unpleasantly early in the morning. Then they turned inland and strolled up the Kirkgait past the lawyer's house, where Neil Campbell slipped away with a murmured excuse, and inspected the church of St Mary and St Bruoc, half a mile from the castle.

'Not bad,' said the mason critically. 'These tombs are good. Old-fashioned work, but well done. And that arch is well shaped. Sir William tells me he is also chaplain of St Bride's, on the hill yonder. Shall we go and hear Vespers there?'

Gil, having no strong feelings on the question, agreed to this, and they made their way unhurriedly back down into the town and up to St Bride's. This was a diminutive structure, scarcely bigger than St Chattan's, with a box-like nave and smaller chancel, and even the mason felt no pressing need for a longer look after Vespers. Leaving Sir William preparing to say Compline before a probable congregation of two old women, they went out to sit in the wooden porch and look out over the water, watching the cloud-shadows climbing up and over the round hills of the mainland.

'We look north here,' said the mason. 'There is yet another arm of this river. It must have more arms than an octopus. Well, I suppose we have finished our enquiries.'

'I wonder,' said Gil.

The mason turned to look at him. 'You are not sure?'

'I am not sure. I can't put my finger on it but something doesn't fit.'

'Will you confront James Campbell tomorrow?'

'We have uncovered so much that we must.'

'I have wondered how we can make an arrest. We have no authority in the burgh and so cannot employ the serjeant, but we are only two and can hardly overpower a determined man – particularly if his friends also resist.'

'This occurred to me too.' Gil closed the chapel door as Sir William's voice rose in the opening words of the Office. 'Some of the apparitors might act in the matter. I must consult my uncle.'

And he had to find an answer to give his uncle as well, he thought. He had hoped the answer might make itself clear overnight, but this had not happened. Certainly he had not slept well. The straw mattress, as the mason said, had more than straw in it, and Sir William had snored the whole night and Maistre Pierre for a large part of it. And what was the message the hind brought?

'Gil,' said the mason. 'Gilbert.'

Gil looked up.

'I have a proposal to make. I have a marriageable daughter and you are a single man. How would you wish to marry my daughter?'

Gil stared, and felt the wooden bench of the porch shift under him with the whole of St Bride's Hill.

'I . . .' he began, and his voice dried up. He swallowed. Had he really heard that?

'Not, of course, if you do not wish to be married,' said Maistre Pierre. 'But it seems to me it would be a good match.'

'I . . .' began Gil again, and recognized, with glorious clarity, the hind's message, the *next step* he had asked for. 'I can – I can think of nothing I would like more, and almost nothing of which I am less worthy.'

'Oh, well,' said Maistre Pierre. 'That is well, then.' He put out his hand. 'We are agreed in principle, yes?'

'Well,' said Gil blankly. 'Yes. But Alys? How does she feel about marriage? About me? I am six-and-twenty, she is not yet seventeen, she scarcely knows me.'

'Alys,' said her father, 'came home on May Day and told me she had seen the man she wanted to her husband. When I said, Well, *chérie*, but he might be married, she said, No, father, for he is to be a priest. But I think he doesn't want to be a priest, says she, so he might as well marry me.'

'How did she know that?' Gil wondered.

'She knows everything,' said the mason. 'She is not, perhaps, as pretty as her mother, but I think she is wiser. But there you are. Clearly she affects you. And you? Do you affect her? Is there some feeling there?'

'Je désire de voir la douce désirée . . . I wish to see the sweet desirable woman: she has everything, beauty and science,' Gil quoted. 'I have thought of her day and night since I first saw her. But I am not – Pierre, I have no land, no means. How should I keep a wife? What would I bring to a marriage?'

'Yourself,' said the mason, 'warranted sound in wind and limb, your profession, your descent. Your learning and, if you will forgive me, your attitude to Alys's learning. Alys herself will be well dowered. These are matters for your uncle and me to discuss. If we are satisfied, so may you be.'

'And what my uncle will say –'

'He was in favour of the idea when I spoke to him. Are you trying to cry off already?'

'God, the old fox –!'

Gil began to laugh, and took the hand which the mason was still offering.

'You have turned my life round with a few words,' he said, and realized he was trembling. *'My hert, my will, my nature and my mind Was changit clean right in another kind.* I am finding it difficult to grasp such a shift in my fortune.'

'Do not try,' said Maistre Pierre seriously. 'Let it be. You will grow used to it soon enough. Meantime, I think Compline is ended, since there is no singing to slow matters. Sir William will be with us shortly, and we can go back to those appalling mattresses.'

Chapter Twelve

Matt was waiting on the strand at Dumbarton when the *Mary and Bruoc* beached just after Sext. Gil felt astonishingly glad to see him; he was a familiar figure, one of the remnants of his childhood, like Maggie, and it was reassuring to find him here in the midst of change.

'Thrown out of all the ale-houses?' he asked, wading out of the shallows. Matt grunted in reply, and gave the gallowglass the hostile stare of a small man for a tall one. 'And have you found any word of Annie Thomson?'

'Aye,' said Matt.

'Is she safe?' asked the mason, turning from bidding farewell to the master of the *Mary and Bruoc*. Matt nodded, and Gil was conscious of a strong feeling of relief.

'Well?' he said. 'Where does she live? Is she in Dumbarton?'

'St Giles' Wynd. But . . .' said Matt.

'But what?' asked the mason. Gil, more familiar with the man's taciturn nature, simply waited.

'Toothache,' said Matt finally.

'The poor lassie,' said Neil with ready sympathy.

'Bad?' asked Gil. Matt nodded. 'Bad enough to prevent us questioning her?'

Matt shrugged, and turned away to walk along the shore. Gil followed him, trying to concentrate his mind on what he must say to the girl.

He felt quite different this morning. He had slept, badly, two nights in these clothes, and certainly had acquired fleas from the infamous straw mattress, and yet his body felt cleaner than the wind which blew through his hair. His feet in the soggy boots were as light as the wood smoke spiralling up along the shore where someone was heating a tar-kettle. And beach and burgh, rock and hills, the smells of seaweed and tar, seemed as new and unfamiliar as if he had cast up on the shores of Tartary or Prester John's country. He could not gather his thoughts at all, although that might be down to lack of sleep, or to the dream, which would not leave him.

He had lain most of the night in Sir William's loft chamber, listening to his two companions snoring, and to the occasional rattle of rain on the slates of the chapel above his head, imagining strange and glorious ways in which he could earn land and money to support a wife. To support Alys. None of them, he had to admit, was practicable, and he had eventually fallen asleep, and dreamed that he was sailing a small boat, just big enough for one, across billows of grey ribbed silk. A rope in his hand led to a sail bluer than the sky. The boat sped on, until he came to a high rock rising out of the folds of silk. Seated on its crest, Euphemia was combing a lock of her long yellow hair and singing. At her side was an armed man, entangled in another yellow lock; as the boat slid past he raised a mailed fist in salute, or in farewell, and Gil saw without surprise that it was his brother Hugh. He looked back, but the boat sailed on, followed by the singing. The annoying thing was that he knew the tune, and he had woken trying to remember the words.

'Do you know this one?' he said to Maistre Pierre, and whistled a few notes. The mason joined in, nodding.

'We sang it. The other night at my house, you remember? A new song Alys had from somewhere. *D'amour je suis désheritée . . .*'

'I remember. *I am dispossessed by love,*' Gil quoted, '*and do not know who to appeal to. Alas, I have lost my love, I am alone, he has left me . . . to run after an affected woman who slanders me without ceasing. Alas, I am forgotten, wherefore I am delivered to death.*'

'What has brought that into your head?' asked Maistre Pierre, at his most quizzical. 'I hope it has no bearing on the present?'

'I don't know. Oh, none upon Alys or the – the matter you broached last night. Merely, I dreamed of Euphemia Campbell singing that.'

'Hardly likely,' said the mason.

'She is singing like a ghillie-Bride – an oyster-catcher,' said Neil, who had apparently taken Gil for his lord and protector. 'High and thin and all on one note.'

'It keeps coming back to my mind. Matt! Where are we going?'

'St Giles' Wynd,' said Matt, jerking a thumb towards the vennel that led inland.

They could hear the screaming as they picked their way along the busy High Street, and when they turned in at the entry under the figure of St Giles the sounds echoed hollowly in the vault. A little knot of neighbours was gathered along the wynd outside the house, nodding and exclaiming, and as Matt pushed his way through someone looked round saying hopefully, 'Here's the tooth-drawer!'

'That's no the tooth-drawer,' said someone else. 'He's away across the river to St Mahew's to see to a horse, he'll no be back before Vespers. Oh, my, will you listen to that, the poor lassie.'

'What is it?' asked the mason. 'What is wrong?'

'A lassie with a rotten tooth,' said someone else. Several voices explained how the girl's mouth was swelled the size of a football and she couldny eat or speak.

'And her minnie waited till this morn to send for the tooth-drawer, and found him out of the town.'

'Why'd she wait so long?'

'The lassie wouldny have it. Aye, aye, she's regretting it now.'

Gil, listening to the screams, felt it unlikely that the sufferer had thought for anything but her pain.

251

'Is it Annie Thomson?' he asked.

'It is that,' said someone. 'Here, widow Thomson, here's a man asking for Annie.'

'If you're no the tooth-drawer I don't want you,' said the widow Thomson, appearing in her doorway. She was a big-framed, bulky woman, with a strong resemblance to the girl they had seen in Glasgow. 'I don't know, there's been as many folk asking for her since she came home, and the worse she gets the more folk come asking.'

'Who else has been looking for her?' Gil asked quickly.

'Him yonder, for a start,' said the widow, pointing at Matt, who ducked hastily behind the mason. 'And a black-avised fellow in a green velvet hat came round the door yesterday stinking of musk, seemed to feel all he had to do was show enough coin and she'd tell him some story or other.' She flinched as another scream tore at their ears. 'I ask you, maisters, how could she speak to anyone?' She wiped her eyes with the end of her kerchief. 'What she needs is that tooth drawn, and then she can get some rest.'

'Then maybe we can all get some rest,' said a voice from the back of the crowd. 'Two days this has been going on.'

'I wish we could do something,' said Gil helplessly.

'I could,' said Matt suddenly.

Gil stared at him. 'Can you draw teeth, Matt?'

'You can draw teeth?' asked the widow. 'Oh, maister, if you could help my lassie!'

'He will need someone to hold her down,' said the mason in practical tones.

'Aye.' Matt nodded at Gil. 'You can help,' he said firmly. At the sound of the word, the crowd around them began to break up like a dandelion-clock, but Matt put out a hand and seized the sleeve of a bowlegged man in a carpenter's apron. 'Pinchers,' he said, and held out his other hand.

*   *   *

The next half-hour or so was among the most unpleasant Gil had ever spent. Inside, the house was small and dark and smelled of peat smoke, rancid bacon and illness. Matt took one look, scuffed at the earth floor, shook his head and said, 'Out in the street.' He looked about, past the oblivious girl writhing and sobbing in the bed. 'Chair?'

'Maister MacMillan's got a fine chair he'd maybe lend us,' said the widow. She hurried off to see to this. Matt stepped into the street and looked at the crowd, which was gathering again.

'Rope,' he said. 'Clean clouts.'

People ran to and fro, and these were produced. The chair was set on a level patch in front of the house door, and Annie was carried out, struggling and screaming, and tied down. It took four of them to restrain her, the mason and Neil Campbell as well as Gil and Matt himself, with a great deal of advice from the onlookers, and it was clear that even a new tarred rope was not going to keep her still. Her face was indeed badly swollen, and she was conscious enough of her surroundings to offer considerable resistance when Matt tried to look at the tooth.

'It's one of the big ones,' said her mother anxiously. 'One of the wee big ones, not the great big ones, if you take my meaning, maister. I was packing it with pigeons' dung pounded with an onion, but it never did any good.'

'Oh, no, no!' said the mason, hanging on to a flailing wrist. 'The pigeon being a bird of Venus, its dung generates heat, excellent to draw a gumboil but not in this instance –'

'Ah!' said Matt, peering into the swollen tissue. 'There!' He let the girl's mouth close and succeeded, with a few gestures, in placing his helpers in the most useful manner, despite complaints from the crowd that the mason's broad back was obstructing someone's view. Pliers in one hand, he got behind the screaming, squirming girl, issued a word of command, and grabbed her head in an arm-lock, forcing her jaw open with his left thumb precisely as Gil had seen him do to a horse.

There were a few minutes of hectic action. There were screams, and scuffling and sobbing, and then some really unpleasant noises. Gil, intent on keeping Annie's shoulders as still as possible, was aware of the feet of the onlookers closing in. Then suddenly, all the noise ceased and the girl stopped struggling. Gil, wondering if he had gone deaf, let go and straightened up.

Matt was holding up a bloody morsel in his pliers. The girl was lying alarmingly still and was quite white where she was not already bloodstained, but as her mother hurried forward with a cry of, 'Annie! Oh, my lassie!' her eyelashes fluttered. The crowd was commenting freely and loudly on the success of the operation.

'Clouts,' said Matt, handing the pliers to Gil, who took them reluctantly. With a little difficulty Annie was persuaded to open her mouth, and Matt mopped gently at the mess, pausing to point out the amount of pus on the cloth.

'Oh, maister, how can I thank you!' said the widow, patting her daughter's hand. 'What's your fee?'

Matt shrugged.

'I hope there's no trouble with the burgh tooth-drawer,' said Gil, beginning to untie the knots in the rope.

'Well, if he'd been here when he was wanted,' said someone behind him.

The carpenter reclaimed his pliers and went out into the High Street, and the rest of the crowd, the entertainment over, began to drift after him. Annie was helped back into her house, her mother still exclaiming about a fee, and Matt delivered some terse advice which Gil expanded for him.

'Make well-water hot, mistress, and put salt in it, and have her hold it in her mouth and spit it out – don't swallow it – for the space of three Aves, three times a day till it stops bleeding. And feed her on broth for a day or two.'

'What will that do?' the widow asked suspiciously.

'The salt will draw out the excess humours,' said the

mason quickly over Gil's shoulder, 'which is what has been causing the swelling.'

'Should she no be bled?'

'The tooth-drawer might want to bleed her,' said Gil diplomatically. He handed the coiled rope back to its owner at the door, and turned back to the widow where she was heaping blankets on the shivering girl. 'Mistress, did you tell me someone was asking for Annie yesterday?'

'Aye, I did.'

'Did you get his name? Or what he wanted to ask her?'

'I did not. He'd some story about a boy and a bang on the head, but I'd more to worry about than a Campbell in a green hat. There, then, my lassie, lie there and get warm. It's over now, poor lass.'

'He was a Campbell, was he?'

She paused in tucking the blankets at Annie's feet.

'Oh, he was a Campbell all right. You'd only to look at him.'

Sitting in a nearby ale-house, they stared at one another.

'Poor lassie,' said Neil again.

'Thank you, maisters,' said Matt.

'And we still have not questioned the girl,' said Maistre Pierre. 'I would say it will be a day or two before she is fit to talk. Do we wait here for that?'

'No need, I think,' said Gil. 'I have learned enough from her mother.'

'What, that James Campbell was here asking for her? How does that help?'

'We know he has an interest in what she heard or saw,' Gil pointed out.

'But we knew that already.'

'And now we know that he does not yet know what she saw.'

'Ye-es.' The mason eyed Gil, scowling.

'Are ye for ordering, maisters?' demanded the girl at Matt's elbow.

'Yes, indeed,' said Gil. 'There is something I want to do in Dumbarton, but if we get a bite here, we can be in Glasgow for a late dinner. What can you offer us, lass?'

David Cunningham came down to the door to meet them, spectacles in hand.

'Well, well,' he said as Gil dismounted. 'Here's a surprise. I'd not have looked for you before Vespers. Welcome back, Gilbert. Welcome back, maister. You'll eat with us? Maggie has something ready, I dare say. Aye, Matt.'

Matt, gathering up reins, merely grunted. The gallowglass, silent, was keeping his horse between himself and the gateway of the Sempill house.

'I thank you, maister, but no,' said Maistre Pierre. 'I am anxious to get home to my daughter. After all, she will soon be leaving me,' he added.

'A drink of ale, to wash the dust from your throat, then?' suggested the Official, his thin smile crossing his face in answer to the mason's significant grin. 'Maggie! And shall we see you later today, then? John Sempill has been sending twice a day to ask when you'll be back. I think it would suit him to get this matter sorted with the bairn. Tam can go down to tell the harper, if we can arrange a tryst.'

Maggie was already bustling forward out of the kitchen gate, a tray in her hands. Gil, taking a pull at his beaker, realized with surprise that it contained the good ale, the stuff she rarely brewed. Is this for me, he wondered, or for the mason who will be visiting frequently this week, no doubt.

'For you, of course,' said his uncle, when the mason had clattered away and they went into the house. 'I happened to mention the mason's approach, and she was greatly moved. She is gey fond of you, Gilbert. I hope your bride can brew as well.'

'I'm told she can bake and brew with the best,' said Gil.

'And had you good hunting in Rothesay?'

'I did, but it's good to be back. William Dalrymple sends his salutations. Sir, if John Sempill is to be here before Vespers I must talk to you, but before that I must shift my clothes and wash off the dust. Will you excuse me?'

'Come to my chamber once you are clean. You are aware, I take it, that you have lost your hat?'

'Have I? It must have fallen off. Likely when Matt drew the lassie's tooth.'

His uncle paused in the door to the stairs, raising his eyebrows.

'You have clearly a lot to tell me,' he said.

Maggie looked up as Gil entered the kitchen.

'You might have warned me you were bringing a Campbell back with you,' she said. The Campbell, seated in a corner, ducked his head in embarrassment and took a bite of bannock and cheese. 'And so you're to be wed, are you, Maister Gil?'

'So it seems,' said Gil. 'Are you pleased?'

'Oh, aye. It'll get you out from under my feet.' She thumped at the dough under her hands. 'And you'll no be so far away, you'll can visit your uncle, I've no doubt. Is she bonnie? I've seen her at the market, but no close to.'

'I think so,' said Gil.

'That's what matters. And I've heard she's a rare house-wife, which is more to the point.'

'She runs her father's household, which is a large one, and does it well, from all I've seen. Maggie, I must wash. Can you spare William to fetch more water?'

'I can,' she said doubtfully, looking at the kitchen-boy, who was hunkered down by the window staring vacantly at the gallowglass. 'Tam's faster, but he's still down at the harper's. It takes William a long time, and I'll need him soon, to turn the spit for tomorrow's dinner.'

'I can be turning the spit,' offered Neil Campbell.

'There's water hot,' said Maggie, accepting this. 'Get you in the scullery, Maister Gil, and shift that beard, in case the lassie comes up the hill with her father before Vespers. A three days growth is no way to commend yourself to a lass before you're handfasted. You can fling that sark out here when you're done and I'll put it to soak. And then I'll have a dish of eggs ready for you.'

To be fed, washed, shaved, combed and clad in clean linen simply accentuated the strange feeling of lightness Gil still felt. Kissing Maggie, who told him sharply to save that for his own lass, and clapping the startled gallowglass on the shoulder where he sat turning the spit, he sprang up the stairs to the hall and checked by his uncle's oratory. On impulse he slipped behind the curtain, remembering the last time he had knelt here. Just as on that occasion, he found the words would not come, but this time only a boundless gratitude, which he offered up until he felt it turn to gold as if in sunlight and float away from him.

He knelt for a while longer, feeling the unseeable sunlight almost tangible behind his closed eyelids. When it faded he rose, signing himself, and went on up, crossing the solar to his uncle's chamber.

'Ah, Gilbert,' said his uncle. 'What is this about a lassie with toothache?'

'The lass we were to find in Dumbarton,' Gil answered. 'The same lass we missed in the Gorbals. When we got to her house today we found her screaming with a rotten tooth, and Matt drew it for her. Did you know Matt could draw teeth, sir?'

'I did not. Likely it's a thing he learned away at the wars in Germany. He has already asked for a day off tomorrow to go to Dumbarton.'

'I suppose he wants to see how she does.'

'No doubt. And you, Gilbert? How do you do? This proposition of Maister Mason's likes you, does it?'

'I can think of nothing I would like better,' said Gil, as he had to the mason, 'and almost nothing of which I am less worthy.'

'Well, well.' His uncle looked down at his book, unseeing, for a moment. 'I had hoped to deacon for your first Mass, Gilbert, but do you know I find I would rather say a wedding Mass for you and christen your first bairn.' Gil murmured something. 'There are too few of your father's name left. Aye, I think you will do better out in the world, providing we can find you something to live on.'

'That is what worries me,' said Gil. 'However well Pierre dowers the lass, I cannot live on her money. I'm a Cunningham, after all.'

His uncle shot him a sharp glance, and nodded.

'You are a Cunningham,' he agreed. 'The lands out by Lanark are lost to us, I think, but there is property here in the burgh that does near as well, I can let you have in conjunct fee. The rents are all in coin, of course. As for income, I have one or two ideas. Let me ask about, Gilbert.'

'May I know what they are?' Gil asked politely. 'You could say they concern me, sir.'

He got another sharp glance, and the corner of David Cunningham's mouth quirked.

'You could say so. Let me see. It is possible that Robert Blacader will consent to your employment here in the Consistory as we had planned, though you are in minor Orders only. You could hang out a sign and practise as a notary in the burgh, though I cannot see you growing rich at that.'

'Nor I,' agreed Gil, thinking of Alexander Stewart's house with the tumbling children by the peat fire.

'Since as Maister Mason's son-in-law you will get your burgess ticket almost as a wedding-gift, you might find a post as one of the burgh procurators.'

'What, and speak for poor devils taken up for theft?'

'Or speak on the burgh's behalf in the same case,' his

uncle concurred. 'I have friends, and some influence, Gilbert. Let me continue asking about.'

'I should be grateful, sir. I am grateful,' said Gil, still aware of the unseen sunlight, 'for everything you have done for me these past years.'

'Well, well,' said his uncle again. 'You're a good boy, Gilbert. Your father would have been proud of you.' He closed his book, and opened it again at random. 'Now, tell me about your hunting in Rothesay. What did you raise? Sit down, for mercy's sake, and tell me about it.'

Gil, hooking a stool towards him with his foot, sat down and gave a concise account of the interviews with the lawyer, Mariota Stewart and the gallowglass. His uncle heard him attentively, asking the occasional question.

'And the lassie in Dumbarton,' he said at the end. 'What did you learn from her?'

'I had no speech of her,' Gil said, 'but her mother reports that James Campbell of Glenstriven came looking for a word with her yesterday, with no success.'

'Did he so?'

Uncle and nephew looked at one another consideringly.

'John Sempill will be here shortly,' said Canon Cunningham after a moment. 'No way of knowing, of course, how many of his household will come with him.'

'No,' agreed Gil. 'I wonder, sir, might we borrow a couple of the apparitors from the Consistory?'

'They will have gone home by now,' said his uncle, glancing at the window. 'No, we must make do with Tam, I think. And perhaps Maister Mason will bring one of his fellows with him. I wonder will he bring the lassie, hm?'

'I hope he may,' said Gil, feeling his face stretch into a fatuous grin. The image of Alys rose before him, in her plain blue gown with her hair down her back. He dragged his mind back to the point at issue. 'There will be the harper's sister, of course. I'd back her against an army.'

'Ah, yes, the harper and his sister. What are we to agree for the bairn, who is the main point on the agenda?'

'I have no idea what my principal will ask for.'

'You must get a word with him as soon as he arrives.' The Official rose, and Gil stood politely. 'I wish to be sure the bairn will be reared fittingly, and his property decently overseen. If that is in jeopardy I will say so.'

'Understood, sir.' Gil followed his uncle from the room and down the stairs. 'Do we meet here in the hall?'

'Considering the numbers, I think we must.'

Shouting down the kitchen stair for Tam, Gil began to move benches. Shortly, despite his uncle's directions and Tam's inclination to ask about Alys rather than lift furniture, he had an impromptu court-room arranged, with the great chair behind a carpeted table, and the two benches set on either side. He was hunting through the house for more stools when he heard a knocking at the door, and Maggie's heavy feet descending to answer it.

Gil contrived to reach the hall with his latest find just as the mason stepped in from the stair, followed by a complete stranger in a French hood and a black brocade gown, wearing a string of pearls which gleamed in the light from the windows.

Gil's jaw dropped, and the mason advanced on the Official and spoke.

'Good evening to you, Maister Cunningham. May I present to you my daughter Alys?'

When she moved forward, of course it was Alys. Straight-backed and elegant, she curtsied to Uncle David. If his feet were rooted to the floor just inside the hall door, how was it that by the time she straightened her knee and raised her head, he was at her elbow?

'Well, well,' said his uncle. 'Here's as bonnie a lass as there's been in this house since it was built, I think.'

The old man took Alys's hands, embraced her, kissed her, as was an older relative's right. Could this be jealousy, Gil wondered, barely aware of the nursemaid jiggling the baby at the mason's back.

'And here's my nephew,' said Uncle David.

She turned, and their eyes met. Her hand was in his.

'Take her in the garden,' said his uncle. 'You have a quarter-hour.'

In the centre of the garden, in full view of the hall windows, the green mound was dry enough to sit on, but Gil took off his gown and spread it anyway, then handed Alys to the seat. Her silk brocade rustled as she sat down, and gave off a scent of cedarwood. He kept hold of her hand, and stood looking down at her. She looked up, a little shy, her face framed by the black velvet folds of the French hood.

'You truly wish to marry me?' Gil said at length. She looked down, blushing slightly, then up again to meet his eyes.

'Truly,' she said with that directness he admired so much. 'And you? You truly wish to be married? Not to be a priest?'

'You know the answer.'

The apologetic smile flashed.

'I would still like to hear it.'

'I wish to marry you,' he said earnestly, 'more than anything else I have ever had the opportunity to do. I have never felt like this about anybody before. I think I must have loved you from the moment you spoke to me on that stair by the Tolbooth.'

'I too,' she said. 'From that moment.'

'Alys,' he said. He sat down, and somehow she was in his arms.

'Gilbert.'

Her mouth, innocent and eager, tasted of honey under his.

When the mason interrupted them he swore they had had half an hour.

'And Sempill is here, with his entire household, I believe,' he said cheerfully, 'becoming more thunderous by the breath, and the harper is sitting like King David on a *trumeau* ignoring everything while his sister mutters spells at his side.'

'A merry meeting,' Gil said. Alys was putting her hair back over her shoulders, so that it hung down her back below the velvet fall of her hood. He dragged his eyes from the sight, and said more attentively, 'Sempill's entire household, you say? Who is there?'

'Sempill and his cousin, Campbell and his sister, the other gallowglass, the companion – why she has come I know not, unless as some sort of witness –'

'Right.' Gil drew Alys to her feet. 'Go with your father, sweetheart. I must get a word with Maggie first, then I will come up.'

Her hand lingered in his, and he squeezed it before he let go, drawing a quick half smile in answer, but all she said was, 'Is my hood still straight?'

'Square and level,' her father assured her. She took his arm and moved towards the house, her black silk skirts caught up in her other hand. Gil turned towards the archway to the kitchen-yard, where the mason's man Luke was drinking ale with the Official's Tam.

Maggie's face fell when he entered the kitchen alone.

'And am I no to get a sight of your bride?' she demanded.

'And she's well worth seeing. You'll have the care of her later this evening, Maggie,' Gil promised, 'for I think things may get a little fractious upstairs. For now, I have an errand for you. And you, Neil, I want you to stay here handy until I call you.'

The gallowglass, seated by the fire with a leather beaker of the good ale, merely grinned, but Maggie scowled and objected, 'I've to take wine up for the company.'

'I will do that. You get over the road and get Marriott Kennedy to help you search for that cross you never found.'

Her gaze sharpened on his face.

'Uhuh,' she said, nodding slowly. 'And if we find it?'

'Bring it to me, quiet-like.'

'I'll do it,' she said, and went to the outside door where her plaid hung on a nail.

'Maggie, you're a wonderful woman.'

Her face softened.

'You're a bad laddie,' she said, and stumped out of the house.

Gil reached the hall with the great jug of claret wine and plate of jumbles just as John Sempill leapt to his feet snarling, 'If he's no to compear we'll just have to manage without him. Oh, there you are! Where the devil have you been? Vespers must be near over by now.'

'I was concerned with another matter,' said Gil, setting wine and cakes down on the carpet on his uncle's table. 'Have some wine and come over to the window and instruct me. Maggie has gone out, sir. Will you pour, or shall I fetch Tam up?'

Sempill, a cup of good wine in his hand, seemed reluctant to come to the point. Gil simply stood, watching him, while he muttered half-sentences. At length he came out with, 'Oh, to the devil with it! If he'll let me name the bairn mine –'

'By "he" you mean the harper?'

'Who else, gomerel? If he'll let me name it mine, without disputing it, then I'll settle Bess's own lands on the brat immediately, and treat it as my sole heir unless I get another later.'

'That seems a fair offer,' said Gil. 'Who gets the rents? What about your conjunct fee?'

'That's mine, for what good it does me,' said Sempill quickly. 'I suppose the bairn or its tutor gets the profit from the land, which willny keep a flea, I can tell you, so that's between the harper and the nourice.'

264

'You do not contemplate rearing the child yourself,' said Gil expressionlessly.

'I do not. You think I want another man's get round my feet?'

Gil looked across the room at the assembled company. On one bench was Ealasaidh, dandling the swaddled baby, while Alys waved the coral for the small hands to grasp at and the harper and the mason sat on either side like heraldic supporters. As he looked, the mason broke out in a volley of sneezes. On the other bench, in a row, one Sempill and two Campbells drank the Official's wine in a miasma of conflicting perfumes and discussed, apparently, the marriage of a cousin of Philip Sempill's wife. Euphemia cast occasional covert glances at the rope of pearls which glimmered against Alys's black Lyons brocade. In the background, Nancy on one side, Neil's brother Euan and the stout Mistress Murray on the other, waited in silence. Canon Cunningham was sitting in his great chair, watching the infant, who was now grabbing at the fall of Alys's hood.

'Do you wish to stipulate who is to rear the child?' Gil asked.

'I'll let the harper decide that,' said John Sempill generously. 'He'll likely be more confident leaving it with someone else. Of course if it's someone he chooses, he can settle the bills,' he added.

'That's clear enough.' Gil drank off the rest of his wine and gestured towards the makeshift court. 'Is there anything else you wish to tell me? Shall we proceed?'

Sempill nodded, and walked heavily over to sit beside his mistress. She had decided to grace the occasion in tawny satin faced with citron-coloured velvet, which clashed with Sempill's cherry doublet and gown and turned her brother's green velvet sour. A large jewel of topazes and pearls dangled from a rope chain on her bosom, and more pearls edged her French hood. Finding Gil watching her, she favoured him with a brilliant smile, showing her little white teeth, and tucked her arm

265

possessively through Sempill's. Gil was reminded sharply of his dream. Well, Hughie is certainly gone now, he thought.

Gil took up position at the end of the bench, beside his client, and nodded to his uncle. He should, he realized, have been wearing a gown. The green cloth gown of a forespeaker, buttoned to the neck like his grandfather's houppelande, would have been favourite, but failing that his decent black one, which he must have left in the garden, would have lent dignity. Too late now, he thought, hitching his thumbs in the armholes of his doublet. Perhaps I can imagine one. Or full armour, in which to slay dragons.

'Friends,' said David Cunningham, rapping on the table with his wine-cup. 'We are met to consider a proposal made by John Sempill of Muirend, concerning a bairn born to his lawful wife when she had been living with another man, namely Angus McIan of Ardnamurchan, a harper –' Ealasaidh stirred and muttered something. 'Who speaks for John Sempill?'

'I speak for John Sempill.' Gil bowed.

'And who speaks for Angus McIan?'

'I am Aenghus mac Iain. I speak for mine own self.' The harper rose, clasping his small clarsach.

'And I speak on behalf of the bairn. Is this the child? What is his name?'

Ealasaidh, rising, said clearly, 'This is the boy that was born to Bess Stewart two days before Michaelmas last. His name is Iain, that is John in the Scots tongue. Yonder is his nursemaid, who will confirm what I say.'

Nancy, scarlet-faced, muttered something which might have been confirmation.

'Very well,' said David Cunningham, 'let us begin. What is John Sempill's proposal for this bairn?'

Chapter Thirteen

'John Sempill of Muirend proposes,' said Gil, from where he stood by Sempill's side, 'to recognize the bairn as his heir. If he does so, he will settle its mother's property on it –' At his elbow, John Sempill glared defiantly and point-lessly at the harper. Beyond him, Euphemia suddenly turned to look at her brother, who did not look at her. '– so that it may be supported by the income deriving. The bairn will be fostered with someone agreeable to Angus McIan, and the said Angus will be responsible for any extra dis-bursements not covered by the income.'

'Ah!' said Ealasaidh. The harper made a hushing move-ment with the hand nearest her.

'It is a good proposal,' he said. 'It is a fair proposal.' Euphemia stirred again, and her brother's elbow moved sharply. 'There is things I would wish to have made clear. I may choose the fostering, but who chooses the tutor? Is it the same person? Does Maister Sempill wish to order the boy's education, or shall we give that to his tutor? And how if Maister Sempill changes his mind, one way or the other? Is the boy to be wrenched from a familiar foster-home to be reared by the man who cut off his mother's ear?' Euphemia giggled, and her brother's elbow jerked again. 'Is his foster-father to find himself unable to feed a growing child because the income has been diverted?'

The old boy can talk, thought Gil. Euphemia and her brother were glaring at one another.

'I speak for the bairn,' said David Cunningham. 'I stip-ulate that once the fosterage is agreed, John Sempill and

Angus McIan both swear to abide by the agreement. Likewise once a tutor is agreed both swear to abide by that agreement. Both these oaths to be properly notarized and recorded. And when the property is transferred it is entered into the title that John Sempill renounces any claim to it.'

Boxed in, thought Gil. He bent to say quietly to his client, 'Well? Do we agree?'

'Aye, we agree,' snarled Sempill. 'I need this settled.'

'We agree,' said Gil.

'I am agreed also,' said the harper. Euphemia was now sitting rigidly erect, staring over Ealasaidh's head. The lines between her insignificant nose and pretty mouth were suddenly quite noticeable.

'Then let us consider,' continued Canon Cunningham, 'where the bairn is to be fostered. There is an offer from Maister Peter Mason, master builder of this burgh, to foster him in his household.'

'He's offered?' said John Sempill suspiciously. 'Why? Why would he do that?'

'I have taken a liking to the boy,' said Maistre Pierre, his accent very marked. 'Regard it as an act of charity, if you will.'

Alys smiled at her father. Sempill breathed hard down his nose, and the Official, looking from one side to the other of his makeshift court, said, 'What do you say to this offer, Maister McIan?'

'It is a generous offer,' said the harper, 'for that I know well it was made before the matter of the boy's income was mentioned.' At Gil's side John Sempill cursed under his breath. 'I am agreeable. I will abide by this arrangement.'

'And I,' said Sempill harshly.

'And I propose,' said the harper, before David Cunningham could speak again, 'that Maister Gilbert Cunningham be named the boy's tutor, to stand *in loco parentis* until he be fourteen years old and to see after his fostering and rearing and his schooling and learning.'

There was a pause, in which the baby made a remark. Ealasaidh answered him in soft Gaelic.

Well, thought Gil. And where did McIan learn Latin tags?

'I hardly think I am the best –' he began.

'On the contrary,' said the harper. 'You are a man of learning, well connected in this diocese, well able to judge if the boy is being managed as he ought. I am greatly in favour of it.'

'Yes,' said John Sempill happily. 'I agree.'

Gil, detecting the note of revenge, kept his face blank.

'Then we are past the first hurdle,' said the Official, 'for both these suggestions are agreeable to me as the bairn's adviser. The next point to consider is the property which John Sempill will settle on the bairn, renouncing any claims which might proceed from his marriage to the bairn's mother.'

'Aye,' said John Sempill sourly. 'Only I don't have the papers for it, since Bess took them when she left my house. Not that it'll do ye much good,' he added.

'It was not your house,' said Ealasaidh, not quite under her breath. The mason sneezed.

'I have seen the papers she had,' said Gil. He produced the inventory and tilted Alys's neat writing to the daylight. 'There is a house in Rothesay and two farms at Ettrick. The house I believe is let to a kinsman of the Provost of Rothesay's wife, who is not keeping it in repair. The farms are also let. The rent on the house is five merks, a hen and a creel of peats yearly, the rent on the farms is five merks and a mart cow, with a half-merk maill yearly. Each,' he added.

'Eh?' said John Sempill. 'Each? Do you mean Bess was getting that much rent all this time?'

'Surely not,' said Euphemia in her high, pretty voice. 'That would be fifteen merks a year, let alone the – ow!'

Her brother put both hands on his knees and remained silent. Philip Sempill said, 'You never had that amount from the land in Bute, John!'

'No, I never,' agreed John Sempill flatly.

'Whose responsibility is it to collect the rents?' asked the Official.

'Sempill's,' said James Campbell.

'They go to James,' said Sempill in the same moment. Their challenging stares met. 'Except the rents that went to Bess, to buy harp keys with,' he added in a suggestive snarl.

Euphemia giggled again. Her brother's green velvet elbow moved sharply, and she showed her teeth at him. The harper sat impassive.

'Is it agreeable to Bess Stewart's kin,' asked the Official, 'that these properties pass to her bairn, with arrangements for the rent to be paid directly to his foster-parent?'

'Her kin have nothing –' began Sempill.

'It is not,' said James Campbell of Glenstriven, as if he had been waiting for this. 'I am married to her sister Mariota Stewart, and I submit that if John Sempill alienates these properties they should be offered first to my wife.'

'It is none of your –'

'If Bess had died before she disgraced herself –'

'Which, St Catherine be my witness, I wish she had!' exclaimed Euphemia piously.

'You keep out of this,' said her brother. 'If she'd died before she went for a harper's whore, Mariota would have got her Stewart properties.'

'I'd have seen you in court first!'

'I'd have taken you there with pleasure.'

'Bess never had no rent off her lands in Bute,' said Ealasaidh loudly. Both men turned to look at her. The mason sneezed again.

'What are you saying, woman?' demanded Sempill.

'Och, what does a singing tramp know,' began James Campbell.

'You miscall my sister, do you, *Mhic Chaileann*?' said the harper quietly.

'I am saying Bess never had any money off Bute but what she brought away with her,' said Ealasaidh doggedly.

'And that was what little she had by in the house. She was saying, if we had waited till St Martin's tide she would have had more to bring that was her own rents.'

'Hold up here,' said Sempill. 'Are ye saying she never brought anything but the coin that was in the house? What about the plate-chest? There was plenty in that.'

'Plate-chest?' said Ealasaidh. There was no mistaking the blank surprise in her voice. 'How would she be taking a plate-chest off Bute, and me not noticing?'

'Well, she never left it behind,' said Sempill. His pale eyes turned to Campbell. 'At least, so I was tellt. Well, good-brother?'

Gil stepped back quietly from the shouting.

'Euan,' he said to the waiting gallowglass. The man, intent on the argument, jumped and looked up at him. 'Go down yon stair to the kitchen and fetch your brother up to me.'

By the time Neil sidled into the hall, James Campbell had reached the point of accusing Ealasaidh directly.

'And what price did you get for it, you and her? Plenty of silversmiths in Edinburgh would ask no questions, though it had the crest on it.'

Ealasaidh was on her feet, spitting Gaelic. Beside her, Alys was hugging the baby, who was becoming alarmed by the noise. The harper cut across his sister with a single calm sentence which made all the Gaelic-speakers in the room flinch.

'I must ask you to speak Scots in this court,' said the Official, apparently forgetting where he was for the moment.

'I ask the court's pardon.' The harper rose and bowed in the direction of Canon Cunningham's table, his dark-browed face very solemn. 'I have said, I am a harper, and I can determine the truth of the matter.' It appeared to be a threat.

'There is one here,' said Gil, cutting in smoothly, 'who can tell us more towards the facts.'

271

'Euan Campbell?' said his master. 'What does he know?'

'They were asleep when she left,' said Campbell of Glenstriven. 'She got out of a window, no doubt with help from this ill-conditioned woman –'

The harper said something, quietly, to his sister. She bowed her head and restrained herself. Gil said, 'I have seen this window.' James Campbell turned to look at him, his jaw dropping. 'It is this size,' Gil continued, measuring the air with his hands. 'I have not seen the plate-chest –'

'It was this big!' Sempill demonstrated. The dimensions appeared quite similar.

'But we are asked to believe that this woman climbed out twenty feet above the ground, from a window scarcely big enough to accommodate a laddie, let alone a grown woman fully clothed, taking with her a box at least the size of the window and containing near thirty pounds of plate, as well as coin and jewels.'

'Forty pounds of plate at least!' Sempill corrected.

'I have the inventory,' Gil said, looking at another of the parchments in his hand. 'Twenty-seven pounds, ten and a half ounces. There were never any marks of a ladder found, so she either jumped or climbed down a rope with this box –'

'She must have lowered it first to whoever helped her,' said James Campbell desperately.

'And landed in the spreading white rose-bush which grows under that window.' Euphemia giggled, and was pinched savagely by her brother again. 'Shall we hear a different version? Not Euan Campbell but Neil can tell us more about that night.'

He beckoned the gallowglass forward, and got him launched with difficulty on the account he had given on Sunday evening. While the halting explanation went on he looked round the faces. On this bench, John Sempill in steadily rising fury, Euphemia critical as if she was listening to an old tale badly told, her brother in gathering alarm, Philip Sempill with the expression of a man waiting

272

for a cannon to go off. On the other, the mason absorbed, Alys watching the baby (she looked up, and their eyes met for a moment), Ealasaidh intent, her face softening as she remembered the escape, and her brother beside her, clasping the harp, still as King David on a church doorway. In the great chair, his uncle was watching the gallowglass.

'And I never laid eyes on it again,' the man finished.

'Lies – all lies!' said James Campbell, a second before Sempill said,

'Right, James. Where is it?'

David Cunningham beckoned to Gil, and when he approached asked quietly, 'What is the significance of the plate-chest?'

'It is certainly missing,' said Gil. 'The contents belonged to her first husband's family, and were to revert to them, so someone owes them the value of twenty-seven pounds of silver.'

'And ten and a half ounces,' the Official added, watching the growing argument before him. At the point where Philip Sempill leapt up to restrain his cousin, Canon Cunningham banged sharply on the table with his wine-cup. Even muffled by the table-carpet the sound was enough to distract the combatants.

'I am not certain,' he said in his dry voice, 'that this discussion is relevant to the point at issue, which is I believe to establish what lands belonged to Elizabeth Stewart, deceased, in the Island of Bute, and which are now to be assigned to her son.'

'May it please the court,' said Gil, following where his uncle led, 'I think it is relevant, since if the money and other rents did not reach John Sempill and did not reach Bess Stewart they must still be owing to someone, and might be said to belong to the bairn.'

'And what about the land in Kingarth?' said Philip Sempill, sitting down. 'And was there not another stretch in Rothesay itself? Where are the rents for that?'

'The conjunct fees. I had the rents off those,' said Sempill grudgingly, 'for what they're worth.'

'The land at Kingarth,' said Gil, referring to the parchment again, 'is valued at eight merks and a weaned calf, besides the toll on the rents taken at St Blane's Fair, which my informant estimated at a considerable sum.'

'What?' Sempill stared at him. 'And I suppose there's a goldmine on the plot on the shore?'

'No, but there is a very handsome barn on it,' said the mason, 'used by a cartel of merchants whose turnover is probably a thousand merks a year, I would guess.'

'The barn? You told me it was the next toft!' John Sempill's hands were at his brother-in-law's throat. James Campbell flung himself backwards off the bench, rolling over as he landed to come up with his dagger drawn. Euphemia screamed, but Philip Sempill got between them, stripping off his gown to use as a defence.

'Be seated, maisters!' said David Cunningham sharply.

'I sent you on the rent,' said the laird of Glenstriven, ignoring him. 'I sent you it with that pair of perjured caterans.' He jerked his head at Neil, who was in front of the table, stooping to retrieve the scattered wine-cups. 'It should have reached you.'

'Oh, aye, it reached me. Eight shillings reached me for the two properties at Candlemas. Less than two merks and a half for the year, that makes. Where's the rest, James? Where's the rest? Is that what your fine education and your foreign travel does for you? Is that what studying law in Italy learns you?' He tried to push his cousin aside. 'Let me at him, the cheating –'

James Campbell cracked.

'Oh, there was more than that, John. I sent it to Euphemia.'

'James!' She leapt to her feet, her hands at her bosom, her eyes luminous with martyred virtue, the image of a little saint accused before Caesar. Sempill turned to her.

'Where's the money, Euphemia?' He held his hand out, as if expecting her to produce it from her bodice.

'I – I gave you all James sent me,' she said, tears quivering in her voice. 'Don't be angry with me.'

'I'll be as angry with you as I choose to be,' he snarled, face to face. 'What did you do with the money, Euphemia?'

'I gave you it, John!'

'That you did not,' said her brother. 'Most of it's on your back, high-kiltit hussy that you are. How much do you think she paid an ell for that satin she's wearing?'

'Is it so?' said Sempill, advancing on her. She gave back another step. 'Keep my rents back, would you, and then come winding round me begging for this and that jewel, with me scraping and pinching to find the money I owed the Crown –' He snatched the gaud hanging at her waist and yanked at it. She screamed, but lurched forward against him. Philip Sempill was there again.

'Sit down, please,' he begged them, 'as we are bid. Sit down and discuss this properly.'

Now there's a vain hope, thought Gil. His sleeve was tugged. He looked round, and found one of the gallow-glasses beside him, directing his attention to the kitchen doorway.

Maggie stood there, beaming broadly, one red fist clenched.

'Easy,' she said when he reached her. 'A wee secret drawer in the bottom of her jewel-box.'

'Secret?' he said, startled.

'You don't hide much from Marriott Kennedy. No that secret,' she admitted. 'And did you know the woman Campbell has a troutie in the well?'

'She does, does she? Did Marriott tell you that?'

She nodded, and opened the fist to show him her trophy: a plain gold cross, smoothly shaped and sweet to hold.

'And this was with it,' she added, and showed him a little key in her other hand. He took key and cross, and kissed her.

'Well done, Maggie. Wait here a moment, will you?'

He crossed behind the Official in his great chair, barely noticing Mistress Murray, who was swelling like a threatened hen and glaring at Maggie. Alys looked round as he approached her.

'Bring the bairn,' he said quietly, 'and come away. There may be a bit of a squabblement shortly.'

'I want to watch!' she said, following him back round to the kitchen stair. 'It's like jousting, isn't it? You're defending the truth against all comers.'

Gil, quite charmed by this view of matters, introduced her to Maggie and dispatched the pair of them downstairs cooing over the baby, with instructions to send Tam up. Then he turned back to the fray.

It appeared at the moment to be a four-handed shouting-match between both Sempills and the Campbell brother and sister, each taking on all comers. Nobody else was attempting to speak, which was probably just as well, he reflected.

The mason caught his eye and nodded approvingly, then sneezed again. Drawing a deep breath, Gil moved forward, and placed the cross on its ribbon on his uncle's table, the key beside it.

'What is this?' asked David Cunningham.

'Evidence,' said Gil deliberately, 'of who killed Bess Stewart, and therefore also Bridie Miller.'

'Eh?'

'What did you say?'

Sharp exclamations from Philip Sempill and James Campbell. Ealasaidh, identifying the cross from the far end of the bench, was speaking in an urgent undertone to her brother. Sempill and Euphemia were still shouting.

'I thought you wanted me to have nice things!'

'Not to that tune, you light-fingered bismere! How much have you had? What have you cheated me of? Tell me that!'

'Lady Euphemia!'

Campbell of Glenstriven said something vicious in Gaelic which made Ealasaidh nod, pursing her lips. Euphemia turned to look at him, flung a glance so swift at the table that Gil would not have seen it if he had not been waiting for it, and clasped her hands at her throat.

'Oh, I am breathless!' she said. 'I am faint!' She dropped gracefully into her brother's arms, an effect badly marred by his pushing her away and dumping her unceremoniously on the bench. Mistress Murray hurried forward, with another dark look at Gil, and began patting hands and exclaiming.

'If the lady is not well,' said Canon Cunningham, 'should we adjourn?'

Gil shook his head at him over the roiling mass between them. John Sempill emerged from it, his cousin at his elbow.

'What's that you say, Gil Cunningham?' he demanded. 'Do you know who killed Bess? Who was it? Was it no the Italian?'

'If you sit down, I will explain,' said Gil.

'I thought we were sorting who took the plate. And the rents,' he added, with a savage kick at his mistress's ankle.

'All this excitement's not good for her, Maister Sempill,' Mistress Murray remonstrated.

'I'll be a lot worse for her yet,' he threatened, and Euphemia moaned faintly.

'It's all linked,' Gil said.

Sempill glowered at him, but sat down, pushing Euphemia along. She was now drooping on her companion's bosom with little fluttering movements; unimpressed, Sempill said, 'If you can't sit up straight, go and lie on the floor. Philip and James want to sit down.'

'I am ill,' she said plaintively. 'I feel sick.'

'There is a garde-robe in the corner,' said Gil. Euphemia rose, and tottered towards it, supported by Mistress Murray. The sounds which emerged from behind the curtain suggested that she was indeed throwing up.

'Come on, then, man,' said John Sempill. 'Who killed Bess?'

'I, too, wish to know,' said the harper.

Gil, bowing to his uncle, surveyed his audience.

'Bess Stewart came up the High Street,' he began, 'on the evening of May Day, with Euan Campbell. Not Neil,' he added to John Sempill, who looked blankly at him. 'She was seen by more than one person, including James Campbell of Glenstriven, who was tousling a lass in a vennel near the Bell o' the Brae and made some effort not to be seen by her. I don't know whether he was successful.' Both Sempills turned and stared at James Campbell, who was staring in turn at Gil, the colour rising in his face. 'Euan left her in the clump of trees opposite the south door of St Mungo's and went into the kirk to tell John Sempill she was waiting for him.'

'We know all this,' growled Sempill. 'Get to the point, man.'

'Campbell of Glenstriven, leaving his limmer in the High Street, followed Euan into the kirk.'

'There's a sight too many Campbells in this tale,' muttered Sempill.

Gil, who had felt this from the start, nodded, and went on. 'I was near to your party in the kirk. I saw both these two arrive. I saw Campbell of Glenstriven slip away briefly and return. I saw other comings and goings.'

'I went away to pray before St Catherine,' said Euphemia wanly, returning.

'I saw you before her altar. The one I did not see go away, the one I had my eye on every few verses, was the lutenist. He cannot have killed Bess Stewart.'

'Why did you not –' began John Sempill, and stopped.

'You gave me little chance, John. You were aye quick with your hands.'

He looked at the faces again. The harper's face turned towards him, Ealasaidh staring sourly at the opposite bench, the mason intent. His uncle watching without expression, the way he did when a witness was about to become entangled in the facts. Philip concerned, James Campbell with a faint sheen of sweat on his upper lip,

John Sempill looking baffled. Euphemia, wilting elegantly on a stool near the kitchen stair, her waiting-woman bending over her and glaring at Gil. Checking that Tam was nearby, and Neil by the other stairs, Gil continued.

'Bess was not in the trees when we all came out of Compline. She was already dead, inside the building site of the Bishop's new work. Archbishop,' he corrected himself. Ealasaidh made a small angry sound, and her brother put one hand over hers. 'Whoever killed her had probably come out of the kirk, enticed her into the building site, presumably to be private, knifed her, and then gone back into the kirk. Unless it was a reasonless killing, and it seemed too carefully done for that, it had to be someone who knew her.' Gil counted off. 'You yourself John, James Campbell, Philip, Lady Euphemia, all came and went. I knew, at first, of no reason why any of the others should wish to kill Bess Stewart, and I did you the credit of believing that you would not have summoned her publicly and then murdered her secretly.'

'Oh, thank you,' said Sempill ungraciously.

'I found her the next morning, and was charged with tracking down her killer. Maister Mason here, also concerned because it was his building site, has hunted with me. It has not been easy.'

'Get on with it, man!'

'The kirkyard appeared to be empty, but there were in fact two witnesses, a young couple still a-Maying. What I think happened was that they found Bess's plaid where she had hung it on a tree so that her husband would know she was not far away. They decided to make use of it for greater comfort in the masons' lodge, against the side of the Fergus Aisle, and I think they overheard some of the conversation and the killing. They may have looked, and seen murder committed by a wealthy individual, one of the baronial classes who could be assumed to have the backing of powerful people, people who could be a threat to a mason's laddie and his sweetheart. The two of them certainly fled. The boy broke his skull running into a tree, and has been able to tell us nothing. The girl got away.'

Gil exchanged a glance with Maistre Pierre, who pulled a face and nodded.

'I think the burden of guilt must be shared here. If we had not hunted so openly for Bridie Miller, who was the boy's previous leman, she would be alive yet. She had quarrelled with the boy on Good Friday, and spent May Eve in the kitchen and part of May Day with her new lover.' He looked at James Campbell, who was now staring fixedly at his boots, still sweating. 'The boy had a new lass. Her name is Annie Thomson, and we have traced her in Dumbarton.' Was it imagination, or did Campbell's eyes widen briefly?

'Bridie Miller was killed at the market on Thursday. She had been persuaded to step aside to a place where many of the girls go to ease themselves. She was killed in the same way as Bess Stewart, by a fine-bladed knife, with no sign of a struggle. It could have been a separate killing, but two killers abroad in Glasgow at the one time, with the same method of killing, seemed unlikely. Most of your household, John, was down the town that morning, but you and Philip can swear for each other, Lady Euphemia was with her lutenist, and I saw James Campbell myself near the Tolbooth about the time Bridie was killed.'

Campbell's eyes did flicker this time.

'We know all this,' said Sempill again. 'Get to the point, in Christ's name!'

'Then the serjeant came to arrest Antonio.'

'I feel sick,' said Euphemia again, raising her head from her companion's bosom. They all paused to watch her sway towards the garde-robe. Maistre Pierre sneezed.

'Antonio was killed,' said Gil elisively, 'and therefore could not be questioned. Nor could he swear to anything he did or did not do or see.'

Sempill frowned, staring at him.

'By this time I had eliminated yourself and Philip, John.' Philip Sempill looked up with a crooked grin. 'I went down to Bute to discover who benefited, and dislodged a fine mess. I had the wrong philosopher. Not Aristotle but Socrates: there is always a previous crime.'

'Thank you for nothing,' grunted Sempill. 'I'd have caught up with it eventually.'

Gil, suppressing comment, counted off points again.

'I found there was evidence of misdirected rents, more than one version of what happened the night Bess Stewart left Bute, the curious story of the plate-chest, and one name that kept coming up in all these inconsistencies. It is clear to me that you and James Campbell of Glenstriven have a lot to settle between you, John.'

James Campbell leapt to his feet, his whinger hissing from its sheath. The narrow Italian blade appeared as if by magic in his other hand, and he backed wide round the Official's table as if he had eyes in his heels.

'I'll take at least one of you with me,' he said. 'Who will it be? It wasny me that killed Bess, or Bridie, the poor wee trollop, and I'll prove it on any of you that cares to try. Come on, then.'

There was a tense silence, into which the harper said something calmly in Gaelic. Then Ealasaidh sprang up with a cry of fury and hurled herself, not at Argyll's grandson but the other way, towards the door which Neil guarded. Gil whirled, to see her grappling with the gallowglass and shrieking vengefully in Gaelic. He ran to intervene, and she fell back, ranting incoherently.

'She is gone, she is escaped, this hallirakit kempie, this *Campbell* has let her go! Let me by, you ill-done loon!'

'She bade me,' stammered Neil. 'I thought it was Maister James we was after, I thought –'

At the foot of the stairs the house-door slammed. Gil stared round, and saw the curtain of the garde-robe still swinging, and met the triumphant gaze of Euphemia's waiting-woman. He stepped hastily to the window, flinging the shutters wide.

'Leave her,' said John Sempill. 'Get on with it. Are we to

take my good-brother or no, and are you going to be at the front of the assault?'

'No,' said Gil, 'for it was not Campbell of Glenstriven that killed your wife.'

'Well, if it's Euphemia we're after, she'll not get far. Is that her down at the gate now?' Keeping one wary eye on his brother-in-law, Sempill came to join Gil at the window.

Across the street Euphemia had just succeeded in opening the gate of the Sempill yard. Hitching up her tawny satin skirts, she slipped through the gap and made straight for the house-door. She was half-way across the yard when the second tawny shape emerged from the kennel.

'*Ah, mon Dieu!*' exclaimed the mason behind Gil as the mastiff bounded across the cobbles, silent but for its dragging clanking chain.

'Saints keep us, the dog!' wailed Mistress Murray. 'Oh, my poor pet!'

Euphemia turned her head just before the jaws closed on her arm. Gil got a glimpse of her horrified face before she went down, screaming, under the weight of the huge beast. Bright blood sprang on the tawny satin of her sleeve as Doucette, pinning her prey with one massive paw, let go Euphemia's arm to go snarling for the throat.

'Help her, maister!' shouted her waiting-woman. She turned, darted at James Campbell, her black veil flying, and tugged at his sleeve. 'Call the brute off! Save her!'

'She's past helping,' said Campbell, shaking her off.

'In Christ's name!' Gil exclaimed, making for the door. Before he reached it a hand seized each of his wrists.

'Leave it,' said Ealasaidh at his left through the screaming.

'If she killed Bess,' said Philip Sempill at his right, 'this is her due.'

The screaming turned to a dreadful gurgling which sank beneath the mastiff's snarls. The dog was now shaking her prey as easily as some monstrous terrier.

'Ah, well,' said John Sempill, staring out of the window. 'It wouldny have been legitimate anyway.' As Mistress Murray fell at his feet in a moaning heap and across the road the yard was filled by horrified shouting, he added, 'She should never have teased that dog the way she did.'

Chapter Fourteen

'We will have to reconvene,' said David Cunningham, 'to determine the questions of the bairn's future still unsettled.'

'Another day, I beg of you, maister,' said the harper, as his sister put the little goblet in his hand. 'I at least have had enough of great deeds for one day.'

'I, too,' muttered Ealasaidh. She accepted wine herself from the Official, and sat down.

They were all in the garden in the evening sun, with the replenished jug of wine and a plate of cakes. John Sempill and his household had gone home. Gil had felt it was typical of the man that he had asked no further questions. Euphemia's guilt was clear enough to him in her flight. Euphemia's brother also seemed to accept the fact, although he had been more intent on defending himself and casting blame on her in the matter of the missing rents. It seemed, indeed, as if Mistress Murray was the only person to feel any grief for her fate, and that appeared to be mixed with dismay at the loss of her own living.

Canon Cunningham was initiating a discussion with the harper on the differences in the law of inheritance on either side of the Highland line. Gil paid little heed to the polite exchange; his attention was being drawn to the other side of the garden where the mason and his daughter were in intense conversation. Alys's head was bent, and he could not see her face, but Maistre Pierre's expression was stern. Overcome by a sudden feeling that it was now his responsibility to chastise Alys if anyone was going to, Gil set down his pewter goblet and made his way between the box-hedges, his footsteps light on the gravel. As he approached, Alys turned and walked away, rapidly, aimlessly. The mason looked at her retreating back and moved towards Gil.

'Who would be a father?' he complained. 'She has been a rational intelligent mortal since she could talk, but suddenly now she is betrothed –' He bit off the next words.

'Is something wrong?' Gil asked, with a return of the familiar sinking in his stomach. Has she changed her mind? he wondered. Perhaps Euphemia's fate –

'No. She'll come round,' said Maistre Pierre. 'That was an impressive performance just now, Gilbert. You made all very clear – and with your uncle watching, too.'

'He trained me,' Gil pointed out. 'But Alys –'

'I should let her be.'

'But what's troubling her?'

'She is mumping,' said the mason in exasperated tones, 'because she was excluded from that singularly unpleasant scene a little while ago. She feels she had a right to be present.'

Gil looked from his friend, bulky and indignant in the big fur-lined gown, to Alys, slender and indignant in almost identical pose at the other end of the path.

'I have to deal with this,' he said, half to himself.

'She'll come round,' said the mason again. 'Leave her.'

'You have sixteen years' advantage over me,' Gil pointed out. 'You came to terms with her long since. Alys and I have all our terms to settle, and this is certainly a clause which demands negotiation.'

'Well, your diplomacy is clearly more polished than mine.' Maistre Pierre looked beyond Gil at the wine and cakes. 'Negotiating with your uncle is taxing enough for me. You go and make terms with Alys, if you feel you must.'

Filling two goblets with watered wine, Gil avoided the stately legal discussion and made his way to where Alys was pacing slowly along another of the walks, her brocade skirts brushing over the gravel. Stopping in front of her, he held out a goblet.

'A toast with you, demoiselle,' he said formally. She turned her head away. He held the goblet forward so that the backs of their hands touched. 'Alys,' he said, more gently. 'What ails you, my sweet?'

'Nothing,' she said, with an attempt at lightness.

'It is the duty of a good wife,' he pointed out, 'to speak the truth to her lord at all times. I assumed I was getting a good wife, and if it's going to be otherwise I think I need to know it now.'

She looked at him uncertainly round the fall of her hood. Her face was pale and pinched, the narrow blade of her nose outlined sharply against the black velvet. He smiled at her, and put the goblet into her hand.

'If you won't drink a toast, shall we walk?' He indicated the path beyond her. She set her other hand on his wrist and turned to walk with him between the beds of primroses and cowslips. Gil found himself thinking, suddenly and irrelevantly, of the primroses growing wild on the steep banks of the burn at Thinacre, where the Cunningham young had scrambled to pick handfuls of the flat, sweet-scented flowers for their mother's still-room. These were slips of the same growth, brought in on the cart when the tower-house was cleared. And there had been primroses by the well at St Chattan's, when he saw the hind, he recalled, and recognized that the images were not irrelevant at all. This was part of *the next thing* that he had asked for.

'Tell me what troubles you, Alys,' he prompted.

She paced on, carrying the goblet of wine, and at length said, 'You have offended Maggie.'

'Maggie and I are old friends. She'll come round.' But that was what the mason had said of Alys. Am I wrong about Maggie too? he wondered.

'Nevertheless,' said Alys, with another shy glance round the hood, 'you have rewarded her ill. She had done an unpleasant task for you, and you repaid her by shutting her in the kitchen away from the excitement.'

'I gave her the care of the bairn and of you,' said Gil. She turned her head away. 'Is that it, indeed? Your father said you were mumping at not seeing the excitement –'

'I was not mumping,' she said clearly.

'It's the kind of thing parents say,' he agreed, 'to reduce us to their power. Did you really want to see Euphemia torn to pieces by the dog?'

'No,' she said, with an involuntary shiver. 'But I wished to be present while you explained what happened. I know you'll tell me how you discovered it – won't you?' She turned to look up at him. He nodded. 'But Maggie and I should have seen how they all heard your account.'

'What – you think it was your right to be present?' he said, startled.

'It was certainly Maggie's.'

'And yours?' He found he was looking at the back of her hood again. 'This is the nub of it, isn't it, Alys?'

'I suppose it is,' she admitted after a moment.

'Then put your case to me, and then I will put mine, and we will both judge between them.'

'But how can two judges agree? It takes three to sit on the bench in Edinburgh.'

'One and one make three,' he said fondly, 'but I hope not until a year or so after we are wed.' He heard the little intake of breath. 'No, here are only two judges, so we must either agree, or agree to disagree. Come, Alys. You speak first. How was it your right to be present?'

He moved on as he spoke, leading her through the gate in the hedge, out of the formal flower garden to the kailyard on the slope below it. The burgh lay at their feet under its haze of smoke. The bell of Greyfriars began to ring for Compline before she spoke.

'I also helped you to gather the facts of the story,' she said at length.

'So did a number of other people who weren't there,' Gil observed.

'But most of those had duties elsewhere. You sent me from your side,' she said, trying to suppress indignation.

'I thought it would be dangerous,' said Gil, annoyed to hear himself on the defensive, 'and I was right. How could I take the risk, for you or the bairn?'

'But you took it for yourself.' She was looking up at him now. 'Is that, after all, how you see marriage? That you have to be responsible for me as if I was a baby? I can run a house and bear children and do all the hard work, but outside the house I cannot look after myself or think for myself?' She stopped by a bed of feathery turnip-sprouts and turned to face him properly. 'That wasn't what you said before. Do you remember? *Women have immortal souls,* you said, *and were given the ability to seek their own salvation. How can they do that if someone else takes responsibility for their every deed and thought?'*

He stared at her, his thoughts whirling, recognizing again that this girl had a mind like Occam's Razor. And she remembered everything he said to her. She misread his silence, and looked away again, out over the burgh. Another bell was ringing, possibly the Blackfriars'.

'I do not mean to be an unruly wife,' she said earnestly. 'Only, I thought you valued me for my mind, that you would allow me to think for myself, to make my own decisions, and now at the first moment there is a conflict you set me aside completely. That is different from Griselda's marquis, but it is just as belittling. Women are not little mommets, to do things you admire and imagine for us and then be put back on the shelf. And you never thought, till the last moment, of it being Euphemia who had killed Bess Stewart,' she went on. 'We can be wicked as well as good.'

He was silent. After a moment she looked round at him.

'That is the sum of my case. I think.'

'In principle,' he said slowly, 'you are perfectly right. If you can think for yourself inside the house you can do so outside, and I must let you do so, or give you a good reason why I should overrule you. The scene in my uncle's hall just now was rather more than exciting. James Campbell had his whinger out, there was nearly fighting, Euphemia had stabbed two women already. There was some danger. I thought that was a good reason to keep you back from it, but I can see that we should have discussed it first, however briefly. Will you forgive me?'

Her smile flickered and was gone.

'But in practice, Alys, you must acknowledge, there may not always be time to discuss it. There may be occasions when I have to act for your safety without consulting you, simply because I am taller, or stronger, or more experienced in fighting.'

'That I understand,' she admitted. 'Though I do not like it.'

'I don't expect you do, but I hope you will accept it and discuss it later, as we are doing now. As for making decisions,' he went on, 'I have a less exact memory for my own words, but I am very sure I said something about marriages where *the wife is allowed to think for herself and decisions are made by both spouses together.*'

'You mean,' she said slowly, 'that we should have decided jointly whether I should stay to watch you expound the murder?' He nodded. 'Then may we also decide jointly whether you should go into danger without me?'

'Going into danger is a man's task in life,' he pointed out. 'As well expect to discuss with me whether you should open the bread-oven.' Her smile flickered again. 'Alys, I have told you how I see a marriage, and you have quoted my words back at me. How do you see it?'

'As a partnership,' she said promptly. 'Different, but equal.'

'I think we can agree on that.' He looked down at her. 'A debate, in which both spouses have a voice.'

'An equal voice?' She was looking at him directly again, her expression intent. The pinched look had gone, and her colour had improved. He smiled at her.

289

'If each has an equal chance of being right,' he said, 'then the voices must be equal.' He realized he was still holding the pewter goblet. 'Now will you drink a toast, demoiselle?'

She looked in surprise at her own.

'Where did this come from? Yes, a toast, maistre.'

They linked wrists. She gazed up at him across the rims of the two little cups.

'To good fortune,' she said.

'To partnership,' he said.

They drank the wine.

'And the next time?' said Alys.

'The next time,' he said, and it felt like an oath, 'I will keep you by my side. If I can reasonably do so.'

'Do you promise me?'

'I will get my uncle to put it into the contract.'

He put his arms about her, feeling the warmth of her flesh between the bones of her bodice, but she held him off for a moment with a hand on his chest, gazing up at him with that direct brown stare. The scent of cedarwood rose from her brocade.

'I have a lot to learn, haven't I?' she said at last.

'We both have,' he said. 'We'll learn together, Alys.'

She smiled blindingly at that.

'We both have,' she agreed, and put up her face for his kiss.

They went back through the hedge as the light faded, to find the legal discussion still raging, while over the herb-bed by the house wall the mason and Ealasaidh were sniffing crushed leaves and exchanging remedies.

'But creeping thyme is best for slow maladies,' said Maistre Pierre earnestly as they approached, 'because of its nature, clinging close to the ground.' He turned to greet his daughter, but whatever he would have said was interrupted as the house-door was jerked open from within.

'Here's Maister Philip Sempill,' said Maggie crossly, stumping out of the house. 'Wanting to know how you knew. And if you're wondering about the bairn, it's asleep in my kitchen, with its nourice.'

'I know I'm intruding,' said Philip Sempill apologetically behind her, ' but I can't rest till it's clear to me.'

'Come join us, Maister Sempill,' said the Official resignedly. 'Bring a light, Maggie, and bring more wine and a cup for yourself.'

Gil, somewhat reluctantly, drew Alys forward into the group as it gathered, settled her on a bench before anyone else could claim it, and poured out wine.

'When were you sure?' asked the mason, taking a handful of little cakes. 'I was not certain until she ran away.'

'To be honest,' admitted Gil, 'nor was I. It could have been James, all along.'

'But it wasn't,' said Philip Sempill, pleating the taffeta lining of one wide blue sleeve with the other hand. 'I must admit, I thought it was.'

'Make it clear to us,' said the harper. He seemed to have shed a great burden of anxiety. 'What happened?'

'She must have known Sempill had sent for Bess, and why,' Gil began obediently. 'I thought at first that was the reason Bess died, to make it easier for Sempill to sell some of the property in Glasgow, but it wasn't that, and it wasn't the fact that Euphemia was pregnant and hoped it would be Sempill's heir either. Sempill might not have known till I told him, but her brother certainly did, that her child could never have been legitimate.'

'So it was the money,' said the Official.

'Yes. And possibly the plate, though I think her brother had that,' Gil added. 'We may never know its fate. I dare say there are silversmiths all over Scotland who would melt it down and never ask about the crest. She simply feared that if Sempill spoke to his wife he would discover that she had never had any of the rents from Rothesay. And you only had to look at Lady Euphemia to tell she was an expensive woman.'

'I've always wondered how John could afford her,' said Philip Sempill.

'So she borrowed Antonio's dagger, went out of St Mungo's during Compline, and called Bess over. They were kin by marriage, Bess had no reason to be suspicious. Euphemia coaxed her into the Fergus Aisle so they could sit on the scaffolding, or maybe so she could throw up in privacy, for the traces were there.' By his side Alys stirred, but said nothing. 'Then she knifed her, seized her purse and the gold cross to make it seem like robbery, skelped back over the scaffolding and into the kirk for a quick word with St Catherine –'

'I wonder what the holy woman was making of that?' said Ealasaidh heavily.

'Quite so. And after the service, when they all went out, she gave Antonio back his knife. I saw him sheathing it. I was just on their heels going into the kirkyard.'

'How did she know how to strike so deadly?' asked the mason. 'Or do you suppose it was luck? And why the musician's dagger and not her own?'

'Not simply luck, for she killed Bridie the same way. I think one of her lovers may have taught her how to use a knife. It is the kind of thing she would have relished knowing.' Not Hughie, he thought. Surely not Hughie?

'Her own knife is – was a small one,' Philip Sempill observed. 'I saw it often at mealtimes. I suppose the Italian's was better suited to the task.'

'Would a woman think of such a thing?' asked Maistre Pierre.

'Euphemia would,' said Sempill firmly. 'She was drawn to knives, and blood. When one of the men cut his hand on a broken crock, Mally could scarce bind it up for Euphemia getting in the way staring.'

'I remember, her reaction to the Italian's blood was yet stronger,' said the mason.

'She must at some point have checked the purse,' Gil continued, 'probably on her way back into St Mungo's, and found only a few coins, a key which must be the key to Bess's box, and the harp key, which she dropped or threw away. The purse went on the midden. Maggie found the cross and the other key, hidden in a secret place in her jewel-box until it should be safe to bring them out. I expect if Sempill had ever got his hands on Bess's effects she would have coaxed the box from him and made use of the key.'

'She cannot have seen Davie and his girl, I suppose, though you told me she claimed to have done so,' said Maistre Pierre. 'No doubt she was alarmed when we began to search for Bridie Miller.'

'She must have enticed Bridie into Blackfriars yard in the same way,' Gil continued. 'The girl was easy enough to identify, she was telling the whole market what a narrow escape she had had, and she would be flattered by a lady who asked her advice about where she could be private. Euphemia had taken care to dress differently. On May Day evening she was wearing a hat, and the next day and also when I met her in the market on Thursday she was wearing a linen kerchief, a monstrous thing which changed her appearance completely. Like the Widow in Dunbar's appalling poem – *schene in her schrowd and schewed her innocent*.'

'I had never seen her wear such a headdress before those two days,' said Philip Sempill. 'It surprised me, I can tell you.'

Gil nodded.

'She can't have stopped to find out whether the poor lass saw anything, she simply got rid of her as quickly as possible. I suppose it is characteristic that she also took the few pennies Bridie had on her, as she took Bess's coin, though it would scarcely pay for a finger of one of her gloves. The scent on Bridie's kerchief puzzled me, until Mariota Stewart said something about Euphemia's perfume smelling different when it was stale.'

'Aye,' said Maggie. 'That was the other thing, Maister Gil, only you were so quick to be rid of me. All the clothes in her kist smelled like that, and it wasny the same as when it was on her at all.'

'I noticed that often,' said Philip Sempill.

'And I've noticed that, fresh or stale, it makes Maister Mason sneeze, just as hawthorn flowers do. And then the serjeant arrested Antonio. I also bear some guilt for what happened then, because I know John Sempill, I should have been quicker to realize what he would do.'

'No, Gil. I know him even better,' said John Sempill's cousin, 'and I was taken by surprise too. Euphemia should also have known what would happen.'

'I think she did. She had known John well, and for a long time, and think how economical to get one lover to execute the other. What would the Italian have told if he was put to the question? He didn't look to me like a man who could withstand the thumbscrews or the boot.'

'That would have silenced his music,' said the mason. Ealasaidh flinched, but the harper did not stir.

'I never asked her point-blank, but I expect she would have sworn that he was with her all the morning Bridie was killed. If he was questioned, he would have told all he knew about her movements, both when Bess died and when Bridie died. I suspect he was also the father of her child. John's success has not been notable in that way. So Antonio had to go, and as Maister Mason says, her reaction to the spilt blood was powerful. What sticks in my craw is that the poor devil begged her to help him, addressed her as *Donna mia cara*, dear my lady – and that was his reward.'

'Poor devil indeed,' said Philip Sempill. 'I will say, I knew what was happening – that she had taken the Italian to her bed – and I hoped John never found out, but I never looked for it to end that way.'

'Then we went to Rothesay and discovered this large-scale pauchling of the rents. As I said, I had eliminated you and John both by then, but I was still thinking in terms of James Campbell, and every word I heard seemed to confirm it.'

'To me, too,' agreed Maistre Pierre in answer to Gil's raised eyebrow. 'But I cannot understand yet how Maister John Sempill never recognized the – what is your word? –

pauchling. Embezzlement. He must have known what his land was worth.'

'John doesn't read very well, Grammar School or no, and he's not a great thinker,' said Philip, grinning. 'I tried to suggest the rent was a bit low, but he's so taken with James's education, and yours, Gil, that he would never entertain the idea that things might not add up.'

'And so you knew it was the good-sister,' said the harper.

'When she ran, I knew,' said Gil. 'Something I learned in Dumbarton set me thinking things through again. James Campbell had been there looking for Annie Thomson, and gone away without speaking to her because she was demented with a rotten tooth, poor lass. Her mother described him, and identified him as a Campbell. Now, if he was guilty, he knew what she might have seen, he had no need to question the girl publicly, and every incentive to make contact with her secretly and do away with her like the other lassie. Since he had tried to contact her quite openly, I could infer that he was not guilty, but had a reason for wanting to know what she had seen or heard the evening Bess died. So I began putting things together – there was that, and a conversation I had with Euphemia Campbell the day Bridie was killed when she knew far more than she should have done, and Mariota's remark about the perfume – and began to think perhaps I knew the answer. But until Euphemia saw the cross and ran, it was simply the most likely explanation.'

'I knew,' said the harper calmly, 'when I reminded the company that I am a harper and can determine the truth. All who understood me were in decent awe, but Euphemia Campbell was frightened. I smelled it.'

'I knew at Bess's funeral,' said Ealasaidh.

'What?' said Gil.

'She was waiting, out in the church,' she said remotely. 'My sight is good. I saw her in the shadows, waiting until we were done with touching the body. Why would she do that if her conscience was clear?'

'It would have helped if you had told me,' Gil said.

She turned a considering gaze on him. 'Would it?'

Perhaps not, he acknowledged.

'Do you think, sir,' he said, touching the harper's wrist, 'that we did uncover the truth?'

'I do,' said McIan harshly. 'Justice has been served here.'

'But what an end she met,' said Maistre Pierre. 'Torn to pieces unshriven.'

'She would have been held in the Bishop's jail,' the Official pointed out, 'and tried, and if found guilty executed by drowning.'

'And is that right, maister,' said Maggie with interest, 'that they haveny found her arm yet?' Philip Sempill grimaced, and shook his head. 'Likely it'll be in the dog kennel.'

'Has the dog been disposed of?' asked the mason.

Sempill, getting to his feet, laughed sourly. 'You do not know my cousin John, maister. Fortunately for them, the servants do, and the stableman had enticed her away with some meat with aniseed and tied her up. No, John sees no need to dispose of a good guard dog simply because it did what he requires it to do. He's more put out because James Campbell will not bear the cost of his sister's burial. It'll need a sizeable donation to get her buried in holy ground, considering, and James says she was John's problem in life, she may stay his problem in death. And for all John's already sent to Dunblane last week, to let John Murray know he's got an heir, he won't see a plack of the old man's money till he's gone. He'll have to sell that gaud she was wearing to coffin her.'

'And it'll need to be a coffined burial, by what I'm told,' said Maggie.

Philip Sempill grinned wryly, and turned to bow to the Official. 'I have taken up enough of your time, sir. I will take my leave of you, now that I understand what happened. I agree with Maister McIan. We have seen justice here.'

Gil saw him through the house and down to the door. He paused there, a hand on the doorpost.

'I wanted her, Gil,' he said abruptly. 'I would have married her, but Campbell of Glenstriven, as her good-brother, preferred to take John's offer. My Marion's a good lass, but . . .' Another crooked grin. 'She's not Bess.'

'I'm sorry,' said Gil inadequately.

'Bess Stewart was a bonnie woman, and a bonnie singer, and I saw her dwindle into a silent thing, feared to move when he was in the room. I would never have treated her like that.'

'She can maybe rest easy now,' Gil offered.

'Not yet,' said Philip Sempill, narrowing his blue eyes, 'but I tell you, I will take care to exact the next part of the revenge out of your territory.'

Gil considered him.

'Do that,' he said, clapping him on the shoulder, 'and good luck to it.'

When he returned to the hall he found the rest of the company had come in from the garden and were taking leave in various ways. The harper, with one hand on his son's head, was reciting a sonorous blessing in Ersche while the baby regarded him with huge solemn eyes from his nurse's arms and Nancy herself yawned and blinked sideways at all the people.

'We must arrange a fresh tryst with John Sempill,' said Canon Cunningham. 'I have just agreed a time with Maister McIan. And you and your lassie must be properly handfasted, with witnesses. We must agree a time for that too.'

'I look forward to it,' said the mason.

'The sooner the better,' said Gil, drawing Alys aside. She looked up and smiled at him, so he kissed her, and quoted, *'Her fair fresh face, as white as ony snaw, She turnit has, and forth her wayis went.* Sweetheart, you must go now. I think I will sleep on my feet soon.'

'It has been a long week,' she said.

'It has been an even longer day. I have sailed across

the water, helped Matt draw a rotten tooth, procured the death of a murderer, been handfasted to the wisest girl in Scotland, and mended our first disagreement. At least I think we have mended it.' He looked down at her anxiously. She nodded. 'Good. And that has set a precedent.'

'Precedent?'

'That when we disagree, we can settle it by debate between us.'

Her smile flickered again, elusive as a wren in a hedge.

'If there is time,' she said, and put up her face to be kissed.

When all the company had gone he gathered up the wine-cups and took them down to the kitchen. Maggie was entertaining Matt with a lively account of the evening's action which appeared not to suffer by the fact that she had not seen the centrepiece.

'And they'll keep the dog,' she added. 'Savage creature, I don't know how they could live with it.'

'Poor brute,' said Matt.

'And is that right, Maister Gil, that the bairn's to be fostered with Maister Mason?'

'So it appears,' said Gil, deducing from this that he was forgiven. 'And I'm to be its tutor.'

'So you'll start married life with a family.'

'I'll not be the first man that's happened to,' he said, setting the wine-cups down on the table. 'They don't usually come dowered with a lachter of properties in Bute, but if the rent from that pays to wash the tail-clouts, Maister Mason may be thankful.'

'That's a good lassie you've chosen,' she said, her face softening. 'And bonnie manners with it. Mind you,' she added, 'she's a sharp one. I think she'll tame you as readily as you'll tame her.'

'I still can't believe my good fortune,' he admitted.

'When?' said Matt.

298

'When will the wedding be? When I can afford to keep a wife.'

'She'll wait for you,' said Maggie. 'She'll do, Maister Gil. Your minnie will be pleased.'

Avoiding a conversation with his uncle, who seemed willing to go over the entire argument of his accusation again, Gil climbed to his attic and opened the shutters without lighting his candle. It was dark by this time, though greenish light in the sky still outlined the hills away to his left. Some of the shapes looked familiar now. Nearer at hand, the Bishop's castle (Archbishop, he corrected himself) and the towers of St Mungo's loomed dark. Nearer still, candlelight in the windows of the Sempill house showed three pairs of hands and another game of Tarocco.

He stood looking out for a little while, as the cards went round, thinking of the events of the day, and the long game of Tarocco that had been the evening. Not to Alys, not even to his uncle had he admitted how undecided he was. He had not known whether it was James Campbell he was looking for, or Euphemia, or even one or other of the gallowglasses, right up to the point where Maggie had handed him the cross.

Well, he thought, I have jousted for Truth, and won. And not only for Truth, it occurred to him, watching the play at the lit window. For Hugh, and for his Sybilla, poor girl, who was now avenged. No wonder his brother had saluted him in his dream. And also for Bess Stewart, who escaped a grim future and found love, however briefly, in her broken vows. (As I have done, he thought, and St Giles send it lasts longer than Bess's happiness.)

Down in the dark between the Sempill house and the gate, the mastiff Doucette grumbled to herself about something. The curfew bell had rung long since. Windows were darkening along the street, fires were smoored for the night. The shutters were fastened tight at the window on the floor above the card game, where he had watched Euphemia wrestle with her lover, when he had still thought he was bound for the priesthood. But now I have a girl, he thought, who wrestles with her mind. We will debate the state of our marriage between us. And after the marriage-debate, there would still be the marriage-debt to settle, an extraordinarily satisfying thought. He thought of the warmth of Alys's slender waist between his hands, and the sweet innocence of her kisses.

He closed the shutters and began to undress. Tomorrow they would settle matters with the mason.

Tomorrow he would see Alys.